CAPTIVE

Tony Park was born in 1964 and grew up in the western suburbs of Sydney. He has worked as a newspaper reporter, a press secretary, a PR consultant and a freelance writer. He also served thirty-four years in the Australian Army Reserve, including six months as a public affairs officer in Afghanistan in 2002. He and his wife, Nicola, divide their time equally between Australia and southern Africa. He is the author of fourteen other African novels.

CAPTIVE
TONY PARK

PAN BOOKS

First published 2018 by Pan Macmillan Australia Pty Ltd

First published in the UK in 2018 by Pan Books
an imprint of Pan Macmillan
20 New Wharf Road, London N1 9RR
Associated companies throughout the world
www.panmacmillan.com

ISBN   978-1-5098-7655-6

Cartographic art by Laurie Whiddon, Map Illustrations

Pan Macmillan does not have any control over, or any responsibility for,

A C

Visit **www.panmacmillan.com** to read more about all our books
and to buy them. You will also find features, author interviews and
news of any author events, and you can sign up for e-newsletters
so that you're always first to hear about our new releases.

For Nicola

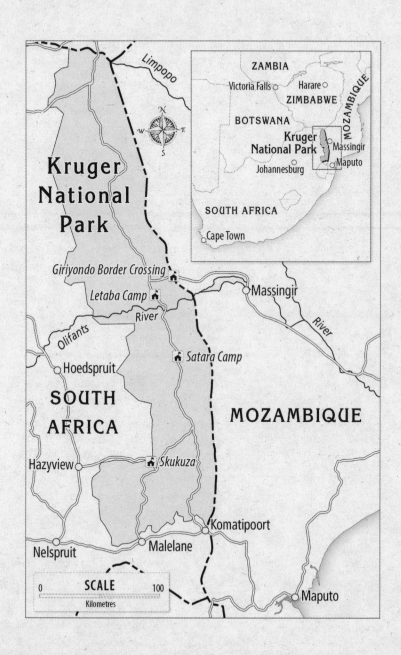

Author's note

The problems facing Africa's wildlife seem almost as numerous as the number of non-governmental organisations trying to protect and conserve it.

I am a supporter of several charities taking very different approaches to these issues, including anti-poaching, relocation of wildlife, conservation and demand reduction. There is no single solution to the problems of poaching and the illegal trade in wildlife products.

The organisations and people depicted in this novel may bear similarity to real-life bodies and individuals, but I assure you they are not based on any person or group.

Prologue

Nsele was scared of nothing, nobody. Not lions, not leopards, not hyenas nor even the wild dogs, who were professional killers. What he lacked in height he made up for in attitude and ferocity.

He was a killer, and no one messed with him.

But he knew when it was time to run. Nsele leapt over a fallen log and scrambled under a thornbush. He felt no pain from the barbs that tried to hook him. He was invincible, he was young.

But he was scared.

Behind him his pursuers had taken to a vehicle. The Land Rover bounced over the open *vlei* of dry golden grass, flattening stems and lurching in and out of a landscape cratered by the sinking feet of elephants passing through here during the last rainy season. The black soil had hardened now into a hundred thousand potholes.

It didn't slow him. Nothing could stop him.

If they cornered him, somehow, somewhere, he would kill them and their deaths would be vile and bloody.

If they wanted to kill him they would have done so by now. They had guns, and they'd had a clear shot at him, but they were still in pursuit. They wanted him alive.

Nsele had evaded traps in the past, amateurish affairs that were easy to circumvent and easier still to escape from. He would not be taken easily.

He ran and he ran, but the men were faster. Nsele scurried up and over a termite mound, but when he started sliding down the far side he saw he had run into a trap.

There, in front of him, was another open-topped Land Rover, parked and waiting. A man stood in the open rear with a dart gun.

'Honey badger!' The driver of the vehicle pointed at Nsele.

Nsele turned and tried to get over the mound again, but the dart left the weapon with a *pffft*, and Nsele felt a pain in his arse.

Chapter 1

South Africa, the present

Kerry Maxwell looked out of the window of the Embraer jet and gasped. She turned to the man in the khaki uniform of the South African National Parks across the narrow aisle. 'It's a giraffe!'

He smiled. '*Ja*, a big bull.'

'Sorry,' she said, feeling a little self-conscious. 'You must see giraffe every day.'

He laughed, his big beer belly shaking. 'I wish. I work in Pretoria in an office mostly; I'm almost as excited as you to be back in the Kruger Park. This your first visit?'

She nodded. 'I'm *so* excited.'

'Do you mind if I ask, where are you from?' His accent was Afrikaans. 'China?'

It was her turn to laugh. 'No, Australia. I'm part Vietnamese.'

He looked over the top of his reading glasses. 'You know, sadly, much of the rhino horn taken from animals that are illegally killed here in the Kruger Park ends up in Vietnam.'

'I know.' She didn't think the man meant offence. 'Actually, I'm involved with a charity dedicated to saving the rhinos. That's why I'm here. I've come to learn more about the problem. The charity is all about reducing demand in Vietnam, and I've travelled there to work as a translator with our people who are placing anti-poaching advertisements in the news media.'

He smiled. 'Good for you. We can't win this fight with guns and bullets on the ground. My name is Danie.'

She shook his hand. 'I'm Kerry-Anh, though people just call me Kerry. Anh was my mother's name, she was half-French, half-Vietnamese.'

'Was?'

'She died, of cancer, two years ago.'

'So sorry for your loss. That is a beautiful name, Kerry-Anh. Do you work for this charity fulltime?'

'No, I'm a lawyer. I work for a firm in Sydney, but I'm taking two months' long service leave. I try to help out in my spare time.'

'Then welcome to South Africa. Where will you be staying?'

'I'm first going to volunteer for a month at a wildlife rehabilitation centre at Hoedspruit.'

'Ukuphila Wildlife Orphanage?'

'Yes, that's the place. I read on their website that the name means "life" in Zulu. I'm going to be working with a veterinarian. Dr Baird.'

Danie shook his head. '*Eish*, that Graham Baird.'

'What does that mean?'

He smiled. 'You'll find out. Try and catch him before midday, though.' The man pantomimed taking a sip of a drink from a bottle.

Kerry sat back in her chair, a little disconcerted. *What have I got myself into?* she wondered.

*

CAPTIVE

'That's the Lebombo Hills over there in the distance, Doc. The Kruger Park's on the other side, across the border,' the helicopter pilot said into the intercom.

Graham Baird felt queasy. It wasn't the flying – he'd been in and out of choppers for twenty-five years, since his time as a conscript in the South African Army and had a fixed-wing pilot's licence. It was the beers last night. And the red wine. And the Scotch. And the brandy. He hadn't expected to be flying today.

Graham burped. 'I was working as a vet in that area before you were born.'

'Whatever, Doc,' said the pilot, Retief, who Graham thought looked about sixteen.

On the rear seat of the helicopter, next to Graham, was his plastic fishing tackle box full of drugs and darts, and some traces and lures in case he ever got the chance to hunt for some tigerfish in Mozambique's rivers.

He was very familiar with the Kruger National Park, having worked there for the national parks board in his youth, but nowadays nearly all his work was done in and around the Timbavati Game Reserve and other neighbouring privately owned safari land on the western border of Kruger. Today, however, he was far to the east, on the Mozambican side of Kruger.

The Kruger Park, as big as the state of Israel, had been expanded even further in recent years across the border into Mozambique. The whole conglomeration was known as the GLTP, the Greater Limpopo Transfrontier Park.

All that meant to Graham Baird these days, however, was more space for poachers to hide in, and more dead and injured animals. He loaded a dart with M99, the potentially lethal opium derivative he'd need to sedate the elephant if they found it.

'Last report had the baby elephant somewhere around here, running up and down the old fence line,' Retief said.

Graham looked out the open side door, scanning the ground. It was a forlorn hope trying to find a lost baby elephant in all this bush, but his friend Juan Pereira, the owner of the newly developed lodge on the Mozambican side of the park, had been alerted to the calf's plight by one of his guides, who had encountered it while taking some well-heeled American visitors on a game drive that morning. The visitors were investors in the lodge and had, by good fortune, arrived in a helicopter – the one Graham was in now.

As luck would have it – although his flip-flopping belly protested he was anything but fortunate – Dr Graham Baird had been visiting the lodge at Juan's invitation to perform surgery on his dog, which had been seriously mauled by a leopard.

Graham looked up and scanned the horizon. He saw a swirl of black dots against the clear blue dry-season sky. They looked almost like a disjointed tornado. 'Vultures, to the north.'

'OK, Doc. I see them. You think that's the baby's mom?'

'Could be.'

'Bastards,' Retief said.

Graham felt the same. It was bad enough having to deal with the scourge of rhino poaching on an almost daily basis, but in recent times there had been an upsurge in elephant poaching. It was hopeless; the killing never ended.

Retief headed in the direction of the vultures and the elephant carcass came into view. Retief settled into a hover nearby and they both searched the surrounding landscape. 'Hey, there's the baby! To the west.'

Graham shifted his binoculars. The distraught calf ran in circles.

'Call the ground team,' Graham said. 'Give them the coordinates. We're not far from the lodge and there's a game-viewing road nearby. Shouldn't take them long to get here.' As soon as the two vehicles arrived, Graham would dart the elephant and then Juan could take it to wherever and whatever he had planned for it.

'Roger, Doc. How about we take a bit of a joy flight while we wait for them?'

Graham rolled his eyes. 'I'd rather die. Keep it straight and level.'

Far to the north the sun glinted on water Graham realised was Massingir Dam, on the Olifants River. He closed his eyes and laid his head against the padded insulation on the rear bulkhead of the chopper.

'Doc!'

Retief's voice roused him from the micro-sleep he'd fallen into. 'What now?'

'I've got people ahead, crossing a *vlei*, running.'

Graham lifted his binoculars and followed the pilot's directions. He picked up the men, half-a-dozen of them, running through the waist-high golden grass of the floodplain. Two of them were burdened with long, curved ivory tusks.

'Put me through to the ground team,' Graham said. Retief patched him through. 'Juan, it's Graham. We've got six poachers in the open, about a kilometre southwest of the coordinates we gave you for the elephant, over.'

'Copy, Graham,' Juan said above the noise of his Land Rover's engine. 'What are they carrying?'

Retief keyed his microphone. 'Looks like three with AK-47s, two carrying the tusks and the remaining guy with the tools.'

There was a pause on the other end. 'Graham, I've got one rifle, my .375.'

'Where's your nearest anti-poaching patrol?' Graham asked.

'Eli Johnston's working fifty kilometres south of us today. With the state of the roads here it will take him nearly two hours to reach you.'

Graham had met Johnston, a former US Navy SEAL who had left the military to devote his life to hunting poachers.

'I'll be out of fuel by then,' Retief said. 'I've got maybe thirty minutes remaining.'

'Best we can do is keep them in sight for as long as we can,' Graham said. 'Juan, see if you can raise Eli or the police in any case.'

'Roger.'

Retief cut in again, using their private intercom. 'I'm going to buzz these guys, scare them.'

Graham shared the pilot's frustration, but not his impetuous youth. 'All I've got is my nine-mil pistol. I smuggled it into Mozambique.'

Retief reached under his seat. 'Take mine as well.' He passed a Glock 17 back to Graham.

Graham held a pistol in each hand. 'What am I, Wyatt Earp?'

The pilot threw the helicopter into a steep banking dive. 'You are now, partner.'

Graham tensed his whole body as the ground raced up towards them. Retief levelled out and the long grass on the floodplain flattened under the downwash. Graham saw the poachers dive in fear.

Retief was foolhardy, but Graham couldn't fault his courage.

'They're not going to fire on us,' the pilot said. 'They don't want to risk getting in that much shit.'

'I'm not so sure about that,' Graham said. 'How about you back off, China.'

'Negative, Doc.'

Retief turned tightly one hundred and eighty degrees, and came back for another low-level buzz. Graham saw two of the poachers pop up, their AK-47s pointed at the helicopter. 'They're firing.'

Graham heard the ping and thud of bullets penetrating the skin of the helicopter. He put both hands out in the slipstream and started firing back, the two pistols blazing as they passed over the men below. A bullet whizzed between Graham's legs and he yelled with fright.

'Sheesh, that was too close,' Graham said. It was terrifying, yet at the same time exciting. Graham was momentarily taken back to his time in the army.

He looked back, the wind catching his hair. The poachers were running. The helicopter lurched sickeningly to the right. Graham stuck one pistol inside his open shirtfront and grabbed onto the seat. 'Retief, what's going on?'

'Doc . . .'

'What is it?' Graham leaned forward and saw the blood.

'I'm hit.'

Graham looked around him in the back of the helicopter. He saw a first aid kit clipped to a bulkhead and wrenched it free. 'Hold on.' He climbed awkwardly between the pilot and co-pilot's seat.

'Got to find somewhere to put her down.'

The helicopter slewed from side to side. Blood was spurting from the top of Retief's thigh and his face was getting paler by the second. Graham fell into the co-pilot's seat. He reached over and put his hand on Retief's leg. 'It's your femoral artery. Shit.'

Retief tried to smile. 'What happened to "reassure the patient", Doc?'

Graham unzipped the first aid kit and the contents tumbled out into his lap and onto the floor. He found a wound dressing and ripped it open. When he lifted his hand from Retief's leg the blood kept welling. He placed the dressing over the bullet hole. 'Can you lift your leg?'

'Not unless you want us to crash. I can see a clearing . . . up ahead.'

Graham kept pressure on the wound. 'Hang on, you'll be OK.'

Retief coughed and blood ran out of his mouth.

Graham used his free hand to feel behind the pilot. When he pulled away from Retief's shirt he saw fresh blood on his hand. The bullet that hit him must have passed through his leg, nicking the artery, and carried on up into his body.

'Can't . . . can't keep my leg steady. Brace . . . brace, Doc.'

Graham looked up and saw that the helicopter had tilted almost onto its right side. The ground rushed up at him. There was the sound of screeching metal as pieces of the rotor blades sheared off and flew at crazy angles as the helicopter smashed into the ground.

Chapter 2

I can take the meat off for you,' said Lawrence, the Shangaan safari guide who had picked Kerry up from Skukuza Airport.

'Thank you,' Kerry said.

They had stopped at a picnic spot, a place called Nhlanguleni, which Lawrence explained was near the western border of the Kruger Park, and he had produced ham and cheese rolls from a cooler box for lunch. Kerry had politely explained that she was a vegetarian. She took a travel-sized bottle of hand sanitiser out of her daypack and thoroughly disinfected herself before eating.

The light seemed brighter and the sun even hotter than either Australia or Vietnam, the two countries she was most familiar with. The sky was a perfect endless blue. The picnic site was a clear patch of raked dirt with a few big trees for shade. There was no animal-proof fence, just a log and pole affair that Kerry suspected was more to stop people wandering. A few sets of green tables and chairs were occupied by families laying out food for lunch.

Lawrence pointed. 'Look.'

'Oh my God, it's an elephant!' She had seen zebra, wildebeest, and more beautiful giraffe already that morning, along with what seemed like thousands of impala, but this was another first.

'Yes, we have many elephants in the Kruger Park,' Lawrence said. 'Some people say we have too many.'

Kerry raised her camera and fired away as the big lone elephant sucked up a trunkful of water from a man-made cement waterhole, set in an open plain about a hundred metres from the picnic site.

'How can you have too many elephants? They're a threatened species.' Kerry realised she hadn't put sunscreen on so she found her bottle and applied a liberal smearing of SPF 50 to her face and hands.

Lawrence stood beside her. 'That is true. Elephants have disappeared from much of Africa, but in places where they are protected, like the Kruger Park, their numbers grow and grow each year. Parts of Kruger are suffering from elephants eating too much.'

A herd of zebra trotted across the plain and closed, nervously, on the waterhole. The elephant turned and took a few steps towards them, sending the skittish animals galloping with a spray of water from his trunk. They returned, though, once the elephant had drunk his fill and ambled away.

'It's breathtaking,' Kerry said. She swallowed hard, experiencing a sudden foolish thought that she might cry.

Lawrence looked at her. 'Don't worry, I have seen people shed tears at the sight of their first wild elephant.'

They packed up and drove on. This, to her mind, was Africa as she had pictured it, with the harsh thorny trees giving way to open plains of golden grass.

'Keep your eyes open,' Lawrence said. 'This area west of Satara Camp is very good for cheetah. They favour these savannahs.'

Kerry stared into the heat haze, willing a big cat to appear, but they reached the Orpen Gate without a sign of the predator. She told herself she had plenty of time to see all Africa had to offer.

*

Graham came to and smelled smoke. He lifted his head and his vision swam as he felt the pain, worse than any hangover he had ever experienced.

Something electrical was shorting. He caught the odour of burning plastic. 'Retief,' he croaked.

There was no answer from the pilot next to him.

'Retief!' He shook the pilot, then placed two fingers on his neck. No pulse. 'Shit.'

He fumbled with the buckle for the pilot's harness and dragged him free of the wreckage. He rolled the younger man onto his back and started CPR.

'Come on.' Graham moved from breaths to compressions, but got no response. Retief was dead. He heard voices. They were men, speaking Portuguese, calling to each other.

Graham shivered. It was the poachers. The ground crew from the lodge would be coming by vehicle. The men who had downed the helicopter would not want to leave any witnesses. He reached into his shirt for the pistol, pulled it out, and ejected the magazine. His wild gunfire had left just three rounds.

He went back to the wreckage of the helicopter and hurriedly searched the rear compartment, snatching up the only other weapon he could find: his dart gun. The other pistol must have fallen out of the helicopter during the crash.

Graham did a quick check of Retief's shirt and shorts, but the pilot had no more ammunition. Graham looked down at Retief and crossed himself, then limped away from the helicopter.

When he reached a clump of thorn trees he dropped to his knees and wriggled into the dry undergrowth.

Three men armed with AK-47s came into view, moving with the professionalism of soldiers on patrol. Graham guessed that the other men, those carrying the tusks and the tools they had used to remove them, must have carried on towards their base or destination, leaving the armed men to investigate the crash.

The first gunman searched the helicopter, including Retief's body, and after helping himself to the pilot's wallet, called his comrades forward. They talked to each other in Portuguese as they ferreted around the crash site.

One poacher, an older man with tight curls of grey hair, circled the wreckage, his eyes on the ground searching for spoor. He called to the others. The youngest-looking man in the group, perhaps still a teenager, joined him, while the third stayed by the helicopter.

The youth looked at the tracks the older man was pointing out and then both looked up, following the trail towards where Graham lay. The old man put his hand on the younger one's arm to caution him, but the youth shook off the touch and started heading Graham's way.

Graham was a hundred metres or more from the wreckage, too far for an accurate pistol shot. He picked up the Dan-Inject dart gun he had been about to use on the baby elephant, took aim through the telescopic sight and centred the crosshairs on the young man heading his way.

The youth paused, then pointed directly at Graham and yelled something over his shoulder, in Portuguese, to the older man. The boy raised his rifle and started to take aim.

Graham pulled the trigger. The dart flew true, and the young man fell. Graham changed weapons as the other two men, calling to each other, raised their assault rifles and opened fire.

The elder of the group hung back, but the man who had been checking out the downed helicopter ran forward. Graham stood, wrapped his left hand around his right and fired a shot at the man coming towards him, aiming for the centre mass of his body. The man fell backwards and lay unmoving. Graham dived for the ground and rolled, then crawled for the cover of a fallen tree.

The old poacher fired a wild burst of three rounds from his AK-47 then turned and ran.

Graham fired his last two bullets at the fleeing man, but neither shot found its mark. He stayed in cover until the man was out of sight.

He stood, dusted himself off and walked to the young man he had darted. The boy was immobilised, but still conscious. He blinked twice.

Graham knew he should draw up a syringe of naltrexone, the same drug that paramedics administered to heroin addicts who had overdosed, to reverse the effects of the dart. His tackle box was somewhere in the wreckage.

He jogged to the helicopter and paused, briefly, to look at Retief's body. In the back of the helicopter he found his tackle box full of drugs, but it had come open on impact and phials, syringes and ampoules were scattered everywhere. By the time he had found and drawn up a syringe of naltrexone, and made it back to the poacher, the young man was dead.

*

Kerry and Lawrence pulled up at the reception office of Ukuphila Wildlife Orphanage, near Hoedspruit.

Kerry walked into the thatch-roofed building which was painted a similar khaki hue to the bush she'd been passing through all day. She was tired, but pleased to be at her destination. Except there was no one at the reception desk. She rang a bell on the counter. As well as housing a variety of birds, animals and reptiles, Ukuphila's grounds also included a dozen two-person accommodation units. Kerry saw a white-board behind the counters that bore the heading *Chalets*.

Next to the numbers one to twelve were various surnames. Oddly, hers wasn't there; perhaps, she mused, the board had yet to be updated.

Lawrence came in behind her, pulling her wheelie bag.

A portly lady walked slowly through a doorway from a back office. 'Hello, how are you?'

'I'm Kerry Maxwell. I'm here for the month-long volunteer program with Dr Baird.'

The woman seemed miffed at something. 'Ah, but Dr Baird, he is not here today.'

Lawrence and the woman exchanged what seemed like extended words of greeting in their language and Kerry wondered if she should have been more polite, instead of coming straight to the point.

'Can you tell me when he'll be arriving?' Kerry asked.

The woman shrugged.

Kerry looked back at Lawrence, but he just smiled. Kerry took a deep breath to still her growing impatience. 'OK. Perhaps I can check in to my room and you could let me know when Dr Baird arrives.'

'Your name?'

Kerry took a deep breath. 'Maxwell.'

The woman clicked a computer mouse and looked at the monitor.

'There is no one by that name booked with us.'

Kerry leaned over the reception counter. 'Let me see.'

The woman frowned at her, but turned the monitor slowly her way.

Kerry scanned the names. 'I'm not here. You look busy.'

'We are fully booked. There is a wedding happening tomorrow.'

'You mean you don't have any accommodation for me?' She felt her heart rate start to rise. 'I sent my money to Dr Baird and he confirmed my booking.'

16

'Dr Baird, he is not here.'

Kerry felt a panic attack coming on.

*

Graham Baird drank slowly but steadily all the way to the town of Massingir.

Juan had picked him up and taken the bodies of Retief Potgeiter and the two poachers Graham had killed back to his lodge, where they had collected Graham's Land Rover. Graham followed the lodge owner on the drive to town where they would have to report to the Mozambican police. Graham wasn't looking forward to the inevitable bureaucratic marathon that would ensue, so he worked his way steadily through a sixpack of warm Dois M beers as he drove in order to prepare himself and to steady his nerves.

Massingir was dominated by the dam of the same name, a low but five-kilometre-long wall that held the Olifants River in check for a while on its journey from South Africa into Mozambique.

The town had sprung up around the dam and was, year by year, eating up more of the surrounding bushland. There were high hopes that one day tourists would flock to the lake created by the dam to fish and view game, but for now a good deal of the money that paid for the newer houses and the four-by-fours that honked and bumped their way around Massingir came from poaching.

A Mozambican poacher could make well in excess of the country's average annual income from the proceeds of shooting one rhino across the border in the Kruger Park, while the kingpins who supplied the animals' horns to the Vietnamese middlemen were akin to local royalty.

Graham crumpled an empty beer can and tossed it on the floor of the passenger side of his Land Rover, where it clanged against the first three. He had a nice buzz on, though it wouldn't be enough to see him through the day.

Juan led the way past market stalls that were selling tomatoes and second-hand clothes donated by well-meaning do-gooders overseas, and pulled up outside the town's police station.

Graham parked behind him and got out.

'Stay here, for now, my friend,' Juan said, then went inside.

Three police officers filtered out of their bunker with Juan. They clustered around the *bakkie* loaded with the bodies of the dead poachers. Retief was wrapped in a green waterproof poncho in the rear of Graham's Land Rover.

The policemen chatted among themselves, one took notes, and a couple took pictures with cheap Nokia phones. They came to Graham and the one who seemed to be in charge started berating him.

'He says you are to be charged,' Juan said.

'Then tell him I am very sorry for any offence I have caused to the peace-loving people of Mozambique, but now is the time for me to go back across the border to South Africa.'

Juan did some translating. 'The officer says this is not possible, for now.'

It was hot. Sweat streamed down Graham's face and he thought it could be the beers evaporating from him. He felt light-headed.

The senior policeman was taking notes now, still speaking only in Portuguese.

Juan looked Graham in the eyes. 'He says one of the men you killed was the little brother of a local politician, Fidel Costa.'

'Hah!' Graham said. 'You know as well as I do he's the biggest criminal in town, and supposedly the local rhino poaching kingpin. What are they charging me with, manslaughter?'

Juan shook his head, his expression grim. 'Murder.'

Chapter 3

Kerry was fuming. With no accommodation available at the Ukuphila Wildlife Orphanage, Lawrence had driven her to the only place in Hoedspruit he could think of that would have a room available.

She was in a place called Raptor's Lodge, a collection of self-contained accommodation units on the edge of the Raptor's View wildlife estate, a housing development set in the bush and populated with animals as well as people. It would have been very pleasant if she didn't feel like a landlocked castaway.

Her Australian mobile phone was picking up a roaming signal. She tried the Ukuphila number for the third time that afternoon and Thandi – she was now on first-name terms with the receptionist – answered.

'Is there any more news about where Dr Baird is, when he'll be coming back?'

'Ah, I have some bad news and some good news answers for you.'

Kerry sighed. 'Good news first, please, Thandi. I need some.'

'The good news is that I have found your booking. The problem is that we were not expecting you until this time next *month*. I think this is Dr Baird's mistake. He can be – how should I say – less than attentive to detail, particularly after lunch. I also now know where Dr Baird is. His friend, Juan, the lodge owner he was visiting in Mozambique, called just now.'

'And?'

'And that is the other news – the bad news. Dr Baird is in prison in Mozambique.'

Kerry plonked herself down in one of the cane chairs in the small lounge room of her unit. 'Where? What's he done?'

'Ah, he is in Massingir, in Mozambique. He has been charged with murder.'

Kerry was speechless. How could this be happening to her? She took a deep breath and tried to think straight. Kerry realised she had so far only been thinking about herself.

'What was Dr Baird doing in Mozambique?' she asked Thandi.

'He was trying to save a baby elephant whose mother had been killed by poachers. Dr Baird's helicopter was shot down by poachers. The pilot died in the crash and Dr Baird was involved in a gun battle with the criminals.' Thandi relayed the news in the same tone as she might have if Dr Baird was stuck in traffic.

Kerry felt like she'd been physically floored for the second time in as many minutes. Here she was worried about her ruined holiday while a man who put his life on the line to save Africa's wildlife was rotting in a third-world prison.

'Do you have a number for this Juan guy?'

'Of course.'

'Good. Give it to me, please.' Kerry scribbled down the number. 'Thanks, Thandi.'

Kerry dialled the number and a man answered in what she assumed was Portuguese. She introduced herself and explained who she was.

'Ah, I'm sorry to hear about your predicament,' Juan said.

'I wish I could tell you Graham will be out of prison soon, but the justice system in my country moves very slowly. I'm doing what I can behind the scenes.'

'Does Dr Baird have a lawyer?'

'Alas, no,' Juan said. 'I'm not sure I can find a good lawyer to represent him and, anyway, I know from my own dealings with my friend Graham that he is not a wealthy man. I usually end up covering his bar bill. However, I'm also having cash flow problems. I'm going to ask the police if Graham can perhaps pay a fine – what you might call a bribe – but even if they agree I'm not sure where we would raise the money if it is expensive. For a murder charge it is likely to be extortionate.'

'I'm a lawyer,' Kerry said.

'You are?'

'Yes.'

'Then perhaps you could . . .'

The call ended. Kerry called Juan again but there was no answer, just a recorded message in Portuguese, repeated in English, telling her that the phone user was out of range or not in contact. She made five more attempts to call Juan, but could not get through.

'Damn.' Kerry felt helpless, but she was not only concerned for herself. A man was in trouble and needed legal help. She phoned Ukuphila again. 'Hello, Thandi?'

'Yes?'

'Do you know where I can rent a car to drive to Mozambique?'

*

The rum was at room temperature, which was to say, close to boiling.

The cell smelled of old sweat and recent urine and the odours, like Graham himself, were ripening in the stifling October heat. Juan had smuggled in a bottle of Tipo Tinto, home-brewed

21

rum sold in old plastic Coca-Cola bottles. The spirit was like sandpaper going down, but it was the only thing keeping him half-sane, as in half-drunk.

Graham willed himself to be patient. Juan would be pulling strings in the provincial government offices. It would just take time; Africa time.

A cockroach scuttled from out of the drain hole in the stained sink in the corner of the cell, looked around, twitched its antennae, then retreated.

'Wise move, China.' Graham raised his bottle to the departing bug. 'The sewer's cleaner. Probably smells better, as well.'

Graham heard voices speaking Portuguese. Keys rattled in the lock and a warder opened the door. 'Come.'

He stood, his nose rankling at his own odour, and followed the policeman down a corridor with stained walls. They went into an office. A policeman sat at a battered wooden desk, his white shirt straining at the buttons over his corpulent belly. The man smoked while he perused a handwritten file. He looked up.

'*Doctor* Baird,' said the seated officer.

'Sit,' said the warder. 'I will make the translation.'

The officer, older and clearly more senior, spoke in Portuguese, his words as sluggish as the blades on the ancient desk fan that squeaked as they failed to make headway against the humidity.

'This is Capitão Alfredo. He says you are in big trouble.'

'Don't worry. Tell him I'm innocent.'

The younger officer translated and Captain Alfredo regarded him through heavy, sleepy lids. 'Guilty,' the captain said in English.

'I want a lawyer,' Graham said.

The captain stubbed out his cigarette in an overflowing ashtray, listened to the translator, then shook his head. He spoke again.

'The captain, he says there is no need for a lawyer, or a trial. He says he is able to deal with this matter with a fine.'

Graham nodded. He'd expected, hoped, this might be the case. His number one priority was to get out of this stinking place and back to South Africa, not clear his name in the eyes of the Mozambican justice system. 'Ask him how much.'

There was a discussion between the two officers.

'Five thousand,' the warder said.

'Meticais. Sure, no problem.' Graham didn't even bother bargaining. The price was too good to be true.

'Unfortunately not.'

'Rand?'

'No, US dollars,' said the warder.

'What!' Graham didn't have anything like that much money. 'That's criminal. My life's not worth that.'

'The captain takes offence at your words.'

'Well, tell him some more words from me. How about he . . .'

Captain Alfredo held up a hand and spoke low and slow to the translator.

'The captain says you would be wise to consider paying this fine. He says there are other men in Massingir who might want to come and visit you.' The warder moved behind Graham and grabbed his upper arm, motioning for him to stand. It was time for him to go back to his cell. 'You would not like these visitors.'

Chapter 4

Kerry left Letaba Camp in the Kruger Park at dawn, just as the security gates opened. At the four-way stop she turned right, to the north.

She gripped the steering wheel of her rented Corolla hard and her eyes swept left and right, looking for elephant or other game that might suddenly jump out from the mopane trees into her path.

Off to her right a herd of buffalo, perhaps two or three hundred of them, were plodding, single file, towards a concrete trough at a man-made waterhole fed by a windmill-driven pump. She slowed, but didn't stop to take a picture. Yesterday she'd been in a kind of limbo, heading from the Kruger Park's Orpen entrance gate north to Letaba Camp.

On her afternoon drive through the reserve, at a sedate pace dictated by the speed limit, she had almost convinced herself not to go to Mozambique, and rather just enjoy the spectacular wildlife and scenery around her. The countryside from Orpen to Satara, the first camp she'd stopped at, was sparse and open and she'd been treated to a sighting of a cheetah. She had watched, barely daring to breathe, as the cat had stalked an impala, then showed itself and gave chase. Puffs of red dust had erupted like mini explosions, signalling where the cheetah's paws hit the ground. It had turned, dramatically, using its long tail as a rudder, and made a desperate lunge for the impala, but the lucky antelope had got away.

At Letaba Camp she had stayed in a rondavel, a round hut overlooking the wide sandy banks and glittering blue river of the same name. A dainty bushbuck, a milk chocolate brown antelope with white icing stripes, had walked up to her while she'd sat at a little table outside her chalet, beseeching her for a snack with its big glistening eyes. She'd seen signs warning tourists not to feed the animals, so she hadn't.

Over dinner at the camp restaurant, while she'd watched a big bull elephant drink, Kerry's doubts had surfaced. She'd spent a restless night and, thanks to a mix of jetlag and apprehension, had woken at five, before her alarm went off.

And now she was heading to her second African country in three days. Mozambique.

The road she followed climbed up into the Lebombo Hills, which marked the physical barrier between South Africa and Mozambique, and eventually led her to the Giriyondo border post. The formalities on the Kruger side were painless, though slower once she drove through the short no-man's land into Mozambique. There were forms to fill in, for her and her rental car, an expensive visa to purchase, and she had to produce documents and a letter from the hire company to prove she had permission to take the car out of South Africa.

Kerry showed the customs officer on duty that she was bringing nothing into the country then set off through the Mozambican side of the reserve. Here there was less game but she drove through forests of towering mopane trees. She guessed that one side effect of the poaching that had plagued this part of Africa in decades past was a lack of megafauna, such as elephants, to thin

25

out the vegetation. It seemed a sad irony that while the Kruger Park, according to Lawrence, had too many elephants, on this side of the border there seemed to be very few.

Kerry passed through a village and an exit gate from the park and finally drove onto the low, curving wall of Massingir Dam. She took it slowly, and forced herself to breathe deeply and calm herself for whatever she might encounter next.

Massingir itself burst her peace bubble. Children ran alongside her car, shouting and holding their hands to their mouths. The buildings looked ramshackle, either decaying old colonial edifices of brick and cement or shacks made of salvaged anything. Here and there were new structures with whitewashed walls and tin roofs, bureaucratic beneficiaries of foreign aid, but for the most part the residents and businesspeople of the town appeared to inhabit the south side of the poverty line.

Though not everyone.

A horn blared behind her and Kerry saw a black BMW X5 four-by-four in her mirror, flashing its lights at her and doing its best to mate with her rear bumper. She slowed and pulled over. The big car, with its dark tinted windows, roared past her.

A little further down the road she saw a new Range Rover and, somewhat incongruously, a low-slung Audi Q5 parked next to it. A few people in this dusty corner of Africa clearly had money to burn.

Kerry pulled over and checked her GPS, trying to find the police station. It was on Google Maps, but she couldn't quite tell which street she was in. A banging on her window gave her a fright. It was a small boy. Kerry wound down the window.

'Police. Er, *Policia?*' she tried.

The boy nodded. '*Sim.*' He pointed to a road ahead and crooked his hand to the right.

'Thank you. *Obrigado.*' She recalled the Portuguese word for thank you from a trip to Macau long ago with her parents. She missed her mother, still, terribly. What would her father think of her being here, on her mission? she wondered. It would be better to tell him when she got back to Australia.

The little boy was running after her as she drove off, doing his best to keep up with her, waving his hands. She wondered if she should have given him money.

Kerry slowed again and saw a large building on her right. It was surrounded by a wire fence, and a man in a white shirt with what looked like police insignia sat on a wooden stool by a gate. He had an assault rifle cradled on his lap. Kerry swallowed hard.

*

'Visitor.'

'What?' Graham Baird blinked and coughed. The cheap rum had stripped his throat. He went to the steel door. When it opened he had to blink again. Standing in the gloomy, smelly corridor was a young woman in safari clothes. She had jet-black hair, almond-shaped eyes like a cat's, and honey-coloured skin.

'Dr Baird, I presume.' She forced a smile at her own joke.

'Howzit. Do I know you? I hope so.'

'My name is Kerry-Anh Maxwell.' The corners of her mouth turned down. 'I was supposed to be staying with you right now at Ukuphila.'

'You were?' Graham scratched his head. Her accent sounded Australian, not quite what he'd expected. The penny dropped. 'Oh. I thought you were due next month, or something like that. I'm supposed to be in Zimbabwe next week.'

'Er, no, Dr Baird, I was supposed to be with you now, in South Africa. We can discuss all that later. I'm a lawyer, I've come to help you.'

Graham burped and was slightly ashamed of the invisible wave of stale booze that washed over Kerry. 'Well, Miss . . .?'

27

'Maxwell.'

'Miss Maxwell, I'm afraid there's not much you can do for me. I can't afford the bribe the cops here want to let me go, so I definitely can't afford a lawyer.'

She looked around the cell, and back at the warder, who was leaning on a wall in the corridor behind her. 'I know you can't afford legal representation; your friend Juan told me already. So what do you intend on doing?'

He shrugged. 'Wait. This is Africa; sometimes that's all you can do. If you spoke to Juan then you probably already know he's trying to pull some strings for me.'

Kerry pursed her lips. 'I don't think you heard me. I'm here to represent you. I hear you killed a poacher.'

'No, I killed two.' Graham sighed. 'Like most foreign volunteers you think you can change the world, but I don't think you heard me, either. This is Africa.'

She put her hands on her hips. 'What's that supposed to mean – that justice doesn't count and that you don't deserve a fair trial with legal representation?'

'Pretty much.'

She stomped a foot.

Graham laughed. 'Did you just stomp your foot?'

'Don't mock me, Dr Baird.'

'If I were you, Miss Maxwell –'

'Kerry-Anh or Kerry for short.'

'All right. If I were you, Kerry-Anne –'

'It's Anh, not Anne. It's Vietnamese. Try Kerry if that's too hard to pronounce.'

'Well, Kerry, my advice to you is to go back across the border to South Africa and enjoy the rest of your holiday. Oh, and please don't shoot any more of our rhinos on your way out of the country.'

She strode across the cell to where he was sitting and raised her hand. Graham recoiled, but was too late. She slapped him, hard, on the face. The guard in the corridor chuckled.

*

Kerry stepped back. She was shocked and surprised, and embarrassed. She had never hit anyone in her life. She was amazed that this dishevelled man, who smelled of alcohol and acrid sweat, had got under her skin so quickly.

But she was not sorry. 'How *dare* you, you racist, arrogant, ungrateful criminal.'

'Hey, I'm not a criminal.' He rubbed his cheek. 'Quite a right hook you've got there.'

'You took my money. I was supposed to be spending a month with you, right now, helping you tend to injured wildlife.'

'Sure. I'm the only injured wildlife here at the moment. I don't think I would have survived a week with you, lady.'

She looked down at him. 'Can't you be serious about anything?'

'You want to come to Africa and save the cute little animals?'

She bridled again. The man was impossible. 'I want to do something. I want to help stop the slaughter.'

He ran a hand through his lank, greasy, greying hair. 'Well, I was part of the slaughter yesterday. I saw a good man die and I killed a couple of others. That serious enough for you?'

Now she saw the pain in his eyes and wondered if the redness wasn't just from the alcohol he'd been consuming.

'Visiting is over,' said the guard in the corridor. He walked into the cell and put his hand on Kerry's elbow.

She shook him off. 'Don't touch me.'

'I'd listen to her, comrade,' Baird said to the guard. 'She's dangerous.'

Kerry started to leave, but turned back to the man on the concrete bed. 'Dr Baird . . .'

29

'Graham.' His voice was softer now and his big frame sagged. 'And I'm sorry, for what I said before.'

'Thank you, for what you're doing, trying to save wildlife.'

'Don't thank me. And do what I told you. Go back to South Africa. I'll be all right. They'll get sick of me here after a while, and if I'm not out of here by next week I'll get your money back to you, somehow.'

'I didn't realise how traumatic all this must have been for you. I'll get you released.'

'Whatever.' He lifted his hand in a half-wave and Kerry walked out of the cell.

He was infuriating, she thought, but he had just been through a trauma. Kerry had come too far to give up just yet.

Chapter 5

Graham touched the skin on his face, which was still hot from her blow. She was something else, this Kerry Maxwell. He remembered the name now, from the email bookings. He hadn't been sure at the time if the name was male or female. Now he knew.

The guard opened his door. 'You have visitors.'

'Again? Tell that bloody lawyer woman to leave me alone.' He meant it; he wanted her to go back to South Africa and forget him, not to mention the money he owed her.

Two men walked in. They wore jeans and, despite the heat, leather bomber jackets that bulged under each of their left armpits.

'Let me guess, you're from the South African embassy, come to give me consular assistance and get me out of here?'

'Leave,' one of the men told the guard, who nodded and obeyed. The man closed the door. He was older than his companion, and although Graham had only caught a glimpse of the grey-haired poacher who had fled from the gunfight at the scene of the chopper crash, Graham was now sure this was the same man.

The temperature climbed with the addition of two extra bodies in the cell, or perhaps, Graham thought, it was the sudden sense of fear that flooded his body.

The two men stared down at him.

'Can I help you gentlemen?'

They moved on him, but despite his age Graham hadn't lost all the reflexes honed through years of rugby and the occasional pub fight. He took them by surprise, sucker-punching the younger one on the right, smashing his fist into the man's nose. The man fell back, gasping with pain. The victory was short-lived, however, as the older man delivered two hard punches to Graham's kidneys that made him stagger.

Graham rounded on the man who had hit him, but his opponent was faster than his friend had been and ducked out of Graham's reach. Graham charged at him, but before he could land a blow he felt a stab of pain at the back of his head. He fell to his knees, then dropped to all fours.

He rolled to escape the kicking he was sure was coming, but when he looked up he saw that the older man had drawn a Tokarev pistol and was pointing it at him.

'Who are you?'

'Judge, jury and executioner. You killed the boss's brother. The sentence is death.'

'Costa.'

The man smiled and raised his gun.

'Hell,' Graham said. He thought of the hearts he'd broken, the wife he'd lost, the men he had killed. So this was how it ended.

The door to the cell swung open.

All three of them looked around.

The warder opened fire with a burst of Portuguese and gesticulated at the gun. Graham hoped he was telling the man to put the pistol away and not pull the trigger. Behind the guard was the senior officer who had interviewed Graham and asked for the bribe.

The warder spoke in English. 'The capitão asks if you are truly a doctor, as it says on the charge sheet.'

'I am.' Graham left out the bit about him being a veterinarian.

'The captain's wife, she is having a baby and there is trouble. You must come.'

Graham couldn't believe his luck. 'All right.'

The thugs who had been beating him protested, but the captain seemed to outrank the local poaching kingpin, at least here in the police lock-up.

There was loud arguing in Portuguese, but Graham recognised the deep voice of the captain overruling the grey-haired man who the warder had called Luiz. Graham's guard kept him inside the cell until the ruckus had ended, then propelled him down the corridor.

Graham raised his cuffed wrists to his eyes as he stumbled outside into the bright African day. The rear door of a Toyota double-cab *bakkie* opened and Graham climbed in, sighing pleasurably at the relief the air conditioning offered him.

The captain sped off. He spoke rapidly in Portuguese to Graham's guard and turned briefly to glare at him from the driver's seat.

'The capitão, he say that if his baby or wife dies then he let those men kill you.'

'Right,' said Graham.

*

Kerry had found a place to stay, a small lodge with simple but clean chalets.

The owners of the camp, an Afrikaner couple, were welcoming and friendly and tried to sell her on the idea of a birding or fishing cruise on Lake Massingir. She politely told them she had work to do.

Kerry found that her mobile phone couldn't pick up a roaming signal in Mozambique, but she was able to log on to the camp's slow satellite internet to check her emails and Facebook. There was a message from her father, Bruce, saying he was worried he hadn't heard from her and that he would check Skype each evening in the hope that she could call.

She took a deep breath and opened Skype. Even though she was thirty-two she was the youngest child and her father still treated her like a baby. Kerry realised he had become even more protective of her since her mother had died.

'Kerry. There you are.'

It was good to see his face again and she waved at the screen. Her father was looking good; tanned, with his steel-grey hair neatly trimmed. He had been in a bad way after her mother had died, but he was working hard at getting on with his life. 'Hi, Dad.'

'How's the safari going? Seen lots of animals?'

She could see the relief in his face. She wondered if she should tell him where she was. 'It's been great. I've seen heaps.'

'But?'

'But what?'

'Hey, I've known you all your life, kiddo, I can tell when something's worrying you. You've got that look.'

'What look?' Damn, he always could see through her. 'I'm in Mozambique, Dad.'

'But what are you doing there? The itinerary you emailed me didn't say anything about Mozam-bloody-bique; you're supposed to be in some wildlife orphanage patting cheetahs or some shit like that.'

His face was turning red. When her dad got cranky he started talking like a soldier again. Kerry had known this would happen. Still, she was a grown woman and she didn't need her father's permission to visit a different country. She could have lied to him but that wasn't how they worked as a family. Quickly, before she backed out, Kerry told her father about Graham Baird and how she was hoping to represent him.

Bruce raised his hands, palms up. 'What the hell am I going to do with you, kiddo? You're taking on some third-world legal system in a country where you're not even licensed to practise law?'

'Dad, I've got to go.'

Just then the internet connection dropped out. Kerry had time to wave to her father, and then he was gone. He was right, of course, she was totally out of her jurisdiction, not to mention the fact that she was a tax lawyer and had never defended someone accused of a crime.

The internet connection returned, but she didn't try to contact her father again on Skype. Instead, she sent him an email reassuring him she would be fine. She hoped she would be.

Kerry still had Graham's friend Juan's mobile phone number, but when she tried it she found that once again she couldn't get through. She looked up his lodge online and sent Juan an email saying she had seen Graham and would like to talk to Juan. She told him where she was staying and gave the number of the lodge, hoping he might have more luck calling from a landline, assuming he had one.

Kerry gathered her bag and her car keys and decided to go back to the police station and find the man in charge.

*

Capitão Alfredo, the officer in charge of Massingir police station, hugged Graham and kissed him on both cheeks.

Graham broke free of the captain's sweaty embrace, walked out of the officer's house and leaned against the wall. He exhaled and looked at his hands. They were washed, but still shaking. The baby, named Dina, was crying her healthy little lungs out inside. He absent-mindedly patted his shirt pocket.

'Cigarette, yes?' the captain said, appearing beside him and noticing the gesture. Graham nodded. 'No, we have cigar. For baby!'

'*Sim*,' said Graham, using one of the few Portuguese words he knew. Before the captain returned to the house, Graham grabbed his arm. 'Telephone? Please?'

The captain hesitated, then smiled and pulled a mobile phone out of his uniform shirt pocket. He went inside.

Graham's brain had been addled by a good many substances over the years, but he prided himself on his ability to remember telephone numbers. He called Juan.

'Graham? You're lucky to get me. The phone signal has been down lately. Are you still in prison?'

'No. I'm at the station captain's house. His wife was having a breech birth and the local doctor and midwife were both away, or busy, or something. I delivered it.'

'You delivered a human baby?'

'Don't sound so incredulous. I handle difficult animal deliveries all the time. I'm better qualified than some local GP quack to deliver a breech baby.'

'All right. What do you want me to do?'

'Come get me?'

'From Capitão Alfredo's place? OK. I know where that is.'

'Good. Hurry.'

'Ten minutes.'

Graham ended the call just as the captain re-emerged, beaming still, and handed him a Cuban cigar and a bottle of Laurentina Lager. Graham opened the beer and let the policeman light up his cigar, then returned his phone.

'Cheers, yes?'

Graham clinked his bottle with the captain's, but the officer then ushered him inside again with a hand in the middle of his back. Relatives and friends were talking fast and loud in Portuguese and xiTsonga.

The captain was talking to the warder who had been keeping an eye on Graham. They weren't looking at him so Graham backed slowly towards the front door and slipped outside once more.

'Come on, come on,' Graham said under his breath, scanning the street for sign of his friend.

After a couple of agonising minutes Juan's four-wheel drive rounded a corner and came speeding towards the house. Just then, Graham felt a hand grab his shoulder. His heart sank as he turned and saw the captain, who had hold of him, and the warder next to him.

'The captain, he want to know where you are going?'

'Um, nowhere,' said Graham. Juan had pulled up outside the house, engine idling.

The captain reached into the top pocket of his uniform shirt and pulled out a green South African passport and Graham's mobile phone. He spoke in Portuguese.

'The captain, he say that if you do decide to go somewhere, you might need your passport. Also, he say you should go quickly, and no come back to Mozambique for maybe one year. People at the border will be looking for you soon if you try to come back. Fidel Costa's cousin is a senior officer at Giriyondo border crossing. You should be quick.'

Graham nodded and took the passport as the captain let go of him. He shook hands with both policemen and got in the waiting truck.

'Go!' he said to Juan.

Chapter 6

The cemetery was becoming too crowded. There were so many fresh graves, Fidel thought, that if one squinted a little it looked like a freshly ploughed field. The only thing that grew in abundance here in this harsh land was the body count.

Luiz stood next to him, as he had for several other funerals. The old tracker was now the closest thing Fidel had to a direct family member. The pallbearers, the other men Fidel's younger brother Inâcio had been with on the day of his death, slowly lowered the coffin into the gaping wound in the red soil.

Fidel drew a breath. He would not cry in front of his soldiers, but that did not mean he was incapable of grief.

The civil war had robbed him of his mother, father and sister, and his childhood. *SIDA*, as Portuguese speakers referred to HIV-AIDS, had taken two uncles, and his wife had been killed in a car accident in a collision with a drunken driver. Luiz, a friend and wartime comrade of his father, had trained and mentored the young Fidel as he rose through the ranks of the liberation army, and had been something of an uncle to him.

Fidel's early life had been driven by a desire for revenge, for his family and later his wife – he'd had the driver of the car that killed Gracia murdered. Later he had turned to money in an attempt to buy his way out of his grief.

'He was a good boy,' Luiz said, when the priest had finished.

Fidel looked at the open hole, trying, but not quite able to picture his little brother inside the box.

'He was stupid. He should have listened to you, rather than running towards the veterinarian.' Fidel put a hand to his eyes and took a deep breath to try to stifle the scream that was fighting to escape from his lungs. 'But I loved him so much.'

'He knew the risks. We all do.'

Fidel looked around the cemetery. The spaces between the old cement graves of the Portuguese colonials had long since been dug up and filled with the victims of the *SIDA* plague, but many of these new mounds were the unmarked resting places of young men like Inâcio, who had crossed the border into South Africa in search of their fortune. More than five hundred men had been killed while illegally hunting rhino in the past ten years, and a good many of them lay here.

Fidel held the brim of his Panama so tightly he thought he might destroy it. It did not do to show weakness in front of his lieutenant, but the grief was roiling inside him. 'He was more like my son than my brother, Luiz. He didn't need to die.'

Luiz shook his head. 'Not for money. But he did what young men need to do, prove themselves as warriors. Whether it is shooting a RENAMO dog or a rhino, or driving a car too fast or fucking too many whores, young men will take risks and some of them will die.'

Fidel shook his head. 'There was no need.'

'You were the same,' Luiz said. 'You couldn't wait to get to the war and fight for the cause.'

'No,' Fidel corrected him, 'I fought to avenge the deaths of family members. Inâcio wanted for nothing. You saw the car I bought for him.'

'That is why he picked up the AK-47, why he went to the bush.'

Fidel looked into the older man's eyes. They were looking rheumy and Luiz was losing weight. Fidel, who was educated enough to take precautions and rich enough to afford the occasional virgin, wondered if Luiz, despite his age, was succumbing to the virus. 'I don't understand.'

'He was the boss's brother, Fidel. You are right, he did not want for money, but he lacked respect.'

'Who didn't respect him?' Fidel clenched his fists. 'Tell me, and they will answer to me.'

Luiz shook his head again, as if Fidel was the slow pupil who still struggled to understand the formula on the chalkboard. 'He wanted your respect.'

Fidel's vision began to swim. He wanted to cry, to scream, to pull his hair out, but he could not; these were the actions of women, not men, not commanders. He took a deep breath and summoned the memories from his youth, of the days, weeks and years after the deaths of most of his family, and the cleansing that had come through the kick in the shoulder from the recoil of his rifle, the smell of the cordite in his nostrils, and the warm red blood on his hands. He relaxed his hands.

'We need to talk business,' Fidel said. Money, like revenge, would not extinguish grief, but it could pave over it for a while.

'Yes?'

'The South African government has changed its regulations relating to the trade in rhino horn. Their environment minister is allowing limited numbers of horns to be traded within South Africa's borders. If this is the thin edge of the wedge and free trade comes then I want to be part of it.'

'Pah,' Luiz spat. 'I am a tracker and a hunter, not a farmer.

Besides, you know the Vietnamese. They demand we take the ears and the tail of the rhinos we kill so that they know the horn comes from a wild animal killed in the bush, not one that has been reared like a cow and had its horn harvested.'

'I am working on something,' Fidel said, 'that will give us access to captive rhinos. What we do with them, and their tails, ears and horns, will be up to us.'

Luiz looked unconvinced. The gravediggers were hovering nearby, waiting to begin the business of robbing Fidel of the last vestiges of his family. 'But what will you do now?'

'Now? Kill Graham Baird.'

*

Kerry arrived back at the police station but when she walked inside there was only one officer there, a young woman who continued studiously reading a newspaper, even as Kerry coughed for attention.

'Hello? Excuse me,' Kerry said.

'*Por favor, eu não falo Inglês. So Portugues.*'

'No English?'

The woman shook her head.

'Dr Graham Baird? I want to see the doctor.'

The woman shook her head. Kerry turned at the sound of footsteps behind her.

'Good afternoon, miss, can I help you?'

The man who addressed her in nearly flawless English was well dressed in a tailored shirt and trousers and a Panama hat. He was handsome, with a neatly trimmed moustache and engaging dark eyes.

'I'm here trying to visit someone who's in the cells, a Dr Graham Baird, but this woman doesn't speak English.'

The man spoke in rapid Portuguese and the policewoman replied, this time immediately and respectfully.

'The officer says that only relatives of the inmates are allowed to visit.'

Kerry thought quickly. She'd had no problem getting in to see Baird earlier, but a different officer in charge obviously meant different rules. 'Can you tell her I'm his fiancée, please?'

The man raised his eyebrows. 'Really? You are to be married?'

She didn't know what business it was of his, but felt she should keep the conversation going. 'Yes, really.'

The man translated and the woman shrugged and spoke some more.

'Ah, Miss . . .'

'Maxwell.'

'Miss Maxwell, the officer now says that if you are the doctor's wife-to-be then you may visit him, but there is a small problem.'

'Oh? What's that?'

'The doctor is no longer here.' The man conversed some more with the female officer. 'He went with Captain Alfredo, the man in charge of the station, to the captain's house. There was a medical emergency, apparently. I am here to see the captain and I know where he lives. I can take you there.'

Kerry was unsure of what to do. She had a methodical, analytical mind and prided herself on being able to solve complex problems and juggle multiple tasks at the same time, but Africa was bringing her undone. The man standing next to her was polite, but she wasn't in the habit of following complete strangers. 'Can I ask who you are?'

He smiled and gave a little bow of his head. 'My name is Fidel Costa. I am a businessman and local politician; I serve on what you would call the local council. The officer here will vouch for me, I'm sure.' He spoke to her again in their language.

The police officer looked to Kerry and nodded. '*Sim*,' she said, which by the vigorous nod of her head Kerry realised meant 'yes'. 'Big man.'

Kerry felt reassured and she followed Fidel out into the blinding sunlight.

*

One of Juan's safari guides drove Graham's Land Rover through the Parque Nacional do Limpopo and met them on the road to the Giriyondo border crossing.

Graham kept wiping sweaty palms on the side of his grubby trousers as he waited to clear customs and immigration. Graham hoped Fidel Costa's cousin hadn't yet received word to keep an eye out for the South African veterinarian.

Juan stayed in the car park on the Mozambican side of the border until Graham emerged, surrendered to a perfunctory search of his vehicle by the bored customs officer on duty, and then gave a thumbs-up and got in his vehicle.

Graham drove through to the South African side and felt like kissing the woman from the Department of Home Affairs who stamped his passport and welcomed him home.

One of the rules relating to travel through the Giriyondo border post into South Africa was that people using it had to book a night's accommodation in the Kruger Park. This was to stop long-distance lorries and passenger buses using the national park as a short cut to and from Mozambique's Indian Ocean coast. There was a South African National Park office at the border and Graham was able to book a rondavel at Letaba Camp. He would have preferred to drive all the way home, but he figured a night in the park, playing tourist, would give him a chance to chill out before going back to work.

Before getting back into the driver's seat he went to the car fridge in the back of his four-by-four and took out a Long Tom can of Castle Lager and popped it. He drank deeply as he drove into the Kruger Park and then let out a satisfied, celebratory burp.

The sight of hippo sunning themselves on the wide sandy banks of the Letaba River and a bull elephant feeding by the side of the road helped calm him. At the camp he checked in and went to his accommodation, via the camp shop where he bought more beer and a steak to *braai* for dinner.

In the hut he plugged in his mobile phone to charge the battery and stripped off his filthy clothes. Several messages beeped at him. Thandi had tried him a couple of times, letting him know that Kerry Maxwell was looking for him.

He wondered how the woman was faring; he hoped that she, too, had returned to South Africa by now. She would be angry that he hadn't told her he was out of prison and that she had wasted her time; he would have to find a way to keep her calm until he could refund her money.

She was pretty, so the thought of making amends with her was not unappealing. Graham felt bad about the way he had dismissed her. He'd been half-drunk on the rotgut rum, but he had been unnecessarily rude to her.

He took a beer into the shower. She would get over it.

When he finished washing, Graham lay down naked on top of the bed. He fell asleep immediately and it was dark when the sound of his phone ringing woke him. He groaned, rolled over and saw Juan's name on the screen.

'Howzit?'

'Fine, Graham, and you? I take it you're safe in the Kruger Park?'

'I am, thanks. Sheesh, what time is it, man?'

'Ten o'clock. Do you know a woman by the name of Maxwell?'

Graham rubbed his face and took a sip of now-warm beer. 'Kerry, yes. We met briefly when I was a guest of the Mozambican government.'

'She called and emailed me, asking about you and how she could help get you out of prison.'

'So? She's a do-gooder.'

'She left a message for me to call her at a lodge in Massingir. I did, just now. They're worried about her. She booked for dinner but never returned to the lodge. Either she's skipped out without paying her bill or she's gone missing.'

Graham digested the news. 'She's a lawyer, so she's not going to leave town without paying. Also, she doesn't strike me as the type who'd savour the night-life of Massingir – too prissy.'

'What do we do?'

'Check with the lodge again in the morning, see if she showed up.'

'All right. And I'll go to the police station tomorrow and see if they saw her this afternoon,' Juan said.

'All right. Be careful, my friend.'

'Always.'

Graham finished his beer and drifted back into a fitful sleep, but was woken at midnight by his phone. He answered the call.

'Dr Baird?' asked a male voice.

Damn it, he wasn't going to get any sleep this night. 'Who's this?'

'We have your fiancée.'

'My what?'

'Your wife-to-be.'

'I don't have one. Is this a joke?'

'No joke. We are going to kill her unless you bring money.'

'I'm telling you I don't have . . .' Graham felt sick to his stomach as he realised who the man meant.

'Miss Maxwell. She is here. Listen.'

Shit, Graham said to himself.

'Dr Baird,' the Australian woman sniffed. 'I've tried telling them we're not engaged, but it doesn't seem to matter. They're threatening to kill me.'

Graham slapped his forehead. How had this happened? He tried to collect his thoughts. 'Have they hurt you?'

'They roughed me up a bit, pointed a gun at me. This is all very traumatic, you know?'

'Yes, of course. But you're OK, physically?'

Her tone changed. 'I've been a hell of a lot better! Call my father, he's –'

The phone was taken from the woman again.

'Dr Baird, you killed two good men, their families are grieving. You have cost people a good deal of money. You will compensate us for this. You will bring one million rand across the border. You have forty-eight hours, otherwise we will start cutting this pretty woman.'

'No, wait, I don't have that sort of money. Anyone who knows me will tell you that. I'm broke, man.'

'No problem. The woman will die then.' The man ended the call.

Graham sat on the edge of the bed and turned on the light. He called Juan, waking him, and explained what had happened.

'If I try to cross the border at Giriyondo again Costa's cousin will grab me,' Graham said.

'Maybe that's what all this is about.'

'Yes, that's what I thought, too,' Graham said. 'Can you try Captain Alfredo tonight?'

'I'll try, but you saw him when I collected you – already had a couple of beers in his hands. We might just have to trust the cops in the station.'

'*Ja.*' The thought didn't fill him with confidence. 'Can you put the call in?'

'Will do.'

Kerry had asked him to call her father, but she'd been cut off before she could give him any more details. Graham checked the emails on his phone and found one from his friend, Sarah Hoyland, a charity fundraising consultant who specialised in pairing people who were prepared to pay to be volunteers with worthy causes in Africa. It was through Sarah's website that Kerry's trip to Ukuphila had been organised. In the attachment Kerry had completed he found next of kin details for a Bruce Maxwell, Kerry's father, in Canberra. Graham took a deep breath and dialled the number.

'Hello?'

'Mr Maxwell, hello. My name's Dr Graham Baird. I'm a veterinarian in South Africa and your daughter . . .'

'I know exactly who the bloody hell you are. Where's Kerry? Did she get you out of prison? I have to say I'm not very happy about this set-up you're running over there, mate.'

There was no hint of affection in the last word Bruce Maxwell had spoken. In fact, it sounded to Graham more like the gravelly voiced man wanted to rip his head off.

'There's a problem, Mr Maxwell.' When he'd finished explaining what had happened, there was silence on the end of the line. 'Mr Maxwell? Are you there?'

After a few more seconds the man spoke, low and slow. 'I am. But tomorrow morning I'll be in South Africa on the late night flight from Perth. And then watch out, because if anything happens to my daughter in the meantime I'm going to kill you, Dr Baird.'

Chapter 7

Bruce Maxwell surveyed the dull browns and khakis of the bush below him as the SA Express aircraft turned and lined up for its approach to Hoedspruit's Eastgate Airport. He was as alert as he could be after the international flight and domestic connection. He prided himself on his soldier's ability to sleep anywhere, but his concern over Kerry had limited him to naps and nightmares. A wave of heat washed over him as the flight attendant opened the door, and Bruce was taken back instantly to a time forty-seven years earlier, when he was nineteen and had first set foot in Vietnam.

A slovenly long-haired man in khaki, shirt half-in, half-out, boots scuffed, was waiting in the small terminal. 'Baird?'

Graham stroked his nicotine-stained grey beard nervously then thrust out his hand. 'Mr Maxwell, it's good to meet you.'

Bruce didn't move to return the greeting. 'Any news about my daughter?'

'I've been in touch with the Mozambican police. They've been searching for Kerry. They questioned the last person she was seen with, a local politician and businessman named Fidel Costa, but he says he has no idea what happened to her after he dropped her outside the local police captain's house.'

Bruce stared into bloodshot eyes. 'You think he's lying?'

Graham nodded. 'I killed Costa's little brother, a poacher. I think he's got your daughter.'

Bruce tossed his camouflage hiking pack, his only bag, into the back of Baird's Land Rover then squared up, eye to eye with the veterinarian. Bruce had risen in the ranks after Vietnam and later accepted a commission and made it to major. He closed the gap between them and used the low, even tone of voice that was far more menacing than parade-ground bellowing. 'You're responsible for my daughter being kidnapped and you're going to help me find her. Understand?'

'I . . .' Graham began, stumbling over his words, 'I'm sorry, but I think Costa wants me. If I cross the border, I think he'll try and take me, as well.'

Bruce was close enough to smell the stale alcohol and the fear coming off the man. 'I. Don't. Give. A. Fuck.'

Graham gave a small nod, but didn't flinch. 'If they take me, they won't release your daughter. Costa thinks he's untouchable.'

'I've got money,' Bruce said, 'but I'm not interested in negotiating with amateur blackmailers. I'd deliver you to the man myself if I thought it would help get my daughter back.'

Baird shrugged. 'He thinks your daughter and I were engaged to be married. I think that's why he took her, as a way of getting to me.'

Bruce poked the other man in the chest and Baird was sensible enough not to try and resist. 'If you laid a hand on her –'

'I didn't.'

'Did you serve in the South African defence force?'

'South-West Africa – Namibia. Military intelligence.'

Bruce snorted. 'Well then, you can help me plan, if nothing else.'

Baird nodded.

'I'm going to get my daughter back and you're going to do what I tell you.' From his shirt pocket Bruce produced a list he had written on the flight to Hoedspruit. 'I'm going to shower and get a couple of hours' sleep, and by the time I wake up I want you to have done some shopping for me.'

Graham looked at the list and shook his head. 'Or what?'

'Or I'll gut you and dump your body at Mr Costa's front gate. Then I'll kill him as well. Got it?'

The veterinarian swallowed hard. 'Got it.'

Bruce clapped him hard on the arm. 'Good man.'

*

Graham cleared the bachelor's clutter of beer cans and a pizza box from his dining room table and spread out the map of the Kruger Park and adjoining Mozambique that Bruce had asked for.

Piled on his sofa was as much of Bruce's shopping list as he had been able to fill. He had Google Earth open on his computer on his work desk in the corner.

Bruce emerged from Graham's spare room, towelling his hair dry. Graham saw the firm pectoral muscles, the sixpack, the faded tattoos from wars past. Bruce cast his eye around the room. 'Where's my gat?'

'Your what?'

'My rifle.'

Graham threw his hands up. 'A gun's not that easy to find, even in South Africa. I've got you a camouflage uniform from a friend who runs the local anti-poaching unit, combat web gear, compass, hunting knife, even a set of night vision goggles that I must return intact under pain of death.'

'None of that gear's much good if I can't shoot anyone. They tell me this country's awash with guns. Get me a rifle, an R5 if possible.'

'Eli's sorting you a rifle.'

'Who?'

A knock at the door interrupted them. Graham opened it. The man who came in had dark curly hair and the top of his mop brushed the doorframe. His shoulders almost filled it sideways. He carried a big zip-up vinyl dive bag.

The man walked in and extended his free hand, which Bruce shook. 'Eli Johnston, sir.'

'This is the other thing on your list,' Graham said, 'someone who knows the area around Massingir. Eli runs the anti-poaching operations on the Mozambican side of the border in the private reserves south of the Parque Nacional do Limpopo.'

'How do you do, sir?' Eli set down his heavy bag.

'A Yank?' Bruce said.

'SEAL Team Six, retired chief petty officer, Mr Maxwell. Been in Africa going on three years now, most of that time in Mozambique. I'm sorry to hear about your daughter, sir.'

'Call me Bruce. Baird's told you what I need doing?'

'He has.'

'And you're happy to help us mount an illegal cross-border raid. Mind if I ask why?'

'Your daughter's in trouble and a good pilot's been killed, but I've also lost men across the border in Mozambique to these people. Added to that they're slaughtering defenceless wildlife for cold hard cash. To tell you the truth, Bruce, I'm getting a little tired of playing by the rules.'

'Fair enough. Now tell me something I don't know.'

Eli went to the map and bent over, a considerable way, to poke a long thick finger on the table. 'Fidel Costa is one of three local kingpins running the rhino horn trade in this part of Mozambique. He's recently branched out into elephant ivory.'

'Where does he live?'

Eli pointed to the town of Massingir. 'He has a villa here, big place, and what's ostensibly a farm about ten klicks out of town, here. He's got a big house there and accommodation for the poaching teams he runs.'

Bruce rubbed his chin as he studied the map. 'How many teams?'

'Up to five teams of three or four.'

Bruce shook his head. 'A small bloody army. You know all this, so supposedly the local cops know it too. Why don't they act?'

Graham weighed in. 'Costa is connected; he has a network of people on the take. The South African military has all this intel, but they're not allowed to pursue poachers across the Mozambican border or mount operations there.'

'Just like the Taliban scooting over the border into Pakistan from Afghanistan, or the North Vietnamese hiding in Cambodia and Laos,' Bruce said.

'Exactly.' Eli went to the computer screen and clicked on the satellite picture, enlarging it. 'You'll see here the farm is accessed from a rough winding gravel road that leads to a tar road about two klicks away.'

Bruce leaned in closer to the screen. 'Hills there?'

'Yep,' Eli said. 'Granite *koppies*, Afrikaans for rocky hills. Good place for an OP as you can see all the farm buildings from there.'

'That's what I was thinking. How do we insert, that's the question?'

'Long walk from South Africa even if you jump off near the border, inside the park,' Eli said. 'And there's a risk you could bump into a South African anti-poaching patrol or get eaten by a pride of lions.'

Bruce nodded. 'And the doctor here is too chicken to drive across the border in case he gets picked up.'

Graham decided he'd had enough of the insults. 'I'll fly you.'

'I was going to ask you about that, Graham,' Eli said.

'I've got access to a Bat Hawk, a light sports aircraft similar to an ultra-light, that's used for anti-poaching operations on the local game reserves. I use it sometimes to look for injured animals and I fly the occasional patrol flight as a volunteer.'

'You'll be in even deeper shit in Mozambique if you get caught,' Bruce said.

'No worse than I would be if I went across as a tourist. Anyway, I owe it to your daughter.'

'Too right you do,' Bruce said, his face returning to his trade-mark scowl. He went back to the computer and studied the satellite image of the farm again.

Graham looked over the older man's shoulder. 'I'll put down on the road, then we can hide the aircraft somewhere.'

'No,' Bruce said. 'You drop me on the road close to Costa's farm then fly away somewhere safer and put down. We'll have radios and I'll call you when I'm ready for extraction.'

'Too risky,' Eli said.

'Got a better idea, Yank?' Bruce asked.

'Yup.' Eli unzipped the dive bag.

Chapter 8

Kerry cursed Graham Baird out loud as she finished the last of her maize meal porridge. She was still hungry, but pushed the stringy chicken to one side of her plate then dropped it on the floor of the prefabricated metal storage shed.

As she had come to expect, she heard the clank of the padlock being unlocked and the squeal of the door as José, the young man who was guarding her, looked inside.

'What is wrong?'

'I've finished my food and I hate that man who killed your friends,' Kerry said.

José, who had confessed to her that he was just seventeen, nodded. Kerry had been deliberately trying to befriend him.

'The boss says I am not to talk to you any more,' José said.

'I won't tell.'

José looked over his shoulder, as if checking for his master, then back at her. He frowned. 'No talking. Please.'

'I'm scared, José. I'm worried you're going to kill me because that stupid South African man is too poor to bring the ransom.'

'Please.'

'Please, it's not your life that's in danger.' She raised her hands to her eyes and coaxed out some sobs.

José stepped into the room. It was dark, with no windows, but fiercely hot under the African sun. She peeked through her fingers and saw that the teenager was looking at her body. *Good*, she thought.

Kerry sniffed. 'You have to help me, José.'

'I cannot do that. I would be killed. You should not have come to Mozambique to help that man. He is a murderer.'

'I *know*, and I don't care what happens to him.'

José looked over his shoulder again. 'Please, no more talking.'

Kerry let her head hang down despondently, and it wasn't all for show. She had felt helpless, alone and terrified when she'd first realised she was being kidnapped. She assumed that the politician who had helped her at the police station, Fidel Costa, was, in fact, her captor and José's 'boss'.

After she had met Costa at the police station she had followed his Range Rover, in her rental car, to a house in the back blocks of town. They pulled over and got out then Costa told her that this was Captain Alfredo's house and that he would also come in and see the police officer, but first had an errand to run. Costa had left and Kerry had knocked on the door of the house. There was no answer, but as she stood there two men in ski masks jumped from some bushes and grabbed her and put a hood over her head.

Less than five minutes after she had last seen Costa, she was bundled into an air-conditioned vehicle with soft leather seats; it seemed clear to her the politician had lured her into a trap.

The man who had questioned her also wore a ski mask, but she was sure the voice had been Costa's. Her imagination had run riot, thinking she would be tortured, raped, perhaps killed.

Kerry didn't feel as badly towards Graham as she had made out to José, but she wanted to position herself as the innocent victim in all this, to try to win her guard's sympathy.

José was about to leave. 'Please, may I have some more water?' He looked around her cell. Her water bottle was empty.

'And I need to go to the bathroom.' She stood up, defying him. He pointed to the corner of the room. 'We gave you a bucket.'

'I can't do that,' she said, and it was not far from the truth.

He squared up, his machismo returning. 'Well, that is too bad for you.' José walked out and closed the door behind him.

Kerry heard the padlock being slotted into place. She leaned her back against the hot metal wall and slid down until she was sitting. She put her hands over her face and started to cry, for real.

*

The following day Eli drove across the border from South Africa to Mozambique, taking the long way, south to the Komatipoort border crossing, then to Maputo, and north to Massingir.

Bruce and Graham waited for more word from Costa, but there were no more demands. It was time to act.

When the sun was low, turning the grassy airstrip on a private game reserve outside of Hoedspruit into a ribbon of molten gold, they readied themselves for take-off and battle.

Bruce slung the AKMS assault rifle, a modern version of the venerable AK-47 that Eli Johnston had sourced for him, over his shoulder, barrel pointing down. The AKMS had been designed with a folding metal stock, which made it easier for Soviet paratroopers to stow when jumping into battle, and Bruce would be doing just that.

'A friend of mine's been wanting to sell me his old 'chute for a long time,' Eli had told Bruce the night before as he had unzipped the dive bag and pulled out the freefall parachute. 'Hopefully it'll be good for at least one more jump.'

'You don't need a few pointers or some sort of refresher about how to use a parachute?' Graham had asked.

Bruce fixed him with emotionless eyes. 'Some things you just don't forget.'

The way Bruce had stripped, cleaned and reassembled the rifle was also testament to fact that there were some things age did not dull.

'Eli will light up a stretch of road for you five kilometres from the farm. You can land there and wait for my call,' said Bruce.

'I know, I know,' Graham said.

Eli would be providing logistical assistance for the mission. He had a radio-controlled drone, funded by donations from abroad, to use against poachers. It was fitted with FLIR, a forward-looking infra-red camera. Eli would fly it over the farm to give Bruce real-time information. If something happened to Graham's aircraft, Eli would pick up Bruce, and hopefully Kerry. If things went according to plan, Graham would pick up Kerry and fly her to South Africa. The Bat Hawk could only carry two people, so Bruce would meet up with Eli after the raid, spend the rest of the night with him and then Eli would drop Bruce close to the border of the Kruger Park. Bruce would walk through the bush to the South African side and Graham would pick him up in his vehicle and then smuggle him out of the park.

Bruce adjusted the parachute on his back and tightened the buckles as much as he could.

'This is crazy,' Graham said.

'Yes,' Bruce said, 'but my daughter's life is at risk.'

*

A herd of elephants churned the surface of the Olifants River white as they ran through the shallows, startled by the noise of the low-flying Bat Hawk as Graham flew over the border.

We're invading another country, he thought to himself. Bruce was stony-faced beside him, the old soldier betraying no emotion.

Graham followed the river for a while, then turned off to the south to skirt the town of Massingir, whose lights glowed in the distant east. He started to climb.

There was the occasional light below indicating a settlement of some kind in the bush, but Graham relied on the satellite navigation device in front of him to tell them when they were over a spot a kilometre from Costa's farm. On Google Maps they had identified an open grassy *vlei*, which Bruce would use as his drop zone.

Graham pointed to the screen and ahead through the windscreen. Bruce nodded. He had seen the clearing.

Bruce unbuckled his seatbelt, turned to Graham, gave him a quick thumbs-up, then clambered out of his seat and tumbled into the night sky.

*

Fidel Costa drove with no lights on. He was close to the South African border and he knew the military and national parks people on the other side would have observation points on *koppies* and other high ground.

The South Africans also operated helicopters fitted with FLIR at night.

Fidel stopped his double-cab Nissan Navara, turned off the engine, got out and listened. His three-man team in the back of the truck knew better than to make a sound. They waited for his all clear, and Fidel was just about to give it when he cocked his head.

He scanned the night sky over the Kruger Park but, oddly, the faint drone of an engine was not coming from across the border but from behind him. He turned one hundred and eighty degrees and confirmed his guess. That was strange. The Mozambican parks people or police were not operating aircraft in this area at this time.

His men followed suit, another three pairs of eyes scanning the sky.

'What do you think?' he asked Luiz. Despite his age, which was somewhere between sixty and seventy, Luiz had the best eyes and ears of all his men, which made him an invaluable tracker.

'Aircraft. Like the one the American uses sometimes.'

Fidel nodded. Eli Johnston was one of their most annoyingly effective enemies, having foiled several poaching forays. The American occasionally had use of a privately operated Bat Hawk, the same type of aircraft the South Africans used to patrol the Kruger Park.

'You two, stay in the truck,' Fidel commanded the shooter and bearer. 'Luiz, in the front, with me.'

Something was not right on this night. Fidel would not drop off his team so they could walk across the border in search of rhino, not because he was concerned they might be captured or killed, but because he suspected someone was snooping in his backyard.

*

Bruce Maxwell made a perfect landing in the dry grass of the open *vlei*. He collapsed the canopy of the parachute, bundled it in his arms, and took it to the tree line where he stashed it and covered it with dry branches. *Still got it*, he thought to himself; the rush of a successful jump was still there, but it was no time for a celebration.

He took the handheld GPS he had borrowed out of his pocket and checked the coordinates for Costa's farm. It was a one-kilometre walk.

Bruce moved at a steady pace, taking care to watch his footfall so that he didn't snap a dry twig or kick a rock. He felt the tingle of adrenaline charge his senses. He paused by a stout tree, moving from one source of cover to the next, and checked the GPS again. He was on track.

*

Four kilometres from where he had dropped Bruce, and six hundred feet above ground level, Graham Baird wondered if he was lost.

He checked the GPS screen in the Bat Hawk once more and assured himself that he was on track. Eli Johnston should have been somewhere on the road below him.

'Trident, this is Eagle, over,' he said into his radio for the fourth time, using the call-signs he and Eli had agreed on – Eli's after his old Navy SEAL badge. 'Nothing heard, out.'

'Eagle, this is Sabre,' came a voice in his headset.

'Go, Sabre,' Graham said. Sabre was Bruce's call-sign, harking back, apparently, to Bruce's days in an SAS Sabre Squadron.

'Where are you?' said Bruce.

'I'm over the rendezvous point, but there's no one here.'

'Shit happens. Put down where you can and await further orders.'

Graham's nerves were stretched to the limit and he was dying for a drink. Anything could have happened to Eli. He could have come across some poachers, had a breakdown or a flat tyre. Graham checked the fuel gauge. He couldn't afford to loiter about in the air indefinitely.

He carried on another kilometre, then climbed and turned in preparation for landing on a deserted road in the middle of Mozambique.

*

Ahead of him, Bruce could see a hill rising up out of the otherwise featureless bushveld. It was the *koppies*, an outcrop of granite boulders and trees they had identified on the satellite image.

Bruce quickened his pace and made it to the first of the smooth rocks. He started to climb the boulders but found the climb harder than he expected. It was a warm night and by the time he reached the top of the outcrop he was sweating and gasping for air. This, he conceded, was his body reminding him of his age. But the view below him was worth the effort. Not two hundred metres away was a man-made clearing with four buildings around it.

He shrugged off his pack and pulled out the night vision goggles. Bruce saw movement in the open square and focused on it. A man with an AK-47 was walking to the smallest of the four buildings. Bruce heard the sound of metal clanging and a high-pitched voice coming from the compound. His heart pounded hard.

*

'Water! Water! Water!' Kerry kept banging on the metal door of her cell until José relented and came to her.

She stepped back as he undid the lock and opened the door. He thrust a warm litre bottle of water into her hands.

'Toilet?'

José sighed and, as before, instinctively looked over his shoulder. As he turned Kerry noticed the black leather pouch on his belt, a holder for a Leatherman multi-tool.

'Bucket.' He looked back at her and pointed to the corner of her cell with his rifle.

'I'm *desperate*.' She peeked over his shoulder.

'The other men will see you. I will be in trouble.'

'There can't be many of them,' Kerry said.

'There are . . .' He scowled at her. 'You do not need to know how many other men are here.'

Well, at least I know he's not alone, Kerry thought. 'Please, José, I'm feeling sick. I need to go to the toilet.' She doubled over and groaned for effect.

Kerry glanced up and saw José checking behind him again. 'I can't,' he said, but Kerry detected a note of uncertainty in his voice.

She lurched, one arm outstretched for support. José caught her with his free hand, his other still holding his rifle. Kerry reached around with her other arm, clinging to him, and flicked open the cover of José's Leatherman. He lifted her then pushed her away. 'Please, José.'

'All right, quickly.' He opened the door for her and she stepped out. He raised his rifle with two hands and she walked in front of him, towards the tin-roofed brick building that she assumed was Fidel's house here.

Kerry looked around and saw two long buildings that looked like dormitories, each with a row of five windows and doors. Lights shone in three windows in one building while the other was dark. A cooking fire glowed in front of the occupied building and a three-legged pot sat on the coals.

She headed towards the big house, but José told her to turn right. They went around the back to a small outhouse. It was little better than her bucket.

There was a small window above the toilet, but it was too high for her to escape through. When she'd finished she washed her hands and came outside. 'Thank you, José.'

'Hurry.' He pointed back to her cell with his rifle.

Kerry heard voices and looked across to the dormitory room with the lights on. She saw a man in shorts and a football shirt step out. He had an AK-47 slung over one shoulder. He leered at her as she walked past, and she quickened her step. He said something in Portuguese to another man, who pushed past him from inside to get a look at her. The second man laughed then whistled at her, but the two voyeurs then lost interest and returned to their rooms.

As Kerry walked up the three steps back into the storeroom where she was being kept she deliberately tripped and sprawled forward. She cried out. José cursed in Portuguese, but followed her in and bent over and extended his free hand to help her up.

'Are you trying to trick me?' José asked her as she reached for his hand.

'No.' Kerry tried to grab him with two arms and got her fingers under the flap of his Leatherman pouch. She could feel the metal on her fingertips as she pulled the Leatherman tool free.

'Get off me! Stand by yourself.' José shoved Kerry away. Kerry doubled over and unfolded the Leatherman's blade out of sight. When she turned, José's inner gentleman had returned and he reached out to help her up. Instead of grabbing his hand, however, Kerry grabbed the barrel of his rifle.

José pulled the trigger.

Kerry felt the steel of the weapon in her left hand go from cold to cooking as she swung around with José in a deadly dance. She managed to slide her hand down to the wooden foregrip of the rifle before her skin was burned, but held on. His eyes were wide with surprise as if he'd been caught off guard. He kept his finger depressed on the trigger and as they spun bullets punched holes in the shed wall. As quickly as it had begun the barrage of gunfire was over and the rifle was emptied. Kerry arced her right hand around and plunged the blade down somewhere into his back. José screamed in pain, dropped his AK-47 and fell to his knees, frantically reaching for the knife still stuck in his body.

Kerry ran.

*

Looking through his night vision goggles Bruce saw bright plumes of light from the muzzle flash of a rifle at the same time as his ears registered the chillingly distinctive pops of an AK-47 being fired on full automatic.

A woman's high-pitched scream echoed through the night, and just as his wife, Anh, had been able to distinguish the yells of their kids from a cacophony of a dozen others, Bruce knew it was Kerry crying out.

He hauled himself to his feet and hopped down the *koppies*, from boulder to boulder like the sure-footed klipspringer antelope that called these rocky hills home.

Once down he broke into a sprint, thorny acacias scoring his face and hands as he ran through the thick bush. He heard shouting as he closed on the farm buildings. Bruce couldn't face the possibility that he was so close to saving his daughter, only to lose her while he watched from his observation post.

He was not the nineteen-year-old bundle of muscle and testosterone who had gone off to Vietnam to fight, but nor was he unfit, so it was surprising to him that he suddenly found the running so difficult.

Each bound was becoming shorter, slower, and his heart was pounding. His fear for Kerry should have propelled him faster, adrenaline charging his aching limbs, but instead he was fighting for every single breath. The sound of his heartbeat pounded in his ears. Bruce saw lights through the bushes ahead. He carried on, his legs feeling like they were encased in lead. He had to get to his daughter.

When he reached the edge of the clearing two men emerged from a building, one shrugging on a shirt. The other wore a football top. Both carried AK-47s. To his right was the hut in which he'd seen the muzzle flashes. A man was in the doorway, calling to the other two; he was also armed.

The reflexes and skills he had honed in the jungle kicked in. Pain shot up his left arm to his chest, but Bruce had enough energy left to raise his rifle and take a sight picture of the closest of the pair of men. Just as the man noticed him, Bruce squeezed the trigger twice and the man went down, two holes in his chest.

Stunned, but quick to act, the second man raised his rifle and let off a wild burst. Bruce felt the rounds cleave the air beside him. It took all his strength to hold his AKMS up and steady, but he fired twice more and saw the man fall.

Bruce tried to call Kerry's name, but the word came out half-formed, as a groan. He pivoted to the right, seeing the third man come down the stairs from the hut, taking aim at him. Bruce fired, but a spasm of pain overtook his body and his shots went wide. The other man opened up.

Bruce fell to the ground.

Chapter 9

Graham was standing by the Bat Hawk, on the road, when he heard the distant gunfire. The shots continued.

'Sabre, Trident, anyone, can you hear me, over?' he said into his radio. Of Eli there had been neither sight nor sound.

Bruce had given him explicit instructions not to fly to the access road of Costa's farm until he gave the word. The gunfire had stopped. Graham weighed up his options and thought through a range of scenarios of what might have happened. Bruce's radio could have been malfunctioning, Eli's likewise, but the gunshots were not part of the plan. Bruce's idea was that he would reconnoitre the camp, with the help of Eli's drone and airborne infra-red camera, and then the ex-SAS man would sneak into the camp, free his daughter and make his silent exit. Bruce would *neutralise*, as he put it, any guards silently.

His mind made up, Graham got back into the Bat Hawk, started the engine again and took off. As he turned towards the farm he heard static in his headphones and the faint sound of Eli's voice.

'Eagle . . . this is . . . contact.'

Graham concentrated on following the road below while trying to make out the indistinct call on the radio. It sounded like Eli was in trouble. A contact was a military term for a gunfight.

'. . . I repeat, two men wounded, vehicle immobilised.'

'Trident, if you can hear me, I copied that you are not mobile, over,' Graham said. Eli's reply was drowned out by static. 'I am heading to the farm. I heard shots fired there.'

Graham tried Eli a couple more times, but there was no further word from the American. He devoted his attention to the ground and located the junction of the road on which he had landed and the rutted access track to Costa's farm. He turned left and followed the winding route to the politician's spread.

He saw lights ahead and descended to not much higher than treetop level, popping up to clear the granite *koppies* Bruce had intended to use as his observation post. When he descended again he was over the compound. He saw two bodies on the ground and a figure crouched over another prone man. In the moonlight he saw the person's face. It was Kerry. She waved frantically at him and pointed to the smallest of the buildings. As Graham looked over his shoulder he saw a man step from behind the shed and raise a rifle. The muzzle flash winked brightly and Graham heard and felt a couple of bullets rip into the fabric of the flimsy aircraft. He banked hard and tried to climb.

*

Kerry had run to her father, amazed to see it was him firing the rifle, and fallen to her knees. She had run her hands over his body and face, searching for bullet wounds.

But she had found none. Bruce was lying in the dust and his face had turned an odd colour. 'Dad, talk to me.'

Kerry had been initially scared by the noise of the low-flying aircraft but had waved a warning in case it was someone coming to her rescue. The pilot was gone before she could try and make out who it was. José, however, had shown himself; the knife in his back had not debilitated him as he reloaded his rifle and opened fire at the departing machine. Kerry, enraged by all that had happened to her, picked up her father's folding-stock rifle.

She had fired an AK-47 once, at a shooting range while on a family holiday to Vietnam and this weapon looked basically the same. But José had seen her and now that the aircraft was gone he was striding across the compound towards her. As he walked he removed the second magazine from his rifle, tossed it away, and reached into the canvas satchel hanging around his neck for a fresh load.

'Stop!' Kerry shouted.

'You tricked me and stabbed me,' he said. He slotted the new magazine home in the rifle. 'I don't care if the boss wants to keep you alive, I'm going to kill you.'

'No, José, please stop. Please, just let me go, my father needs help.'

He looked at the prone man, then to the bodies of the other two men. 'Your father? He just killed one of my cousins. And now, you . . .'

Kerry saw the fury in the young man's eyes. She brought her father's weapon up to her shoulder. 'No!'

José mirrored her actions. Kerry pulled the trigger. The rifle bucked, slamming into her shoulder, but at least one of her bullets hit home. José pitched backwards into the dirt. There was silence.

Kerry let out a primal cry and dropped the rifle, wanting no more of this killing. Her head was spinning and she felt like she just wanted to curl into a ball. This madness, the kidnapping, the killing could *not* have happened to her. Through her panic and terror, she looked down at her father and fought to regain control of herself. She lay her ear against his mouth. She put two fingers to his neck and when she picked up his pulse it seemed terribly slow. He was clutching his left side and though he was trying to talk he couldn't form his words. She remembered him, now, coming back from the doctor not long before her mother had died, telling her that the 'quack', as he had called their GP, had warned him to lower his cholesterol intake and stop smoking, or suffer the consequences.

'Fit as a fiddle, I am,' he'd said.

Kerry wiped away the tears that filled her eyes.

'Can't . . . can't breathe,' he managed to say.

She adjusted her father's head to open his airway and blew two long breaths into his mouth. From the corner of her eye she saw his chest rise and fall.

'Come on.' Her father was clearly having a heart attack and she didn't know what else to do. He was breathing, but for how much longer she had no idea.

*

Graham brought the Bat Hawk around again. He flew with one hand, every muscle in his body tensed and waiting for the impact of a bullet; in his other he held his pistol, cocked and ready. He could not leave Kerry alone again.

Graham had to land as close as possible to the farm. He took a low pass over the open *vlei* Bruce had parachuted into. There was no telling what the surface of the ground was like. Graham overflew the clearing once more, turned back and prepared to land.

His first touchdown resulted in him hitting a mound which sent him lurching into the air again. He braced himself again as the wheels settled a second time. It was like driving over an endless series of speed humps but eventually the Bat Hawk slowed to a stop. He cut the engine.

From under his seat Graham grabbed his veterinarian's bag. He'd hoped he wouldn't need it, but he was glad now that he'd brought it with him. He wasn't licensed to treat human patients, but on occasion he'd found himself the closest thing to a medical doctor when accidents had happened out in the bush. Bag in one hand, pistol in the other, he ran in the general direction of the farm compound.

*

Fidel Costa smelled blood and cordite on the wind. They had re-joined the main gravel road back to Massingir just as another *bakkie* had been coming from their right.

Fidel had noticed, in the moonlight, that the other vehicle was driving fast, with only its park lights on. He had switched off his engine and called to his men to ready their weapons.

Through his Chinese-made night vision binoculars Fidel had picked out the distinctive silhouette of the American Eli Johnston's anti-poaching vehicle. It had high seats in the back for his men, his dogs and extra driving lights mounted on the roof. Fidel could see two men on the rear seats, rifles across their laps.

'They are moving fast, towards my place,' he told his men. 'Fire at my command.'

When Johnston had come into range they had opened up on him and Fidel had the satisfaction of seeing the vehicle veer and skid off the road, then plough into a grove of thorn trees. There had been a couple of shots fired in their direction, but the barrage of AK-47 fire he and his men had directed at the anti-poaching patrol silenced them.

Rather than staying and finishing them off, Costa had started his engine and sped off in the direction of his bush home. He had stopped whatever part they were playing in the night's strange events.

Just after leaving the stranded *bakkie* he had seen an aircraft, a Bat Hawk, fly low over them. They were travelling with no lights and if the pilot had seen them he gave no indication.

They were out of mobile phone range, so Fidel tried the radio in his vehicle. There was no answer from his men at the farm. He pushed the accelerator pedal to the floor.

*

'Kerry!'

Kerry was panicking. 'Over here,' she yelled.

Graham Baird stumbled through a clump of bushes and sprinted over to her. He fell to his knees. 'Where's he hit?'

Kerry shook her head. 'Heart attack, I think. His doctor was worried about it.'

Graham nodded and opened a leather bag he had brought with him.

'What are you doing?' Kerry said while continuing to compress her father's chest. 'You're an animal doctor.'

He rolled up her father's sleeve, fitted a tourniquet above Bruce's elbow and took out a cannula from his bag. He slid the needle into a vein in the crook of Bruce's arm, then drew it out, leaving the cannula in place. Graham snapped the end off a plastic bottle, filled a syringe from it and squirted the liquid into Bruce. 'This is saline, to make sure the line's clear.' He snapped the end off a vial and drew up another syringe.

Her father seemed barely aware of what was going on, but he was breathing. 'What are you sticking in him now?'

'Epinephrine – adrenaline – we use it in animals just the same as doctors use it on humans who've suffered cardiac arrest.' Graham injected the drug.

The effect of the drug was instantaneous. Bruce coughed, blinked, looked at Graham then reached up and grabbed his shirtfront with two hands. 'Where's my daughter?'

Kerry bent over him and kissed him. 'I'm here, Dad. I'm fine, and so are you.'

Graham drew up another syringe. 'I'm going to give you some

morphine as well, Bruce. We've got to get you to hospital as soon as possible.'

Bruce sat up and Graham injected him in the arm. 'Take Kerry. That's . . . that's the plan.'

Graham shook his head. 'The plan didn't survive, Bruce. Eli's in some kind of trouble. He's got injured men. He didn't make the rendezvous point. I got half a radio message from him.'

Bruce reached for his belt and took his radio. 'Call him, again, on mine.'

Graham took the radio. 'Kerry, I landed not far from here. Help me get your father there.'

'One sec.' She jogged across to José's lifeless body and, swallowing the bile that rose in her throat, bent down and retrieved his rifle. She went back to her father and Graham.

'I'm fine,' Bruce protested, but he was unsteady as Kerry and Graham brought him to his feet.

'Lean on me, Dad.' She put his left arm over her shoulder to support him and Graham got under the right. Kerry carried José's AK-47 and Graham slung Bruce's rifle around his neck. Graham tried the radio as they walked as fast as they could away from the compound and through the thorny bush.

After a couple of attempts, Eli answered. Bruce held up the radio so they could all hear the American.

'I've got two men wounded, one seriously, and my pick-up's been totalled. I've got a vehicle inbound from Juan's lodge to get my men to the clinic in Massingir. We were shot up pretty bad. It was a white Nissan – Costa's.'

Kerry felt her father's body start to shudder as they emerged into a clearing. She saw to her relief that Graham's flimsy little aircraft was parked in the grass. 'Dad?'

'Ease him down, he's convulsing,' Graham said.

Kerry felt the fear almost overcome her. 'What do we do?'

Graham opened his veterinarian's bag again and rummaged through it.

'I'll give him a sedative.'

'No,' Bruce managed to say through gritted teeth. His fists were clenched. 'Leave me, with a rifle . . . Get Kerry out of here.'

'No, Daddy!'

'Yes, you have to . . .'

Her father's body was racked with violent shudders. Graham jabbed another needle into his arm and depressed the plunger. Kerry held her father tight in her embrace until he started to calm.

'What do we do now?' she asked Graham.

He looked her in the eye. 'If I don't get your father to a hospital in South Africa as soon as possible he's not going to make it.'

Kerry looked at the little aircraft. 'Let me guess, no room for three?'

Graham shook his head. 'Not a chance.'

Chapter 10

Fidel moved from body to body. All three of his men who had stayed behind at the farm were dead, and the woman was gone.

Luiz, the master tracker, was looking about for a spoor. He stopped and changed position to keep the tracks he had found between him and the moon. He pointed to the ground.

Fidel went to him, near the edge of the compound. 'What can you see?' he asked in Portuguese.

'Three people. Two men, one woman. One man is injured.'

'Follow them.'

After calling his other men to him, they moved fast through the bush, Luiz barely stopping to check a broken twig, some flattened grass or the occasional boot print visible in the dirt. Ahead of them, out of sight, they heard an engine cough into life.

'Hurry,' Fidel commanded Luiz and his other men. They ran towards the noise. As they entered a clearing, Fidel looked up, and silhouetted against the ivory moon was the Bat Hawk aircraft. Anger coursed through him. 'They have gone.'

They all stood there for a moment, watching the aircraft turn and head west, towards South Africa.

'Yes,' Luiz said, 'but only two of them.'

*

Kerry stopped running. She was breathing hard, but she was fit, a legacy of her regimen of jogging three days a week back home in Australia. She held up the GPS Graham had taken from her semiconscious father. On its screen she could see she was still heading in the direction of the arrow, to the southeast, where Eli Johnston and his men were stranded.

The radio clipped to her belt squawked. She paused, fighting hard for breath, and listened to it. 'This is Sabre,' she said, having adopted her father's call-sign, 'say again, please, Trident.'

'Sabre, I've launched the drone, over,' Eli said.

Apart from when she had first been taken hostage, Kerry had never felt so alone in her life. But to her great relief, Graham had managed to reach Eli before taking off into the night sky with her father, and Eli had been in contact with her, encouraging her, but also warning her to use her father's radio sparingly to conserve the battery. He had told her that he would be using his surveillance drone as soon as he could ready it to fly, to help guide her to him.

She scanned the sky in the direction she was heading. 'I'm looking, but I can't see it.'

'Shouldn't take too long,' Eli said. 'I'm getting a feed from the FLIR camera on the drone now, so I can see in the dark, and pick up anything or anyone moving.'

Kerry was moving again now, as fast as she could through the bush, following the arrow on the GPS unit. Periodically she looked up, and the next time she did so she saw a dark shape. 'I see it,' she said into the radio.

'And I see you,' Eli replied. 'Keep on track, on the course you're following. I'm going to fly a circuit around you to make sure the coast is clear.'

Kerry stumbled and nearly fell, but kept on jogging.

*

Graham pushed the Bat Hawk to its limits and when he picked up a phone signal, crossing the Kruger Park south of Letaba Camp, he called a doctor friend of his who lived at Raptor's View.

The doctor, Bongi, was tired and grumpy at first, but intrigued enough by the severity of Bruce's condition and Graham's odd call for him to meet them at a private airstrip to agree to come out in the middle of the night. He had also called Ukuphila, telling Thandi what he needed.

Graham lined up for the landing. The doctor's Range Rover cast its headlights down the grassy airstrip, along with two other vehicles from the wildlife orphanage.

'Cardiac arrest, Bongi. I've given him epinephrine and ketamine as a sedative.'

Bongi raised his eyebrows as he quickly checked Bruce.

'It's all I had.'

'I must get him to hospital, asap.'

'Can I leave him with you?' Graham asked.

'Where are you going?'

'Back to where I came from.'

'Should I ask where?'

Graham clapped the doctor on the arm. 'No. Thanks, Bongi.'

Graham called to Thandi, who drove the orphanage's *bakkie* over to the Bat Hawk.

'I have the fuel, Dr Graham.'

'Thank you, Thandi. I need to top up and go. Please help Dr Bongi get Mr Maxwell into the Range Rover.'

'*Yebo*, Dr Graham.'

Graham filled the Bat Hawk's fuel tank by hand, sweating as he hefted the twenty-litre jerry cans. Within twenty minutes of landing he was taxiing down the grassy airstrip. He took off and banked sharply to the east, heading back to Mozambique.

*

'Sabre, this is Trident,' Eli Johnston said over the radio.

Kerry slowed her pace but did not stop. 'I'm here.'

'You've got four tangos on your six, over.'

'Speak English, for goodness' sake.' Kerry instinctively looked back as she jogged, but in doing so she missed an exposed tree root. She tripped, sprawled headlong and cried out in pain.

'Four men following, maybe two hundred metres behind you. Are you OK?'

Kerry groped in the dry leaf litter and found the radio she had dropped. 'I think so. I fell over.' She tried to stand, but winced and dropped back to the ground. 'My ankle. I've twisted it.'

'You have to keep moving,' Eli said. 'They're gaining on you. They're all carrying weapons. I –'

'Can you come to me, Eli?' she pleaded, forgetting radio security.

He coughed through the static. 'I . . .'

'What is it? What's wrong?'

'I took a bullet, nothing too serious, but I can't get to you in time.'

Kerry forced herself to stand. The pain in her ankle was agonising. She found a slender fallen tree branch and used it as a walking stick. 'I'm moving again. I'll come to you.'

'Roger that. Sorry I can't be of more help, ma'am. Your friend just called; he's dropped off his package, safely, to a doctor, and he's on his way back.'

Kerry allowed herself one small sigh of relief. At least her dad was in good hands. 'I'm going as fast as I can.'

'Go faster. I can see them . . . on . . . on my screen. They're gaining on you.'

*

Graham spoke to Eli on the radio as he approached Massingir. He turned off before the town to avoid being seen by any police who might be stationed at the dam.

'You say it's four men after her?' Graham asked. Eli's voice was softer, almost a hoarse whisper.

'Roger that. And they're closing on her.'

'Have you got a fix on her?'

'Affirmative.' Eli read out the GPS coordinates of where his drone was orbiting and Graham punched them into the satellite navigation device on the Bat Hawk.

'Talk me in, Eli, I'm nearly there.'

'There are two *koppies* in the area.'

Graham saw the hills, like dark pimples. 'Got them.'

'The tangos are passing between them now.'

Graham scoured the bush ahead and saw movement. If Eli hadn't given him the reference he might have missed it. He broke left, then changed course, so that he would fly a line between the two outcrops. Graham put the stick between his knees and reached under his seat for Bruce's AKMS. He yanked back the cocking handle and let it fly forward, chambering a round.

*

'Graham?' Kerry said into the radio, not bothering any more with the ridiculous code names. 'Is that you?'

'It is, over.'

'I can hear your aeroplane, but the men behind me are getting closer.' She couldn't hide the terror from her voice.

'Kerry, you're not far from the road. It's maybe three hundred metres further from the two rocky hills you just passed between. Get there and I'll pick you up.'

Her ankle was on fire and every step was agony. She didn't know if she could go on.

'Your dad is fine, Kerry. You can do this.'

She hobbled on, but lost her footing again and fell. She dropped the rifle and it clattered to the other side of a rock. Kerry crawled towards it, then paused. She cocked her head and heard footsteps.

'Graham, they're coming for me.'

*

Graham cut his airspeed to as low as he dared without stalling. He looked down at the moonlit bush below. He held the folding-stock AKMS one-handed.

He saw movement and pulled the trigger. The rifle bucked crazily but he kept his finger down as he overflew the two figures. He had no idea if his wild firing had hit anyone, but it had the effect he desired. The men stopped running and turned their rifles on him. Bullets chased him, zinging and slapping through the fabric-covered wings as he increased his airspeed and climbed.

*

'Kerry, listen to me,' Eli Johnston said into the radio.

Having retrieved José's rifle, Kerry reached for the radio and turned down the volume. 'I hear you,' she whispered back.

'Look back in the direction you just came from. Can you see a big dead leadwood tree, with no leaves, like it's been burned or struck by lightning?'

She stared at the ghostly silhouettes around her. 'I don't know that type of tree, but, yes I see a big burned-looking one.'

'One of the targets is approaching that tree. Is your weapon ready to fire?'

Squinting in the gloom, she checked José's rifle. 'Yes.'

'You've got to take him out, Kerry, he's almost on you.'

Take him out? This could not be happening to her. This was vastly different from killing José. That had been instinctive, a sudden life or death reflex action. Now, she was about to kill a man, deliberately, in cold blood. *I'm a tax lawyer*, Kerry wanted to scream. She steeled herself and tried to steady her rapid breathing. 'I'm ready, Eli.'

'He's close to the tree. Aim to the right of the trunk, about four feet off the ground.'

'OK.'

'Pull the trigger when I tell you.'

*

Luiz paused as he approached the dead leadwood tree. He listened. There was the sound of whispering on the faint breeze and the hiss of a radio. The woman – he could tell it was her by the tracks – was close.

She had stopped moving, as there was no noise of her shoes slapping rocks and breaking twigs as there had been last time he had paused to listen. He knew she was armed, but she was just a woman.

Luiz snapped his fingers, summoning another of Fidel's men forward. The man came to him, ready for orders.

'The woman is close, just ahead,' he whispered. 'Be careful, try and take her alive if you can.'

'*Sim*, Luiz.'

The man stepped slowly around the wide trunk of the ancient tree, rifle up.

And then he died.

*

Graham allowed himself a small cheer when he heard over the radio that Kerry had hit one of the poachers.

Eli gave him a fix on the other men. He could only see two moving. Graham lined up for a second strafing run and, having reloaded, once more flew the gauntlet of their fire from below.

Kerry was moving and close to the road, according to Eli. Again, Graham felt the flimsy little aircraft take hits, but he let out a wilder cry of elation when he passed over them without injury to himself. The road was ahead of him now and he brought the Bat Hawk down and landed.

'Graham, Graham, I can see you,' Kerry said over the radio. 'I'm behind you.'

He turned the Bat Hawk, only just clearing the trees on either side of the road, and taxied until he saw her hobble out from cover. He stopped beside her and she was half-in when he heard more gunfire and felt a bullet fly over his head. Kerry had her rifle up as he picked up speed, and emptied her magazine at their pursuers as they lifted off.

When they were clear of the ground and headed towards South Africa Graham reached over to Kerry. She looked at him and grabbed his hand and squeezed it. They looked at each other for as long as they could.

'Eagle, this is Trident, over.'

'Eli, how are you, man?' Graham asked.

'I've had better nights, but I can see the vehicle from Juan's lodge heading my way now, full speed. Cavalry's coming, and the remaining tangos are walking the other way. Me and my guys should be OK.'

'Good to hear, Trident,' Graham said. 'I'll check in with you later.'

'Roger that. Safe travels.'

The wind in the open cockpit cooled them as their shared adrenaline high wore off. The sun was coming up behind them, bringing warmth and a red-gold wash to the bush below.

They cleared Kruger Park airspace but over the Timbavati, almost with Graham's hometown of Hoedspruit in sight, he noticed the fuel gauge needle fall into the red.

Kerry saw him tapping the dial. 'Trouble?'

The engine coughed. 'We must have taken a bullet in the fuel tank.' With that the propeller stopped turning.

'Graham, no!'

'We'll be OK,' he said. 'I won't let anything harm you, Kerry.'

They shared a glance, then Graham looked around. Off to their right was a grassy airstrip used to ferry well-heeled visitors in and out of some of the Timbavati private game lodges. There was an open-topped Land Rover parked at one end of the strip. Animals grazed on bush airstrips and their long open spaces were favourite hunting grounds for cheetah.

Graham banked and lined up for the landing.

'Strap yourself in, as tight as you can,' he said to Kerry.

They glided in, losing altitude at a rate that made Graham doubt his earlier optimism. They came in over a line of trees and Graham's whole body tensed as the Bat Hawk's wheels brushed the uppermost dry branches of a knob thorn.

But then they were down.

They bounced and rolled along the strip and the safari guide driving the Land Rover started up and came towards them. When they came to a halt Graham, doing his best to steady his hands, helped unstrap Kerry and took her hand as she climbed out.

The half-dozen tourists on the back of the truck, dressed in safari outfits and muffled against the chill morning air in scarves and beanies, broke into spontaneous applause.

'Now that looked like a close call,' said the guide.

'You don't know the half of it,' said Graham gruffly.

The guide asked his tracker, who sat on a seat perched on the front of the vehicle, to unpack the vehicle's breakfast supplies.

Kerry stood in front of Graham and looked up into his eyes.

'I'm so sorry,' he said to her.

'You saved my life, and my father's.'

He reached out and put a hand on each of her shoulders. 'And you came to Mozambique to try and save me.'

Kerry smiled. 'Let's call it quits.'

A champagne cork popped and the tourists cheered and gathered around them as Graham and Kerry hugged.

'Welcome to Africa,' he said to her.

Chapter 11

Nsele the honey badger's life was dictated by routine, his horizons limited by grey concrete walls and a wire fence.

For twenty years he had been imprisoned in Australia, but that was not his home. He should have been living free under clear blue African skies. Nsele paced, up and down, up and down.

Soon it would be time to eat. Food was the only thing he had to look forward to.

That was his life, pacing and eating. Nsele's captors were not unkind to him, but nor did they understand him. They did, however, have a healthy respect for him.

In fact, they feared him.

When the guard who fed him came to the prison, Nsele curled his lip. He would not cower before these people, even though they held him. He thought he could detect the scent of fear in the man who slid his food through a metal grate. The man backed away, a little too quickly. He was new. The more experienced warders gave him a wide berth.

While food was all he had to look forward to, there was one other thing that kept Nsele active, kept him engaged and kept him busy – the thought of escape.

He gnawed on a beef bone that was already starting to smell. Nsele didn't care. He was tough and he had a gut that could digest just about anything.

This evening, however, something interesting happened. A brown snake, an Australian native, slithered in through the wire mesh fence. The reptile reared up at him, droplets of venom dripping from its wickedly long teeth. Nsele was not tall and the snake's head was above him, poised to strike.

Nsele watched the snake. When he moved his head from side to side, so too did the horrible hissing mouth. Nsele stood his ground. He was afraid of nothing, no man, no beast, but this was perhaps the scariest thing he had seen, even during his two previous breakout attempts.

He had made it out of the place where they kept him, over the walls of the tiny space that passed as his exercise yard. During a fierce wind storm a branch from a eucalyptus tree had broken off in the gale and been blown into his prison. He had dragged and pushed the heavy limb, rolled it to the wall and, using all his strength, raised it until it was vertical. He'd then been able to use it as an improvised ladder to scale the wall.

However, as soon as he had climbed the first wall he had found himself confronted by the rest of the prison. He had run past inmates, as forlorn or as nasty as he was. They had called their taunts and their threats at him. He hadn't understood these foreigners, of course, but he knew menace when he heard it.

Nsele had no idea where to go, but he'd followed his nose along a winding pathway towards what might have been the entrance. Like now it had been dark and there had been few lights, but he had good night vision. He had come to a gate and started climbing it, stretching, swinging and jumping to the next higher crossbar.

But then he had been spotted. A guard on night duty had seen him and rapped the bars of the gate with a stick, trying to scare him. When more guards were summoned he had led them on a merry chase around the rest of the prison, but they had cornered him eventually. He'd come at them like a tiny tornado, and although they'd finally managed to wrestle him down, he'd left more than one of them bleeding.

Nsele kept watching the snake, and it would have been hard for an observer to tell who was hypnotising whom. Their heads swayed in unison and Nsele stilled his fear, bided his time and waited.

Then Nsele struck.

He reached for the snake and pinned it down, narrowly avoiding the scrape of a fang. He rolled, to try and get behind the head, but the snake was quick as well. It wriggled and slithered under him and wrapped its long body around him, entangling him.

Nsele grabbed and, not having any sort of weapon, he used his teeth. He bit into the cool skin and chomped down, trying to draw blood.

The snake's body convulsed and bucked, and its considerable strength pushed Nsele off balance. No sooner had he been able to get to his feet and try and gain purchase than he was on his back again. He shook and shimmied to try to loosen the reptile's grasp. It was almost as if he was spinning around inside his own skin. Finally he broke free from its grip.

Far from done, the snake reared back its head and struck. This time Nsele had dodged when he should have weaved and he yelped as the fangs pierced his back, twin hypodermics shooting poison into his body.

But Nsele was not dead yet and it would take time for the venom to work its way through his bloodstream. The pain focused him, and Nsele used the split second that the snake's fangs were still inside him to roll again and strike again himself. He grabbed that creature around its girth, between his jaws.

Nsele bit down with all his strength and shook his head from side to side. The snake's body flailed in the night air and cracked like a whip.

The serpent went limp between his teeth; Nsele had broken its back.

Panting, he let the dead creature fall from his mouth then collapsed beside it. Nsele knew he should probably eat the snake, having killed it, and draw strength from its huge body.

Instead, however, he felt a numbness supplant the pain as his nervous system began to shut down. The ceaseless noise of the traffic and honking of horns from outside the prison's walls began to dim.

At last, he heard silence, and felt at peace. His last thought was of the day he had been captured, in his home. Africa.

*

Sarah Hoyland sat at the desk that had been allocated to her in the Sydney office of the Animals Without Borders wildlife charity, opened her MacBook and checked her emails. The NGO operated out of a serviced office in North Sydney, an internal suite with no windows. It was important that potential donors she might bring to the office didn't think the organisation had *too* much money.

Sarah's digital inbox was full to overflowing. She'd been increasing her Facebook posts in the lead-up to some big announcements and the traffic was coming in, from people wanting to donate, offering to help, or just asking for more information. Other than the chief executive officer, Fiona Murray, who had started Animals Without Borders, Sarah was the only other person in the office who was paid for her work – the rest of the staff were volunteers. As a professional fundraiser Sarah's job was to get more people from around the world and all walks of life to donate money to the cause. In addition to the hourly rate she charged Fiona for her expertise Sarah had negotiated a success fee in her contract – the more cash people handed over, the more money she received. She had also been brought in to raise the organisation's profile in various African countries, especially South Africa.

That was the point of social media and public relations, of course – to garner support for the cause she also passionately believed in – but the more she did, the greater her workload became.

She sighed as she scrolled through the list of messages, knowing that much of her afternoon would be spent in the office responding to all these people.

One message caught her eye. It was from Graham Baird. The time on the message showed that it had only been sent a few minutes earlier.

Sarah looked at her watch. There was an eight-hour time difference between east coast Australia and South Africa, which meant that it was about one in the morning in Hoedspruit.

Sarah shook her head. She opened the email and judged from the typos that Graham was probably drunk. He asked her how she was and apologised for not replying to her last four emails. His excuse made her heart lurch. He had been in prison in Mozambique.

Her last message to him had been angry, telling him to get his act together because she needed his input for the meetings she was having in Australia with the people from the New South Wales environment ministry and the Downunder Zoo, a private facility with an impressive collection of African wildlife in the state's central west. She had a temper and she had been hard on him.

Sarah logged into Skype and saw that Graham was also online. She started a video call.

'Howzit, Sarah,' he said when his face came up on the

screen. 'Thanks to the marvels of modern communications technology you can now criticise me face to face.' He took a drink from a big glass with a Kenyan Tusker Lager logo on it. The beverage inside wasn't beer, however. Sarah knew Graham well enough to guess that it was probably a triple brandy and Coke.

'Very funny,' she said. 'I wouldn't have been so nasty if I'd known you were in prison. Which customer did you rob?'

Graham put a hand over his mouth to cover a mini belch. His cheeks were red and his forehead glistened with sweat. 'I'll have you know I risked my life to save a damsel in distress.'

'Sure, sure,' she said. 'Seriously, are you all right?'

He waved a hand. ''Course I am. What do-gooding are you doing now?'

'Well, if you'd read my emails you would know that things are on track to bring the sable antelope over, but there's another animal the Downunder Zoo over here wants us to take home to Africa.'

'What is it?' he asked.

'A honey badger.'

Graham raised his eyebrows. 'Serious?'

'Very. It's called Nsele.'

'Zulu for honey badger,' Graham said.

'I know. Original, right? True to form it keeps escaping from its enclosure and its keepers are terrified of it. The fierce little bugger was bitten by a brown snake the other day, but he killed the snake, tried to eat it, fell into a coma then eventually woke up. Nsele's popular with visitors, but he's a headache. The zoo people privately can't wait to get rid of it. They've all but said they want us to take it as a show of good faith, and, to be fair, something of a test case in moving animals from Australia to South Africa.'

'It's hardly an endangered animal,' Graham said. 'Anyway,

how's the weather there? It's damn hot here, can't wait for the rains to start.'

She was about to tell Graham about the rain when a figure moved into view behind him. It was a woman with dark hair, and wearing short pale blue pyjamas that showed off slender arms and legs.

The woman held up a glass of what looked like water. 'Graham, do you have any ice?'

The accent was pure Australian twang.

Graham partially lowered the screen, and Sarah was left looking at the keyboard of Graham's computer.

'Sorry to interrupt,' the woman's voice said from the background. The sound was still on.

'Oh nothing, nothing at all. Just work.'

'Um, sorry, again,' the woman said. 'This is kind of embarrassing. I'll leave you to your privacy.'

'Graham!' Sarah yelled.

'What?'

'Who's that woman?'

Graham burped, raising the screen again so that the room swung back into view, then waved a hand across his face. 'That's the one.'

'Which one? You're drunk.'

'Am not. The one I rescued.'

'The damsel?'

'Yes.'

'What's she doing at your house, half-dressed?'

'She's a volunteer – you should know, you sent her. And she's mostly dressed. Pyjamas. In this weather it's acceptable attire.' He burped again.

'Oh,' Sarah nodded. 'That's Kerry Maxwell?'

'Kerry-Anh Maxwell,' Graham corrected.

Sarah told herself that if he was up to some hanky-panky with a volunteer he would have tried harder to hide it, or been more indignant. Instead he was smiling at her.

'Graham . . .'

'Sarah . . . If there had been anything going on here do you think I'd be so flippant?' He moved his face closer to the screen and lowered his voice to a conspiratorial tone. 'Between you and me, she's a bit of a cold fish. I think she might even bat for the other team.'

'Why, because she hasn't fallen for your charm?'

He looked over his shoulder, theatrically checking if the coast was clear, then leaned in close to the screen. 'Vegetarian.'

He leaned back in his chair and laughed. Then, seeing the scowl on her face, he ran a hand down in front of his face, wiping away his smile. 'Sorry. I'll be good now.'

'Hang on,' Sarah said, 'you said you had to rescue her? You're not opening me up to a lawsuit are you, Graham Baird?'

'No, no, no; storm in a teacup. The girl's fine. So, what exactly do you want from me? I saw your email asking me to contact you.'

'I'm bringing the honey badger to South Africa and I need you there to look after the animal and make sure it's fit and well before we release it at a media event.'

'Where's Vergel with two "e"s? Isn't he your celebrity vet?' Graham said. 'He can do all the checks on the honey badger for you, and be your talking head. He's good at that.'

Sarah shook her head. 'No, he can't. He's in hospital.'

'Why?'

'Vergel's got malaria. He came down with it two days ago. He was shooting a documentary in Zimbabwe a couple of weeks ago, around Victoria Falls, and he reckons he picked it up there.'

Graham sat bolt upright and seemed instantly sober. 'How is he, Sarah? Do the Aussies know what they're doing?'

'Relax, Graham, he's in good hands and yes, they do know

about the disease here. He was supposed to do some media interviews in Australia prior to us leaving with Nsele, but I've had to cancel all those. I really need you, and the coverage in South Africa, Graham.'

Graham nodded, though Sarah could see his face was pale. Graham of all people knew how serious malaria could be in its various forms and she felt a pang of sympathy for him. He forced a smile, though, trying no doubt to get back to his old drunken self. 'Damn bad luck. No TV vet for the Aussies.'

Sarah ignored the sarcastic barb. Graham and Vergel Worth did not get on, even though they worked together often. Vergel had a reality TV show called *Extreme Vet*, which showcased his work with big game in Africa, and Sarah suspected Graham was jealous of Vergel's success, wealth and good looks. Sarah had once had a fling with Vergel, before he had taken up his position as Animals Without Borders' honorary vet, but he was married and they had agreed it had been a mistake. After it was well and truly over she had invited him to work for the charity. He was great for public relations and fundraising, a household name in much of the world, handsome, witty and an excellent vet.

'Damn bad luck is right. He was going to be my keynote speaker at the Cape Town dinner.'

'Yip, well, that's the way the cookie crumbles.' Graham took another long gulp of his drink.

A pop-up notification at the top right of Sarah's screen caught her eye. It was a Facebook post, from Eli Johnston, another fine-looking specimen of a man. Sarah clicked on the link and her eyes must have widened considerably as she read the post.

'Are you looking at dirty pictures on the internet?' Graham said.

'Ha ha. I'm not like you, Graham. Did you know Eli Johnston was wounded in a gun battle in Mozambique?' she asked.

'Do I know?' It was Graham's turn to widen his bloodshot

eyes. 'I was there. Eli was supposed to be the ground element for my operation in Mozambique. Fidel Costa ambushed him and shot up Eli and some of his guys.'

'Fidel Costa the politician? In a gunfight?'

Graham shook his head. 'Oh, no, Costa's too clever to be out in the bush pulling the trigger himself, but it was his men.'

'That's a relief,' she said.

'Why?'

'Oh, nothing,' Sarah said. 'I'll tell you later. Now what happened in Mozambique?'

He sighed. 'I killed a couple of poachers, got thrown into prison and your earnest volunteer, who happens to be a lawyer, tried to get me out. In the process she became detained and I had to rescue her, with the help of Eli and the girl's father.'

'Graham!'

'Calm down, Sarah.'

'Don't bloody tell me to calm down!' She clicked on Eli's Facebook post.

'OK,' she said, speed-reading. 'Eli's concentrated on the attack on his men – and himself – and mentioned an operation to free an innocent hostage taken by a poaching kingpin. My volunteer. Shit, Graham, what have you got me into?'

'She's fine. You just saw her. One of the men I killed was Costa's brother. He was trying to lure me back to Mozambique by holding the girl hostage, but everyone's fine now, sort of.'

'Sort of, Graham?' Sarah gripped the arms of her chair.

'Eli's probably left out our names so the authorities in South Africa or Moz don't start asking questions. Costa has friends in high places in their government – it's how he's stayed out of prison even though everyone knows he's guilty of rhino poaching – and he could make trouble for Kerry and her father Bruce, who entered the country illegally. As did I, of course. Between us we broke maybe a couple of dozen laws, which isn't bad, even for Africa.'

Graham laughed, but Sarah's mind was turning over the new information. She had broken a few laws herself, when she lived in Mozambique, but was on the straight and narrow these days. Sarah had driven overland tour trucks in Africa and ended up on an island off the coast of Mozambique where she had, for a time, become involved with a former British military officer who was leading a gang of modern day pirates. There were some things she had done that she hoped would never come to light given her new career as a fundraiser, but what she saw in Graham's story was not something to be covered up – far from it.

'You never check Facebook, do you?' she asked.

'Do I still have an account? In my defence, I do "tweet" occasionally.' Graham made air quotes with his fingers. 'I find Twitter a good source of news and links to porno sites.'

'Graham! Behave. Listen to this.' Sarah called up Eli's page again and read from his post. *'Kudos goes to our anti-poaching operatives who held their ground and returned fire in the face of a fierce ambush, and to Juan Pereira and his staff who patched me up. They probably saved my life.'*

'A tad melodramatic, but it's the truth,' Graham said.

'This is gold, Graham.'

'Stop talking in Australian,' he said to her. 'In English, woman, or Afrikaans at least.'

'Don't call me woman. You know I hate that, and all that "my girl" South African rubbish.'

'Have a drink.' He raised his glass and drained it. 'I need a top-up.'

'No, Graham, just a minute. Hear me out.'

He looked at his watch and started to stand. 'It's Captain Morgan time.'

She held up her hands. 'Stop.'

Graham sat back down. 'I love it when you're forceful.'

94

'Shut up and pay attention.'

'Yes, miss.'

'The stuff Eli has posted is pure gold when it comes to tugging on the heartstrings of donors, and raising money for our cause. That's a real live report from the front line of the war against poaching.'

Graham picked his nose.

Sarah wagged a finger. 'I'm warning you, Graham. Listen to me. I need you for the honey badger job, but I also want to fly you to Cape Town.'

'What for?'

'Like I said, Vergel was supposed to be the guest speaker at my fundraiser there. I've got all sorts of politicians and people coming, plus some zoo people from Australia attending a conference there at the same time.'

'Um, no.'

'Why not? I've just offered you a free trip to one of the most beautiful cities in the world.'

'I like Hoedspruit, thanks.'

'Graham, come on!'

'I don't like public speaking, the limelight and all that.'

'You'll be fine, Graham. There are some tricks I can teach you about addressing a crowd of people.'

'Such as what?' He sounded dubious and instantly sober.

'Imagining everyone in front of you is naked.'

'I do that all the time.'

Sarah sighed. She then wondered if she had spoken too soon. However, she thought of the two hundred–plus people who had paid good money to see television's bush vet, Vergel Worth, and she shuddered. She did *not* want to have to refund all that money.

'Graham, please tell me you'll come to Cape Town, to talk at our function.'

He rubbed his stubbled chin. 'Honestly, my girl, I'm not

interested.'

'Don't call me that.' Sarah played her trump card. 'What about money.'

He blinked. 'You didn't say anything about cash.'

'The television vet was going to be paid an appearance fee. He'll have to claim that back on his travel insurance now, lost income and all that.'

'Hmm,' Graham said, and she could see the sparkle in his eye.

'Twenty thousand rand.'

Graham gave a low whistle. '*Eish.*'

She held back a smile. The appearance fee was actually twice that amount, but Graham didn't need to know that. She wondered if he even realised just how big an international star Vergel was.

'It's yours, if you come.'

He shook his head. 'No.'

'Come *on*, Graham. I know you could use the money and I'm asking this as a friend.'

'No.'

'Graham!'

He held up his hands and smiled. 'Relax, Cinderella. You can go to the high roller's fundraiser and I don't need your money. Pay for the flights and my accommodation and,' he raised his glass and clinked the ice cubes, 'this stuff, and you've got yourself your talking monkey.'

'You don't want the money?'

He shrugged. 'Give it back to the cause. There have been hardworking saps and armchair conservationists around the world raiding their piggy banks to help you – help us – so it seems wrong to take their cash.'

Sarah ignored the thinly veiled criticism of Vergel. 'Thank you. You've got me out of a bind, and possibly reminded me why I like you. Also, since you're coming to Cape Town, I need you to do a check on half-a-dozen black rhino at a small private game reserve not far from the city – Vergel was going to do that for me as well. I'm working on a project to relocate them to another country to start a captive breeding program.'

'Where are they going? Australia? You were working on relocating some of them over there, weren't you?' Graham asked.

'Can't tell you right now as it's hush-hush, but I'll be announcing it in Cape Town.'

'Intriguing, and I'm happy to give your rhinos the once-over. Look forward to seeing you soon. All of you.' Graham shifted in his chair, grinned, and half closed his eyes.

Sarah couldn't miss the unmistakable sound of a fart. She shook her head and ended the call. She went back to Eli Johnston's Facebook page. She re-read his account of being in the gunfight with poachers. There were a few pictures he had posted with the story. One showed a ranger standing in the open, firing a rifle – probably during a shooting practice, she imagined, but an action shot like that would help gather more likes. There was another shot of Eli, in hospital, bare-chested with a bandage around his arm. His skin was smooth, possibly waxed, and Sarah wondered what it might be like to run her fingers over that. Graham's torso was covered in too much wiry salt and pepper hair.

Next she typed 'Kerry-Anh Maxwell' into Facebook's search window and soon found there was only one woman with that name, who was also a friend of Graham Baird.

Sarah went to Eli's post and hit Share so that it came up on her Animals Without Borders Facebook page, and then started to tap in her own caption.

Amazing report from anti-poaching warrior Eli Johnston on his gunfight with poachers in Mozambique. What Eli wasn't able to report, for security reasons, was that Animals Without Borders' *own assistant veterinary surgeon, Dr Graham Baird, was also caught up in that action. Graham was in a helicopter that was shot*

97

down a few days ago by poachers, also in Mozambique, and personally killed two of the gang that had been slaughtering elephants. To top all that off, after escaping unlawful imprisonment and making his way back to South Africa, Dr Baird then went back over the border to rescue a young wildlife volunteer, Kerry-Anh Maxwell and her father, Bruce Maxwell.

'Yes,' Sarah said to herself. 'Gold.'

Chapter 12

Kerry woke to the sound of her phone ringing.

'What the bloody hell's going on?' her father said by way of greeting.

Kerry rubbed her eyes. 'Dad? What's up?'

'Face-bloody-book, that's what's up. What are you playing at?'

Kerry swung her feet off the bed. She hadn't even been sure where she was when she opened her eyes, but now she remembered. She needed to go to the toilet. Holding the phone to her ear she opened the bedroom window. Her father was still in hospital, where he had been given an angiogram and had a stent inserted. As far as she knew he was doing fine.

'I have no idea what you're going on about, Dad.'

'Your name's all over the internet, all the stuff about you being kidnapped, about the bloody vet coming to get you. Eli's really worried for you.'

'Hold on, hold on. I need to wee.'

'TMI, as the young people say. Call me back. I'm on my Aussie phone and it's costing me a fortune.'

Kerry rolled her eyes as she walked passed the litter of Graham Baird's evening – a pizza box, empty beer cans and a half-demolished bottle of rum. There was a pair of underpants hanging over the back of a dining chair.

In the bathroom she checked her phone. 'Shit.'

Her Facebook account had been bombarded with messages from friends and relatives wanting to know how she was, and if her father was OK. A couple of friends had shared a post from Sarah Hoyland which, Kerry saw, was actually a re-share of something Eli Johnston had posted. Kerry quickly read the posts and most of the comments and as she did so she felt her anger start to rise. She called her father back.

'Dad, I don't know how that woman got all that information.'

'Well,' Bruce huffed, 'she's obviously a buddy of your no-good friend Graham Baird. He must have told her everything that happened and she's spilled the beans. This is a serious breach of what we used to call operational security in the army. She's practically told the world how we violated Mozambique's borders and your name – and mine – are out there for anyone to see.'

Kerry felt her anxiety rising. 'Damn. Maybe I should contact a lawyer here, get some advice. I might need one in any case to help me with the car hire company – my rental car is still in Massingir and I'm facing a huge bill to have it brought back to South Africa.'

'Don't bother about lawyers and cars. Get back to Australia. Today. See if you can change your flights and head back to Sydney this evening.'

'I've still got more than six weeks left of my stay in Africa, Dad, and I'm not ready to go home. I'm shaken by what happened, of course, but now that I've learned so much more about the poaching problems here I want to help out more than ever.' Her father shook his head and Kerry knew what she was saying was counterintuitive. As terrifying as her ordeal had been it had also exposed her, firsthand, to the seriousness and violence of poaching in Africa and made her even more aware of the need to fight it. If she left now, while people such as Graham and Eli stayed in the fray, then what sort of person would that make her? Added to that she realised she had become hooked on the continent and its wildlife and landscapes in a very short time. 'But what about you?'

'I'll be fine,' Bruce said. 'Doc says I'm on the mend. Besides, I've got Eli here to keep me company. His medical aid insurance company flew him from Mozambique to South Africa to treat his gunshot wound and he ended up here in Nelspruit in the same hospital I'm in. Apparently a lot of people who get sick or hurt in Mozambique end up here because it's the closest decent hospital on this side of the border. He's ropeable, too, love. Eli's very annoyed that someone put all that info on Facebook about you.'

'I can't say I'm overly happy about it, either. I'll ask Graham about it when he gets out of bed.'

There was a pause on the end of the line. 'Kerry, please don't tell me . . .'

She laughed. 'Oh, no way. Come on, Dad. There's no way I'd sleep with him.'

'Sleep with who?' Graham asked.

Kerry turned and saw Graham, dressed only in a pair of chequered boxer shorts, scratching his groin.

'Got to go, Dad. See ya. I'll call you later.' Kerry hung up before he could say anything else.

'Graham, have you seen Facebook?'

He shifted his scratching to his stubbled chin, and then around to his rear end. 'As a rule, no.'

Kerry thrust her phone towards him. 'Read that.'

'Let me get my reading glasses.' He plonked himself down on the tattered couch and started rummaging under the pizza box. 'I know they're here somewhere.'

Graham found his glasses and put them on. 'Oh, dear,' he said.

'Yes. We're trending. Breaking the internet.'

'Probably good for my business. I might get a few more paying volunteers.'

'I'm not laughing, Graham, and neither is my father. He and Eli are worried we might get in trouble from the Mozambican authorities.'

'Pfft,' said Graham. 'Costa knows me, he knows where I live. If he wants me he'll come for me one day, or send one of his henchmen or poaching gangs, more like it.'

'You're very fatalistic.'

'You have to be, living in Africa. You never know what *kak* is going to come your way next.' Still reading, Graham made his way to the refrigerator.

Kerry snuck a look at him. His general unkempt demeanour gave the impression of a middle-aged man going to pot under his baggy sweat-stained bush clothes but, in fact, she saw he was surprisingly toned. She guessed his work was quite physical, but she had also seen a pair of running shoes on Graham's front porch, and she had noticed a pile of particularly smelly mouldering exercise shirts and rugby shorts in the laundry.

He took a quarter-full plastic bottle of orange juice from the fridge and closed the door, then handed the phone back to Kerry. 'This is Sarah's handiwork.'

'Sarah Hoyland? The woman I booked my stay here with?'

'Yes.' Graham held the juice out to her, but she shook her head. He put the bottle to his mouth and drained it. Kerry cringed. 'That's who I was Skyping with last night. She's a professional fundraising consultant for do-gooder groups, kind of a hired gun who helps charities rake in more bucks and takes a cut as a management fee. She runs that business you booked through, pairing paid volunteers with people like me as a sideline. Her big client at the moment is Animals Without Borders.'

'Oh! I read about them on her website. They do brilliant work, relocating African animals from zoos around the world back here, and sometimes moving endangered wildlife, such as rhinos, to safer havens.'

'I know, I'm their back-up vet. Their main guy is –'

'Vergel Worth. He's gorgeous.'

'If you like the pretty-boy, lantern-jawed type.'

'Mmm, yes please. But tell me more about Sarah.'

'Well, like all do-gooders, she's got her eye on the dollars. Vergel is in Australia with her – she's negotiating with the Downunder private zoo to bring some sable antelope and a honey badger, of all things, back over to South Africa – and he was supposed to speak at some gala fundraisers in Sydney and Cape Town and make all the rich middle-aged matrons swoon and part with their savings to save the furry creatures of Africa.'

'You're a cynic,' Kerry said.

'You think?'

Kerry ignored the sarcasm. 'So why all the stuff about you and me escaping from Mozambique?'

'Vergel's come down with malaria and Sarah wants me to be her ventriloquist's dummy and talk on stage in Cape Town and at some media event dog-and-pony show when she releases the badger into the Kruger Park. The idea is to tug at everyone's heartstrings.'

'Ah,' said Kerry. 'So she thinks people will be interested in hearing about your gunfights with the poachers?'

'And yours, too, I expect.'

'That would explain why she named me in the posts. She had no right to do that without my permission,' Kerry said.

'Sarah subscribes to the old saying that it's easier to ask for forgiveness than permission,' Graham said.

'Clearly. You don't seem very worried by all this.'

He shrugged again. 'Why should I be? I'm not scared of Costa.'

Kerry drew herself up and thrust out her chin. 'Then neither am I. You don't seem too upset about this Sarah splashing your name all over the internet. How come you aren't mad?'

'Oh, I'm not happy, but Sarah knows the one thing that will stop me complaining. Money.'

'You get paid for your work for Animals Without Borders? I thought that was a charity gig.'

'It is, for me at least, but she was going to pay Mr TV Vet some serious coin as an appearance fee. Hero that I am, I'm only asking for my room and board as recompense for wowing the crowd.' Graham ran a hand theatrically through his lank, greasy greying hair.

Kerry raised an eyebrow.

'What are you insinuating, Miss Maxwell?'

Kerry looked him up and down. While his body was lean, the rest of him was a wreck. He rummaged in the mess on the coffee table and found a packet of cigarettes. He shook it and the last one fell out. His eyes gleamed like a kid who had just been told he could have ice-cream for breakfast. Graham picked up a lighter.

'Out . . .'

He glared at her. 'This is my house. You don't like smoking, then *you* go outside, Miss Prissy Pants.'

Kerry saw red. She put her hands on her hips and took a step closer to him.

He raised the flame to the tip and sucked on it. The orange glow mocked her. 'Sarah will want you, next.'

'What do you mean?'

He exhaled, though he blew the smoke away from her. It wasn't enough; she coughed and waved a hand in front of her face. The smoke stank, he smelled of perspiration, and the house was a tip. 'You're part Vietnamese, you're pretty. Sarah is also doing a lot of work in 'Nam; everyone's on the rhino bandwagon, but she's buttering up the Vietnamese government with her plans to relocate African animals. She makes your people feel good about themselves, and not the wildlife criminals that most of Africa think they are. You'll be a perfect token Asian to front her campaign.'

'How. Dare. You.' Kerry raised her hand.

'Want to slap me again?'

'Yes!'

'Ooh, goody. It was strangely arousing last time.'

They stared at each other and then a phone rang. Graham found his iPhone, which had a cracked screen, under a half-eaten packet of Simba chips.

'Howzit. Yeah. OK. I'm coming.'

Graham turned and went back to his room.

'Don't just walk away from me like that,' Kerry said. She was angry at him and the slur he had cast on her background. He was infuriating.

Graham said nothing but emerged less than a minute later. He had put on a pair of shorts and sandals and was buttoning up a stained bush shirt. 'Wild dog. Hit by a car on the road into Hoedspruit. We can continue this later.'

'I'm coming with you,' Kerry said.

He shrugged and checked his watch. 'Suit yourself. I'm leaving in three minutes. The dog's still alive – just.'

Kerry rushed back to her room, took off her pyjamas and shrugged on a shirt dress. She grabbed a pair of shoes and her camera, and went outside. Graham was in his Land Rover and had the engine running. She could see he was putting the truck in gear as she opened the door.

'You don't have any shoes on, Graham.'

'So what? I wear them as little as possible. Hurry up and get in.'

She climbed into the four-wheel drive. Graham let out the clutch and the wheels crunched the gravel drive. They bounced along the Raptor's View dirt roads as fast as Graham dared, although Kerry noticed he didn't break the speed limit. At least, she thought, he cared about not injuring wildlife, even if he paid no attention to hurting people's feelings. She had been almost ready to walk out of his house – she was sure that was what he wanted – but she had come here to help save wildlife and that was what Graham was doing.

For all his faults, and they were many, Graham had a genuine passion for wildlife. It seemed to Kerry that he preferred the company of animals to people. She'd often heard people say they were like that, but had never met anyone of whom she truly believed it, until Graham.

He stopped for a giraffe to cross the road, then sped down the hill and across the low-level bridge of the creek bed that was dry except for a reedy pool. He left the estate, impatient for the boom gate to rise, and then turned right. Each four-way stop in the town seemed to increase his level of frustration and anxiety.

When he came to the Pick n Pay centre he turned right again and picked up speed as soon as he was away from the town proper.

'Keep your eyes peeled. It's somewhere on this road.'

After a few kilometres a gaggle of three cars parked off on the grassy verge of the main road told them they had found the right spot.

Graham opened the back of the Defender and took out a leather bag. It was the same one he'd had with him at Costa's farm, but in the light of day Kerry could see that it was old and the skin looked like it could have been crocodile – not very PC, but sturdy enough to survive a long time.

'Get that *lappie* off the back seat,' he said to her.

'That what?'

'Tea towel.' She picked up the rectangle of grubby fabric.

The crowd of people standing in a circle broke ranks to let Graham in.

'We've tried to give it some water,' a woman said.

'Step aside, please. Kerry, put the towel over its face, please.'

The dog was weak, barely able to open its jaws. She tentatively hovered over it.

'Just cover its face.'

Kerry dropped to her knees and found that when she did put the cloth over the dog's face, it calmed down.

Graham set about examining the dog, thoroughly yet gently. 'This leg is broken, but it looks like there might be internal injuries as well.' He opened the bag and drew up a syringe from a vial. 'I'm going to immobilise it, then we've got to get it into the truck.'

Kerry ran her hands over the dog's coat. It was a stunning patchwork of brown, black, golden tan and white. 'This is the first wild dog I've ever seen.'

'Well, shame it had to be three-quarters dead. Bastards. There's good visibility either side of the road here; whoever did this must have been flying, or half-drunk, or both.'

Kerry heard the anger in his voice and realised that even amid the chaos and gunfire of Mozambique she hadn't seen him this emotional. He seemed to treat life as a joke, but she could see he was seething now.

Once they had loaded the wild dog into the truck, Graham turned it around and headed towards Ukuphila Wildlife Orphanage, where his surgery was located.

'Where would it have come from?' Kerry asked, looking over her shoulder at the sedated dog. She could see its narrow chest rising and falling, which was something. 'The Kruger?'

Graham shrugged. 'Originally, maybe. However, there's a pack that hangs around this area. They move from Hoedspruit Wildlife Estate to Khaya Ndlovu, then on to Raptor's View.'

'Where you live? Like in among the houses?'

He nodded. 'Yip. Same as the wildlife estate, the dogs get under the fences, come in and have a field day with our resident impalas.

Some people don't like the dogs being around; they say they eat all the game. It's true, they have to eat every day, but when you think there are about one hundred and fifty thousand impala in the Kruger Park alone and about five thousand wild dogs in the *whole* of Africa, I'd say it's not a bad sacrifice to lose a few antelope in support of an endangered species. But some people don't see it that way, and even plenty of game reserves don't want wild dogs for the same reason.'

'And they were persecuted in the past, right?' Kerry said.

'Yes. Farmers used to shoot them on sight, here and in Zimbabwe and South-West – Namibia, that is.' Graham patted the breast pocket of his bush shirt. 'Shit.'

'What is it?'

'I'm out of cigarettes.' He looked ahead, then indicated.

'What about the dog?'

Graham turned off the road and pulled up in front of a bush pub. There were a couple of Hilux *bakkies* parked outside. 'He'll stand a better chance if my hands aren't shaking. You stay here and mind him.'

Kerry shook her head. She didn't relish the thought of riding even the short distance to Ukuphila with Graham puffing away. His vehicle smelled like an ashtray as it was. While she waited for him she pinched her nose with the fingers of her left hand and removed the Defender's actual ashtray from the dashboard with her right. She climbed out of the car with the ashtray and saw that the nearest rubbish bin was by the entrance door to the bar. Kerry made a quick check of the dog and saw that its condition was unchanged.

As she walked towards the bin, Kerry noticed that one of the two other vehicles in the car park had been in a collision of some sort and there was a dark sticky substance on the front bull bar. Then, as she stood there shaking the foul contents of the ashtray into the bin, the plate glass window next to her suddenly exploded outwards.

Graham rolled over in the dirt, wincing in pain, and got to his feet. Two young men came running out.

'And stay out of here, you old drunk.'

'Hey, what's going on here?' Kerry said, hands on hips.

'These two – the one on the right – he hit the dog,' said Graham coldly.

'*Ja*, so what?' The man, no more than twenty, Kerry thought, looked back at him defiantly. 'It's just a fucking dog, man. My old man used to kill them and get paid a bounty.'

'How can you say that? That's an endangered animal,' Kerry said.

'Sheesh.' The man turned on her. He raised his fingers to his eyes and pulled them into a slit. 'Listen to that. It's a Chink with an Australian accent. Doesn't get much worse than that.'

'You take that back.' Graham charged at the man, and ducked under a swinging fist to get his arms around the youngster in a tackle that brought him down.

The other man came over and brought back his foot, preparing to kick Graham. Kerry had darted behind him. She pulled the fingers of her right hand back into her palm, making a pointed fist, drew back her arm and delivered a short, sharp punch to the boy's kidney, just as her father had taught her in a comprehensive series of self-defence lessons he'd given her when she turned sixteen. The would-be kicker howled in pain and grabbed at his back.

The man Graham had tackled was younger, fitter and faster than the veterinarian, and had rolled him over and straddled him. He punched Graham in the face.

Two other young men emerged from the pub. The one Kerry had punched came towards her, his face red with fury. Bruce had taught Kerry that there was a time to fight and a time to run, so now she sprinted for Graham's Defender. She opened the passenger door, jumped in, and slammed the door behind her. Kerry searched around for a weapon. There was nothing to hand so she checked in the cubby box between the two front seats.

She heard the door open and felt a hand grab her on the thigh. 'Get out here.'

Kerry saw a small spray can and grabbed it. As she spun around, she pushed the button on top and a cloud of stinging, choking pepper spray hit the man in the face.

He yelped again like the pathetic specimen he was and tumbled out of the truck backwards, hands clawing at his eyes. In the confines of the Defender Kerry had caught some of the blowback of the spray and tears streamed down her face. Her throat and nose were on fire as she, too, stumbled out, can still in hand.

She staggered across to where the other young man had landed another blow on Graham's jaw. Without warning she stuck the can in the man's face and emptied the contents onto him. He, too, fell over, and Kerry helped him on his way with a shove. She grabbed Graham's hand and pulled him to his feet.

'Get in the bloody truck,' she ordered.

Graham clutched his side.

'Get in the passenger side, I'll drive.'

Graham looked relieved as he hauled himself up into the truck. Kerry was anything but and her eyes streamed with stinging tears. She got into the driver's seat, started the engine, dropped the clutch and planted her foot on the accelerator. The man who had been punching Graham was banging on the side of the Land Rover as she pulled away. Graham stuck his head out the window, gave him the finger and swore at him.

When he turned back to look at her he was grinning wildly, though blood was streaming from the corner of his mouth. 'Now *that* was fun!'

She shook her head. 'You're certifiably fucking crazy.'

'Ooo, good. She swears.' He laughed some more.

'Don't mock me.' She wiped her eyes.

He checked the wing mirror. 'Pull over, they're not following us.'

He found a bottle of water on the floor, picked it up, and when she was safely parked he told her to lean her head back. Graham poured the water liberally over her eyes and she blinked and spluttered as the water went into her nose and mouth, but the relief from the effects of the pepper spray was immediate.

'You fought like a champion, my girl. Well done.'

'I'm not your bloody girl.'

'Well, you did well, and I couldn't have those buffoons insulting your racial background.'

'Why not? You insulted me,' Kerry said dryly.

Graham dabbed his bloodied lip with the tail of his already filthy shirt. 'Yes, but we're friends.'

Kerry looked across at him, wiped her eyes, and burst out laughing.

Chapter 13

Kerry borrowed Graham's Land Rover and drove to Nelspruit, which was about one hundred and sixty kilometres south, on the R40. She had delayed her departure until after lunch so she could watch Graham perform surgery on the wild dog.

Graham had acceded to Kerry's wish to name the dog, which she'd christened Bubba, as Graham had said it was still quite young, probably less than two years old.

'It's alive,' was the best Graham could say about the animal's prognosis. 'You should go see your father; there's nothing more you can do to help me here now.'

Graham had told her that if he received a callout he would use one of the Ukuphila Wildlife Orphanage vehicles, which he usually did when his old Land Rover was at one of its regular visits to the mechanic.

Kerry found her way through the sprawling settlement of Bushbuckridge, then down through Hazyview, White River and on to Nelspruit. Graham had a satellite navigation device so she located the Mediclinic hospital without problem. Her biggest concern was the speed at which many other drivers travelled and the frequent stop-starts of minibus taxis that pulled out in front of her several times without indicating.

In the hospital a nurse gave her directions to her father's ward.

'Knock, knock,' she said.

A very handsome man in pyjamas with a broad chest and a mop of dark curls stood up when she entered her father's private room. A hand of cards lay face down on the table and her father sat on the other side on a chair. He started to stand.

'It's OK, Dad.' She went around and kissed her father.

'How do you do, ma'am,' the other man said in an American accent, 'we haven't officially met, but I feel like I know you already. I'm –'

'Eli Johnston. Lovely to meet you.' Her hand felt tiny in his, but he was gentle with her as he looked her in the eye.

'You were truly a warrior out there in the bush, ma'am. I can see that the apple didn't fall too far from this old tree over here.'

'Watch who you're calling "old", Yank,' her father said.

'Call me Kerry, please,' she said.

'I'll just get another seat.'

Eli walked out and Kerry's eyes followed him.

'Like what you see?' Bruce asked her.

'Dad! Don't be embarrassing.' She sat down where Eli had been.

Bruce snuck a look out through the door then started to lift Eli's hand of cards. Kerry slapped his fingers. 'Stop that.'

'Just like your mum, bloody goody-two-shoes. That crooked SEAL is fleecing me. I won't have a brass razoo left to my name if his winning streak keeps up.'

'How are you, Dad?'

'Me? I'm fine. Can't wait to get out of this bloody place. The doctor's given me some medication that I have to keep taking, but he says I'll live and don't need surgery, thankfully. He asked if I suffered any unusual stress lately.' Bruce laughed.

'Well, take it easy,' Kerry said.

'I didn't expect a holiday in South Africa, but being cooped up in a hospital is driving me crazy. If it wasn't for young Eli I would have broken out by now.'

'He seems nice,' Kerry said.

'You only just met him, but he has that effect on women.'

'I don't mean it that way, and stop being creepy.'

'You should see the way the nurses check him out, all queuing up to change his bandages and give him his sponge bath.'

With that a nurse walked in. She had short spiky blonde hair and was probably in her late forties or early fifties, Kerry thought, with a buxom figure that her rather severe old-style uniform couldn't hide. Bruce smiled broadly.

'Shower time, Tamara?' Bruce said.

'Ag, Mr Maxwell, I'm getting tired of that one.' She consulted the chart at the end of his bed.

'Tamara, this is my daughter, Kerry.'

She lowered the chart. 'Hello. I feel your pain.'

Kerry rolled her eyes. 'You should try living with his jokes for twenty-five years of your life.'

'I would have run away from home,' Tamara said.

'I'm her favourite patient, really, aren't I, Nurse Shepherd?' Bruce said.

Tamara looked at the chart again. 'I see you haven't had a movement for two days. I'm going to recommend an enema.'

'Hang on! Wait, I went . . .'

Tamara let out a laugh that was more like a snort. She turned to Kerry. 'Was he always so easy to trick?'

'Always. Dad, behave yourself, at least while I'm here.'

'Oh, he's not that bad, really,' Tamara said. From inside the pocket of her tunic she pulled a brown paper bag. She looked around and passed it to Bruce, who put it under his pillow. 'Don't take all your medicine at once, Bruce.'

'Thanks, Tammy.' He winked at her and Kerry thought she saw the nurse's cheeks blush as she nodded to Kerry then walked out.

'Jeez, Dad, you're here to get better. What is that, Scotch?'

'Nope, some local rotgut brandy they call Klipdrift. Tamara swears by it.'

'You're incorrigible.'

Eli came back into the room. In one hand he carried an armchair that looked like a feather in his grip and in the other he had a bouquet of flowers.

'Steal those from room 35 where that bloke died last night?' Bruce asked.

'Very funny. I went to the gift shop, that's what took me so long.'

'Well flowers or not, you still can't top and tail with me tonight,' Bruce said. 'I know what you navy types are like.'

Eli ignored him and turned to Kerry. 'These are for you, with my apologies.'

'Oh, Eli, you didn't have to do that. You've got nothing to be sorry for.'

'Yes, I do. I was back-up and fire support in Mozambique and I couldn't be there for you. I feel bad that you had to go through what you did after Bruce found you. It must have been terrible enough being locked up, but then to have to . . .'

Kerry took the flowers and sniffed them. 'They're lovely. Thank you, but you really don't have to apologise. And after all, if you hadn't had that drone of yours overhead I might have been a goner. You actually saved my life, after all.'

'This is all very touching,' Bruce said as he reached under his pillow and slid the small flask of brandy from the bag. 'Fetch some glasses, Yank, and let's have a drink.'

'Bruce, you shouldn't have alcohol in here,' Eli said.

'You Yanks are all so damned puritanical.'

'No, I mean you should give it to me. I'll hide it for you.'

'Ha ha, very funny. Pass me that glass.'

Bruce poured three measures of brandy. 'Cheers, everybody. Here's to a close shave, and to life.'

Kerry wrinkled her nose, but took a sip, then coughed. 'Gross.'

'Your mother was a cheap date too, that's one of the many things I liked about her.'

There was a loud cough from the corridor and Eli craned his neck to see through the door. 'Drink up, it's the bad guys.'

Bruce upended his glass and drained it in one swallow, then put the plastic cup on his bedside table. Kerry looked around, found a pot plant and tipped her liquor into it. Eli stood and kept his hand behind his back.

Nurse Tamara Shepherd and a young doctor in a white coat with a stethoscope around his neck walked in. Tamara coughed again. 'Sorry, doctor, I have a bit of a tickle.'

'Then stay away from the patient, please, nurse. Mr Maxwell, it's time for your examination.'

'Come on, Kerry,' Eli said, 'let's get some air, give your dad a little privacy.'

'Sure, back soon, Dad. Be *good*.'

Tamara rolled her eyes.

Kerry followed Eli out. 'How are you doing?' she asked him.

'I'm OK,' Eli said. 'I took a bullet but luckily it didn't hit anything vital. I've had worse.'

'You *have*?'

'Just war stories. Doc says I'll be good to go in a day, maybe two.' He led her to the hospital cafe. 'Coffee?'

'Sure, anything to get the taste of that rotgut out of my mouth. Cappuccino, please.'

Eli got the coffees and Kerry found them a table. When he

came over she saw he was still carrying his cup of brandy. He sipped some of the coffee then topped it up with the alcohol. He looked clean-cut and fit, but he was a military man and she knew from her dad and her time growing up on army bases that they could get up to no good, no matter how straight they looked.

'Your dad's a great guy.'

'Yes, he is. I haven't had a chance to properly thank you. I know you helped Dad and Graham get everything they needed to come and get me, and you put your life on the line.'

'It was nothing. I'm just glad you're safe.'

He had a look of sincerity and he held her eyes with his, even as he took some more coffee. She needed to get back to small talk; his eyes were enticing. 'So, do you head back to Mozambique once you're discharged from hospital?' she asked.

'Nope, afraid not. I have to go to Cape Town. I've got a fundraiser there.'

'You make it sound like a chore,' Kerry said.

'Kind of is, for me. I'd rather be in the bush. But some friends of mine with a band are organising a concert to help raise money to fund my anti-poaching unit, so I have to put in an appearance. It's coinciding with a conference for zoo and national parks people from around the world.'

'I heard,' Kerry said. 'Graham's been asked to speak at an event there as well, apparently.'

'But aren't you supposed to be working with him as a volunteer?'

Kerry rolled her eyes. 'Well, you know Graham, I guess. I'm just getting to know him. It seems like everything I thought I'd be doing in Africa is subject to change. I wanted to see Cape Town at some point on my trip – I had thought it would be at the end – but if he's going down there for his fundraiser then maybe I'll go as well.'

'It is a beautiful city, and you may as well see as much of Africa as you can before you have to go back to home and work.'

'I hear you,' Kerry said. 'I like my job, but I keep thinking there must be more to life.'

'Your pop says you're a lawyer, and a damn good one.'

'Well, he would say that, he's my father. It's mostly corporate stuff, but I've done the odd pro bono case and I get more satisfaction out of helping people who can't afford to pay than minimising the tax paid by big businesses.'

'And Africa?' Eli asked.

Kerry sipped her coffee. 'I didn't know what it would be like, and what happened in Mozambique was a complete nightmare, but . . .'

'But?'

'It was like seeing the wild dog – Graham and I rescued this wild dog that had been hit by a car near Hoedspruit – it was tragic and so sad, but to see this wild animal that up until an hour or less before the accident had been roaming free, in among people's houses, but still living this sort of normal life, was just . . . I don't know . . .'

'Awesome, but in the real meaning of the word,' Eli said.

She looked into those dark eyes again and she saw a reflection of how she felt. He was smitten, in love, addicted – not to her, but to this place. 'It feels like I've changed, like I've been bitten by something, or I've drunk something or breathed something in.'

'Africa.'

'Yes. Even with all that's happened I have no desire whatsoever to go back to Australia. I've known since I was a little kid that I wanted – needed – to go to Africa, but I'm worried, Eli. I think I'm hooked.'

'Hey, if you were free, perhaps we could catch up when I'm in Cape Town, maybe hang out?'

She leaned back in her chair. 'Did you just ask me on a date?'

'Well, your dad thought it would be OK.'

'Excuse me?'

Eli shuffled in his seat. 'I mean, I asked him if it would be OK if I asked you if we could . . . if I could ask you if we could maybe . . .'

His shyness, coming from such a big, strapping handsome man, was endearing, but Kerry couldn't hold back her feelings of annoyance. 'You discussed me, with my father?'

'Hey, Kerry . . .'

'Hey, nothing. This isn't Africa, I mean, it is, but we're not Africans. You don't have to offer him a herd of cows or something before you go out with me!'

Eli put his hands up. 'No, no, no, that's only when we get married.'

'When?'

'Oh, no. I mean *if*. *If* we get married.'

'Crikey, are you asking me to marry you now?'

'No!'

'Eli, can you understand that I feel like an object, being discussed by you and my father? I'm thirty-two years old.'

'Shoot, I'm sorry, Kerry. Your dad did warn me that you'd be like this. I . . .'

'He *warned* you about me?'

'Well, not so much warned me as advised me.'

Kerry stood up. 'Eli, I want to thank you for being there for me in Mozambique and I'm sure you and my father are getting on well as mates, but I am not some commodity to be traded.'

She turned and walked back the way she had come. She was ready to give her father a piece of her mind. The doctor who had come into the room was walking down the corridor towards her.

'Miss Maxwell.'

'Kerry. How is the old goat?'

'Your father is recovering well and he'll be fit to fly home in a day or two.'

'Oh. Thank you, doctor.'

'Hey,' said a voice behind her.

She turned and saw Eli. He had caught up with her on his way back to his room, or Bruce's, or wherever he was heading.

'Is everything OK?'

'Yeah.'

'I want to apologise, Kerry.'

She felt bad, seeing his soulful eyes. 'I overreacted. I do that sometimes, sorry. I think I inherited my dad's temper.'

'I watched a rugby game with him last night – Australia versus South Africa – and I thought he was going to throw a vase through the TV screen at one point.'

Kerry laughed. 'That sounds like Bruce.'

'I just saw my doctor, in the cafeteria. He was looking for me.'

Kerry reminded herself that Eli had been wounded by gunfire in a mission to try and save her, so she should ease up on him. 'What did he say?'

'Good news. I'm clear to check out whenever I want.'

'Well, good for you. Where will you go?'

'I know some folks, the Strydoms, who have a B&B here in Nelspruit. I just gave them a quick call. They've got space, but they're in Johannesburg. Their gardener will let me in; I just need to organise myself a ride.'

'I can take you, I guess.'

'Cool,' said Eli. 'Where are you staying?'

'Um, to tell you the truth I hadn't thought that far ahead. Graham said I could keep his Land Rover for a couple of days if I needed it, but I thought I might drive back to Hoedspruit tonight.'

Eli checked his watch. 'It'll take you a couple of hours at least and it'll be getting dark when you pass through Bushbuckridge.'

'That's the big town I passed through on the way, right?'

'Yep, that will be the one.'

'Is it dangerous to drive there at night?'

'You would have seen the traffic, with all the minibus taxis?'

'I sure did,' she said.

'It gets worse in the evening, with people coming home from work. Plus, there's the risk of cows and dogs wandering onto the road and, as you get closer to Hoedspruit, even wildlife.'

Kerry nodded. 'Yes, Graham said to be careful driving after sundown. He actually suggested I stay here in Nelspruit if it got too late.'

'Good advice. Hey, I can call my friends back and see if it's OK for you to stay in one of their other rooms if you like? It's clean, self-contained and not expensive.'

Kerry weighed her options. In his awkward way Eli had possibly asked her out on a date, if she came to Cape Town. He was young and handsome and she wondered if he thought that maybe if they stayed in adjoining rooms in a B&B that something might happen. It wasn't the worst thought in the world, but after everything she had been through Kerry felt like she wanted to be somewhere safe. Oddly, right now, that seemed like Graham's place. Graham was an objectionable man, but he hadn't tried anything inappropriate with her. Sex – even the remote prospect of it – was the last thing she needed right now.

'That's a really nice offer, Eli. It's funny for me being here in a city. Every night I've spent in Africa so far has been somewhere wild – even Graham's housing estate has animals wandering about. They have a resident leopard. It'd be weird to go to a bed and breakfast place in Africa. Thanks for the offer, but I think I'll drive back to Hoedspruit.'

Eli looked a little hurt, but recovered from it quickly. 'Well, take Graham's advice and drive really carefully, OK?'

'Deal.'

Chapter 14

Bruce Maxwell had been a light sleeper most of his life, ever since Vietnam. He woke and it took him a moment to remember where he was, in hospital.

Everyone in the family knew that if they had to wake him, they were never to shake him by the shoulder or anywhere near his face or he would spring up in bed and, more often than not, grab the waker by the throat in a vice grip.

'Touch my feet,' was the order of the day when it came to waking Bruce. He'd told Tamara Shepherd the same thing. She was a looker, Bruce thought. She was mildly flirty, but that was probably just her indulging him, he thought. Tamara – Tammy – was an Afrikaner though her late husband, she had told him, had been an English-speaking South African and she'd kept his surname. He liked her accent.

Bruce drifted back to sleep and was vaguely aware that he was dreaming.

He was back in Vietnam, not on patrol but in the rear area base, in the Australian Special Air Service base in Nui Dat. He was wandering past the open-sided green mess tent, his leather and canvas American jungle boots sloshing through mud puddles. He felt sad and annoyed. How, he wondered in his slumber, had he ended up back in this bloody place again? Where was Tammy?

Bruce sensed danger.

He couldn't work out why he was in Vietnam again, after all these years. He couldn't see any of his old comrades around, but he had the feeling he was being watched, that there was someone lurking between the rows of tents. Each had a wall, halfway up, made of sandbags, to give some protection from incoming mortar rounds.

Although this was their rear area base, there was no front line in Vietnam; the enemy was everywhere. Bruce heard a movement and someone stepped from the shadows.

He opened his eyes, sat up straight and found he was in a bed; a starched white sheet falling from his sweat-soaked body. But it was dark, gloomy, like the shadows of his dream. His hand shot out and grabbed something, someone, and there was a muffled yelp.

It was a dream, Bruce told himself, but, no, maybe it wasn't, because the woman he was holding, her forearm in the iron grip of his hand, was Vietnamese. A spy. In a white coat. It didn't make sense.

'Mr *Maxwell*,' the woman hissed. 'Let. Me. Go. It's OK. You are safe. I am your doctor.'

Bruce looked around, doubly confused. The room was dark, illuminated only by the glowing lights of the monitor he was attached to.

He blinked and looked at the woman. She was small, harmless, pretty. For a second he thought of his late wife. He relaxed his grip.

'I . . . I don't know you.' He rubbed his eyes, coming out of his deep sleep.

'No. I am Dr Nguyen. Sally.'

Now that he could focus he saw that she couldn't be much older than her early twenties. That wasn't unusual, he thought; it seemed to Bruce that whenever he'd been in hospital in Australia the whole place had been staffed by people who should still have been in school.

'Where's my normal doctor?' Bruce asked.

'Oh, he is on the day shift. I am the night duty doctor,' she said.

'Hmm. Well, I'm fine, Doc.'

She smiled. 'You let me be the judge of that, Mr Maxwell.' She came to him and laid her hand on his forehead. She was short so she had to lean over him. He smelled her perfume; it was sweet and girlish.

'I saw a girl here yesterday while I was making my rounds – she looked part Asian.'

'That was probably my daughter, Kerry,' he said. Her coat was open and her small but firm breasts were straining against a simple black T-shirt underneath.

'She is very pretty.'

'She had a beautiful mother.'

'Had?'

'She died, cancer.'

'Oh, I am so sorry, Mr Maxwell.' She put a hand with long scarlet fingernails on his chest, and Bruce felt his old heart pump a bit faster. In his condition that probably wasn't a good thing.

She was a cute girl, but there was something not right here; especially her touching him in that way.

'I need to give you some medicine,' she continued.

'What? I get my meds during the day; Nurse Shepherd brings them, not the doctor. I'm just going to call the duty nurse.'

'She's busy, I saw her on the way in here to do my rounds,' Sally said, taking a step back from him.

Bruce looked her up and down. The nurses here in South Africa wore what would be considered in Australia an old-style uniform, and they had identification cards on lanyards, ditto the doctors. Sally Nguyen, if that's what her name was, had nothing of the sort visible.

'Where's your ID?' he asked her.

She smiled. 'Oh, Bruce, I don't need ID.'

That did it. He picked up the call button attached to a cable lying next to his pillow. He pressed it and the light outside his room lit up.

'We'll see what the nurse has to say.'

Sally gave a little giggle. 'Oh, Bruce, I told you, the nurse is tied up right now. I'm here to make sure you get *better*.'

Bruce was about to call out when he saw Dr Nguyen's fingers go to the belt of the short khaki shorts he could now see she was wearing under her laboratory coat. She undid the belt, then the top button.

'What the flaming hell is going on here?'

'Oh, Bruce,' she said in a tone that flowed like warm honey. 'I think we both know I'm not a doctor.'

'Then who, what are you?'

'I'm your get-well present, Bruce.'

'What?'

'You have a friend? American? His name is Eli?'

'Maybe.'

She looked up, seeming to search her memory as her zipper paused at half-mast. 'Johnston. That's right, isn't it?'

Bruce was open-mouthed for a couple of seconds. 'What about him?'

'He sent me with a message. He said to tell you, "This is for Mozambique, to say sorry for letting you down".'

'The cheeky bugger,' Bruce said. 'Where are you from, Sally, if that's your name?'

125

She giggled again. 'Oh, Bruce, I think we both know my name is not really Sally. But you can call me doctor if that turns you on.'

Sally unzipped all the way, let her shorts fall to the floor and then stepped out of them. She was wearing a red G-string. She shrugged off her coat, twirled it once on one finger then tossed it so that it landed on the visitor's chair.

Bruce didn't know what to make of this. It was a hell of a surprise. Eli had struck him as a mister nice guy, one of those straightlaced Yanks who went back to base for a bit of bible study after a day shooting terrorists. He might have misjudged him.

'Ah, Sally . . .'

'One second please.' She turned and bent over, giving him a view of a very pert bottom as she snapped open an old-style leather doctor's bag that he hadn't seen sitting on the floor. 'Time for your examination, Bruce.'

She stood, now with a stethoscope in her ears and a little black zip-up clutch bag in her hands.

'I'm sorry.'

'Oh, don't be sorry, Bruce. You'll be happy. And don't worry about the night nurse. Eli spoke to her and she let me in. Everyone is in on this present to you.'

That explained why no one had responded to him pressing the call button, he supposed. What kind of a hospital was this? He reached under his pillow and drew out the flask of brandy and unscrewed the cap. He took a swig and offered the bottle to Sally.

She shook her head. 'I'm on duty, Bruce.'

He laughed so hard some of the fiery spirit spurted out of his nose. He coughed and wiped his mouth. What the hell, he thought. He put the cap on the bottle and hid it under the pillow again.

Sally came to him and slowly undid the top three buttons of his pyjama top. She reached a hand inside and found his nipple and give it a little pinch. He jumped in his bed and hoped she didn't give him another heart attack. He felt himself start to stir. There was life in the old dog yet, he told himself, rather pleased with the reaction.

Sally breathed on the round disc of the stethoscope to warm it up and put the zipped bag on the bed beside Bruce.

He smiled as she leaned over him. 'Be gentle with me.'

She tittered and put the end of the stethoscope on his chest. 'You still have a heart.'

He laughed. She unzipped the little black bag. 'What's in there?'

'Oh, just some special doctor things. Nothing to hurt you, Bruce. Big strong man like you . . .'

From the bag she took out an eye mask; it looked like the kind they gave you on airlines to sleep on night flights. 'You want me to wear that?'

'What you can't see can't hurt you, Bruce.' Sally leaned over the bed and her small breasts rested against his chest. Bruce smiled.

*

Jorge Silva checked his phone. The SMS from Sally, the hooker, simply said *In*. That told him she had bypassed the nurse on duty and was completing her mission.

He had tailed the Land Rover with Kerry Maxwell in it from the hospital car park. The woman had Eli Johnston with her and Jorge followed them to a bed and breakfast place in Steiltes, an up-market suburb of Nelspruit high in the hills above the city. The American got out and waved goodbye. Jorge sent an SMS to Sally, giving her the address. She would deal with Johnston the same way she was dealing with Bruce Maxwell right now.

He followed the woman out of Nelspruit and through the plantation forest–covered hills between White River and Hazyview. They were passing through a stretch of banana farms. Jorge had been a sugar cane farmer with a property at Hectorspruit, in the south, but he had gone bankrupt and his wife had left him thanks to his gambling addiction.

Jorge liked wildlife, but he had looked at the large number of rhinos wandering the national park and the insane amount of money that was being paid for horn, and he had come up with a plan.

Security was tight and getting tighter at the park, but a white South African farmer of Portuguese descent who visited the park nearly every weekend and sometimes during the week attracted only the most cursory of checks from the security men and women on the gate. He knew most of them on a first-name basis.

Jorge had personally killed three rhinos on his own in the past, his rifle hidden under a mound of cooler boxes and luggage in the back of his vehicle, but it had become too risky to carry on like that – the security checks had intensified, even for him, and sometimes there were sniffer dogs on the gate.

In response to the increased security, one Sunday afternoon he had taken a drive in the park and then detoured onto one of the no-entry roads. These roads were used by national parks rangers to patrol the unseen parts of Kruger, and to fight fires. Out of sight and a few hundred metres from the main road that led to Crocodile Bridge gate, he had got out of his car and started to dig.

In the deep hole he'd buried a big, one-hundred-litre cooler box, and into that he had placed two disassembled rifles, a .375-calibre Czech hunting rifle and an AK-47 he had taken as a souvenir from his days fighting in Angola nearly thirty years earlier. He had wrapped them in oil-soaked rags and left a good supply of ammunition for each weapon, then closed the cooler box, covered it with plastic bin liner bags for extra protection, and filled in the hole. He had placed twigs and leaves and a big rock on top of the cache and marked the location with his handheld GPS.

On three successive trips Jorge had brought shooters with him – Mozambicans who had worked on his farm. He chose those who had served in the military during the Mozambican civil war, or those who had grown up in the bush and knew a thing or two about tracking and poaching. He'd told the security guards on the gate that he was rewarding his workers, giving them their first ever visit to the Kruger Park, for a weekend. These visits had coincided with the full moon, the hunter's moon.

When Jorge had checked into his accommodation, either at Malelane Camp or Crocodile Bridge, he had done so alone. He had left his farm workers at the site of the cache, with a mobile phone.

Jorge would then spend the afternoon driving around the park. He rarely had to venture far from where his rifles and his trigger men were waiting; there were many white rhino in this part of Kruger. When Jorge found a suitable specimen – he was a man of principles so he mostly tried to find an old bull with a big horn, rather than a female with a calf – he would return, collect his shooter, and then drive him to a spot near where he had seen the rhino.

Jorge would then leave the men there, and head to his accommodation unit. While Jorge made his *braai*, drank his beer and his brandy and Coke and chatted to his fellow campers about how *lekker* the bush was and how terrible was the problem of rhino poaching, his erstwhile farm worker would be following the chosen rhino through the bush, waiting until it was far from any road where a ranger on patrol might see them. The man would then kill the rhino, take its horn, and then return to the place where the cooler box was buried. The weapon would be cleaned, disassembled and reburied, and the horn wrapped up and placed in a backpack. The next morning, just after the gates opened at dawn, Jorge would go and collect the poacher and his booty. It was a good system and it worked well.

That was, until Fidel Costa got wind of what Jorge was up to.

One Sunday, Jorge returned to the site of his buried weapons and walked into an ambush. Four poachers, heavily armed and led by a dapper-looking man in civilian clothes, were waiting for him. His farm worker was tied and gagged on the ground near the freshly unearthed cooler box. Jorge had been marched deeper into the bush at gunpoint and told to sit on a log.

Fidel had told him, as he sat waiting to die, that his days as a freelance poacher were over. The good news, Fidel told Jorge, was that if he started working for him taking rhinos, he could keep his life, and still earn good money. Jorge really couldn't refuse, although he had not willingly signed up for the extra jobs Fidel expected of him, like this one.

Jorge couldn't have grabbed Kerry Maxwell in the hospital car park – there was too much lighting and security, and she'd had an ex-Navy SEAL with her. His plan was to follow her and take her somewhere along her route – he assumed she was heading back to Hoedspruit where, he had been briefed, she was staying with Baird, the veterinarian. It was a long drive and he guessed she would stop somewhere on the way.

The R40 came to a T-junction on the outskirts of Hazyview, and Kerry, with Jorge behind her, followed the main road, to the left, towards Hoedspruit. Hazyview had grown in a rapid, ramshackle way in the past twenty years, from little more than a couple of farm stalls and a small supermarket to a bustling jumble of low-rise malls, shops and roadside businesses.

The Maxwell woman slowed, as if searching for something, and turned right onto the R536 and then left into Hazyview Junction, a new shopping mall that hadn't been there the last time Jorge had been to the town.

She parked as close as she could to the Wimpy, which was still open, and Jorge stopped his Volkswagen Amarok a few spaces away. Kerry spoke to a car park guard, then went into the burger place. The same guard sauntered over to Jorge, who lowered his driver's side window and lit a cigarette.

'I will check your car nicely, boss,' the young man said.

Jorge shook his head. 'I'm staying with my *bakkie*, waiting for someone.' He reached across into the footwell of the passenger side of the Amarok and picked up a couple of empty Coca-Cola cans and the wrapper off a Pick n Pay pie. 'But take these to the bin and I'll give you five rand.'

'Sure, boss.'

When the guard took the rubbish Jorge opened the glove compartment and took out a bicycle spoke he had brought with him for just such an eventuality.

Chapter 15

Graham was bored, and a little drunk and maudlin.

He had brought a sixpack of Black Label lager with him to Ukuphila with the intention of having a few beers when he finished work, then getting a lift home to Raptor's View. Things hadn't gone according to plan.

Desmond Hennessy, the eccentric old man who owned Ukuphila, had gone to a wedding in Hazyview, and Silke, the German volunteer who had been at the wildlife orphanage long enough for Des to trust her as a part-time manager, was at the clinic. She'd come down with severe flu symptoms in the afternoon and Graham had ordered her to go and get a malaria test. Silke had tested negative but was feeling terrible, so Graham had told her to go home and assured her that he would look after the place until Des got back from the wedding dinner.

After operating on the wild dog and seeing Kerry off to Nelspruit, Graham had tended to a Bateleur eagle. It had been brought into Ukuphila by a South African National Parks honorary ranger, Dave Corlett, who had been on his way to the

Kruger Park to do his weekend duty when he'd found the bird under a powerline outside of Hoedspruit.

'Looks like he flew into an electricity cable,' Dave had said. Graham occasionally played a round of golf at the Hoedspruit Air Force Base course, which was open to civilian members, and Dave was a regular on the greens and in the clubhouse. He had emigrated to South Africa after retiring from the police in the UK, and he and his wife had a house on Raptor's View estate. Honorary rangers were part-timers who did volunteer work in South Africa's national parks, easing the load on the fulltime staff. The beautiful eagle had escaped electrocution, but it had broken a wing.

Graham got up, turned off the television in the office – there was nothing on except *7de Laan* in any case – and decided to go outside for a walk. He took his last beer with him, husbanding it by taking only the tiniest of sips.

It was a nice night out. He wondered how Kerry was doing. She had sent him a message to let him know she was driving back from Nelspruit.

He was concerned about her driving at night so he called her and she answered, on speaker. 'Hi, Graham, yes, I'm still alive.'

'It's not you, it's my Land Rover I'm worried about.'

'You're all heart.'

'That's the first time anyone's ever said that to me.' He laughed. Graham explained what had happened to Silke. 'Can you come by Ukuphila and pick me up? Des should be home from his function by the time you get here.'

'Sure, no problem. See you soon.' Kerry ended the call.

A hyena whooped, and for want of any other plan and to take his mind off females – human ones at least – he walked towards the enclosure where a motley clan, of sorts, had been thrown together by circumstance.

133

Des had a varied collection of animals and birds. Some were orphans that had been brought in by farmers or the local nature conservation authorities, others had been involved in accidents outside the national park and adjoining game reserves. Des's commitment to the natural environment was unquestionable; he would rail like an old-time preacher spouting fire and brimstone sometimes, literally frothing at the mouth when he told visiting tourists and school groups about the perils facing wildlife in the twenty-first century.

Much of the content of Des's messages about habitat loss, poaching and pollution was lost on most tourist visitors however, who were probably only there to pat the resident cheetah, Roxy, but Des liked to think that occasionally someone took notice and, even better, took some positive action towards conservation.

Graham looked through the wire fence into Roxy's enclosure, but she was asleep, which was normal for a cheetah at night.

Jamu, the orphaned leopard, was a different cat altogether. He paced up and down as Graham passed him, and bared his fangs. Jamu, in Graham's opinion, should not have been at Ukuphila. Although Des had raised Jamu from a cub, Graham was sure that, given the slightest chance, the leopard would have clamped his jaws tight around his owner's neck and suffocated him and then fed on him.

Des maintained that Jamu couldn't be released into the wild, and in theory he was probably right. Jamu had been captive-bred, at a small private petting zoo that had since closed down. Such places were thankfully going out of vogue in South Africa. There was no place in Africa, in Graham's view, for captive-bred lions, leopards or any other cats, for that matter.

Graham paused and watched as Jamu reached out with his right front paw and touched the single strand of electrified wire that ran at ankle height along the leopard's side of the enclosure fence. Jamu snatched his paw back. He was, as was his habit

134

several times each day, checking to see if the current was on. Des had a back-up generator in case the mains power went out. Graham couldn't imagine how many thousands of times Jamu had tested the fence. He had no doubt that the day the cat found that wire dead, he would scale the chain-link fence in a few short bounds and then crawl over the three high-voltage strands at the top of the fence.

The whooping of the hyenas intensified as Graham got closer to them and they picked up his scent.

'Hello, you bunch of ugly, slobbering, stinking misfits,' he called to them. 'Yes, yes, yes, I love you all.'

They crowded along the fence as Graham walked past them and around the side to the first of two sliding gates. The hyenas followed him, showing their excitement with tails raised like bushy feather dusters.

'Howzit, my beauties.'

Graham took out the orphanage's set of master keys and unlocked the padlock on the first gate, opening it then pulling it closed behind him. He slid the lock into position, but didn't re-lock it.

When he undid the second gate and walked into the enclosure, the hyenas crowded around him, sniffing and nipping at him. The youngest, Jade, started nipping at his ankle.

'Hey!' Graham swung around and grabbed Jade under her forearms, lifting her up in a bear hug. He held her back to him so she couldn't reach around and bite him. He lowered his face to her smelly fur, placed his mouth over her ear and bit down hard. He growled as he spun in a circle and shook her ear in his teeth as she yelped.

The others in the clan cackled and whooped with joy at the spectacle of Graham teaching the cheeky youngster a lesson. He spat out fur and tossed Jade from his arms, sidestepping to stay clear of her.

Graham hadn't been cruel to Jade, he had simply treated her like one hyena would another – though nowhere near as painfully. He sat down on the ground and the matriarch of the small clan, Gina, came up to him. She sniffed him, from just a few centimetres away, and her calmness washed over the group, who milled around Graham.

'Hello, my girls.' He reached out a closed fist and Gina sniffed, then licked it.

He marvelled at them, at their close-knit family with its rigidly enforced pecking order. Gina had been brought to Ukuphila by the Limpopo province nature conservation authorities after she had been trapped on a farm.

She was a wild animal that had probably escaped from the Timbavati or one of the other private game reserves in the province, and when Des had put her in with his other hyenas, who were all captive-bred, she asserted her dominance over them in a frenzied, bloody rampage that had lasted less than half an hour. She had then mated with one of the subservient males in the group and Jade was her first offspring.

Graham hoped that Des might one day agree to his proposal that the clan be let loose on a private reserve somewhere that did not have any resident hyenas. Graham was confident that Gina could lead her blended family in the wild and teach them to become self-sufficient. She and her kind were incredibly intelligent animals, far more so than lions.

Graham sat, oddly at peace, as the hyenas relaxed or wandered around him in the dark. He felt no fear of them and they accepted him, almost as if he were one of their own.

Gina, who had plonked herself down proprietarily next to Graham, suddenly jumped to her feet. She put her head up, sniffed, then ran for the fence. Her subjects followed her.

Graham was also on the alert now.

He stood, dusted off his bum and moved to where the clan was.

'Dr Baird,' a voice called.

The hyenas whooped in reply.

Graham made his way to the fence. 'Who is it?'

'Charles. I am the new night security officer.'

While Graham worked out of Ukuphila it was rare for him to stay overnight, so he did not know all of the night shift. The man, Charles, was standing in the shadows about twenty metres away. Graham made out the dark peaked cap of the security guard's uniform.

'Very new; when did you start, Charles? What happened to Elphes?'

'I started work just yesterday. Elphes met with a serious accident. He was the victim of a hit and run driver and is in hospital with a broken pelvis.'

'Good lord. Poor fellow. What's up, Charles?'

'There is a problem,' Charles continued.

'Come closer.'

'I am scared.'

'Of what?' Graham asked. What was the point of a chicken security guard?

'Of those *mpisi*. Witches ride on the backs of those things and you should not be in with them, Dr Baird.'

Mpisi was the local word for hyena, and it was none of this fellow's business to tell Graham what he should and shouldn't do – even if he was right. 'All right. I'll come out. Just give me a minute. What's the problem, anyway?'

'One of the alarms on the fence has gone off.'

Gina continued her whooping.

'Quiet, my girl,' Graham said, but Gina kept up her call, flanked by her family, and stayed at the fence, fangs showing, drool falling from her chops, as she confronted the guard in the shadows.

'Quickly, please, Dr Baird.'

137

'All right, all right.'

Graham went through the first gate and pulled it closed.

'The alarm was very close to where the rhino is, with her calf,' Charles said, and there was no hiding the panic in his voice.

Graham was worried as well. He would have to get a firearm out of Des's strongroom. The key was on the bunch in his pocket. Graham didn't bother locking the hyenas' internal gate and when he came to the external gate he remembered the padlock was the kind that had to be locked with a key, rather than snapped shut. He fumbled on the ring, looking for the right one. 'Oh, bugger it.' He didn't have time. He slipped the lock into its hole and left it there. That would be fine for the moment.

Charles beckoned. 'Hurry up, please, Dr Baird.'

The man was annoying him, but he was unarmed and had probably come to the same conclusion as Graham – if it was rhino poachers who were after Des's old cow, Grace, and her impressive horn, which was as long as a man's arm, then they would be heavily armed.

'All right, all right. I'm coming.'

Graham jogged to Charles, who fell in behind him. *Typical*, Graham thought, and then the starlit night turned to black as he pitched forward into the dust and passed out.

*

Fidel Costa saw the torchlight flash three times in the dark and drove up to the gate of Ukuphila Wildlife Orphanage in the BMW X5 he had rented. Charles unlocked the gate and Fidel drove in.

Fidel took a face mask, decorated with a grinning skull, out of his pocket and pulled it on. At the moment he killed Baird he would show the man his face, but first he would have to pass by Ukuphila's security cameras and he did not want to be subsequently recognised. He got out of the BMW.

'Baird?' Fidel asked.

'In the rhino enclosure, boss, as you ordered. He is still unconscious. I have tied him for now, in case he wakes.'

'Good work.' Charles, his man, had been infiltrated into Ukuphila thanks to a favour owed to Fidel by a distant relative by marriage who ran the security company that supplied the guards to the wildlife orphanage. It had been a costly exercise, organising the hit on the regular nightwatchman, Elphes, and while the regular guard had not been killed he was in hospital, which allowed Charles to take his place.

Fidel would have revenge for the death of his younger brother. Losing Inâcio had been akin, as far as Fidel was concerned, to a parent losing a child. He had seen comrades, friends, killed in war and fail to return from poaching missions, but this was different. Perhaps it was because he had hoped for a better, brighter future for his little brother. Whatever the cause, his quiet rage seemed unquenchable. Graham Baird would not only die, he would die in shame, his memory forever sullied. Even more, he wanted Baird to feel the pain of losing someone he cared for, right before the veterinarian himself died.

Charles led the way past the various animals and birds to the boma made of logs stout enough to contain the fully grown female white rhino and her latest calf. Charles had corralled the baby rhino into a separate part of the enclosure. It whined pitifully, pining for its mother. Fidel ignored the annoying sound.

'Start cutting,' Fidel said.

Charles nodded and climbed over the wooden post-and-railing fence. Inside he found the saw he had already taken from the tool room. The white rhino lay on her chest, a blindfold over her eyes. She was immobilised, but not unconscious. Next to her, beside Graham Baird, was a Dan-Inject dart gun, which had been used to tranquillise the rhino.

Fidel looked around and saw a bucket, probably used to bring food to the rhinos. He took it to a nearby standpipe and filled it with water. He hefted the bucket over the boma fence then climbed it himself. On the other side he carried the bucket to where the veterinarian was lying and set it down.

From the pocket of his bush jacket Fidel, who was wearing soft leather driving gloves, took out a Makarov, a Russian-made pistol that dated from the long, bloody civil war in Mozambique. Baird was lying on his side; his wrists and ankles were bound.

Fidel got down and put his right knee on Baird's arms. The unconscious man started to stir. Fidel looked to Charles and saw he was halfway through sawing off the rhino's horn. 'Faster.'

'Yes, boss.' Charles redoubled his efforts, and wiped sweat from his eyes with his free hand.

Fidel, meanwhile, put the Makarov in Graham's right hand, and threaded the man's index finger through the trigger guard. Graham came to just as Fidel used Baird's finger to fire a round into the air. Birds squawked and animals erupted into call at the clap of man-made lightning that too many of Ukuphila's residents remembered.

Baird tried to turn the pistol on him, but Fidel knelt hard on Graham's right arm and his fingers opened. Fidel snatched the gun back, stood and backed off a step. Then he looked to Charles, who was three-quarters of the way through sawing off the rhino cow's horn. 'Enough.'

Charles stood and wiped his brow with the back of his hand, then pulled out his shirt tail and used it to thoroughly wipe the handle of the saw he had been using. He brought it to Fidel.

'Open your hand, Graham. Charles will put the saw in your hand and you will grab hold of it.'

Graham looked up at him. 'Fuck you. Fidel Costa? Is that you? Have you finally grown the balls to do your own dirty work?'

'You murdered a young man, Dr Baird,' said Fidel through gritted teeth. 'You shot him with one of your darts and you let him die, just like this rhino will die very soon. You look confused.'

'You're setting me up? No one will believe I darted this rhino and tried to cut off its horn.'

Fidel shrugged. 'Why not? It's happened before. The money this useless keratin, fingernail material, commands in Vietnam has corrupted far better men than you, even other veterinarians like yourself. And anyway, you won't be around to tell your version of events. You will die in shame.'

'*That's* what this is about? You can't just kill me, you want everyone in town to think I was crooked?' He laughed.

'Yes, Graham, that is what I want everyone to think. If I simply murdered you then people would figure out who was behind it. You would be a martyr, a cause célèbre, a posthumous poster boy for the save-the-rhino campaign. People would donate money, there would be investigations and enquiries and fingers would be pointed.' Fidel dropped to a crouch to close the distance between them. 'Believe it or not, Graham, the authorities in Mozambique are starting to get serious about rhino poaching. The president is under pressure, and not even I can rely on his patronage if the shit, how do the Americans say, hits the fan over your death. So, my best option is for you to pass into history like the useless, drunken little failure that you are.'

'Hey, I'm six foot three. Who are you calling little?'

Fidel laughed. 'I salute you, Graham. Joking to the end. Now grab the saw, please.'

'Kiss my arse.'

Fidel shook his head, then stood. 'Then we must do this the unpleasant way.'

He took out an iPhone, pressed in a number and then activated the phone's speaker.

'Yes?' said a voice, impatient.

'You are with her, Kerry Maxwell?'

'Yes, but you said no names,' the man said in a whisper.

'I need to use the names for a minute, I have someone here who needs to know we're serious.'

Jorge paused, which was understandable. 'The woman got a flat tyre. I'm *helping* her right now.'

'Good. My instruction to you was that it was to be quick, clean, that my main focus, my main target, is the man I am with now.'

'Yes,' Jorge said. 'That is correct. I was just about to SMS you for the final go-ahead.'

'I've changed my mind,' Fidel said. He looked to Graham and smiled. 'Take your time with the woman. Have some fun with her before it ends.'

Another pause. 'Yes. OK.'

'Unless I call you back within two minutes to countermand this order.'

'Understood.'

Fidel ended the call. 'You see, Graham, I've thought this through. You're all going to die – the Maxwell woman, her father, you, Eli Johnston. I just want you to know that if you don't do as I tell you, your friend Kerry will suffer unnecessarily. I want you to feel what it's like to lose someone you care about.'

Baird was seething. Charles held the saw by the blade, the handle within reach of Graham's fingers. He reached for it and took it in his right hand.

Fidel re-dialled. 'Cancel that last order, just kill her.'

Graham stared up at him.

'You see, Graham, I am a man of honour.'

*

Bruce felt the light hospital blanket move and then a small hand found its way into his pyjama shorts. He started; the touch was electric. It had been a long time since he'd been caressed by a woman.

'You like?'

142

He was already stirring. 'Oh, yes, I bloody well like all right.'

It was just her fingers, which was something of a relief. He didn't know what she had in that little black bag of hers, but his imagination had almost got the better of him.

Her other hand was resting on his right one, which sat on top of the covers. He had a drip attached to a cannula in the top of his hand. Her fingers brushed his, lightly.

'What are you doing?'

'Nothing, Bruce. I just like to touch you. Is that OK?'

'Hmm.'

'No peeking, OK?'

'Well, OK, if you insist.' He closed his eyes under the mask.

'I want to make you happy.'

Bruce felt a moment of guilt, remembering his wife, but then told himself there was no harm in this. He had no intention of letting it go too far, and in his condition it probably wasn't a good idea. He'd just lie back and enjoy a little attention from this bizarre present.

It was still a surprise, coming from Johnston. Bruce thought about how Eli had asked his permission to go out with Kerry, as though he were some Amish farmer or something.

Eli setting him up with a hooker didn't make sense.

'Oh, Bruce, you are very big.'

This was all too weird, he thought. He reached for the eye mask.

Chapter 16

Gina's ears pricked up as soon as she heard the loud boom. As a wild hyena, unlike the less worldly members of her clan, she knew that where there was gunfire there was usually food.

She loped to the gate and her posse followed her, as they always did. She nosed the bars near the lock and the gate started to slide open. She had almost escaped once before, when one of the keepers had forgotten to lock the internal gate. She had been able to lead the clan around Ukuphila but the gate on the exterior perimeter fence had been locked.

Now, Gina came to the second of the sliding gates on her enclosure. She sniffed it and smelled the man, the one with the shaggy beard who had an odour very different from that of other humans, more hyena-like. It was one of the reasons she tolerated him and one of the reasons she had accepted him into her odd little family of misfits.

Gina nudged the gate a few times. Something was loose. The padlock had been slipped into its hole, but it hadn't been locked. Gina banged her head against the metal, then grabbed a bar between her teeth and worried at it. The lock vibrated out and landed in the dust with a thud. With a final shake Gina started the gate sliding and Jade and the others whooped with joy.

Freedom.

Gina scampered out, then stopped, raised her head and sniffed the air and listened. There were human voices, and a cry of pain. More good news. Where there was distress there was also food. But Gina had lived through enough encounters with humans in the outside world to know they were dangerous.

She turned to her clan, growled low to keep them in line, then moved stealthily but quickly through the shadows.

They passed the lion enclosure and the big, stupid round faces stared at them through the wire fences. Oh, how she would like to break in there and teach them a lesson; but there was no time for that now. A pair of wild dogs, roused by the noise, ran up and down within the confines of their enclosure, and whined and yelped at the hyenas. Gina tossed her head at them. Silly creatures.

Ahead, Gina saw a shiny four-wheeled machine, a man with a light – two men, in fact – and the open gate that led to the rest of the world. Her eyes, however, followed the track of the torch's beam.

There, in the dirt, was the smelly man, the one who cared for them, one of her family.

*

Nurse Tamara Shepherd looked at her watch. It was nine in the evening. The seat opposite her in the Mediterranean Restaurant in the Riverside Mall shopping centre was as empty as it had been when she had arrived, five minutes early, at 6.55.

He hadn't even left a message.

Such were the perils of internet dating, she assumed. She had met, in the flesh, three men from the Afrikaans-speaking website, and while none of them had proved to be a good match – one married, one drunk, one still getting over a divorce – at least they hadn't stood her up. This was a first.

Henk, Mister No-show's name, was a schoolteacher. He had remarked more than once, in the course of their online chats, that she struck him as a very self-assured woman. Was he intimidated by her? She wondered if she had said anything to scare him off.

Tamara drained her glass of wine, checked her watch and her messages again, then called the waiter over and asked for the bill. He gave her a sympathetic smile, but she didn't want his pity. The salad she had ordered while she was waiting was barely touched. 'Can you put it in a packet for me, please.'

With her doggie bag she left the restaurant, feeling the eyes of a couple of dozen strangers on her, some mocking, some understanding.

She went to her car, sniffed, wiped her eyes and checked her makeup in the rear-view mirror. Her eyeliner was smudged. Her husband had died in a car accident five years earlier and the last of her three children had gone off to university six months ago. The thought of going home to her empty house was depressing.

Tamara sat for a moment before starting the car. She wondered if Bruce Maxwell had been serious.

'*Breakfast at Tiffany's* is on tonight,' he'd said to her before she'd finished work at four that afternoon. She'd been in a hurry to get home and get ready for her date, even though she'd had hours to do so. Each afternoon since he had arrived in the hospital he had asked her to drop by and see him after work. His invitations had ranged from watching rugby games to playing hands of poker and helping him with the crossword. She had laughed off all of them.

'I'm busy,' she'd told him that afternoon.

Bruce had raised his eyebrows. 'Hot date?'

'Well, as a matter of fact.'

'Oh, well . . .'

She had noticed his change of demeanour immediately.

'I wish you all the best, Tammy.' He had picked up the diminutive of her name from the other nurses, and she didn't mind him saying it in his broad Australian accent. 'I hope you have a really lovely evening. He's a lucky bloke.'

His sincerity had disarmed her. Normally she had to deliver a stern rebuke to him, but this evening she had simply said, 'Thank you, Bruce, that's very nice of you to say so.'

Visiting hours were long over, but as a senior nurse she could enter the hospital anytime, twenty-four hours a day, in case she was called in for an emergency. As she was now single and alone she had also put her hand up to do extra shifts, such as when one of the other nurses was ill.

Tamara turned on the interior light in her X-Trail and rummaged in her handbag. Underneath the .38 Smith & Wesson revolver her late husband had given her for personal protection was her eyeliner. She took it out and fixed her makeup. She had never had cause to use the gun – things were pretty safe out here in the lowveld – but living all on her own and working irregular shifts she carried it with her, just in case. She figured it was like insurance: you would only really need it the day you didn't have it.

Tamara put her makeup away, started the engine and drove out of the shopping centre car park. At the intersection she would have turned right to head home, but instead she turned left, towards the hospital.

*

'Oh, Bruce, you worry too much,' Sally whispered, catching his hand as he reached for his eye mask. 'Time almost is up. Lie still please. I have a surprise for you.'

Surprise, my arse, Bruce thought to himself. Her hand was on his wrist, stilling him, but it was his other hand he was now aware of – the one with the drip in it. He was getting the same feeling he got when the doctor or the nurse injected something into it. He felt the sensation of cool fluid flooding into his vein.

Bruce went to move his other hand, but Sally was pressing down on it. She was surprisingly strong for such a little thing, and for some reason he felt immediately weak. He struggled.

'Goodbye, Bruce.'

She released her grip, but when he tried to lift his hand it felt like it was encased in lead. He reached for his eye mask again and found he barely had the strength to raise it. When he saw the gloom of the room he blinked, as though a bright light had been flashed in his eyes. He made out Sally, standing, but swaying in his vision, or so it seemed.

'Syringe . . .' he managed to say, though the word sounded like it had come from someone else's distorted voice.

'Drugs, Bruce. Fun stuff. You won't feel a thing.' The needle was in the cannula.

'Wait . . .'

'No, it won't hurt you, Bruce.'

Bruce thought of Tammy Shepherd. He reached for the call button and pressed it again, but nothing happened. A feeling of dread washed through him. Sally hadn't come here to get him off, she had come here to kill him.

Bruce gritted his teeth and swung his heavy free hand as hard as he could. It was not in his nature to hit a woman – he never had – but he thumped Sally in the chest and she yelped.

'No drugs.'

Bruce saw the syringe, half-in and half-out of the tube in his hand. He reached for it, managed to get his rubbery fingers around it and pulled it out. Then he tossed it on the far side of the bed, away from Sally.

She gave an animalistic growl, snatched up a spare pillow from the guest chair beside the bed and jumped up on top of him. She straddled his chest and covered his face with the pillow.

Bruce flailed at her with his one good hand and tried to sit up, but she had him pinned, good and proper. He tried to think, but his brain was getting hazier by the second. He gave up trying to dislodge her and, instead, snaked his hand between them, under her belly, and reached for his hand that was encumbered with the drip. His fingers closed around the plastic tubing and he wrenched it free. He ignored the pain.

Reaching back, he found the bottle of brandy Tammy had left him, under his pillow. He grabbed it by the neck and smashed it, as hard as he could, against the metal railing that ran down one side of the intensive care bed. On the second attempt he heard it shatter and felt the liquor running down his hand.

Bruce swung his arm in a roundhouse arc and rammed the broken glass into the little body on top of him.

Sally screamed, let go of the pillow and toppled off the bed onto the floor. Bruce uncovered his face and gulped air, then started to swing himself off the bed to make sure the petite assassin wouldn't get up again. But instead he found himself staring down the barrel of a Chinese-made pistol.

'Shit,' he said.

*

Jorge had his orders, but Fidel's suggestion that he might 'have some fun' with the Australian woman had been playing on his mind since the boss suggested it.

He had been told to finish her off quickly, but that was like holding out the prospect of an ice-cream to a small child for doing a good deed and then snatching it away in spite.

Jorge looked down at her, on the ground. Kerry Maxwell was gagged with duct tape and her hands were bound behind her back with a plastic cable tie. She stared at him with wide-eyed terror.

He grinned at her. For a moment he contemplated how far he had fallen in life, from farmer, husband and father to gambling addict, rhino poacher and, very soon, murderer. The simple act of binding and gagging this woman had been arousing. He was about to cross a final line. He saw her not as a human being, but as an object.

It had been easy to subdue her, even if it had taken longer to catch her than he had planned. At Hazyview Junction, when the car guard had taken his rubbish to the bin, he had used the bicycle spoke to make a tiny hole in the sidewall of the left rear tyre of Baird's Land Rover. It was a trick favoured by thieves in Zimbabwe who, having made the puncture, then followed the unsuspecting victim until, eventually, the tyre went flat.

However, Kerry had managed to get out of Hazyview, through Bushbuckridge, and all the way to Klaserie, not far from Hoedspruit, before enough air was gone from the tyre for her to notice and pull over.

Jorge had been behind her and he pulled over too. He had seen the panic mixed with relief on her face when he got out of the Amarok and smiled benignly. 'Hi there, you look like you're in trouble. Can I help?'

'Yes, please.'

As she had knelt to inspect the tyre, he had taken her. Now he had her, at his mercy. The feeling of power, for a man who had lost everything and now lived to follow the orders of another, was exhilarating.

*

Gina lurked in the shadows. She saw the smelly human, the only one of their kind she trusted, lying on the ground. There was another one, standing over him, looking down at him, plus a third.

The man standing over Smelly kicked him, and Smelly screamed.

That was Gina's cue.

She broke from the cover of the shadows and the clan followed her. They had played together for years, fighting over every carcass meal that was dragged in for them. Gina had sparred with them, teaching them how to move, how to run, how to attack, how to defend. The others had never hunted in the wild, but all the time in the enclosures they had been honing their skills and deep within their DNA they were hardwired for the kill.

Gina had played along with the man who had teased them the night before, leading the pack in a chase along the fence. He thought he was tormenting them but with every run their muscles were worked. Every time he stopped and dodged, the others watched how Gina would be a step ahead of him, how she would outflank him.

But now the man was inside a cage and they were free.

Gina led them in through the open gate, past the other man, who stood by the four-wheeled machine. There was no whooping, no advance notice, just the speed of the chase and the instinctive parting of the pack and its instant transition from group of bored captives to cohesive hunting machine.

Gina and Julia, the eldest of the captive females and the alpha member of the clan until Gina's arrival, went right, and Jade, and Bozo and Benno, the two subservient males, hooked around to the left.

Before any of the humans knew what had happened Gina was on the man in the uniform. She clamped her teeth around his right hamstring and bit down, feeling the bones crunch under the 3,700 pound per square inch power of her jaws. He fell, screaming, and the others of her clan danced in glee and greed around her.

Gina growled and Julia led Bozo and Benno back towards the man they had just passed. He had gathered his wits and was sprinting from the scene of the attack. He was halfway into his machine when Julia got to him. The man wore trousers and Julia was able to snap up the hem. She pulled, worrying his leg as he tried to escape. The man kicked and Bozo and Benno whooped and slobbered, getting in the way rather than helping Julia.

The man kicked again and his trousers ripped. He managed to get into the shiny machine and it started to cough and rumble. The hyenas bellowed for his blood. Gina shook the man in her jaws, then dropped him, but he couldn't get far.

The noisy four-wheeled machine started to move towards them, and Gina saw a hand protrude from one side.

Gina sensed danger. She shifted a few steps so that she straddled the lying smelly man, legs either side of his body.

A clap of thunder sounded again. Gina yelped and slumped to the ground, half-on and half-off the smelly man.

*

Graham braced himself for the next shot, which he knew would be for him, but twin beams of light swept up the access road to the enclosure and he heard the growl of an engine.

Fidel Costa, gun still in hand and still wearing his mask, looked over his shoulder as a *bakkie* pulled up and Des Hennessy opened the door. In his hands was a pump action shotgun. Des took aim and fired and the rear window of Costa's four-by-four shattered into a thousand pieces. Costa put the vehicle in reverse and stood on the accelerator. He churned the dust as he raced past Des, who opened fire again.

Fidel must have found it hard to drive and shoot because there were no return shots as Des pumped and fired again and again.

Des let the gangster go and ran towards Graham and the hyenas.

'Get away,' Des yelled at Julia, Bozo, Benno and Jade, who, having been scared off by Fidel's shots had now returned to the lifeless body of Charles, the crooked security guard. Des punctuated his command with a shot over their heads and the hyenas scattered into the bushes.

'Don't . . . don't kill them,' Graham said.

'What about Charles?' Des ran to his man, dropped to one knee and felt for a pulse.

'He was in on it,' Graham said. 'They tried to set me up.'

Des looked to the immobilised white rhino. 'Grace, no, what have they done to you?'

'Untie me, Des, for goodness' sake.'

Gina was whimpering in the dust next to him.

'Of course.'

Des knelt by Graham, took out a pocketknife and cut the tie binding his wrists.

Graham immediately reached into his pocket for his phone and tried Kerry's number, which rang out. 'Shit, shit, shit!'

'What is it?' Des asked.

'Costa had someone following Kerry Maxwell, the woman who was staying with me. He's got a hit out on her as well. She's somewhere between Hazyview and here.'

Graham ran a hand through his lank long hair. He had to think. If he called the police he could be on hold for ages. 'The Land Rover.'

'What?' Des asked. 'You're worried about your vehicle?'

'No, no. It's got a tracking device fitted.'

'You can check on the office computer, Graham, and take my *bakkie* once you locate your Land Rover.'

'Thanks, Des. You need to sort Grace out – draw up a syringe of naltrexone. That will bring her around. And can you sedate Gina and load her into your vehicle? I'll take her with me. I need to treat her as soon as I find Kerry. I'll do it on the roadside if I have to.'

Des handed Graham his shotgun. 'You'll probably need this. I'll call the cops as well.'

*

153

Nurse Tamara Shepherd's high heels clacked on the polished hospital floor as she walked towards the intensive care ward. Most of the lights were off or dimmed at this late hour.

Ahead of her was the nurse's station where she was based during her shifts, but there was no one there. Precious was on tonight, Tamara recalled. Perhaps she was seeing to a patient who had called for help, or maybe was in the bathroom.

By force of habit Tamara could not walk past the station without checking the computer and charts to see how her various charges, including Bruce, were doing. When she walked around the partition and into the cubicle where the duty nurse usually sat she saw Precious lying on the floor.

Tamara raised a hand to her mouth to stop herself from screaming. Precious had a piece of grey duct tape over her mouth and her hands were bound behind her with a plastic cable tie. Her eyes were open but heavily lidded and she was unresponsive. Tamara checked her pulse and confirmed that she was alive and breathing. She laid the back of her hand against Precious's cheek.

She set down her bag on the floor, opened it and fumbled for the revolver which, by virtue of its weight, had made its way to the bottom of the bag under all her clutter. She pulled it out.

She thought of the patients on the ward. There was a young woman who had been in a car accident, a middle-aged man who had lost three fingers in a chainsaw accident, and Bruce. The Australian man had been in a gunfight with poachers in Mozambique. If anyone was going to draw criminals to her ward, then it would be him.

Tamara slipped off her high heels and moved barefoot, silently, towards Bruce's room. When she neared the doorway she heard voices inside.

'Goodbye, Bruce. I'm sorry I have to use this gun and wake everyone up. You have made this very difficult for me.'

'You . . . drugged . . .'

154

Tamara peeked around the door and saw an Asian woman in a bloodied white lab coat pointing a pistol at Bruce, who, though sitting up, was swaying as if he were about to fall.

'Put down that gun,' Tamara said, as she raised and aimed her own. Her heart was pounding.

The Asian woman turned to her, gun hand moving quickly.

Tamara pulled the trigger and the boom was deafening in the confines of the ward. The woman fell to the ground. Tamara screamed and let her revolver fall by her side. She couldn't believe what she had just done.

Bruce was off his bed. The other woman was not dead, however. She sat up and raised her pistol, but before she could get a shot off Bruce had his arm around her throat. A second later the woman was dead, her neck broken.

Chapter 17

Kerry writhed and screamed into her gag as the man grabbed an arm and a leg and dragged her painfully along the bare metal floor of the *bakkie*'s rear load bay. Her clothes were ripped from his initial assault on her and she had been chilled by the rushing wind as she lay in the back of his vehicle, staring up in fear at the night sky.

The man who had pulled over to help her change her tyre had grabbed her, fought with her, then subdued and loaded her into his vehicle and, from what she could tell, he'd driven her down a gravel track deeper into the bush, out of sight of the main tar road she had been on. Now he had stopped and was trying to get her out of the back.

She was terrified. Her imagination tortured her with a variety of nightmare scenarios, including her being taken back across the border to be imprisoned again by Fidel Costa. Or perhaps the man was some random crazed sex killer? No; she had seen the way the man had glanced at her when he'd taken the call on his mobile phone back on the main road. Someone on the other end had been talking about her, she was sure. This was a targeted attack, and she would bet Fidel Costa was behind it.

Kerry was sore and bruised already; she had rolled and banged herself on the metal sides of the truck and several times she had collided painfully with a shovel that rattled around beside her. She kicked back at him, but he dug his fingers into her flesh and she gave a muffled cry of pain.

As he brought her closer to the tailgate she saw that his pistol was stuffed into the waistband of his shorts. He also wore a hunting knife in a sheath on his belt. He would use the gun and the knife to intimidate her, to force her to do what he wanted.

'My boss said I should just kill you,' he said as the skin on the small of her back was gouged and burned from the friction. 'But I've got other plans for you first.'

He held her by one ankle and reached around to his back pocket with his free hand. He drew out another black plastic cable tie, then proceeded to tie her feet together, and, instead of pulling her out of the truck, he pushed her further in again. Then he grabbed the shovel.

'I'll be back for you in a minute. Don't go anywhere.' He laughed.

The man left her in the back of the truck and walked away a short distance. Kerry managed to sit up and saw that he had begun digging.

She shivered with fear. He was digging a shallow grave.

After a while he came back to her and leaned the shovel against the side of the truck. He looked down at her, reached over and ripped her shirt fully open. Kerry cowered as far away from him as she could. He stepped back, reached into his shorts and started touching himself.

She tried to scream but the gag prevented her. He got up into the tailgate, grabbed her bound feet and started pulling her towards him. Again she felt her skin being rubbed raw as her torn shirt rode up.

But as frightened as she was, Kerry was ready for him as well.

The man drew his knife from his belt. Kerry lay on her back, looking him in the eyes.

'You're being brave. That is good. I don't really want to hurt you more than I have to, so if you cooperate this will go easy for you. I might even let you go.'

She saw through his lie, but did nothing to antagonise him. Kerry prayed he wasn't about to cut her, for fun, as he brought the blade down to her legs.

He sliced through the cable tie binding her ankles, sheathed his knife and then grabbed each of her ankles. He dragged her hard, fast, to the edge of the tailgate.

'Don't move.' The man started to unzip himself.

Kerry inched towards him, moving her butt a little at a time.

'Oh? So you want me?' He grinned. 'Yes. Do this for me, and I will let you go.'

She just needed to get closer.

Kerry brought herself up, slowly, into more of a sitting position, her abdominals straining. She stopped so her face was not too close to his.

'Yes. I want to look into your eyes.' He grabbed himself with his right hand and gripped her right thigh muscle, hard, with his left. He smiled again.

Kerry straightened her back, gritted her teeth, and tucked her chin down onto her chest to brace herself, just as her father had instructed her, many years ago when she was a teenager first going out alone. Her next move was to flick her whole torso forward and ram her forehead into the man's nose.

She heard a satisfying crunching of cartilage snapping, and the man screamed. It hurt her, but, clearly, not as much as it did him. The man turned his head, instinctively, to one side, just as Bruce said an attacker probably would after that first blow, so Kerry did as her dad had told her and aimed her second headbutt blow at the top ridge of his cheekbone, near his eye.

That one gave her more pain, but she was firing on adrenaline now and it totally disorientated the would-be rapist. He let go of her leg and lurched. Her dad had said that hitting him there, the cheekbone orifice, he had called it, would shock the nerves in the attacker's brain; a blow there, Bruce reckoned, would also affect the sensory receptors in the stomach, of all places. Her father was right.

The man gasped, doubled over, and vomited. Blood flowed from his mouth and nose.

Kerry brought her legs together, drew back her knees, then shot her feet out like twin cannon balls and delivered a double kick to the side of his head. The man fell to the ground.

Speed, momentum and aggression were key now. She shimmied to the edge of the tailgate and jumped down. With her feet free she kicked him, but without shoes or boots there was only so much damage she could do. Kerry took a breath and steeled herself, mentally, for what her father had told her she would have to do next. As the man rolled onto his back, starting the process of sitting up, she stomped down on his face with the sole of her foot, not once, but three times, smashing his shattered nose with every merciless blow. He howled and pawed at her.

Kerry thought fast. She could stay here and keep kicking him, but with her hands tied there was only so much she could do until she tired or fell over. He was already reaching for the knife at his belt. She had no time to cut her hands free in order to drive the vehicle, so she decided to run.

Those hours running at home in Australia were hopefully about to pay off once more. The road was stony and uneven, but her fear and adrenaline overrode the pain in her feet as she sprinted downhill.

Kerry had to concentrate; with her arms bound at her back she felt unsteady, as if she might topple forward at any moment.

She heard a bellow of rage and pain behind her; no doubt the man was on his feet now, and even if he was in bad shape he had a gun. Kerry crested a rise and in front of her she saw Graham's battered old Land Rover by the side of the main road. Parked just in front of it was an Isuzu *bakkie*. Her momentary relief, however, washed away from her.

Kerry felt the frustration almost cripple her. There was no one in sight near the other vehicle, and no sound of approaching traffic. She couldn't start Graham's truck with her hands still tied and she couldn't see anything lying in or around the Land Rover that she could use to cut the cable tie. She could not even cry out for help.

She looked over her shoulder and saw, on the crest of the hill, the silhouette of the man who had taken her. He was coming for her. Stopping by the truck had cost her precious seconds.

*

Jorge spat blood and bile and used one hand to wipe his streaking eyes. He moved cautiously towards the Land Rover, his pistol up and ready.

'Where are you, Kerry?' he called out into the African night.

Jorge looked around.

He closed on the Land Rover, pistol up and ready. He looked around and under it. There was no one. He had the keys in his pocket. Next, he moved to the Isuzu *bakkie*, twenty metres further along the road. He was even more cautious now.

As he approached the vehicle he took up the pressure on the trigger of his pistol. The windows of the rear cab, he now noticed, were steamed up, as if there was someone inside, breathing heavily. There was no sign of a driver, but perhaps the woman had got in the back and was hiding.

'I'm coming for you,' he said.

He moved closer, his weapon at the ready. There was movement inside. Involuntarily, Jorge screamed when the snarling, drooling face of a hyena, teeth bared, popped into view. He pulled the trigger but his shot went wide.

He was turning to get away and steady himself when he saw a man with a shotgun step from the bushes on the roadside. Before Jorge could take aim, he was dead.

*

Fidel Costa slammed the leather-covered steering wheel of the BMW and cursed in Portuguese.

Maybe it was he who was cursed, he thought.

His African grandmother said hyenas carried witches on their backs in the night, and the way that clan of stinking animals had come to the rescue of the equally repugnant Graham Baird made him wonder, briefly, if the veterinarian had someone or something watching over him. Maybe he was a warlock.

Fidel shook his head. His other side told him it was just luck, and he was having a bad run of it at the moment. He would get Baird; it was just a matter of time. He hoped his other contacts here in South Africa, Jorge Silva and the Chinese-Vietnamese gangster, David Li, had experienced better luck than he.

Fidel called David.

'I haven't heard from Sally,' Li said into the handset by way of greeting.

'She should have been done by now.'

'I agree. She is a professional, in every way.'

'So was the man she was sent to visit.'

'I'll call you when she reports in,' Li said.

'You mean *if*.' Fidel ended the call then dialled Jorge Silva's number.

'*Boa noite*,' said the voice on the other end of the line.

Fidel held his tongue. Jorge Silva was, technically, an underling, but the ex-farmer rarely uttered pleasantries. The man said nothing else.

161

'Who is this?' Fidel asked in English. He didn't want to identify himself or where he was from if it wasn't Jorge.

'John McLean.'

'Who?'

'American joke,' the voice on the end said.

'Sorry, wrong num—'

'Howzit, Fidel, hold the phone. This isn't a wrong number; it's Graham Baird here. I'm just fucking with you.'

'I don't know who you are.'

'Oh, yes you do. Your guy failed, Fidel. He can't come to the phone right now, mostly because I took half his head off with a shotgun round. Oh, and in case you're wondering, Kerry's fine, as is her dad, Bruce. She just called the hospital; the hooker you sent to him won't be turning any more tricks. Also, Fidel, I am very annoyed at you for wounding my favourite hyena.'

Fidel gritted his teeth. He would destroy this phone, which was a burner, one bought illegally and not registered, as soon as he was finished with Baird. 'Listen to me —'

'No,' said Baird, all traces of false bonhomie gone from his voice. 'You listen to me, motherfucker, I'm coming for you.'

Fidel ended the call then broke open the back of the device, took out the SIM card and tossed it out the window of the BMW. He was coming up to Bushbuckridge, the sprawling settlement to the west of the Kruger Park. Here he would lose the vehicle and stay with a distant cousin who also worked for him part-time as a poacher.

No, Fidel said to himself. He would fix Baird, Johnston, the Australian woman and her father. They would not escape him again and he was in no hurry. He would have his revenge for his brother. In time, he would kill them all, but first he might still be able to ruin them, one at a time, ironically by playing them at their own soft-hearted game.

Chapter 18

Kerry looked out the window of the British Airways Boeing and caught a glimpse of the green-blue snake of the Zambezi River that wound its way through the dry khaki bushveld, and Mosi-oa-Tunya, the Smoke that Thunders – Victoria Falls.

The jet turned, paralleling the river for a little while upstream of the falls, and Kerry scanned the waters for elephants that might be crossing, or browsing for food on the banks.

Graham sat next to her, in his trademark bush clothes, which, while frayed at the cuffs, were at least clean. He wore rafter sandals, his concession to civility. She wondered how long it would take him to end up barefoot.

Bruce had been furious that she was not flying back to Australia, but, then, neither was he, despite having been discharged from hospital and cleared to fly.

'Dad, Graham has a job supervising the darting and de-horning of three black rhinos on a private reserve, and will give the animals a thorough check. It's very straightforward. I'll be perfectly fine – nothing can happen to me in Zimbabwe,' she had told him, the day after they had all survived being assassinated, when he was still in hospital but now with a police officer sitting guard outside his room.

'Did you hear what you just said?' her father had replied. 'Didn't they have a coup there?'

'Bruce,' Kerry had noticed how Nurse Shepherd laid a hand on his forearm as she spoke, 'Zimbabwe is actually quite a safe country to travel in.'

'There's something in the water in Africa,' Bruce said as Tamara left the room to check on another patient. 'It makes you all go cuckoo.'

'Well, I can see what the water's done to you,' Kerry countered, nodding towards the disappearing nurse.

'We're just friends,' Bruce said. 'Tammy has a few days off and she has offered to show me around the Kruger Park when I get out of here. All above board.'

'So it's *Tammy* now, is it?' Kerry had ribbed.

Bruce was pleased that she would be out of South Africa for a while, at least, and he had said he reserved the right to 'order' her to fly back to Australia as soon as she returned from Zimbabwe. It was pretty clear, however, that her father was in no hurry to get home either.

Perhaps he was right about there being something in the water, Kerry thought as she checked her seatbelt for landing. The flight attendant walked down the aisle and collected Graham's fourth empty Windhoek Lager can. She gave Kerry a sympathetic look and Kerry just gave an eye roll in return. Graham had assured her they would be picked up at the airport – the game reserve was sending a car and driver – so it didn't matter if he had a drink or two. Kerry had limited herself to one glass of white wine.

The aircraft bucked, thanks to a hot thermal rising up off the baking black runway, and Kerry grabbed hold of the armrest. Graham put a hand on hers and she didn't try to move him away. The truth was, she was still unsettled by the attacks on her and Graham and Bruce, which had also reminded her of the ordeal she had gone through in Mozambique. The police captain investigating the case, Sannie van Rensburg, had said there were SMS messages between the phones owned by the dead prostitute and the man who had tried to kill Kerry, indicating that Eli would have been the female assassin's next target, after Bruce. Without going into details about the illegal cross-border rescue mission, Graham had told the police that he had killed Costa's younger brother in self-defence and that Kerry had been kidnapped but had managed to escape Costa's thugs. He had said he was sure Fidel Costa was behind the attempts, but had to concede that he had not seen the face of the man who had come to Ukuphila to finish him off.

A couple of the South Africans Kerry worked with in Australia had filled her head with horror stories before she'd left home about how she would be carjacked, murdered and/or raped, and she had brushed off their concerns. Kerry was sure that if her itinerary had gone as planned she would have had an incident-free holiday, but meeting Graham, or rather not meeting him when she first arrived, had turned all that – and her world – upside down.

Graham, too, had tried to dissuade Kerry from coming with him, but she had insisted. After all, as Graham himself reluctantly admitted, if he had remembered and honoured her booking to come and work her allotted period as a volunteer at Ukuphila, he wouldn't have taken the job in Victoria Falls this particular week. Kerry had been more than happy to book a flight to see the falls – the only reason she hadn't already was that she was supposed to still be with Graham at the wildlife orphanage.

Graham had promised Bruce that he would take care of Kerry. She had told both of them, when Graham drove to the hospital the morning after the attempted killings, that she did not need to be protected, and nor did she want to be treated like some man's charge.

The fact was, though, that she was glad Graham was there next to her. Kerry was also pleased that she had at least been able to spend some time with her father alone, save for the frequent check-ups from Nurse Shepherd.

'Are you OK, kiddo?' Bruce had asked her, when they were by themselves.

She had shrugged. 'Kidnapped twice, nearly killed, nearly raped, what do you reckon, Dad?'

He'd laughed, and it had been infectious. 'You'll be right, but, trust me on this, if you want to talk about it, sometime later, then don't hold back. To me, to a therapist, it doesn't matter, but don't bottle it all up too long. I did that after Vietnam and it took me a long time to come right.'

She nodded, remembering his dark times – too much drinking, long days and sometimes weeks when he was on leave and wouldn't want to leave the house, her mother's tears, the screams from her parents' bedroom as Bruce lived out his horrors in nightmares and Anh tried to calm him.

'I will, Dad, I promise. Can I ask you something, though?'

'Anything, kiddo.'

'You know how we were just laughing about all this shit, just a few seconds ago?'

'Yes?'

'Is that what it was like for you, in the war? Terrified one minute then laughing the next?'

He nodded. 'Pretty much. Humans are good at putting up defences, black humour and all that. Plus, and this is what you have to be careful of, there's a thrill to it. Winston Churchill went to the Boer War as a war correspondent, and he summed it up by saying something like "There's nothing so exhilarating as being shot at and surviving".'

She thought about his words. She had come to Africa wanting to help save the continent's wildlife, not to be a soldier. 'I get it, but I don't think that life is for me.'

'Good, love,' Bruce had said. 'Take care of yourself in Zimbabwe.'

Next to her, Graham burped, jolting her out of her reverie.

Kerry sighed. The aircraft taxied up to a garish-looking airport terminal that Graham informed her had been built by the Chinese.

Zimbabwe was the third country she had visited since arriving in Africa and thankfully it was on better terms than her trip to Mozambique. When they entered the terminal Kerry, as an Australian, had to queue for and buy a visa before getting her passport stamped. The flight was full, mostly tourists visiting the falls, so Kerry was going to be a while. Graham, like the few South Africans on the flight, was able to proceed straight to passport control.

'I'll see what's happening with our ride and meet you at the baggage carousel,' Graham said.

'OK.'

It was a slow but fairly good-natured business moving from the first of two counters, where she paid for her visa, to the second, where her passport was stamped. It seemed like needless duplication of effort, but she held her tongue and kept her patience. Within twenty minutes Kerry was through.

Graham had found their bags and a trolley, and true to his word he was waiting for her. Kerry spotted two men dressed like guides in khaki bush shirts and shorts; the logo on their shirts said *Tatenda Safaris*.

'That's them,' said Graham. '*Tatenda* means "thank you" in Shona.'

Kerry followed Graham, pushing the trolley which he seemed to have left in her care. Graham greeted the men and introduced Kerry.

167

'Welcome to Zimbabwe,' said one of the men, whose name was Blessed.

'Thank you, Blessed – *tatenda*. Now, which one of you is our driver?' Graham asked.

The two men looked to each other and there was an awkward pause.

'Um, Mr Garth said you would be driving yourself,' Blessed said. 'Nicholas here drove your vehicle to the airport and I now have to take him to Mr Garth's lodge in Hwange National Park.'

'Oh,' said Graham.

'Graham,' Kerry said quietly, 'you've had too much to drink to drive.'

'Shush.'

'Don't you tell me to shush.'

'There is a problem?' Blessed asked.

'No, no problem at all.'

Kerry put her hands on her hips. 'Yes, there is a problem. I'm not getting into a vehicle driven by this man. He's pissed to the eyeballs.'

Blessed looked down at his suede *veldskoen* bush shoes. 'Ah, Mr Garth does not allow us to drive the vehicles when we have been drinking.'

'Good idea,' Kerry said.

Blessed looked to her. 'Perhaps you can drive Dr Baird, madam?'

Kerry looked skyward. 'Yes. Well, I suppose I'll have to, won't I.'

'Stop fretting about nothing,' Graham said.

'Do you at least know where we're going?'

'More or less. Blessed, can you give me directions to the game reserve, please?'

Blessed looked at his shoes again, then at Nicholas and finally back to Graham, though he avoided eye contact. 'Ah, there is a problem.'

'You don't say,' said Kerry, rolling her eyes. 'What is it?'

'A local chief, he has invaded the reserve,' Blessed said to Kerry.

'Oh, no!'

Graham shook his head. 'Damn. The farm invasions are pretty much over in Zimbabwe – there's virtually no more farmland left to take – but now the last-ditch efforts are focused on taking over privately owned game reserves, one of the few uses of land that still makes money for the country.'

'You are exactly correct,' Blessed said. 'The chief and his supporters have blockaded the gates. We flew out the last tourists this morning by helicopter. No one can get in by road. Mr Garth told us to bring a vehicle for you so that you are not stranded.'

'We can try and organise a chopper,' Graham said.

'Perhaps, sir. Mr Garth is in Bulawayo talking to the provincial governor – they went to school together – to see if he can get the chief to leave the reserve, but for now no one is going in or out.'

Kerry could see this was not Graham's fault, but she was left with the feeling, once again, that nothing he was involved in ever seemed to go according to plan. 'So what do we do now?'

Graham shrugged. 'Go get a drink?'

Kerry was exasperated. 'All right, but I drive.'

Blessed escorted them out to the car park and gave Kerry a quick familiarisation of the Toyota Land Cruiser they would be driving for the next two days, or however long they ended up staying in Zimbabwe. Graham seemed to be paying more attention to his phone, which had beeped with a couple of messages. Kerry guessed he was very familiar with four-wheel drive vehicles, unlike her.

The plan had been for them to spend two nights at Garth's game reserve just outside of Victoria Falls and for Kerry to watch the darting and de-horning of the reserve's rhinos. At some point during their stay they – or Kerry at least – would visit the falls. Back in Johannesburg they would pick up a connection to Cape

Town, where Graham would be, reluctantly, speaking at Sarah Hoyland's Animals Without Borders fundraising event after performing a check-up on the rhinos at Kwangela Game Reserve.

They got into the vehicle. 'Is there any point in us staying two nights now?' Kerry asked.

Graham got into the front passenger seat of the Land Cruiser. 'We may as well stay here, unless you want to spend an extra night in Johannesburg.'

Kerry drove through the airport car park, tentatively at first as she got used to driving the big vehicle. It was different from other Land Cruisers she had seen in Australia. This one had been modified, with a big stretched cab designed to take up to nine passengers sitting in three rows of three behind the driver and front passenger. It felt like driving a tank – a fast tank as she found out when she left the car park and turned onto the main road.

'Watch out for speed traps. The cops here are notorious for finding ways to fleece people,' Graham offered, before closing his eyes and settling into his seat.

'I don't even know where I'm going,' Kerry said.

'Straight,' he said without opening his eyes. 'If you get to the waterfall you've gone too far.'

'Where will we stay?'

'No idea.'

Kerry took a deep breath. She had learned that things most certainly did not go according to plan all the time in Africa, but this complete lack of a plan was enough to make her want to scream her lungs out. She gripped the steering wheel hard enough to hurt as she fought to keep her anger in check. She didn't have a guidebook and hadn't begun to look at accommodation online as she had assumed they'd be staying in the game reserve.

As she approached what looked like the outskirts of town, judging by the Zambezi Lager billboard welcoming her to Victoria

Falls, Kerry was stopped at a police roadblock. She had kept a close eye on her speed, so she wasn't worried when the policeman on duty greeted her and asked to see her driver's licence.

'Australia? You are very far.'

'Yes,' she smiled.

'What have you brought me from Australia?'

Kerry was flummoxed. 'Um . . .'

'A sunny disposition and a wish for world peace,' Graham said, opening his eyes at last.

The policeman laughed and waved them on their way. 'Safe journey.'

They drove into town and the first hotel Kerry saw, on the left, was called the Sprayview. 'What's that one like?'

Graham opened his eyes again. 'Last time I stayed at the Sprayview there were no seats on the toilets – someone had stolen them all – and I got food poisoning. Says it's under new management, though. It was always good value.'

Kerry indicated and pulled into the hotel car park. The road ahead looked like it just got busier the closer it got to the water-falls and she didn't fancy manoeuvring the big truck in and out of traffic. The desk staff were friendly and, bearing in mind what Graham had said, Kerry asked to see a room.

To her relief the room she was shown not only had a toilet seat, but looked fresh and neat and newly renovated. The rooms were set in long single-storey rows. The place reminded her of a 1960s Australian roadside motel, but the interiors were classier. 'We'll take two rooms,' she told the desk clerk.

Graham cleared his throat and she looked to him.

'Kerry, I'm a little short of cash.'

'How much?'

'A lot short, in fact.'

'You want me to pay for your room?'

He shrugged. 'I hadn't budgeted on paying for accommodation.'

Kerry couldn't believe it. No, she told herself on second thought. She could.

'Excuse me, madam?' the receptionist said.

'Yes?'

'Ah, I am sorry, but the room I showed you is the last room we have. There is a big conference on in Victoria Falls at the moment – the ruling party's annual congress. We are very busy.'

Kerry exhaled. 'Can you recommend anywhere else?'

The man shook his head. 'I think you will find all of Victoria Falls is full-full.'

The room she had inspected had twin beds. It would have to do.

'*Eish*, I'll take it,' she said.

Graham raised his eyebrows. 'Did you just say "*eish*"?'

'I may have.'

'You're becoming more African by the minute. Welcome to our world, we mean you no harm.'

Kerry was tired from the early start so after they'd checked in she lay down for a nap, fully clothed. Graham slept off his airline beers, lying on his back on the bed next to hers, snoring.

Every time Kerry dozed off the freight train next to her woke her. After an hour and a half she prodded Graham in the ribs. 'I'm going to see the falls.'

He rubbed his eyes and checked his watch.

'Are you coming?' she asked him.

'I need to get some beers for the room fridge, so, yes, an afternoon constitutional will do me the world of good.'

'Is that all you think of, alcohol?'

Graham mulled over the question while picking his nose. 'Food?'

Kerry got up to go to the toilet. 'Sex, too, I suppose.'

'Well, I thought we were going for a walk, but if you've got a minute.'

'In your dreams, buddy.' She went to the bathroom. He was infuriating, but mildly entertaining, in a gross way.

Kerry came out and took her hat and sunscreen out of her bag and put on both. She held the bottle out to him. 'Want some?'

'Never use the stuff.'

'I can tell. You look like an old handbag. Melanoma will kill you, you know.'

'Isn't Melanoma the husband of the Italian girl who works in the deli at Hoedspruit? She fancies me.'

Kerry walked out, making sure she took the key with her. Graham ambled after her.

'Do you think we need to take a cab?' she asked.

'No,' Graham said. 'It's just a short stroll.'

The town of Victoria Falls consisted of one long street leading downhill to the falls, with a few side streets branching off. They passed shops selling gifts and clothing and booking agencies for a host of adrenaline-fuelled pursuits including bungee-jumping, bridge swinging, elephant riding, walking with lions and white-water rafting.

The place was abuzz with tourists, safari guides and a never-ending procession of young men trying to sell them carvings, trillion-dollar Zimbabwean currency notes from the days of hyperinflation and, in hushed tones, *dagga*.

'What's that?' Kerry asked after Graham told a man to leave them alone.

'*Dagga*? Grass. Dope. Weed.'

The man drifted back within earshot of them. He pulled a plastic bag from his pocket. 'Yes, would you like some?'

'Marijuana? My goodness, no!'

'I knew you were square,' Graham said.

'I am *not* square.'

'OK. Want to score?' asked the dealer.

'No!'

173

'Square,' said the man.

Graham guffawed. 'OK, my friend, you can leave us now.' The dealer shrugged and walked off.

'I am *not* square,' she said.

'OK. Don't worry, it was probably oregano, or some such rubbish. The good stuff comes from Malawi in any case.'

Kerry shook her head. She wasn't surprised he knew where to find the best drugs.

Eventually they came to the entry to the national park, where they had to pay a fee in order to view the falls. Further on, Graham told her, was a border post, and then the high level bridge across the Zambezi that led to Zambia, on the other side of the river.

'Two, please,' Kerry said to a national parks employee behind a window.

'No, I'm not coming in,' Graham said.

Kerry looked over her shoulder. 'It's OK. I'll pay.'

'No, it's fine.'

'Come on,' she said.

'No thanks. I've seen the falls before, a few times. I'll wait out here for you, in the car park,' he said in a quiet voice. He glanced away, avoiding her eyes.

Kerry looked at Graham and for once he wasn't cracking a joke. She shrugged. 'Fair enough.'

Kerry paid and walked through into the national park and found her way on a well-marked and busy track. As she neared the edge of the escarpment she felt a light mist caressing her face. This was Mosi-oa-Tunya, the Smoke that Thunders. The smoke was water, rising like a cloud above the falls and visible for some distance. The thunder, too, was growing louder. She felt a hint of excitement in her belly.

But when she came to the first of a number of viewing points on the edge, overlooking the majestic falls, her excitement dissipated. It wasn't the cascading wall of water or the view that disappointed, but rather the fact that apart from a group of Chinese tourists who chattered and snapped beside her, she was alone.

Kerry thought about Graham, sitting outside in the car park, fending off touts, and Eli, in Mozambique, or wherever he was right now. They were, all three of them, dedicated to their work, perhaps married to their jobs, but none of them had a partner.

Graham seemed to have something going on with the Sarah woman who was organising the fundraising for Animals Without Borders, and she imagined Eli had no trouble attracting women, yet none of them was in a traditional relationship. She wondered why that might be. She found a rock to sit on, and took some pictures of the falls with her phone.

Kerry thought about her father. Bruce was a wily one. She had seen the way the South African nurse, Tamara, fussed over him. She was attractive, though perhaps fifteen or twenty years younger than her father. Kerry felt a twinge of something – jealousy perhaps – that Tamara and her father were spending time together on safari, and a pinprick of sadness when she remembered her mother and how happy her parents had been together.

How happy had they really been, though?

She replayed parts of her childhood, good and bad. Her mother was not given to outbursts of emotion – perhaps that was something to do with her upbringing – but by the time Kerry was in her teens her mother was Australian enough and army-wife enough to complain about Bruce's continual absences from home. She had been outright angry when Bruce had told them that they were leaving Perth – he had agreed to transfer from the Special Air Service in Perth to a newly created Commando battalion in Holsworthy, on the outskirts of Sydney. It was the same time he was commissioned, as an officer, so it had been a time of great upheaval for her father, as well as the family.

But they had come through it, because they were a family. Kerry wondered if she would ever find someone and settle down, maybe even have children.

She shook her head to clear it and tried to focus on what was in front of her. From what she could see it was apparent tourists experienced a very different view of Victoria Falls depending on which side of the Zambezi River they were on. From her side, in Zimbabwe, she looked over to a wide rock wall with water cascading down over the sheer cliff across a panoramic frontage. At the right of her view, on the other side of the river, she could see half-a-dozen dozen people splashing about in a pool on the very edge of the waterfall.

This, she recalled reading in the airline magazine, was the Devil's Pools, on the Zambian side of the river. Kerry reckoned her view of the falls was better than that of those kamikaze back-packers in the pools, who were taking selfies and pictures of each other standing on the rim of the waterfall, but by contrast they were clearly having a lot more fun than she.

Was that her life? Was she a spectator, well heeled and organised enough to view one of the world's wonders, but not able to experience it the way the carefree travellers across the river from her were experiencing it?

The events of the past couple of weeks had shaken her, turned her upside down in fact. She had come to Africa expecting – though she would never have thought of it this way – to be an onlooker, watching the barefoot vet, Graham Baird, operating on animals, perhaps saving a couple, perhaps helping out by applying a bandage or bandaid. She had never really imagined she would play any direct part in the saving of Africa's wildlife. She would have gone back to Australia, if everything had gone according to plan, feeling good about herself, happy that she had helped out, but in reality she would have been no more than a tourist who had paid to play veterinary nurse and pet some animals. She would not have changed a thing.

What had happened was that she had been dropped into the war on poaching and seen and felt firsthand the horrors of a life lived on the edge. She had stared death in the face not once but twice, and she had survived.

Yet here she was, a tourist once more, observing an amazing scene while other people lived it. She wanted to be those people on the other side of the river; she wanted the excitement, even the danger. It wasn't for the thrill, it was to feel alive and to feel like she mattered.

Graham and Eli, two very different men with different jobs, were fighting this battle on a day-to-day basis. Now that she had seen what they were up against, had encountered the evil they had to confront every day, she didn't know how she could go back to her safe, sane, predictable life in Australia.

Two of the people on the other side, a man and a woman wearing T-shirts and shorts, stood in the rock pool, water up to their waists and a sheer drop beside them. They embraced and started kissing.

That's what Kerry was missing, someone to share not only this incredible view with, but to share her life with. She got up off her rock and continued following the path along the edge of the cliff.

'Hello, madam,' a man said to her as she rounded a bend. 'Would you like a guide to the falls?'

'No, to life.'

The man paused, speechless for a moment. He smiled. 'You look like a good person. You will find your way yourself.'

Chapter 19

Graham had sent a tout to the liquor shop in the main street of Victoria Falls to buy him a sixpack of Zambezi Lager on the promise of a big tip, and his faith in humanity was pleasantly and at least temporarily restored when the skinny young man returned with the goods.

Graham gave him a five-dollar tip and the street vendor, perhaps feeling the same way, threw in a carved stone pendant on a thin leather thong.

'*Tatenda, shamwari*,' Graham said, thanking his new friend.

'*Fambai zvakanaka*; go well, *baba*.'

Graham touched the brim of his sweat-stained cap and used one bottle's cap to lever open another. He was no one's *baba* – father – and that probably wasn't a bad thing. The Zambezi tasted like a plunge in a cool lake on a hot day. A baboon sauntered past him, eyed the green bottle, then sniffed and jumped up on a rubbish bin. It fossicked for snacks and inspected a cigarette butt.

'Don't,' Graham said.

He reached into the pocket of his shirt and shook his last cigarette from the packet and lit it. He looked at his nicotine-stained fingers. He should probably give up, though what was the point?

Graham was in the shade of a tree but it was damned hot up here, much warmer even than Hoedspruit. He took off his damp cap and dropped it on the ground in front of him, in the sun, upside down so the sun could dry the perspiration a bit.

A party of Chinese tourists, some wearing surgical masks to protect them from Africa, emerged from the national park entry gate. Their leader, holding a pink parasol aloft, marched towards a waiting bus. Most of the lemmings followed but two of them, women with strands of grey in their jet-black hair, lingered at the rear of the column.

One held up an iPhone and snapped a picture of him.

Graham smiled and raised his beer. The other woman didn't take a picture but moved cautiously forward, approaching him as one of the other group members was approaching the baboon.

The woman closed the distance between them and Graham looked up at her, lost for words, as she dropped a US five-dollar bill into his hat, gave a little bow, then turned and scurried away to catch up with her group.

Graham stared down at the green note in his grimy hat. He finished his beer, took another from the sixpack nestled behind him, and opened it. Then he picked up the money, folded it, and put it in his pocket. He didn't know whether to be offended or touched.

'You found the grog shop, I see.'

Graham looked up. The sun was behind her, making him squint. 'I got home delivery. Life's tough in Africa.'

She looked at her watch. 'Well, I suppose the sun is well over the yardarm.'

He held up the remains of the sixpack. 'Join me?'

Kerry shrugged. 'Well, when in Zimbabwe.'

She sat down on the concrete kerb next to him and he opened a bottle and passed it to her.

'Cheers,' Kerry said, and they clinked.

'Tell me,' he said after another sip, 'do I look like a hobo?'

'A hobo?' She screwed up her face in concentration. 'Oh, you mean a homeless person? They haven't been called hobos in the rest of the world since 1929.'

'Whatever. Do I?'

She leaned away from him and gave him a good look. 'Yes. Why?'

'A Chinese lady just dropped five dollars in my hat.'

Kerry laughed and then coughed as her beer went down the wrong way. 'Well, put your hat back out!'

'That's not funny,' Graham said.

'It is. Kind of.'

Graham drank some more beer in silence.

'You could shave. That would make you look slightly less homeless,' she said. 'And do something about that forest of hair in your ears. Why is it that men start sprouting hair in the oddest of places as they get older?'

Unconsciously he touched his greying bristles, and his ears. 'I do shave. Once a fortnight or when crossing borders.'

'Why when crossing borders?'

'So I don't look like a drug dealer or a homeless person to the immigration authorities.'

Kerry nodded. 'The only drug dealer I ever met was clean-shaven and wore an Armani suit, but he was only a part-time dealer. The rest of the time he was a barrister. And that guy today, he was well dressed.'

'Lawyers and touts, same things,' Graham scoffed.

'Lawyer jokes, Graham? Seriously? Plus, you didn't shave to enter Zimbabwe.'

'Normal rules don't apply to Zimbabwe. And I forgot my razor.'

'So, basically, Graham's number one rule is that there are no rules, is that it?'

He thought about that for a moment. 'Yes. Pretty much. I've had rules before, at school, veterinary college, in the army. Rules aren't always good; they don't always guarantee that everything will work out. Some rules were made to be broken, but some rules are there for a very good reason.'

'Well, that clears that up.' Kerry gave a small laugh.

Graham looked at Kerry. There was an innocence about her that hadn't been stolen from her by life. That was good, for her, especially given what Africa had thrown at her already. Perhaps she was one of those people who were made stronger by adversity. She had lost her mother and Graham knew how hard it could be to lose a loved one. But the death of her parent was not her fault.

That was the difference.

'What rules are good?' she asked.

'You're taking a malaria prophylactic? Pills?'

'Yes, I am,' she said.

'Good. You look like the sort who would.'

'The sort who keeps their arms and legs covered and sprays with repellent in the evenings?'

'Yes.'

'Are you mocking me?'

'No.' He managed a smile. 'Not right now, at least. Big towns like Victoria Falls are where there's a high risk of malaria – plenty of people here will be carrying the disease and the mosquitos spread it from person to person.'

'Why are you so concerned about malaria, but happy to drink and smoke yourself to death?'

'Malaria kills about twenty million people a year and it's preventable.'

'Yes, I read that,' she said.

'Well,' he sighed, 'what you didn't read was that my wife was one of those people. She caught cerebral malaria and died.'

Her mouth fell open. 'Oh, Graham. I'm so sorry. I didn't know.'

181

'How could you?'

'I'm so very sorry.' She paused. 'Did you come here with her?'

'Yes. That was the last time I saw the falls, with Carla, my wife. We should be getting back. Come.'

He turned away, not wanting to see her pitying expression any longer.

'Yes, all right.'

'Oh, by the way,' he reached into his pocket, 'I thought you might like this. It's an old family heirloom.' He handed her the carved stone pendant.

'Really? Was it . . . did it belong to . . .'

'The guy who bought my beer for me gave it to me.'

She rolled her eyes, then took the pendant and held it up to take a closer look. 'It looks like a snake with a weird head, like a fish.'

'Yes, that's it. Exactly. It's Nyaminyami.'

'I've seen these, there are guys selling them around the falls.'

He nodded. 'Yes. Nyaminyami is the river god of the Tonga people, one of their protectors. But like all gods he's vengeful as well.'

'How so?'

'The locals say that when the Kariba Dam wall was being built on the river, downstream, to form Lake Kariba, Nyaminyami was disturbed and he was angry. There were unseasonal floods, accidents on the dam and workers were killed. Three men were drowned, and when the construction authorities couldn't find the bodies they went to the local Tonga people to ask for their help in retrieving them, as the grieving families were coming to the site to bury them.'

'How terrible. What happened?'

'The locals said Nyaminyami needed another sacrifice. The government men agreed. A black calf was killed and placed in the river. The next day, the calf was gone – hardly surprising given the number of crocodiles in the river – but in its place were the bodies of the three workers, floating there, three days after they had gone missing.'

'Spooky.' Kerry tied the leather thong around her neck and straightened the pendant.

'Nyaminyami had a wife.' Graham looked away from her bright eyes. 'The locals say they were separated, upstream and down-stream, when the dam wall was built. They say the earth tremors that occurred after the dam was built were Nyaminyami venting his anger and calling for his wife. One day, so the legend goes, he'll succeed in destroying the dam and he and his wife will be reunited.'

'Scary, but sad and romantic all at the same time.'

Graham hauled himself to his feet. 'Africa.'

*

By the time they had walked back to the hotel the sun was disap-pearing, leaving behind a lava-coloured horizon.

Kerry was getting better at ignoring the street salesmen and not feeling like she should buy something from any of them. Predictably, Graham said he would wait in the bar while she went back to the room and showered. She told him that was fine, but when she got to the room she felt a chill as she remembered what had happened on her way from the hospital to Ukuphila. She locked and latched the door and checked the sliding door leading out onto the little verandah area at the front of the room, then pulled the curtains closed.

She felt clammy, remembering the hands of the man on her when he'd grabbed her while she was inspecting the puncture in the Land Rover's tyre.

Kerry took a deep breath and told herself she was safe here in Zimbabwe. There was no way Fidel Costa could know where she was, or reach her. All the same, she showered and dressed in record time.

When she stepped from her room a man emerged from the shadows. Kerry gave a small gasp.

'Is everything all right, madam?'

The man wore the green uniform and cap of a security guard. 'Yes, yes, fine thank you. I didn't see you there.'

'No problem, madam. You have nothing to worry about.'

I wish, Kerry thought. She followed the sound of music and laughter towards the hotel swimming pool. Tables had been set along the side of the pool closest to the restaurant and bar, and these were mostly full. The clientele were tourists judging by the green and khaki. It was funny, she thought, but after what she'd been through she was starting to think of herself more as a local than a visitor. She told herself to get over the feeling of superiority. She went in search of Graham.

She found him inside, in the bar, propped up on a stool talking to the barman, who laughed at something he'd just said. When he turned she saw that his face was happy and glowing now that he was back in his natural element.

'Hello, glad you could join us,' he called. 'What'll it be?'

'Gin and tonic, please,' Kerry said.

'Single or double, madam?' the bartender asked.

'Double,' Graham said.

'Single.' She was irked at his assumption, her sympathy for him vanishing, almost.

'Sorry, my mistake,' he said.

She let her hackles settle. 'No worries.' The barman passed her drink and she took a stool next to Graham.

He drained a Zambezi Lager and signalled the barman for another. Kerry wondered how many he'd had already. Graham took a long slug from the fresh beer. 'Good shower?'

'Great, thanks. The pressure was wonderful.'

'One thing they're not short of here is water.'

'I suppose so.'

'It's great to see this place jumping,' he said. 'Last time I was here I was the only person in the bar.'

'The lack of toilet seats may also have been a factor.'

He laughed. 'Correct. Are you hungry?'

'Starving, in fact. Shall we go through to dinner?'

'Let's,' he said.

They found the head waiter and he showed them to a table for two. The party next to them was loud and Kerry found that the noise grated on her. A few tables down, a group of half-a-dozen Zimbabwean men was serenading a group of tourists with an a cappella version of 'The Lion Sleeps Tonight'.

'Graham, is everything OK?'

He was looking around. 'What? Yes, yes, of course.'

She saw he had been looking at the table on the other side of them. Sitting at it was a young couple in matching safari outfits. They were looking into each other's eyes and holding hands across the table.

'Honeymooners,' Kerry said.

'What?'

'That couple, over there, the ones you were just staring at.'

'You think they're on their honeymoon?'

'Duh. How much have you had to drink?'

He shrugged. 'Not that much. Why do you ask if I'm all right? I'm fine.'

'I just thought, after what you told me today –'

'Oh my gawd,' he interrupted, 'here comes the mariachi band.'

Kerry was confused, but then saw the singers in their white shirts and black trousers taking up position in a semicircle around the young couple. They smiled with delight and the woman took out her phone and began videoing the group as they broke into an Adele number.

'If they ask for requests I'm going to ask for a cyanide pill,' Graham said.

'Grouch.'

'Ha. Waiter? Please may I have another Zambezi and . . .'

'I'm fine,' Kerry said as the crooning carried on behind them.

They looked at the menus and ordered, Kariba bream for her and steak for him.

'I can't stand traditional dancing,' he said, to break the ice again after a couple of minutes.

Kerry looked to the singers, who were finishing up to applause from the neighbouring tables. 'Adele is hardly traditional African music.'

'No, but it's forced and embarrassing. Waiters and waitresses dressed up in tribal stuff. In fact, I don't like entertainment of any kind when eating. I'd rather just have my meal in peace.'

'Well, you can tell them that, they're coming this way.'

Graham looked over his shoulder. 'Gawd,' he said again.

'Hello, lovely people,' the lead singer said to them. 'May we please entertain you?'

'Um, I think we're OK . . .' Kerry began.

'Do you know "Shosholoza"?' Graham said, without looking back at the lead singer who was behind him.

'Of course, sir.'

'Then sing.'

The man beamed at Kerry, who rolled her eyes.

'It's about miners catching a train to work,' Graham said to Kerry.

The group broke into the melodious strains of the song, much more at home with the Zulu words and the rhythm of the anthem that rose and fell, quickened and slowed like the movements of a train gathering steam.

The guests at the other tables turned to watch them as the group hit their stride.

Kerry caught the second half of the song on video, and even got some vision of Graham scowling, arms crossed, in the foreground. When they finished Graham took a US ten-dollar bill out of his pocket and palmed it to the lead singer.

Kerry sat back in her seat. She was surprised. Graham seemed to have no money, usually, but the tip to the singers had been generous. 'That was nice.'

'People here have nothing,' he said.

'You didn't even want them to sing.'

'At least they're doing their best to earn a living.'

Graham called a waiter over and ordered a bottle of South African wine. Their food came and, both hungry, they suspended conversation for the most part while they ate and drank.

Graham seemed, Kerry thought, to have a phenomenal capacity for alcohol, which she guessed he had built up over some time. She, on the other hand, was feeling light-headed after her gin and tonic and two glasses of wine with the meal.

'Phew, I'm stuffed,' she said.

'Me too. Shall we retire to the boudoir?' He raised and lowered his eyebrows a couple of times.

'Behave.' He had tried to be funny, but she sensed he was forcing it this time, almost for her benefit.

They walked back to the room and the security guard bade them good night.

Inside the room Kerry excused herself to go to the bathroom. She was ready to read Graham the riot act, but when she emerged she saw his bed had been stripped of its pillow and bedspread. Graham's bag was no longer in the room, and nor was he.

Kerry opened the hotel room door and peeked outside. She saw that the interior light of the Land Cruiser was on, but then it went out.

'Graham?' she called softly, so as not to wake any other guests.

There was no answer so she walked to the vehicle and put her hands against one of the side passenger windows so she could peer in. Graham was stretched out along the middle back row of seats.

187

His head was buried under the bedspread. His duffel bag was in the front seat.

She turned and went back into the hotel room, not wanting to disturb him.

Chapter 20

Graham woke with the sun streaming in through the Land Cruiser's windows. The seats had been uncomfortable, but he'd had worse beds in his life.

He had drifted in and out of sleep, tossing off the bedspread when it became almost unbearably hot and humid in the confines of the vehicle. He'd snoozed but been woken at midnight by strobing lightning and the boom of thunder. The heavens had dumped what was probably the first big storm of the wet season over the ensuing five hours until just before dawn.

Graham eased his cramped body out of the vehicle and, after a quick check around, released his bladder into the flowerbed outside the room. He zipped up and knocked on the hotel room door.

'Hello?' came Kerry's voice, a little croaky, after a couple more knocks. She opened the door a crack. 'What time is it?'

'Six. Time to get on the road.'

'Where are we going?'

'Well,' he said, mustering as much enthusiasm as he could at this time of the day, 'since you saw the falls yesterday, I thought

189

we might head out into the bush, into Hwange National Park. Unless, that is, you're up for a spot of white-water rafting or bungee-jumping?'

'Ah, no, I'll skip the adrenaline junkie stuff. Some time in the bush would be fantastic, though. Do you want to come in and use the bathroom?'

'I've been.'

'Graham!'

'When in Africa.'

'That's your answer for everything. At least come in and have a shower.'

'Are you suggesting I stink?'

'Yes,' she said.

'Very well.'

He went back to the truck and got his bag, then went inside. Kerry said she had washed before going to bed, so she got dressed while he showered, singing to himself. He didn't really feel cheery, but he knew he'd been having a bad time last night and he didn't want her asking endless questions today on the drive to Hwange, so he did his best to appear like a normal, positive, fully functioning human being.

'Human again,' he said, emerging freshly dressed in yesterday's clothes.

She was already packed. The woman was organised to the point of being infuriating, but he didn't like hanging around when there was a chance to get out into the bush so it suited him fine. They checked out of the hotel and made a short detour to the TM supermarket in town, which had only just opened for the day, to stock up on enough food and drinks for an overnight trip. Then they hit the road.

Graham told himself he felt good. He liked Zimbabwe. The people were friendly, the roads OK, and apart from two police roadblocks where he had to show his driver's licence and prove all the vehicle's lights were working, they had a good run. For the first fifty kilometres of the journey they were on the main tar road between Victoria Falls and Bulawayo. When they turned off to the right, onto a dirt road, they soon entered the Matetsi Safari Area.

Graham figured that if he kept Kerry engaged in enough small talk she wouldn't ask about his behaviour the night before. 'They carry out big game hunting here, on the edge of the park.'

Kerry grabbed the handle on the dashboard in front of her as the Cruiser slewed a little on the wet muddy road. 'Do you want to maybe slow down a little, Graham?'

'No. We're on corrugations and if I slow down you'll get shaken to bits.'

'But this mud . . .'

'It's fine,' he said. He told himself to keep it cheerful. 'In fact, not a lot of hunting is going on here these days because of the political situation, so there's a good chance of seeing game even before we get to the park.'

He was right. Ahead of them he saw a herd of elephants, twenty-five or thirty, crossing the road. As he got closer he slowed and Kerry seemed to forget about the road and his driving as she took out her phone to get some pictures.

The rains could not have come at a better time. The bush looked painfully dry and the elephants threaded their way through mopane trees that had been shredded by previous herds to spindly jagged stumps. Graham lowered the windows and breathed in the heady sweet smell of fresh rain on thirsty soil. New life would come, for the trees, grasses and animals at least.

'I love that smell,' Kerry said.

Graham gave a small smile. He was pleased she wasn't only fixated with the bigger things in the bush, such as the elephants, the last of which now crossed in front of them.

They drove on and signed in at the Robins Gate entrance to Hwange National Park. Ten kilometres further on, after seeing some zebra and kudu, they came to Robins Camp, where they paid their entry fees. Graham asked about accommodation and the ranger in the green-painted, thatched tourist office told them the camp was empty, so they could have their pick. After going through the options they settled on a two-bedroom lodge, a grand name for a clean but basic unit that had two bedrooms, a small kitchen and, unlike the smaller chalets, its own bathroom.

Without bothering to unpack they set off to explore the park.

Unlike Kruger, which was so far Kerry's only other experience of an African game park, Hwange was not teeming with visitors, and Graham was pleased to be able to show her a piece of empty wilderness, and even more satisfied that she appreciated it.

'You're not bothered at all, are you, by coming up here for nothing?' Kerry said as they bounced and skidded along a sticky black soil road called Windmills Drive.

'You mean about not being able to de-horn Garth's rhinos?'

'Yes.'

'Sure,' he said, 'a lot of people think de-horning is the silver bullet to save rhinos – it's not. He wants to eventually release some of his rhinos into the wild, but not having horns won't help them if they get released. If a poacher tracks a rhino and then finds it's been de-horned, he'll kill it anyway to save himself the trouble of following those tracks some other time. I'm worried about the rhinos, but really the point of the de-horning exercise was mostly to impress tourists like you and Garth's guests, and give you some bang for your buck.'

Kerry looked away, out the window on her side.

He realised his error. 'That came out wrong. I think we can safely say you've graduated from tourist to "old Africa hand" given what you've been through.'

She looked back at him. 'You mean I've been through enough trauma to make me African?'

'No, that would take a lifetime. But you're getting there. I'm pleasantly surprised you've stayed the distance.'

'*Pleasantly surprised*? If I thought you'd be good for a refund I might have changed my travel plans and gone off on some *touristy* tour.'

He had put his foot in it again. 'I don't know how to talk to you,' he admitted, surprising even himself with his honesty.

'How do you manage to look after any of your volunteers?'

'It wasn't my idea, taking on paying volunteers. The whole notion strikes me as faintly absurd. Sarah came up with it, as a way of raising money for the Animals Without Borders foundation.'

'Sarah in Australia?'

'Yes.'

'So I was contributing to the coffers of this charity without even realising it?'

'Probably. The website would have told you that your money was going towards "conserving African wildlife" or something like that, right?'

'Hmm, I think so, yes, and there was a link there to Animals Without Borders which is how I found out about them. I could have put two and two together.'

Graham slowed when he spotted a journey of three giraffe. They moved slowly, gracefully, through long golden grass that reached the bottom of their bellies.

'How many volunteers have you had?' she asked.

'Um, well, you're the second.'

'What happened to the first?'

'She ran away after three days.'

Kerry laughed out loud.

'But no,' he said, returning to her original question, 'I'm not bothered that we didn't get to go to the game reserve near Victoria Falls. My ticket here was paid for so it doesn't matter to me where

I am. I may as well be here in Zimbabwe wasting my time as in South Africa wasting my time.'

She looked at him, the laughter replaced by a look of concern. 'Is that how you feel? Is it all so helpless trying to care for wildlife?'

He didn't have the heart to tell her what he really thought. 'No.'

At a stone-walled hide called Little Tom's they got out of the truck and scared an owl out when they walked into the structure. A trio of warthogs wallowed in the mud at the edge of the water-hole in front of the hide. Graham spotted lion spoor outside and around the building. 'Looks like it was here last night.'

The openness and emptiness of this grand national park lulled them into a companionable silence as they carried on their circuitous game drive. Graham was pleased Kerry had stopped asking questions. He glanced at her every now and then, his eyes lingering when she was occupied looking out the window for game. She was beautiful with her black hair, golden skin and her seemingly incongruous Australian accent. He had seen foreigners like this before; they didn't stay foreigners for long. She wasn't in love with Africa – how could one be in love with a place where she'd nearly died twice and been exposed in such a short time to the greed, corruption, cruelty, crime and hopelessness of this continent?

No. Kerry Maxwell was addicted to Africa. The continent had reached out its tendrils, wrapped itself around her heart and hooked her with its thorny barbs.

The next stop on their route was an elevated viewing plat-form called Big Toms. The sun was high so Kerry busied herself making a salad sandwich for herself and ham and cheese for Graham from the supermarket provisions they had put in the vehicle's cooler box.

Graham took his binoculars and climbed the cement stairs to the elevated pole and thatch hide, from where he surveyed the landscape. The overnight rains had formed pools out on an area that had been beaten to dust by the trampling big feet of thousands of elephants coming and going. A pair of elephant bulls, one bigger and with longer, thicker ivory than the other, slurped noisily from a trough to the right of the hide, which was fed by a solar-powered pump. Water from the trough, when it was full, spilled over and into the narrow stream that ran across the front of the viewing hide. The pachyderms were taking it in turns to place the tips of their trunks over the inlet pipe to mainline the clean fresh water coming from the borehole.

Graham checked on Kerry; she kept looking over her shoulder at the elephants as she finished making the sandwiches.

Then one of the elephants stopped drinking, turned surprisingly quickly and raised his trunk in the air. It was the smaller of the two bulls. The animal's sudden change in behaviour alerted Graham, just as it disturbed the older elephant, who raised his big head. The younger bull let out a shrill trumpet blast.

'Stop where you are,' Graham said to Kerry, who was halfway between the Land Cruiser and the foot of the stairs.

'What is it?'

'Shush.' He followed the younger elephant's gaze to the tree line, beyond the beaten ground about a hundred metres behind where the truck was parked in an open-sided boma of rotting logs.

He saw it.

'Graham?' Kerry hissed.

'Quiet. Do not move.' He pointed.

Slowly, Kerry turned her head, then froze, her torso twisted, a sandwich in each hand.

Graham stood at the top of the stairs, knowing that the best thing for him, for both of them, to do right now was to stay rock-solid still as the lion walked towards the water trough – and Kerry.

It was a male, with a big shaggy mane so pale it was almost blond, though the hair turned to black where it approached his chest, signalling that he was mature. He padded defiantly towards the elephants, who were both facing him now, ears out and trunks up.

The lion stopped.

He looked around him and his golden-eyed gaze rested on the vehicle in the exposed car park. He lifted his head.

'Graham,' Kerry said out of the corner of her mouth. She slowly swivelled her head to look up at him.

Graham put up a hand to warn her to be quiet.

The lion trotted forward.

Graham knew he should stay motionless but he was worried Kerry was going to run. If she did, the lion would vector in on her as quickly as a house cat would pounce on a mouse. As it was, the big cat seemed to be tossing up between defying the elephants and coming over to check out the vehicle. Perhaps, Graham thought, he could smell the ham sandwich.

Now was not the time to joke.

The lion followed a route between the elephants and the hide. When he was almost abreast of both – Graham could see Kerry physically shaking, her hands still holding up the sandwiches as if she were about to deliver them – the younger elephant sounded the charge through his trunk.

Elephants, Graham knew, detested lions, and this pair were determined to show the king of the jungle who was the rightful ruler. They left their water and headed for him. The smaller elephant waved his trunk frantically and shook his head so that his ears flapped, but the dominant bull was ready for the kill, ears back, head down and trunk tucked up between his long, deadly front teeth. If they caught that lion they would pulverise him then toss him in the air with a hooked tusk just for fun.

The lion ran a few steps towards them, but his bravado vanished in a heartbeat. He kicked up a mini dust cloud as he skidded to a halt, turned in a bound and ran. His flight, however, took him towards Kerry and the parked Land Cruiser.

Graham used the moment of pandemonium to sling his binoculars and run down the steep narrow stairs, two at a time, very nearly falling and breaking his neck on the bottom step. Kerry shrieked and ran headlong into his arms.

Grabbing her, Graham barrelled the pair of them into the toilet located below the hide and slammed the door behind them.

Kerry slumped against the wall, panting, her eyes wide, a sandwich still in each hand.

'Not again.'

It was his turn to laugh. 'Another near-death experience?'

She nodded, her face pale.

Graham opened the door a crack and looked out. There was the sound of a receding trumpet blast as the younger elephant continued chasing the lion down the *vlei*. The bigger bull, having seen off the intruder, was ambling back to the water trough.

He looked back at her. 'Are you all right?'

'I just realised something.'

'What?' he asked her.

Kerry forced a smile. 'I've just seen my very first lion.'

*

Graham got the truck bogged in the mud as a finale to their eventful day of game driving.

They had stopped at a picnic site called Deteema to stretch their legs, and Graham was taking a short cut across a wide-open *vlei* to get to the dam of the same name. *Vlei*, he explained to Kerry, was a local word meaning plain or floodplain, and that, she thought, should have been a good enough reason not to drive over the low-lying ground after a night's worth of torrential rain.

197

The Land Cruiser went down like a submarine. After finding the recovery gear stashed in the back of the vehicle and working out that the high-lift jack had a problem relating to a bent pin, they also realised it would be a long walk to find any trees or branches big enough to jam under the wheels in the event they were able to lift the Cruiser up. Graham was getting ready to walk back to the picnic site when the attendant, whom they had met earlier, came trudging through the mud, his AK-47 balanced on his shoulder. Luckily, the man had a radio and was in contact with another ranger who, in turn, was working with a team laying a new pipeline from a borehole to the Deteema Dam. They had a tractor with them, which was summoned and, eventually, they pulled the stricken four-wheel drive out of the mud.

They arrived back at Robins Camp just in time, as the sun was setting. Graham lit a fire and Kerry had a lukewarm bath – the wood-burning hot water heater was not quite hot enough. Still it was refreshing, and she came outside, clean and changed, to find Graham sitting in front of the *braai* fire with a beer. He reached into the cooler box, took the top off another Zambezi and handed it to her without standing. Kerry settled into the chair next to him.

The fire was mesmerising, bush television they called it in Africa – and Australia. Somewhat to her surprise, Kerry found she wasn't missing home. Despite all her troubles here, and everything that hadn't gone according to plan, she felt even more strongly than before that she wasn't ready to go back to work, and Australia, any time soon.

She sighed.

'Thinking about home?'

'How did you know?' She sipped some beer. It tasted good after the long but enjoyably eventful day in the bush.

'You've got that look. I've seen it before.'

She smiled. 'I'm not missing it – Australia, that is. I wonder if I'll be able to settle back into my normal routine again.'

He gave a snort. 'A lot of South Africans would kill for the chance to have a good job in a country like Australia. You know, pretty well every white I know in South Africa has had that discussion with themselves – whether to stay or go.'

'What about you?' she asked. It was still warm, even though the sun had gone down, and sticky because of the lingering moisture from the rain.

'Some people leave because they see no future for their kids in South Africa. Others have had bad experiences with crime. Others lose their jobs and can't see a future for themselves.'

'And you?' she pressed.

'I thought about it. My wife wanted to leave, much more than I did.'

'Had you decided to leave, before she passed away?'

Graham stood up. 'I'll go get those steaks and veggie burgers out of the fridge. Fire'll be ready to cook on soon.'

Kerry slumped into her chair. He was a strange man. He was effusive, the life of the party when he was drinking, but he clammed up when it came to talking about himself. He had to be smart, to be a vet, but he seemed content to play the fool much of the time. She would catch him, every now and then, looking away, not from her but more like at something else, or someone else, perhaps from another time. Like he had just then.

She nursed her beer and watched the dancing flames.

Graham came back out and cooked the food on the grill over glowing coals. They talked about their day over dinner and a bottle of red wine. Kerry thought about the lion, how vulnerable she had been, how scared, and yet at the same time how excited.

'Do you ever get scared, Graham?'

He drank the last drops from his glass. 'Of course, sometimes. Not around animals, though. They're predictable, in their own unpredictable way. You know, say, with a lion, that unless you're really unlucky it will leave you alone, unless you get too close to it or surprise it, or if you run.'

'And people?'

'Thoroughly unpredictable,' he said, 'and far more dangerous. That's why it was a good idea for us to make ourselves scarce for a while. Even though this job didn't pan out, it was good timing.'

'But you'll never consider leaving Africa altogether?'

He shook his head. 'This is my home. Crazy, mixed-up, unpredictable, sometimes dangerous place that it is, I've got nowhere else to go.'

Kerry thought about what she had been through – everything Graham had just summed up. She had faced death, yet she had never felt so alive in her life.

Chapter 21

Kerry was first up the next morning. She'd had a restless night, as she always did the evening before she had to catch a flight somewhere.

There were slight variations to her pre-travel dream, but they all ended in disaster – a forgotten passport, sleeping through an alarm, a traffic jam on the way to the airport, all leading to a missed flight. Last night, however, had been a full-blown nightmare in which the man who had hijacked her on the way to Hoedspruit was chasing her again, through the bush. Her legs felt like they were encased in lead and when she gave up running and turned the AK-47 she was carrying on her pursuer, nothing happened when she pulled the trigger. She had awoken bathed in sweat.

To make matters worse, a lone mosquito had found its way in through the ageing national parks–issue net over her bed. With sleep eluding her she had found a packet of bandaids in her cosmetic bag, and while she had patched the hole in the net, all she succeeded in doing was trapping the insect inside with her.

The dawn light was beautiful and a balm on her dream-ravaged mind as she sat outside and sipped a cup of coffee. She went and woke Graham and he took a bath.

While she waited for him she boiled some eggs then went back outside and watched a troop of banded mongooses go about their business. They moved as a family unit, all the while softly babbling to each other in muted squeaks. They inspected the rubbish bins, looked under the Land Cruiser, scratched at the ground here and there, and then scattered in panic in a dozen different directions when they realised Kerry was there. She laughed, and when she sat down they emerged, coalesced, checked her out, and carried on with their business.

Graham, dressed in his dirty clothes, came outside with a cup of coffee. 'How did you sleep?'

She told him about the mosquito. 'It bit me a couple of times, until I plastered more repellent on myself.'

'Listen to me.' His tone was serious.

'Yes?'

'When you get back to Australia, if you are feeling *at all* like you have a cold or flu, or off colour, go straight to your doctor and tell him you've been in Africa in a malaria area. Do you understand?'

She was taken aback, again, by his concern over the disease, even though she now knew where it came from. 'Of course. I've read all about malaria and my doctor gave me plenty of information.'

'Good. Well, just do as you're told.'

Kerry bridled at being spoken to in such a manner, but she didn't reply.

When Graham was ready they loaded the truck and set off for Victoria Falls. Their flight was at two in the afternoon and it had taken them three hours to get to Robins Camp, so by leaving at seven in the morning, which they managed, Kerry was cautiously comfortable that they had plenty of time.

They were driving the road they had come in on and, by Kerry's reckoning, were about halfway to the Robins Gate entry to the park when Graham turned left.

'What are you doing, Graham?'

He gestured ahead and to the right, to a hill in the distance. 'There's an old camp up there, called Nantwich. It's been deserted but a friend of mine has been negotiating with the national parks people to take it over and revamp it as a private safari camp.'

'So?'

'So, I want to take a look, maybe snap some pictures for my friend.'

Kerry held up her watch. 'We have a flight to catch, Graham.'

'Yes, in seven hours. Stop being a worrywart, woman. This is a short cut to Nantwich.'

'Don't address me as "woman".' Kerry frowned. They were crossing what appeared to be an open grassy *vlei* area and Kerry had a sudden flashback to the day before.

'Graham, there's water on the road ahead, puddles.'

'Relax,' he said, and accelerated.

'What are you doing now?'

'Watch this, we'll plough right through.'

Black water fantailed up the sides of the Land Cruiser, spattering the windows, and Kerry gave a shriek and grabbed the handle in front of her as she felt the rear of the vehicle start to slide. Graham started to lose traction.

He reached for a switch. 'I'll put on the difflock.'

The Cruiser seemed to wallow.

'Graham!'

He clung to the wheel. 'Come on, come on.' A second later they were through the wallow. 'There, see, told you.'

'Turn around, Graham.'

He looked at her as the vehicle trundled on. 'I *can't* turn around. The ground will be softer either side of the wheel ruts

203

and we might not back it through that patch a second time.'

She held on for dear life as he accelerated.

They came to another spot where the previous night's rain-water had pooled in twin grooves of the ruts where someone else had become stuck, presumably in the last wet season.

'Oh, no,' she said.

'Quiet.'

'Don't tell me to be quiet!'

Graham hit the puddles at speed and, as before, fountains erupted either side, but this time Kerry experienced the same sickening feeling in her gut as the Land Cruiser's tyres moaned and groaned and the truck slowed to a stop.

'Shit.' Graham revved the accelerator.

'Stop, Graham, you're just digging us deeper into the mud.'

'I *know* that's what's happening.'

'Then why the hell are you doing it?'

Graham left the engine running but opened his door, got out and slammed it.

Kerry took a deep breath. She knew now was not the time to panic, but she also felt like she was in a new version of her travel dream, except this time no amount of pinching would wake her from it. She checked her watch, then opened her door, looked out over the open expanse of grass, and then got out.

Graham was walking around the Land Cruiser. He got down on his knees. 'Bogged to the axles, both rear wheels.'

'Should we call for help?' Kerry took out her phone. 'Nope. No signal.'

'Of course there's no signal, we're in the wilds of bloody Zimbabwe.'

'Don't "of course" me, you're the one who got us in this mess.'

Graham slammed the body of the Land Cruiser. 'Ow.'

'Take a breath, stop and think.'

He ran a hand through his lank hair, then went to the back of the Land Cruiser, opened it and hauled out the recovery equipment. 'Shovel, high-lift jack, little bottle jack suitable for a Nissan Micra, and that's about it.'

'We don't have all day, Graham. We have a flight to catch.'

'I know, I know.' He walked around the vehicle again. He ran his hand down the left side of the vehicle, along a foot rail used by passengers to get in and out of their compartment. 'We can use this as a jacking point for the high-lift jack. I'll get started – you go find some branches. Remember – this part of the park, the Robins area, has the highest density of lions in Hwange.'

'Remember? No one told me that.'

'You'll be fine, just keep an eye out.'

The sun was climbing fast and the sky was clear. With the ground wet from the day before the heat was turning this low-lying stretch of grassy plain into an open-air sauna already. Kerry went to the stunted remains of a mopane tree and, after having a quick look for snakes and her surrounds for lions, started rocking a branch to snap one off. Eventually she had four reasonable-sized branches, which she dragged through the wet grass back to Graham. Her sandals were now filthy and her lower legs were spattered with black goo. She was sweating from the effort and had to constantly wave away tiny little flies that tried to get into her eyes, nose and ears.

Graham was swearing loudly. He had managed to tramp a large rock into the mud next to the left rear wheel, to support the jack. He had taken his shirt off, and Kerry saw the muscles in his back rippling as he worked the jack's long handle. The rock was pushed down into the mud, but, slowly, the vehicle started to rise. Once the tyre had started to come free of the ground's clutches, Graham got to work with the spade. It was clearly hard going, but he managed to make a space under the wheel and in front of it.

'OK, I need those branches. Hurry!'

'I'm hurrying.' Kerry handed him the branches, and watched as Graham carefully slid them under the left rear tyre.

'The problem we have . . .'

'Another problem?'

He glared up at her. 'The problem we have is that there's nowhere on the other side of the body of the vehicle that will support the jack. There's no foot railing, and if I use the jack on the bodywork it will just crumple it. These vehicles are made for transporting tourists on the open roads, not for bush bashing.'

Kerry resisted the urge to scream, *Then why did you take us into the bush?* 'OK, so you're hoping you'll get enough traction from this left-hand side to free the right.'

'That's about the size of it, yes.'

The next problem occurred when Graham tried to lower the high-lift jack. 'Bloody thing's stuck.'

He took out his Leatherman tool from the pouch on his belt and started prodding and poking around the pins and springs on the jack's mechanism.

'My dad took us on a couple of trips into the outback when we were kids,' Kerry said. 'He told us those jacks were incredibly dangerous and . . .'

Something gave way with a loud crack and the vehicle dropped with a clunk. The handle Graham had been pumping earlier shot up, narrowly missing Graham's head. He fell back with a plop, on his bottom, in the mud.

'Clearly,' Graham said.

He tinkered a bit more, carefully, and as he'd suspected the problem was the bent pin in the mechanism, which was slipping out of place every time he tried to lower the jack. Graham gave Kerry the job of holding the pin in place, with the tip of the Leatherman's pliers, as he raised and lowered the handle. When it worked, which was one time in every three attempts, the Land

Cruiser fell another notch down the main shaft of the jack, to Kerry's terror.

Finally, the vehicle was sitting on the logs.

'OK, here goes nothing,' Graham said.

Kerry checked her watch as he climbed in and started the engine. They had already spent an hour trying to prop up just this one side of the vehicle.

Kerry crossed her fingers and toes as Graham put the vehicle in gear and started to accelerate. She saw the tyre on the side they had just worked on trying to gain traction on the mopane branches, but it was spinning. Her heart dropped. She stomped through the mud to the other side of the truck.

The wheel was running free, spinning fast in the mud and kicking up a mist of black sludge.

Graham depressed the accelerator fully.

Both wheels spun and the right side dug down even further into the mud. Graham turned off the engine and got out. Kerry snuck another look at her watch. It wouldn't have been so bad if they didn't have connecting flights through to Cape Town from Johannesburg later that evening. She resisted the urge to vent her frustration, as Graham was doing now, kicking the truck with his bare foot and screaming at the pain caused to his toes. He clutched his hair with both hands and walked around in circles.

'Shit.' He tried to compose himself. 'Well, that was pointless.'

'Graham, we just need to jack up the driver's side.'

'That's easier said than done.'

Graham explained that with nowhere to hook the lip of the high-lift jack on the right side of the truck they would have to dig down under the rear axle instead, excavating a hole big enough to take the large rock he had used as a jacking base, and then fit the tiny bottle jack under the axle and try to lift the stuck vehicle that way.

Kerry was impressed with his practicality, but the reality of getting the job done was not so simple. The extra spinning of the wheels had dug the vehicle down deeper, and the two rear springs and the bottom of the axle were encased in sticky black clay.

'Should we walk and look for help?'

'I thought of that,' Graham said. 'If we don't get eaten by lions then it's six kilometres either way to the gate or Robins Camp. If we make it we've then got to try and organise a tractor, and you saw where their one tractor was yesterday – forty klicks away.'

'Then let's get digging,' said Kerry grimly.

Graham attacked the earth like it had insulted him. The shovel was next to useless in the cloying clay, and in the end they took it in shifts, digging at the mud with their hands and with a large salad serving spoon Kerry had found in the car, excavating a hole not only deep enough to fit the bottle jack, but also the large rock that they needed to place underneath.

Finally they had the rock and the little jack in position. Graham groaned and lay on his back, like a starfish, arms and legs out. Kerry sprawled beside him, her muscles protesting. There was mud in her hair, on her hands, all over her clothes, and on her face. The sun had burned her legs below the hem of her shorts and she had long since kicked off her sandals after tiring of the mud sucking at them.

They allowed themselves a moment's rest, but the hard labour wasn't over. Turning the crank handle was an effort as the black earth was not ready to release the vehicle's springs and axle from its grasp. Graham would turn the handle three or four revolutions then collapse in the sun, from exhaustion. Kerry stepped in, but was lucky if she was able to complete a single turn.

When Graham was turning the handle, Kerry got back in the truck and clawed at the mud and clay on her body with her bare hands. She didn't dare check her watch, which she had taken off and placed in the truck to protect it. Then she lugged a twenty-litre jerry can of water from the back of the vehicle and poured for them both. She splashed water on Graham to try and cool him down, and it sluiced over his body, accentuating his abdominal muscles and biceps. They belonged on a younger, man-scaped body, she mused in a rare flash of good humour.

Graham took another drink of water and groaned and yelled as he gave the jack a few more turns. Then he grabbed the right rear wheel with two hands and it moved when he tried to turn it. 'Yes!'

Graham began to dig around and under the freed wheel while Kerry jogged off to collect more branches from the nearby mopane trees. Within another half-hour they had the branches packed under the wheel and were ready to try again.

Graham looked at her. He was covered in mud, dressed only in a pair of filthy shorts. His few bare patches of skin had been turned red by the merciless sun. She must look the same, she thought.

'I'm sorry, Kerry. I won't let you down again.'

'Just get in the truck and drive.' She smiled at him.

'If this doesn't work I'll take the shovel and walk.'

'Don't talk like that,' she said. A shovel would be no protection against lions and they both knew it.

Graham got into the driver's seat again and started the engine.

Kerry got behind the Cruiser and readied herself to push, not that she thought it would do much good. She took a deep breath as she heard him put the truck into gear.

'Ready?' he called.

'Ready.'

Slowly Graham let out the clutch and Kerry looked down. Mud was shooting back as both rear wheels spun, the tyres failing to get a grip on the branches they had packed under them.

'Shit,' Graham yelled as he got out and slammed the door. He walked back to Kerry, his face sagging with defeat.

'Just try again, Graham. One more time, please. We can't give up.'

He blinked at her, as if not hearing, but then repeated, 'Can't give up.'

'Give it a go.'

He gave a small nod then got back behind the wheel.

She heard the engine rev, high and loud, and then Graham must have dropped the clutch. Kerry heaved against the rear of the truck and, after a brief squeal and hiss of rubber on wood, the Land Cruiser leapt free of the mud like a champagne cork escaping the bottle.

So quick was the departure that Kerry, who had been pushing against the vehicle, fell flat on her face in the mud. She picked herself up and ran after Graham, waving her arms and yelling with sheer delight.

'Go, Graham, go!'

Chapter 22

The band finished its set on stage in the packed room of the Cape Town International Convention Centre.

'Thank you, thank you,' said the lead singer as she put her hands up to try and still the crowd. 'We really appreciate it.'

There was more applause and yelling. Sarah Hoyland surveyed the audience from her prime seat. Eli Johnston's organisers had had to turn people away, but had gladly taken the money most of them would have paid for a ticket as a donation.

By contrast she had two hundred people lined up for her fundraiser the following night at the Table Bay Hotel at the nearby Victoria and Alfred Waterfront. Her event was black tie, corporate types and high–net worth individuals, mostly middle-aged. The screaming fans here, though, were aged seventeen to thirty. Not as much disposable income, but they were passionate, and they were young.

If the ovation for the band had been noisy – they were good and had a single at number eight in the charts – it was tumultuous when the lead singer called Eli Johnston from the wings.

'But here's the man you've really all come to see. Former US Navy SEAL and man candy supreme, Mr Eli Johnston.'

Sarah watched the audience. Most of them, maybe seventy per cent, were female, and it was these young women who went wild as Eli strode out. The boyfriends and single men in the audience, Sarah noted, applauded with muted respect.

'Thank you all,' Eli began, and waited for the screaming and applause to die down. 'You might have read in the news media or seen on TV that some friends and I got into a little trouble recently, in Mozambique.'

He waited for the laughter to abate. His timing was good, Sarah thought.

'I've been in combat.' That settled the fans. The silence left Sarah's ears ringing. 'I've seen friends of mine killed. I've seen people die for religion, for oil, for their country, for a cause, or to save the life of someone else.'

Eli paused and looked around the audience. Sarah saw that every eye was on the handsome American. He hadn't raised his voice; his tone was almost intimate, reaching out to each and every heart and soul in the theatre.

'It's all bad. It's all sad, but let me tell you there is nothing more frustrating, nothing that makes me want to throw back my head and scream at the heavens until I lose my voice than to witness the death of an innocent animal or a lion-hearted anti-poaching ranger for something as trivial, as base, as meaningless or as evil as money. That's what this war is about, my friends.

'It's tangible, this evil, I see it every day in the carcasses of rhinos and, increasingly, elephants, left to rot under the African sun. It's the smell of death, it's the sight of vultures, poisoned so they can't give away the poachers' positions to the good guys; it's tears on the face of a good woman whose ranger husband has been killed or wounded in the line of duty.

'You can hear the evil. It's the high-pitched squealing,' he held up a fist, 'the *crying* of a four-week-old baby rhino as it runs around the body of its dead mother, trying to wake her, searching in blind panic for something, someone, to look after it and to bring its mom back to life.'

Sarah saw tears streaming down faces, young men's Adam's apples bobbing.

'The illegal trade in wildlife products, to make money for greedy people, is worldwide, and it's scary big, guys. Its root cause is a demand for stuff, the body parts of dead animals, birds and reptiles – rhino horn, elephant tusks, the scales of pangolins, the heads of vultures, the coats of leopards. I could go on. We need to stop that demand, and there are good people working on how to do that. But reducing demand and changing people's mindsets can take a generation or two, and Africa's wildlife doesn't have that time. Rhinos aren't safe anywhere in the world, not even in captivity outside of Africa. Just think of that rhino, Vince, that was killed in the zoo in France. This is a world war.'

He paused.

'What we need to do is to fight back!'

The crowd wiped its collective nose and eyes and roared back. 'Yes!'

'I have men and women on the ground who will put their lives on the line, pick up a gun, go out into the African night and fight for wildlife. Will. You. Support. Them?'

'Yes!'

Eli put a hand to one ear. 'I can't hear you, troops, was that a "Hell, yeah"?'

'HELL, YEAH!'

Sarah smiled and fondled the necklace she was wearing. This guy was good. Very good. She'd heard of Eli Johnston, read everything about him she could get her hands on, watched every

213

YouTube video, but she'd never seen him in the flesh, never heard him speak live. He was often in the news media and his fundraising events were legendary in the NGO world for the numbers and youthfulness of the crowds he attracted thanks to his own good looks and passionate deliveries, combined with the presence of big name music groups. Sarah knew, right then as she watched him, that she wanted him. She felt the shiver through her body.

When Eli had finished, the applause had died down and the lights came up, Sarah found her way to the back of the stage and showed the access-all-areas pass on her lanyard to the burly security guard, who stepped aside and let her into a corridor that led to the dressing rooms.

She stepped aside to let the band members pass her, then found a door with Eli's name on it.

He opened the door when she knocked. 'Sarah, I'm guessing?'

'Yes, hi. Nice to meet you, Eli. Thanks for agreeing to see me, and for the backstage pass.'

'No problem.'

'Can I come in?'

'Sure,' said Eli, peeling off some sticky tape that was holding the hands-free microphone he'd used on stage to his ear and neck. 'Like I told you via email, my schedule is packed and I don't have much time. I've got to go out to meet our donors.'

She noticed he didn't say 'press the flesh' or use some other dismissive term such as 'stalkers' when referring to his fans. He was too clean-cut to be true, and even more handsome in real life than his photos on his website and Facebook page. 'I won't take up too much of your time.'

'Well, I'm happy to talk, and your email sounded intriguing, especially the bit about boosting my fundraising.'

Sarah noted the quick once-over he gave her as he spoke, his eyes travelling up from her stiletto heels and sheer stockings along the lines of her little black dress and plunging neckline to her glossy lips. She had dressed to impress.

Sarah pushed a stray curl of dark hair out of her eyes. 'I'll only be a minute, promise. As I mentioned in my email, while I'm a fundraising consultant I'm not here to sell you my services.'

'Then what can I do for you?'

She kept twirling her hair. 'It's more what I can do for you. I wanted to thank you, first, though, for helping to save Kerry Maxwell in Mozambique. She actually signed up as a volunteer via one of the fundraising websites that I operate. I hardly need to tell you what it would have done for Animals Without Borders if, God forbid, something had happened to her.'

'Well, Graham was the one who rescued her, twice. I just got my dumb ass shot. We were lucky we didn't lose anyone in the operation. You should thank him.'

'Oh, I will. Eli, I want to talk to you about how I might be able to help you, financially, to provide more resources for your work in Africa.'

'I'm not really looking for a partner.' Eli took his phone from his back pocket, turned it on and checked a message while she stood there.

He was playing it very cool. He sat down in a chair at the dressing table and plugged his phone into a charger. He didn't invite her to sit and Sarah didn't take the spare seat. Instead, she perched on the table, very near to him, but looking down. She'd manoeuvred him into a position where she was dominating him.

'We both know there are too many players in the NGO space in Africa, especially raising money for elephants and rhinos and projects like Animals Without Borders, repatriating animals and moving them out of harm's way. We need to work together more.'

He brought his hands together, fingertips to his chin. 'As a collective sector, yes, I agree.'

'The pot of donor money in Africa and abroad is only so big, and competition's getting fiercer all the time,' she said.

'Also noted. My donors are out there expecting to see me, even as we speak.'

She smiled. 'I know. They're literally panting with excitement. You've got the same demographic as a boy band, Eli.'

He shrugged. 'Yes, but these people want to change the world.'

'Young, idealistic, high disposable income – hopefully. I like your style: the rock concerts, the cult of the idol.'

'I'm a warrior, Sarah, not a pop star.'

She held up a hand. 'I'm not belittling what you do, Eli, far from it, but you looked pretty ripped in that last bare-chested selfie after your workout in the bush pumping iron with those African rangers last week.'

He gave a deprecatory laugh and put his hands up in mock surrender. 'OK, you got me there. What do you want, Sarah, time's ticking.'

'I think we could all work together better and I want to put a formal proposal to you. How would you like to join forces with Animals Without Borders? You'd double your support base – as would we.' She took a step closer to him. 'And, business aside, I'd be happy to discuss possible terms any place, any time with you, Eli. I *really* want to get to know you better.'

He stood and she shifted a little so that she was half sitting, half leaning against his dressing table, hands either side of her, legs ever so slightly apart.

Eli towered over and closed the gap between them even more. She smiled. Sarah decided she really would have sex with him, if it helped seal the deal, or even kept him interested.

'I responded to your email, asking to meet, Sarah, because I know exactly what you're up to.'

'What's that?'

'You're going to use your donors' money to relocate six black rhinos from Kwangela Game Reserve, here in the Western Cape.'

Sarah shrugged. 'It's true, I'm making a major announcement about rhinos at my fundraiser tomorrow night, though I can't say any more than that just yet, unless we were, say, business partners.'

'Don't worry. I know already. And not only am I not going to go into business with you, I am going to make it *my* business to make sure your plan for those rhinos never gets off the ground.'

Sarah shifted on the dressing table. This was not what she had planned. 'Why would you do that?'

'I'm not alone. I'm not the only one who knows what you're up to and is opposed to it. Your plan is either crazy or it's criminal.'

He was staring her in the eye. 'Are you threatening me, Eli?'

Eli straightened and took a step back from her. 'Yes.'

She pushed herself off the table and stood, straightening her dress. 'I would have done just about anything to get you onside with us, Eli.'

He went to the dressing room door and opened it for her. 'I know. That's another reason I don't want anything to do with you, or your other *partner*.'

She jutted out her chin. 'You'll regret this.'

'Not as much as you will.'

Reeling a little, Sarah turned and walked out. Anger started to bloom in her stomach. He was wrong.

Chapter 23

Kwangela Game Reserve, Graham thought, hardly merited the title. It was little more than a tourist trap, the complete opposite of the vast, mostly empty wilderness of Zimbabwe's Hwange National Park where they had been the day before.

Graham had driven like an African taxi driver to get to Victoria Falls Airport in time for them to catch their flight. There had barely been time for him and Kerry to sluice the worst of the mud from their exposed skin using a bucket and a tap in the airport car park where they had left Garth's filthy Land Cruiser.

He and Kerry now rode in comparative luxury in the back of an open-top Land Rover game viewer, enjoying the morning. It was pleasantly warm, the air still tastily crisp, as opposed to the oppressive heat of Victoria Falls, much further north in Africa.

The Cape was like another country, another world. Many of the foreign tourists who visited Cape Town didn't want to venture too far from the hipster cafes and trendy restaurants, or the shops on the Victoria and Alfred Waterfront, not even in search of Africa's big five – lion, elephant, buffalo, leopard and rhino – so Kwangela, a tiny reserve by African standards, gave visitors and locals something of a safari experience.

Bradd, with two 'd's according to his name badge, was their ranger, and although Graham didn't ask, he suspected it was the boy's first guiding job. Bradd was handsome, keen and cocky, as young rangers tended to be.

They came to an electrified fence and Bradd pressed a remote control that opened a barred security gate.

'We've got the black rhinos in the bomas, ready for your check-up,' Bradd said.

He drove a short distance to a stout wooden fence. Bradd stopped the Land Rover and they all got out.

'As I'm sure you know, these guys can be quite cheeky,' Bradd said.

Graham rolled his eyes behind Bradd's back. Kerry punched him in the arm.

True to form, the first black rhino they saw was bristling with attitude. It trotted up to them, raised its head and snorted.

'This is Brutus,' Bradd said. 'He's our number one stud at the moment. We had a few births, but it's not so easy in captivity, and it's a long time between babies.'

Graham nodded. He'd known a couple in Zimbabwe, the Bryants, who ran a rhino breeding ranch. In the wild, black rhino calves stayed with their mothers a long time – eight years – so females did not normally go into oestrus for the same period; at the ranch they weaned the newborn babies off the mothers as soon as they were born and hand-raised them, which had the effect of fooling the cows into wanting to get pregnant again straightaway.

'I'll be sorry to see him go,' Bradd said.

'I can imagine.'

'Why exactly are you getting rid of all your rhinos?' Kerry asked.

'Money,' said Bradd. 'I can tell you, because you're not tourists, that the owners of Kwangela are struggling to keep the place going. The name means "sunset" in isiXhosa, and unless they cut costs that's the direction we're all riding into. The security bill to protect these rhinos is huge. So when Animals Without Borders offered to buy and relocate them, it was good news for the owners, if not for us guides.'

'Have you lost any rhinos?' Graham asked Bradd.

'None. Our head of security, Michael Collins, is an ex–Rhodesian SAS guy and he's always testing our systems and looking for ways to improve them. He is bleak that the rhinos are going – it also means there will be less need for him and his guys.'

They walked on to the next boma and Bradd pointed to another black rhino. 'This is Thandi. She's completely different from Brutus, very people-friendly.'

On cue, Thandi trotted over to the fence and held her big head up. Bradd reached into a satchel he'd been carrying over his shoulder and took out an apple which he held up to her snuffling, waiting mouth. She grabbed the treat with her hooked upper and lower lips and munched on it, seemingly smiling with delight.

Kerry, with Bradd's encouragement, reached over and scratched her under the chin. 'Hello, Thandi. I know a Thandi back in Hoedspruit and she's beautiful, just like you.'

Graham swallowed hard. He wasn't given to fits of emotion and wondered where the lump in his throat had come from. He'd hardened himself long ago to the realities of his job and the conditions he worked in. He wondered if it was seeing Kerry's pure, innocent joy at being this close to the rhino that had triggered it. Carla had been the same with animals.

'Where are the rhinos going?' Graham asked.

Bradd shrugged. 'Officially, I don't know, but there are rumours. We thought they were going to Australia, but Michael reckons they're going to another African country and he's flipping mad about that. He says South Africa still has the best record for protecting rhinos so he wants them to stay here, somewhere.' Bradd turned to look at Graham. 'You're speaking, in Cape Town, right, at the Table Bay?'

Graham drew a breath. 'For my sins, yes.'

'You don't sound too happy about it. I read somewhere that some people rate public speaking as more terrifying than the prospect of death.'

'Well, given the choice between hunting poachers armed with AK-47s in the bush or climbing into a monkey suit, walking on stage and addressing a couple of hundred strangers, I'd take my chances with the poachers any day.'

Bradd laughed.

Graham wasn't joking.

Still, as he and Kerry patted Thandi and he felt the rhino's hot breath huffing over his hand, he did what he always did when he was in the bush facing danger, what he'd done in the army – he suppressed his fear and told himself to pick himself up and carry on.

He remembered a trip he and Carla had once taken to Zimbabwe. It was funny; being in Victoria Falls with Kerry had brought back the memories but so, too, had seeing Thandi the rhino and touching her. They had gone to the rhino breeding ranch run by his friends the Bryants on that trip, which was supposed to be their last tour around Africa before leaving the continent for good.

Back then there had been plans to release some of those rhinos, bred in captivity, into Zimbabwe's national parks, including Mana Pools, in the Zambezi Valley. All hope of that was gone; decades of corrupt government had meant that country's national parks rangers had not received the funding, resources and backing they needed to stop the rhino-poaching epidemic. Just a few hundred rhinos were left in Zimbabwe, mostly in heavily guarded private reserves.

'Lost in thought?' Kerry said.

'What? Oh, no, nothing.' All hope was gone, he thought.

*

Kerry thoroughly enjoyed her morning, helping Graham where she could as he examined each of the rhinos.

He was no longer gruff or rude to her, at least not deliberately, but she still felt that the more she got to know him the more obvious it was that he was holding something back from her. Quite what that something was, she couldn't put her finger on.

She suspected it was to do with his late wife.

When they had finished at Kwangela they drove their hire car back to the Table Bay Hotel in Cape Town, where Sarah had paid for them to stay. It was a lovely place, Kerry thought, and they could walk from the hotel straight into the shopping precinct of the V&A, as everyone seemed to refer to the Victoria and Alfred Waterfront.

Poor Graham, she thought when they met again in the hotel lobby; he looked like an African tigerfish out of water. He was dressed in his trademark khaki shorts and grubby two-tone bush shirt, still dusty and stained from working on the rhinos. On his feet he wore Rocky sandals. The weather had turned dramatically, from sunny and warm in the morning to grey and chilly in the afternoon. Table Mountain was shrouded in white.

'You must be cold.'

He looked around at the sound of her voice. 'Nothing that would kill me. Although I feel the ordeal to come might.'

'I met Sarah a little while ago,' Kerry said, 'she came to my room.'

'Formidable woman, yes?'

222

Kerry gave a small laugh. 'You can say that. She's very direct. I think she thought that because I'd signed up to volunteer through her website that she could get me to do her bidding.'

Graham snorted. 'Sounds like Sarah. What are your orders?'

'I'm to take you clothes shopping.'

'Yes, ma'am,' he said. 'I thought Sarah might want to supervise this mission herself.'

She thought she picked up a note of disappointment in his voice. 'You and Sarah?'

He looked at her. 'Yes?'

'You're just friends?'

His mouth curled into a smile like a moustache, turned up at the sides. 'Good friends.'

'Oh.'

'That is to say,' he said quickly, 'occasional friends.'

She saw his cheeks start to colour. He was weird.

He cleared his throat. 'Anyway, what's wrong with what I'm wearing?'

'The invitation says lounge suit.'

'I often lounge in this suit.' He raised his eyebrows. 'How much money did she give you?'

Kerry laughed. 'I'm under orders not to tell you.'

'Typical. She knows I'd spend it on booze, cigarettes and fast women.'

'Yes, there was a comment about that as well.'

'I'm perfectly capable of buying my own clothes.' He snorted.

'Of course. Well, perhaps I can just direct you to a department store.'

'That would be fine,' he said.

She could tell he wasn't happy, neither about having to speak nor about dressing up. Kerry couldn't really blame him. She felt pretty much the same, although no one was giving her the rand equivalent of two thousand dollars to shop.

Kerry took him by the arm and they went up the escalators from the lobby and into the shopping mall. They soon found a stylish menswear store.

'All right, you're not a nine-year-old. I'll leave you here. I need to go and buy some stockings.' She opened her handbag and took out the envelope full of cash Sarah had given her. She passed it to him, but held on to it. 'Remember, it's donors' money, Graham.'

He nodded sombrely. 'I know, *Kerry*. Actually, I think it's a waste of their hard-earned coin, but Sarah knows best. She likes to spend a quid to make a quid, or so she tells me. Aiming for the high rollers and all that.'

'Yes,' Kerry said. 'I'm sure she knows best. I'll see you soon.'

'I could rather come and help you buy stockings?'

'Graham.'

'Sorry. I'll be good. This shouldn't be too hard.'

Kerry left him and went to a lingerie store they had passed on the way. When she was done she browsed for a while, looking at shoes, and on impulse bought a pair of boots that she liked the look of. She checked her watch. It had been half an hour, more than enough time for Graham to buy something. She went back to the menswear store.

Graham was sitting on a courtesy chair, a look of total bewilderment plain on his face.

'What's happening?'

He looked up at her and shrugged.

'Graham, what's wrong?'

'What's wrong? I have no bloody idea what to buy or who to ask. The sales assistants look at me like I'm a vagrant and everything I've looked at costs the same as the gross national product of South Africa.'

She felt sorry for him. 'Oh dear.'

'If you go into a menswear store in the lowveld you have two

224

choices: green and khaki. I looked at something before that was called teal. That's a flipping duck!'

Kerry laughed, then controlled herself when she saw his palpable stress. 'Can I help?'

'Please. I'd rather have my left eye gouged out by a buffalo's horn than do this.'

Kerry took the lead and Graham fell in behind her. 'What's your suit size?'

'How the hell should I know?'

She looked him up and down and remembered buying a jacket for an old boyfriend. The coat had fitted well but the man hadn't liked it, or stuck around. He'd resented her for trying to make him look smarter. Kerry had a sudden panic attack. 'I don't know your style, what you like, Graham.'

He smiled. 'Oh, that's an easy one. I have no style.'

Chapter 24

Eli Johnston moved on foot, alone, through the open grassland around Kwangela Game Reserve.

He carried a backpack and in it a commercially available drone. He was dressed in black jeans and matching sweater and beanie, and combat boots.

Ahead of him, he saw the floodlights of the rhino bomas.

*

Sarah told the catering manager at the Table Bay Hotel to put another dozen bottles of French champagne on the bill, just in case. The guests at her fundraiser, the manager had just told her, were hammering the bubbly during the pre-dinner drinks.

'Excuse me, love, do you know where a bloke can get a beer around here?' said a man in a broad, almost comical Australian accent.

Sarah turned. The man had piercing blue eyes, the first thing she noticed about him, and he was immaculately groomed. The salt and pepper hair was cut short but stylishly finished with just the right amount of product.

CAPTIVE

The shirt was crisp, white, simple but elegant. The suit was charcoal, slim-fit, with a pocket square; the dress boots polished. He was trim and handsome.

Sarah's mouth dropped.

'Well, say something,' Graham said.

'It's . . .'

Kerry stepped out from behind Graham and beamed at Sarah. 'I know, a miracle, right?'

'Uh-huh,' was all Sarah could manage.

'Talk about extreme makeover,' Kerry said.

'I didn't recognise you, Graham.' Sarah took a step closer and kissed him on the cheek.

'Control yourself, woman. I know you're only human, but let's not make a scene in public.'

It was him all right. 'You look great.'

'But?'

'What do you mean?' Sarah asked.

'I sense you wanted to add a "but" at the end of that sentence.'

She exhaled. 'Yes. *But*, are you ready to go onstage and address the audience, after they've had their main meal?'

Graham paused and surveyed the room. Sarah saw what he saw, about two hundred people who could each afford two thousand rand a head for a ticket to a dinner in a fancy function room. These were businessmen and women; Sarah deliberately targeted the top end of town in her fundraising. There were lawyers, bankers, doctors, millionaires.

Graham drew a deep breath. 'Never been readier.'

A drinks waiter came to them, bearing a platter. Sarah took a glass of champagne and Kerry a white wine. Graham reached out, his hand hovering near a beer, but instead he took a sparkling water with a slice of lemon.

'Well done, Graham.'

'Woof, woof,' he said.

'Don't be like that.'

He forced a grin and raised his glass. 'Cheers.'

'Cheers,' the women said.

'I reserve the right,' he said after a sip, 'to get blotto after I've finished my speech.'

'And after you've taken questions and mingled with the crowd for a bit,' Sarah said.

'Yes, dear.'

'Stop it, Graham. You're being boring now.'

The master of ceremonies, a comedian, went to the microphone and asked people to start taking their seats.

Sarah felt nervous and it wasn't simply event-evening jitters.

'Is Eli here tonight?' Kerry asked, trying too hard to make it sound like it was a casual enquiry.

Sarah sipped champagne and started walking towards their table. Kerry went with her. 'No. I invited him, but he had something else on tonight. He wouldn't say where it was when I asked, or who he was seeing. There's nothing on his website that indicated another fundraiser.'

'Oh.'

'Don't sound too upset,' Sarah said.

'I'm not.'

'I am, a bit,' Sarah said.

'How come?'

'He's avoiding me. I met him and asked if he would be interested in us joining forces, his anti-poaching army and our Animals Without Borders campaign. He as much as told me to go and get stuffed.'

Kerry raised her eyebrows. 'That doesn't sound like him.'

Sarah put a hand on Kerry's arm. 'You know the public Eli. Mr Clean-cut, polite, handsome-as-hell all-American war hero and animal conservationist.'

'You make it sound like something bad.'

'Oh no, not at all. That's the good in Eli, in all of us. But underneath he's like the rest of us, fighting for a shrinking pool of dollars. He's done the maths, or the math as Americans say, and he knows I need him more than he needs me.'

Kerry looked around the room. 'But look at all these people. It looks like you've got some of the wealthiest people in South Africa here, Sarah.'

She shook her head. 'Five years ago I was pulling crowds twice this size both here and in Australia, and we would make five times what we'll make tonight. I even spotted a couple of my high rollers at Eli's concert last night, albeit chaperoning their teeny-bopper daughters. It's a numbers game.'

'Ladies and gentlemen,' the comedian said from the front. 'Can I have your attention. Please do take your seats. The show's going to be starting soon.'

Sarah was about to sit down when she saw Riaan Coetzee, the owner of Kwangela Game Reserve, making his way towards them against the tide of thronging guests.

When he got to her she introduced him to Graham and Kerry.

'You've got some nice-looking rhinos,' Graham said as they shook hands.

'Thanks. But I've just received some bad news.'

'What is it?' Sarah asked.

'I just got a call from the wife of my head of security, Michael Collins. He's been killed in a carjacking. She's devastated, as am I.'

'That's terrible,' Kerry said.

'Yes,' said Sarah.

'Well, I just wanted to let you know.' Glancing at the comedian on the stage, Riaan excused himself to return to his table and the others took their seats, except for Graham, who held back.

'Call of nature. I'll be in soon,' he said, and walked the other way.

*

229

Eli had unpacked and assembled his drone. He started it and the propellers buzzed. He used the remote to control the unmanned aerial vehicle and brought it up into a hover.

It seemed to be coping OK with the small payload he had fixed underneath it.

The drone rose higher and Eli checked the screen. Everything was going well. While piloting the device, Eli was able to track its progress via the go-pro camera that was also mounted underneath it.

He could see the perimeter fence looming. Eli veered left, setting a course parallel to the fence.

All was set. Eli adjusted the controls and the drone resumed its course, over the fence, above the arc lights and towards its target, the black rhino pens.

Eli followed the line of pens until he was above the one containing the large male, the rhino called Brutus. He slowed the drone into a hover and start to descend.

On the screen he saw the animal trot around in a circle, head and ears up. He could hear the buzz of the drone's rotors, but it took him a few moments to work out that the noise was coming from above. Brutus finally looked up.

Eli pressed a button on the screen and the payload released, dropping the apple so that it landed in the dust right in front of Brutus. The rhino looked down, up again, and, unable to resist the sight and smell of his favourite treat, he lowered his big head and picked up the apple in his prehensile lips. In a second it was gone.

Eli brought the drone up. Brutus followed its climb, his face carrying an almost disappointed look. Eli kept watch as Brutus started to walk. Unsettled, teased by just a single snack, he was confused. He paced his enclosure and Eli tracked his movements.

In time, Brutus's stride became slower, his course more erratic. He stopped, started to sway, and then dropped, first to his front knees, and then his back legs crumpled. He fell onto his side.

Eli was recording.

'Yes,' he whispered, as Brutus rolled onto his side, immobilised.

Eli turned the drone and began flying it back towards him. As he did so he heard the noise of a vehicle engine, coming from behind him. He glanced over his shoulder and saw the twin beams of headlights bouncing over rough ground.

Ahead of him, as well, he detected another noise, like a motor-cycle being revved hard. A spotlight shot out from the vehicle and began sweeping the ground around him.

A siren blipped. 'You. Stop. Stand still! Police.'

Chapter 25

Kerry saw Sarah walking back into the ballroom. She had gone outside to make a call. The mood among the diners was subdued following the news from Riaan of the death of Michael Collins on the way to the function.

Riaan had spoken of his support for the creation of a new rhino conservation and breeding facility. He said he would leave it up to Sarah, in her speech, to say where the rhinos would be relocated to. Riaan said he would be sorry to see the rhinos go, and while Kerry had learned from her visit that he was selling them to the charity to save money and keep Kwangela afloat, she could tell by the quaver in his voice a couple of times that it had not been an easy decision.

'Thank you, Riaan,' the MC said as the applause died down. 'And in a few minutes, as you enjoy your dessert, we'll hear from Sarah Hoyland from Animals Without Borders, who'll be telling us exactly where this precious natural cargo is headed.'

A few people got up from their tables to use the bathrooms and conversation resumed.

'Where's Graham?' Sarah asked Kerry.

Kerry looked around. 'He went out for another cigarette a while ago.'

'I told you to keep an eye on him. He's going to be on straight after me.'

Kerry bridled at Sarah's tone, but she knew the other woman could be quite pushy. 'I didn't think I needed to hold his hand all night.'

'It wouldn't hurt. Look, can you *please* find Graham?'

'All right.'

Kerry got up and left the ballroom. Sarah had annoyed her, but perhaps she was right to be worried. Where the hell was Graham? She saw a man walking and putting a packet of cigarettes into his pocket.

'Can you tell me where the smokers are, please?'

'Sure, out those doors and on your left.'

'You didn't by any chance meet a grey-haired veterinarian?'

'Your guest of honour?' The man laughed. 'I'm here for the chartered accountants' dinner, but I'd rather be at your dinner if he's going to be speaking.'

'Hmm, I'm not so sure about that,' she said.

'Well, he's out there with the smokers all right, though none of them will have any ciggies left if that's what you're after.'

'Thanks.' Kerry didn't know what was so funny. She headed outside.

Graham was holding court, with four people around him, laughing at something he had just said.

'Ah, Kerry, come join us! This is where the cool kids hang out. I never knew accountants partied so hard. We may all die early, but we'll do so laughing.'

'Not funny, Graham. Sarah wants to see you. You're speaking soon.'

'*Sarah wants to see you,*' he parodied in a high voice. 'The schoolmarm beckons.'

Graham put his hand in his right-hand suit pocket as he drew on a cigarette with his left. Kerry heard the clink of glass.

'Graham, what's in your pocket?'

He looked at her, fixing her with his blue eyes.

'Have you been drinking?'

'I'm of legal age.'

'Graham, you said you wouldn't.'

He hiccuped, then turned to his audience, most of whom were looking away in embarrassment. 'Well, that rather gave the game away, didn't it? Just a little something to take the edge off my nerves.'

Kerry grabbed Graham by a forearm and physically dragged him away from the group, whose members laughed as he waved goodbye theatrically.

When Kerry eased open the doors of the function room Sarah was on stage.

'And so, ladies and gentlemen,' Sarah was saying, 'in closing I can say that even though these rhinos have been superbly cared for at Kwangela Game Reserve, here in the Western Cape, it is time for them to do their bit in rebuilding the population of wild free-ranging rhinos that has suffered so terribly in the last fifty years or more, especially in recent times.'

'She's good,' Graham whispered, then hiccuped again.

'Shush,' Kerry said. They made their way to their table and took their seats.

'These rhinos aren't leaving Africa,' Sarah continued, 'but they are going home, to somewhere that needs them more than ever. To Riaan and his team, and in memory of the late Michael Collins who did so much to protect them, rest assured, we at Animals Without Borders will do all we can to ensure that they stay safe, and that their offspring will carry on the name of Kwangela forever. Thank you.'

When the applause died down the master of ceremonies introduced Graham.

He straightened his tie, weaved his way through the room and took the stairs to the stage, stumbling over the last step, but stopping himself from falling. The crowd hushed.

'You were expecting,' he cleared his voice, 'a handsome television star, and instead you get me, an ugly washed-out old has-been.'

The audience didn't seem to know if this was a joke, though someone laughed, too loudly.

'Thank you,' Graham said, looking at the laughing person. 'You might not know it from looking at me in these fancy new threads, but I am the ugly face of the work you support.'

He waited for silence again.

'It was pointed out to me, ladies and gentlemen, by the lovely Sarah Hoyland, whom you all know, that I was too dirty, my clothes too grubby, for you to see me as I normally dress. Now, I could take offence at that, because my bush clothes, which I was wearing until a few short hours ago, are stained and patched.

'They're stained with blood. My shirt was ripped, gored, by the tip of the horn of a female rhino as she died, under my care, a couple of months ago. She was shot and left for dead by poachers and I became covered in blood as I performed an emergency C-section in a bid to save her unborn calf. I failed.'

The audience was hushed. No one dared lift a fork.

'I'm going to be honest with you. I don't know if what we're doing is right, shipping animals from zoos around the world and sending them back to Africa, shipping rhinos from one country or continent to another because they might be safer or needed more in one place than the other.

'I don't know if our government, the private sector, and good people such as yourselves are better off putting money into breeding endangered animals or giving anti-poaching patrols the training, guns and bullets they need to catch or kill poachers.

I don't know if we need more drones and helicopters, or advertising and PR campaigns to convince people they are bloody idiots for wanting rhino horn, elephant ivory, pangolin scales, cycads – yes, even plants – or abalone.'

Graham paused and took a sip of water. Kerry looked around the audience. All eyes were on him, waiting to see what he would say next. Kerry said a silent prayer that he didn't cock this up. Or fart. He was doing a great job so far and had her, like everyone else in the room, on the edge of her seat. Kerry liked that he could be serious and passionate when he had to be.

Graham set down his glass and drew a deep breath. 'The only thing I do know, ladies and gentlemen, is that we are at war, and you fight a war, if you believe in it, with every weapon in your arsenal. You fight it with guns and bullets and helicopters and drones; you fight it with PR and advertising and you hope that you can change what people on TV call "the narrative" and convince the bastards who use all this stuff, who kill to feed their egos and their superstitions, that they are *wrong*. And, as in previous wars, you fight it by protecting the innocents and keeping them out of harm's way, even if that means moving them from one bloody country to –'

Graham was interrupted by Riaan, who moved swiftly up the stairs to the stage. He came to Graham and whispered in his ear.

Kerry felt a lump in her throat as she looked at Graham, then a stab of fear. His face had turned so pale that Kerry was worried he was so drunk he might throw up. Graham's whole body seemed to sag and he gripped the lectern in front of him, seemingly to stop himself from falling.

Graham hung his head and the whole room could hear his raspy breathing in the microphone. 'I must go, but I am tired. I am sick and tired, and I feel the weariness in my bones, and the sadness fills my heart, because this war of mine has now come to your backyard.'

He looked up and out at the audience, red-rimmed eyes scanning them. His shoulders sagged. 'Riaan has just told me that his prize male rhino, Brutus, who many of you would have seen at Kwangela, has just been poisoned. So now I must go back to my war, to see if there is any chance, however unlikely, that we can save Brutus. Thank you . . . thank you for being on my side.'

As Graham left the stage and walked down the stairs, through the middle of the audience, the crowd rose as one. Their applause was deafening, and as Graham passed them Kerry saw men reaching for their wallets and women opening their handbags.

Graham was walking with Riaan, who was beside him, saying something close to his ear so he could hear above the noise.

'Let's get out of here,' Graham said to Kerry as he came to her table.

Kerry stood. 'You want me to come with you?'

Graham stopped. 'Yes. Riaan here says he's organised a helicopter to take us from the waterfront. There's a guy who does game capture for him in between taking tourists for flips. He's standing by.'

Sarah was waiting for them outside, by a chauffeur-driven car. 'Good work, Graham. The crowd loved your talk.'

He stopped in front of her. Kerry thought he no longer seemed drunk. 'An animal may be dying, and you're thinking about money. Also, I'm sorry I missed your speech, but Riaan just filled me in. You're consigning his rhinos to a certain death.'

'We can talk about this later, Graham,' Sarah said.

'I missed it too,' Kerry said, turning to Sarah. 'What's happening to the rhinos?'

But it was Graham who answered. 'Sarah announced, in her speech, that Animals Without Borders, and an "unidentified philanthropist",' he made air quotes with his fingers, 'who wants to remain anonymous, are funding the construction of a rhino breeding and conservation centre in Mozambique, not far from Massingir. It doesn't take a brain surgeon to know that that is the poaching capital of that country.'

Sarah put her hands on her hips. 'As I said, while you were outside getting pissed, Graham, and as you alluded to in your speech, we can't stop poaching with guns and bullets alone. We need to give the people of Mozambique ownership of rhinos and show them that they can make money out of tourism, and that's what this new centre will do.'

Graham shook his head. 'I don't think those rhinos would last five minutes in Massingir even if you had Mother Teresa running the place and Chuck Norris protecting them. As it is, they're destined to be killed.'

'How come?' Kerry asked, looking from Sarah to Graham.

'You tell her,' Graham said. 'Tell her who this "philanthropist" is that you're dealing with in Massingir.'

'We've got a partner in Mozambique, a well-respected local politician and businessman, who will be the chairman of the board of the new centre,' Sarah said.

'Too embarrassed to say his name?' Graham said, goading her.

Sarah said nothing.

Graham turned to Kerry. 'I'll tell you who her "well-respected" partner is.'

'Who?'

Graham was clearly seething, fists clenched by his side. 'Fidel Costa.'

*

Graham pulled off his rubber gloves and tossed them aside. Brutus the rhino was still groggy, walking unsteadily around his enclosure, but he was alive.

Graham's new clothes were a mess, but he didn't care. Likewise, Kerry's stockings were ripped at the knees and her dress was dirty. 'Good job, Graham.'

Bradd, the ranger who had shown Graham and Kerry around Kwangela, had met the helicopter and taken them to the boma. He had been watching on while Graham ministered to the giant animal.

'What was wrong with him, Doc?'

Graham snapped his veterinarian's bag closed. 'Brutus wasn't showing any signs of poisoning, so I assumed someone simply sedated him. I gave him a shot to reverse the effects of the most commonly used drug and he came to. That doesn't mean someone wasn't trying to take his horn.'

'A humane poacher?' Bradd asked.

'Wouldn't be the first time. Early on in this latest poaching epidemic there were reports of veterinarians getting involved in the trade, darting rhinos secretly and taking their horns. Also, poachers with access to drugs have given rhinos a lethal dose of immobilising agents and not bothered with reversing the effect – a dart gun is a silent way to kill.'

'So whoever did this could still have been trying to kill Brutus, quietly.'

Graham nodded. 'Yes, possibly. I've taken a blood sample and that will show us just what was in his system and how much of it there was – whether it was a potentially lethal dose or not. Whoever did this and for whatever reason, the fact is that there's always a risk when sedating a big animal like this one.'

Kerry took her phone out of her handbag and checked Facebook. 'There's already loads of news on here.'

'What are they saying?' Bradd asked.

'The local police held a media conference just now and Sarah's already shared it on Facebook. Oh, my word!'

'What is it?' Graham asked.

Kerry held up her phone and clicked on a video. Graham and Bradd crowded next to her to see the screen. A South African Police Service captain was addressing a media conference.

'This morning police, acting on information received from a member of the public, attended the Kwangela Game Reserve and a man acting suspiciously outside the reserve was taken into police custody.'

'Has he been charged with anything, Captain? What can you tell us about him?' a journalist asked off camera.

'At this stage I can confirm a thirty-two-year-old American man is assisting us with our investigation. He was found to be in possession of a commercially unmanned aerial vehicle – a drone – and a quantity of pesticide poison. Police had received a tip-off that a man was going to fly a device over Kwangela and drop food laced with poison into the rhino bomas. By the time we arrived on the scene a rhino had already been reported as being in distress and a veterinarian was called.'

'Hectic,' said Bradd. 'While you were working on Brutus I was listening to chatter on our radio system. One of the other guides was saying the police had been outside the wire and had arrested someone.'

'Not just anyone,' Kerry said. 'Look at these comments and at this picture.'

Kerry scrolled down through the comments and opened a picture that someone had posted of a man being escorted into a police station between two officers.

'Eli Johnston,' Graham said. '*Eish.*'

Bradd was wide-eyed. 'Him, a poacher?'

'How well do you know Eli?' Kerry asked Graham.

'Reasonably well. Like a lot of Americans, he's a straight shooter, not afraid to tell it like it is, which can sometimes get you in trouble in Africa. The people in charge don't take kindly to foreigners telling them how to do things.'

'He's a man of action, then,' she said.

'Yes, or an arrogant arse, depending on your perspective. I still can't imagine why Eli would want to sedate or even poison a rhino. It doesn't make sense.'

'He raises a lot of money, from what I've been able to see,' Kerry said, thinking out loud.

'Yes and he's hardly going to try to sell humanely harvested rhino horn to raise money. I've been to his base camp in Mozambique. Eli takes the term "Spartan" in its literal sense. He lives out of his old army backpack, sleeping on a military stretcher and eating the same food as his men, *pap* and *nyama*. As far as I know he doesn't have too many worldly possessions and the money he raises goes straight to the fight.'

'If he needed money, though, for whatever reason, it would be far easier for him to kill a rhino in Mozambique or Kruger, wouldn't it, rather than come all the way to the Cape to kill one?' Bradd asked.

Graham nodded, then something Kerry had said struck a chord. He took out his phone. 'He puts all his effort into the fight. Eli's up to something funny, and we need to find out what; I'm going to call the police and see if I can talk to him.'

Bradd's mobile phone rang and he moved away from them and answered the call. Graham was on hold and Bradd returned a couple of minutes later.

'That was Riaan,' Bradd said. 'He said you two must stay here the night, in our luxury safari tents. The chopper had to return to Cape Town and the pilot's been requested to help fly a search for a yacht that has gone missing. If you don't want to stay I am to drive you back to the Table Bay.'

Graham nodded to Bradd, then held up a hand for silence. 'Thanks,' he said into the phone, 'for nothing.' He ended the call.

'No luck?' Kerry asked.

'The police are still questioning him. So, what do you think about spending the night here?' Graham asked Kerry.

'I'm happy to stay.'

He nodded. 'Me too. I've had enough of Sarah's *hospitality*.'

241

Bradd escorted them back to his Land Rover and they drove through the dark to the camp in the middle of Kwangela where overnight guests stayed. If there were any other people there they were fast asleep at this late hour.

'Here's your stop,' Bradd said.

'Thanks, Bradd, this looks fine,' said Kerry. Her time in Africa had made her surprisingly used to the unexpected by now. She would soon be in danger of losing her reputation as a control freak if this kept up, she mused.

Bradd showed them to two permanently erected green canvas tents, set on elevated timber platforms. Each had an en suite.

'These are lovely,' Kerry said. 'Please pass on our thanks to Riaan.'

'Will do. I'll leave you in peace.'

*

Graham found his way to the shower, stripped off and let the hot water pummel him. Ever since his days in the army he'd been a quick washer and he was out in less than three minutes.

'Graham?'

He quickly wrapped a towel around himself and walked into the main part of the tent.

'Sorry,' Kerry said. 'There are no towels in my tent. I was wondering if I could borrow one of yours.'

'Must be because they weren't expecting guests.' They stood there, looking at each other. Graham ran a hand through his wet hair. She had taken her stockings and high heels off, and he couldn't help but notice her smooth bare legs and her feet, which if anything looked too small and dainty for a woman of her height.

'They're little, I know.' She smiled.

'Sorry.'

'It's all right.'

'Graham . . .'

242

'What is it?' He noticed that despite her smile her eyes were misted, and her lip was quivering.

'Graham, I've killed two men in Africa. I was almost raped. And now . . .' She sniffed and a tear rolled down her cheek, 'And now this poor, innocent animal was drugged and put at risk by a man I thought was really nice.'

Little things, such as a quick shower in a tent, could bring back memories of his military service, but so, too, could blood and loud noises, the smell of cordite from a freshly fired rifle and the clatter of a helicopter's rotors. Kerry had probably been through more trauma in the last couple of weeks than in her entire life, and it was only here and now, back in relative safety and tranquillity, that it was finally hitting her. Graham drew a breath. He knew he should comfort her.

She decided it for him, coming to him and putting her arms around him.

He couldn't not hold her. She felt tiny in his arms and her tears were wet on the skin beneath his collarbone. He breathed in the scent of her and while she hadn't yet washed she was no less attractive or arousing.

Don't, he told himself.

But his fingers found the zipper at the back of her cocktail dress.

'Shower here. I'll wait outside for you.'

She tilted her head and looked up into his eyes. 'Just look after me, Graham. Please. Just for a bit.'

His heart, which he'd thought of as a mass of scar tissue, opened up and threatened to drown him from the inside. He kissed her and she returned the tenderness and desire.

Graham lowered her zip and helped Kerry shrug off her dress and step out of it. Her skin was pale against the lacy outlines of her black bra. He kissed her neck, tenderly, forcing himself to take it slow as he undid the clasp behind her.

Kerry gently prised herself away and, with her back to him, took her pants off. She walked towards the shower, but trailed a hand behind her, which he took. Graham let the towel fall from his waist and followed her.

She reached in and turned the water on, and while it warmed up he put his arms around her and spooned her.

'I'm sorry,' he whispered.

'What for?'

'For being me.'

She turned her head to look back at him and reached up and stroked his still-damp hair. 'Don't be. It's what I like about you.'

They kissed then Kerry stepped under the water. As she lathered her hair with shampoo Graham washed her back and then let his hand trail down over the swell of her bottom, massaging it with soapy hands. Kerry arched her back invitingly.

Graham stayed behind her but reached around to wash her front with a bar of soap as she melded to him.

Their mouths met again when she turned to face him and she stroked him, not that he needed any encouragement. He'd been worried for the briefest of moments, that his regimen of too much booze and not enough sleep might have sapped him, but he stirred proudly.

He touched her and it was glorious to be this close to a woman again. He and Sarah had been together a few times, but she'd seemed distant when she'd contacted him from Australia, as if it was OK for her to let herself go when she was visiting Africa, but back home she had too much else on her mind. Perhaps, he thought, she had someone else. It didn't matter.

Graham looked into Kerry's eyes and wondered if he could do this. Not the act itself, but he didn't know if he could – what was the word – *inflict* his troubles on her.

She turned off the taps. 'Come with me.'

Kerry took a towel and walked through to the bedroom. It was

African, down to the leopard-print cushions, which she tossed on the floor, and the mosquito net suspended above the king-size bed. She turned back the covers.

'Just hold me for a bit, OK? I'm anxious.'

'Of course.'

He lay down on the crisp, cool sheets and suffered another pang of doubt, this time that he might fall asleep from the exhaustion and after-effects of his sly drinking at the fundraiser and the night spent treating Brutus the rhino. His body, however, overruled him.

Graham did as she asked and spooned her, marvelling at the slim, smooth body in his arms.

'I'm sorry,' she said into the pillow, and he felt her begin to sob. 'I'm really sorry, Graham.'

'It's fine.' He stroked her hair with his hand. 'Sleep.'

In time his body succumbed as well and he drifted off to sleep.

*

Kerry stirred and for a moment didn't know where she was. She smiled to herself and drifted back to sleep.

When she woke again and checked her phone she saw that it was just before ten in the morning. Graham was on his back, his mouth half-open, snoring lightly. He looked at peace and she realised it made him appear a completely different man. Even when he was cracking jokes there was a nervous edge to him, as though he was hiding from something through his attempts at humour.

She propped herself up on one elbow. What had she been thinking before they drifted off to sleep? She remembered leading him to the shower, naked, teasing him. Did she really want to have sex with him?

There was no doubt he looked way more handsome since she had persuaded him to get a shave and a haircut. His chest rose and fell.

He blinked, then looked at her and smiled. She felt self-conscious.

'I was watching you sleep,' Kerry confessed.

'I was dreaming about you.'

'I'm hungry.'

He rubbed his face. 'Me too.'

'I'm not talking about food,' she said, and even as she uttered the words she wondered where they had come from, who had said them.

Graham's eyes widened, but he had the good grace and good sense not to make a joke.

Kerry leaned over and kissed him and he reached for her. He was, she recalled from before falling asleep, a good kisser. His lips seemed to meet hers perfectly, which was a novel sensation considering some of the men she had been with.

'I love your mouth,' he murmured in between kisses.

It was an odd thing to say but she felt the same way, and just that simple contact was having an effect on the rest of her body. He took nothing for granted, yet he wasn't passive. His hands roamed over her body – her back, her shoulders, her forearms and the backs of her thighs. It was as if he was teasing her, or maybe he just liked the feel of her skin.

She reciprocated, exploring, mapping him, but avoiding direct arousal. Above his groin, which was still under the top sheet, though nicely outlined, she found a scar where his pubic hair began.

'What's this?'

'Cut myself shaving,' he said.

She slapped the skin. 'The truth, Baird.'

'Shrapnel. Angola. I was lucky, some others weren't.'

It was her turn not to push it, even though she wanted to hear more about him, about his history, his life. Maybe there would be time, maybe not. Her world, her life, were orderly, predictable, and while she'd thought she liked it like that, Africa had turned her upside down.

She felt his fingers on her waist, squeezing. There was urgency in his touch, desire, and it spread through her. Kerry moved so that she was on top of him and he looked up into her eyes.

'You're sure?'

She didn't want to say anything in case she changed her mind or he made a wisecrack. Instead, she nodded, and let her body reply.

He was ready for her, as was she for him, and she closed her eyes, savouring the feeling as she lowered herself down on him. When he was inside her, completely, she kissed him again.

'Tell me this is right. It can't be wrong,' she said, opening her eyes.

He looked at her and gave his head a little shake. 'I'm not saying a thing. I don't want to spoil this. I don't want it to end.'

Neither do I, she said to herself as she started to move.

Chapter 26

Kerry and Graham made love a second time and then she fell back to sleep. When she woke, Graham was gone.

She got out of bed and checked the en suite, but there was no sign of him. Kerry felt a moment of relief when she noticed there was a message on the screen of her phone, however when she checked it she found it wasn't from Graham, explaining where he had gone, but rather a missed call from Eli.

Kerry got dressed. Outside she saw a few lodge guests strolling about, and a ranger, whom she approached and asked if he knew where Graham Baird was. The man didn't but he radioed Bradd, who was nearby.

Kerry went to the dining area of the camp and was served coffee. Bradd arrived a few minutes later.

'Where's Graham?' she asked without preamble.

'Oh, I thought you knew,' Bradd said. 'One of the other rangers gave him a lift to Cape Town an hour or so ago. He said he was on an earlier flight than you and not to disturb you. Riaan had already organised your transfer. A driver from a local tour company will come fetch you after lunch.'

'Shit.'

'Sorry,' said Bradd.

'Not your fault.' Kerry finished her coffee and then tried ringing Graham. The call went through to voicemail. She went back to her tent and tried to make herself look presentable. When the car came to fetch her she got in and tried Graham again – still no answer.

As the driver hurtled down the N2 towards Cape Town, Kerry called Sarah.

'Graham's gone,' Kerry said when Sarah answered.

'I know, I just saw him at the hotel. He was checking out, heading to the airport early. He threw his toys out of the cot and walked out on me.'

'I'm not surprised he was upset. You're going into partnership with a rhino poaching kingpin. Are you crazy?'

'No. This is your first trip to Africa, Kerry, and like every bloody do-gooder you reckon you know how to solve the world's problems. I used to live and work in Mozambique. I know how things work there, you don't.'

'I'm not doubting that, but you're plonking this thing right in the poachers' backyard. Fidel Costa tried to *kill* me, and my father, and Eli Johnston, and Graham. For fuck's sake, Sarah, you have literally done a deal with the devil.'

Sarah sighed. 'Costa's a businessman. He knows a good deal when he sees it. The breeding centre and eventually restocking the Greater Limpopo Transfrontier Park are not just about showing the rural poor that there is monetary value in wildlife and tourism, it's about showing the elite, like Costa, that there's a buck to be made in conservation.'

'Converting him, you mean, from poacher to gamekeeper.'

'I didn't say that,' Sarah said.

'No, but you as much as confirmed that you know that Costa is the Don of Massingir. He's just going to double dip on this deal – take your rich donors' money to build this breeding centre and then send his men in to kill its occupants once their horns are big enough to cut off.'

'We'll be de-horning all the rhinos in the centre and eventually releasing some of them into the wild.'

'Releasing de-horned rhinos into the wild won't work; poachers will still kill them,' Kerry countered.

'Oh, so now as well as being an expert on Mozambique after one brief visit you also know all there is to know about rhino conservation, is that it?'

'On that *brief visit*, I was imprisoned by Costa's thugs, and when I got back to South Africa I was almost raped and killed by one of his hired guns. Seriously, this is the sort of man you are going into business with? The horns you cut off will be smuggled out of the country and sold abroad. You know it and I know it. That's if you can even find a buyer for farmed rhino horn.'

'What do you know about the debate on the legal trade in rhinos anyway?' Sarah said.

'I know it's a fallacy that the market can be supplied by the horns of captive-bred rhinos, legally or illegally. Graham told me that poachers have been caught not only with the horns of rhinos they had slaughtered but also the animals' tails and ears. The buyers in Vietnam are demanding proof that the horn comes from wild free-roaming rhinos that were killed – they don't want farmed stuff or horns from de-horned rhinos that are still alive. I can't believe you don't know all this.'

'I know more about this than you ever will, Kerry. Thanks for your support for Animals Without Borders, but I think we can do without your well-intentioned advice from now on. There is a bigger picture here that needs to be focused on.'

'Try me. Go on, tell me your big strategy. How is getting into bed with a criminal going to save a single rhino?'

Sarah lowered her voice. 'All right. Costa's as crooked as they come,' she said. 'You know that, and I know that. But that doesn't mean he can't change.'

'Hah!'

'Hear me out,' Sarah said. 'Everything else has failed. Eli and his anti-poaching rangers – hell, half the South African Army as well – can't catch or kill every rhino poacher. Costa's a major player, and if we can convert him to the side of good and show him a way to make money – legally and quasi-legally – from a de facto rhino farm, then I'll probably stop more poachers than the entire US military could.'

'*Quasi*-legally? Are you listening to yourself, Sarah?'

'You're a stuffed-shirt lawyer. We're talking about Africa. Hell, anyone who lives in Africa and says they've never broken a law is a liar. I used to work at a resort on an island off the coast of Mozambique that was renovated with the proceeds of crime. These days it's a national success story. The owner, an ex-boyfriend of mine, and his wife – another frigging lawyer – put a share of their profits back into marine conservation and preventing illegal fishing. The thing is, the whole place was funded by dirty money.'

'Two wrongs don't make a right,' Kerry said.

'No, but in Africa if you never did business with someone who had done something wrong or illegal there would be no business. Haven't you heard of those stories where ex-poachers are recruited to work as anti-poaching rangers, using their knowledge of tracking and hunting wildlife for good?'

Kerry wasn't sure how much longer she could control her temper. 'Fidel Costa is not some dirt-poor Mozambican who turned to poaching rhinos to try and feed his family; he's a brutal gangster and a career criminal.'

'Settle down. He's also an elected politician, and like all those slimy buggers, or at least the ones who last more than one term, he's learned how to read the mood of the electorate and the times.

He's getting on board with this project because it will help cement his hold on the town of Massingir. He's got his sights set on higher office, maybe all the way to the top, and if I can persuade him to support the cause of conservation now, he'll be a powerful ally to our organisation in the future. So, yes, I'll do a deal with the devil if it will ensure the future of the rhino and Mozambique's elephants. Hell, yes, I'll do that deal.'

At first Kerry had thought Sarah had been duped into this deal, but it was now clear she knew just what sort of a man Costa was and had no qualms about getting into bed with him. Kerry wondered if someone like Costa really could change sides as easily as that, and go straight.

'He's a murderer, Sarah. He tried to *kill* us.'

Sarah said nothing.

'I'm going,' Kerry said, 'and I'm going to do whatever I can to bring your deal crashing down.'

'Nice knowing you,' Sarah said.

Kerry ended the call and her phone rang straight after. She took a deep breath to calm herself. 'Kerry Maxwell.'

'Kerry, it's Eli.'

So much for calm. 'What the hell were you playing at, Eli? Are you in prison making your one phone call?'

'Relax, Kerry. I'm not in prison and I haven't been charged with anything. I wanted to call you to explain what happened. Can I see you in person?'

'I don't know. I'm in a car, heading back to Cape Town.' She could see Table Mountain ahead through the windscreen. The view was crystal clear and the sky a lustrous blue, but she knew that could change in a minute. 'I should go to my hotel and get changed, but if I run into Sarah Hoyland I might kill her.'

'Then how about we meet in town. Please.'

'OK, where? I'll get the driver to drop me, but I must warn you, I look a mess.'

'Doesn't worry me. Do you like Asian food?'

'Love it,' she said.

'There's a restaurant called Haiku, in Burg Street, close to the big craft market.'

'I'll find it, or rather I'm sure my driver will.'

'OK, see you there in half an hour or so, yes?'

'Cool,' she said.

Kerry ended the call, then tried Graham again.

'Hello?'

'Graham, it's Kerry. Where are you? Back at the Table Bay?'

'No.'

'Then where? Did you get my message?'

'Yes, I got it,' he said.

'And were you going to call me back?'

There was a pause, then Graham said, 'No, Kerry, I wasn't.'

She was surprised. 'How come?'

'I'm at Cape Town Airport.'

'But our flight doesn't leave until tomorrow.'

'Change of plans. I'm flying this afternoon. I'm going to Joburg, picking up the honey badger and taking it out to the Kruger Park.'

'Why? I thought Sarah's plan was to release the badger at a media event at Skukuza later this week, after all the veterinary checks had been done on him.'

'Yes, well, I'm a vet, I can check a badger and I don't give a fuck about Sarah's PR plans.'

'Nor about me, so it seems.' Kerry was taken aback, and slightly offended. They had been making love one minute and now he was leaving her ahead of schedule without even bothering to call her. 'Have I done something wrong?'

Graham sighed. 'No, not at all. But I'm afraid I have to end your stay with me as a volunteer.'

'Why, Graham?'

There was silence on the other end of the call.

'Say something, Graham.'

'I've got unfinished business to attend to.'

'Like what? What is so bloody important that you can just walk out on me without even having the courtesy to return my phone message, let alone give me a proper explanation?'

'Kerry.'

'Bloody hell.'

'Kerry, listen to me.'

She wiped her eyes. 'What?'

'You need to be careful, OK?'

'What do you mean? Costa?'

'I'm convinced he's still out to get you, and Eli, as payback for what happened in Mozambique. I'm the cause of it, all because I killed his brother. He's not going to let up. Where are you now?'

Kerry sniffed. 'I'm on my way to Cape Town, to meet Eli. He's out of prison.'

'Good for him.'

'It sounds like he's in the clear.'

'He might be out of prison,' Graham said, 'but he's not *in the clear*, and neither are you. Get him to stay with you.'

'What do you mean by that?'

'Hold your horses,' he said. 'I just mean he's a good man, and he'll keep you safe, no matter what else he was up to. You're not out of danger yet, either of you, but hopefully you will be soon.'

She was puzzled. 'How?'

'Just keep your head low, and tell your father to watch out as well. Also, tell him, please, that even though he didn't like me, I liked him, and respected him. He made you, and for that alone he deserves thanks. Goodbye, Kerry.'

Kerry felt anxious about the strange turn the conversation had taken. 'What are you planning, Graham?'

'Costa wants me, but you and Eli and your father are still on his radar. This is some kind of blood feud, but I'm going to put an end to it.'

'How?' she asked again.

'Let me worry about that. I'm sorry for what I put you through, Kerry.'

Her heart lurched again. 'Graham, you can't just walk out on me like this.'

But Graham had ended the call. Kerry put her phone back in her bag and wiped her eyes. She was hurt, afraid and angry. What on earth was Graham doing?

Chapter 27

Kerry arrived at Haiku before Eli and took her seat at a table for two. Haiku was a moodily lit restaurant about half-full with businesspeople eating lunch. Asian and African chefs were wreathed in steam and there was the shush of metal on metal as aromatic herbs were tossed with other ingredients in woks.

Kerry spotted Eli immediately when he made his way into the restaurant. His clothes were dirty, as if he'd come straight from prison, and he looked a little self-conscious about it as the waitress led him over to her.

Kerry waved when she saw her.

Eli went to her and took her hand.

'Sorry I'm a mess,' he said.

'No, you look fine,' she said. 'I'm the one who looks like she spent the night babysitting a drugged rhino.'

'About that . . .' he began.

A waiter came to them and Eli ordered a sparkling water, the same as Kerry.

'You don't want a beer after your time in prison?'

256

They both laughed when they saw the waiter's raised eyebrow. 'Sure.'

'Two Windhoek Lagers,' Kerry said to the waitress.

Eli sat down. 'How are you doing?'

'Oh, I've been better. Why did you drug that rhino?'

He exhaled. 'Long story, but I'll give you the condensed version.'

'Please. Though I've got no volunteer position to rush back to in Hoedspruit and I'm not flying until tomorrow in any case, so you can take your time if you like.'

'I went to Kwangela, with a drone and a bag of apples, and my task was to illegally fly the drone over the place and drop a few apples into the black rhino enclosures and to film the whole thing from the drone's camera.'

Kerry widened her eyes. 'But why? You could have been arrested. I mean, you were arrested.'

He held up his hands. 'The whole thing was approved by the Kwangela's head of security, Michael Collins. I heard that you heard, at Sarah's fundraiser, that Michael was killed in a carjacking.'

'Yes, that was terrible news. Did you know him well?'

Eli nodded. 'I met him years ago, in Afghanistan, where we both worked as PMCs – private military contractors. Michael was an ex–South African Recce Commando. When he found out I was coming to Cape Town for the fundraiser he asked me if I would help him test the security of Kwangela, by doing a flyover. He knew all about what I was doing. He was also going to call the local cops on the evening of my mission to let them know what we were up to, but I guess he planned on doing that from the road and he never made it. Like a lot of ex–special forces guys, he was big on keeping secrets – no one else at the reserve knew, not even his own security officers. I explained all this to the cops and eventually they sent someone to his office and their

IT people opened his email accounts and they found the email chain from him.'

'You didn't have your emails on your phone?'

'I did, but my phone was stolen some time after my talk at that Cape Town convention centre. I left it charging in my dressing room while I went out to sign T-shirts and caps and stuff for some of my supporters who'd been at the concert. I bought a cheap replacement phone and had a meeting with Michael Collins in the afternoon, before he died, where I gave him my number verbally, so there was no record on my new phone of me calling him.'

'Bizarre. So who tipped off the cops that you would be flying the drone?'

'Beats me,' said Eli. Their beers arrived and they clinked. 'The operation was hush-hush; there was supposed to be no publicity about it. If I was successful in breaching their security, there was no way Kwangela wanted that kind of information going public.'

Kerry mulled this over. 'Well, at least the world will know that your intentions were good.'

Eli shrugged and she saw the worry in his face. 'I'm not so sure. I've been unfriended and unfollowed by hundreds of people on Facebook and Twitter already and there are plenty of rumours flying around, along with accusations that I'm a rhino poacher. I've also had several big-spending donors email me telling me they're reconsidering their funding. The fact that the police went public right after they arrested me, before they even interviewed me, has cost me dearly. There's so much hype in the media about rhino poaching the cops wanted to be seen to have caught an evil poacher before checking the facts. This is a body blow for me, Kerry.'

She could see his point. 'What will you do?'

'I don't know. Get back up on the horse, I guess. I can't hide from the fact that even with the truth out there, this doesn't look good. The operation was never meant to go public, and if that had been Michael's idea I wouldn't have gone along with it. He wanted more money for upgraded security for Kwangela and was going to use my report on my incursion to help justify his budget plans. That was supposed to be as far as it went. People are already saying on social media that I was irresponsible to even get involved in a stunt like this in the first place and I must say that with the benefit of some Monday morning quarterbacking I tend to agree with them.'

Kerry was quiet for a moment. It made a sort of sense, she supposed, but a couple of things still didn't add up.

'Do you think the rhino you were flying the drone over was ever in any danger from what you were doing?'

'None,' he replied, his eyes meeting hers. 'There was nothing in the apple I dropped that could have killed him, just a sedative.'

'*Just?* Graham was angry. He told me that any time an animal is drugged there is a risk. The rhino could have rolled over at a bad angle, stopping blood flow to its heart.'

'Yes, but it didn't. And I was watching it through the camera. If it had gone down badly or been in trouble I would have called someone. Collins wanted a video of the rhino being sedated so he could show to the Kwangela management and shock them into beefing up security. Of course, it was all in vain.'

He looked away then, only briefly, but it was enough to make Kerry think that there was more to this, something he wasn't telling her. She'd seen it before, occasionally, when she was asking clients about their business dealings and tax affairs and she could tell they were obfuscating. She was wondering how to ask him about it when he said, 'What about you, what are you going to do now?'

'Graham told me to be careful. He said I should stick with you, but I guess you're heading back to Mozambique.'

'I am – heading back that is – tomorrow. He must be worried about Costa.'

'You think he'll try to get at us again?'

Eli shrugged. 'I think he was behind my getting arrested, and maybe even had a hand in killing Collins.'

'But why go to all that trouble?' Kerry asked.

'Yeah, good question. I was alone out there in the dark, and if someone knew I was going to be there, they could have just snuck up on me and shot me. Costa might want me dead, but first he wants me shamed. He wanted all my supporters and followers to think I was guilty of the worst crime I could be accused of – poaching.'

Kerry frowned and said nothing for a few seconds. 'He did the same thing to Graham in South Africa. Costa's guy came for him but it wasn't enough just to kill him. Graham was in the process of being set up at Ukuphila, and Costa was going to make it look like Graham had been killed while trying to take a rhino horn. He did the same thing to you.'

'Why?'

'I don't know. Some twisted form of payback, I guess.'

The waitress came back to them and they ordered a selection of dumplings; meat and seafood for Eli and vegetarian for Kerry.

'You know, this plan of Sarah's to move Kwangela's rhinos to Mozambique is ludicrous,' said Eli.

Kerry nodded. 'Yes. She's dealing with a criminal in order to meet her fundraising target.'

'More than that,' Eli said, 'this whole business of moving animals from one country to another or to another continent is a waste of money.'

'Plenty of experts and good, generous people would argue that with you, Eli. History could very well show that the decision to move black rhinos from Zimbabwe to Australia in the 1980s saved the last of that country's rhinos. Also, another charity has

260

done great work bringing antelope and rhinos from Europe back to Africa. What do you think is needed?'

'More boots on the ground and more money.'

'Is it as simple as that?' she asked him.

'No, it's not simple, but it's winnable. The trade in rhino horn is finite, it's not endless, and not necessarily growing. If we had a surge we could cover more ground, gather more intelligence, and interdict more poachers coming into the Kruger Park and its surrounding reserves, which are home to the largest number of remaining wild rhinos.'

'Sounds like a military solution, the kind of thing your American generals pitched to successive presidents in the Middle East.'

'It is, kind of, but it's not just about guns and bullets. We need more for PR, strategic communications they call it these days, to take the fight to the enemy in their home countries, to change their behaviour. Warfare's not just about guns and bullets and tanks and bombs and fighter planes, it's asymmetrical. We fight for control of the minds of the enemy and their supporters, as well as targeting their troops on the ground.'

'I'm pleased to hear you say that,' she said, 'that it's not just about the war in the bush.'

'I'm not some crazy Rambo,' Eli said, holding her gaze. His intense look gave Kerry the feeling that he wanted her to be as passionate about his mission as he was. He wanted to enlist her.

'I don't think you're crazy.' She looked away from him.

'Something on your mind?'

'It's just . . . these past couple of weeks have been unbelievable. I was nearly killed, twice, but I can't get this place, this continent out of my head. And then Graham, well . . .'

'Graham's flaky.'

'That's one way of putting it.'

'Is there something going on between him and Sarah?' Eli asked.

Kerry shrugged. 'Something in the past, I gather, but he won't forgive her for going into business with Costa.'

'That Sarah knows what she wants and she'll do anything she can to get it.'

Kerry raised her eyebrows. '*Anything*? Like what?'

'Well, a gentleman wouldn't tell, but she's a woman who's not afraid to use any means, if you catch my drift.'

'Hey,' Kerry said, leaning back in her chair away from him, 'that's a big call, saying a woman would use sex to further her business interests.'

'I'm not saying there's anything wrong with that. What she does in or out of the bedroom is her business.'

Kerry closed the gap between them, lowering her voice to a conspiratorial level. 'You said she wanted to get into bed with you – business wise; did she also want to get into your pants, Eli Johnston?'

'Like I said, a gentleman doesn't tell.'

'Did you sleep with her?' she pushed.

He looked her in the eye. 'No.'

'I never knew there was this much scandal in the not-for-profit world,' she said.

'It's like any other business. People sleep with each other, fight with each other, try to get ahead of each other. In that respect it's just like the corporate world, I guess.'

'I'm not so sure about that,' Kerry said. 'But seriously, I see a lot of cooperation in the corporate sector. By contrast, I'm learning that the not-for-profit sector is more dog-eat-dog than Wall Street. I wonder if people get involved with charity work because of what it does for their personal worth, their status or even their ego, as much as their passion for the cause. What do you think, Eli?'

'I think I want to go back to the front line. There's more honesty out there in the bush.'

'I'm worried about Graham, Eli.'

He raised his eyebrows. 'You think he's gone off the reservation?'

'If by that you mean I wonder if he's gone a little crazy and is off on some crusade by himself, then yes. I'm worried he's going after Costa to try to keep the heat off you and me.'

Eli rubbed his chin. 'To tell you the truth I feel kind of bad that I dropped the ball in Mozambique when Graham and your dad went to rescue you.'

Kerry sagged a little in her chair. She was tired. 'I could really use a hand, if you'd be prepared to head back to Mozambique via the Kruger Park?'

He stared at her a few seconds, locking eyes. 'OK.'

Kerry smiled and waved to their waitress and asked for the bill. When she had paid, a gesture of thanks to Eli, they both went outside and she used her phone to book an Uber.

The driver dropped Eli at a Protea hotel and, as he made his way towards the breakwater where the Table Bay Hotel was situated, Kerry remembered Eli's earlier evasiveness about the drugging of the rhino. She was grateful he was coming with her, but she was still pretty sure he was hiding something.

Chapter 28

Graham was tired and hungover the next morning.

He had started drinking at Cape Town Airport, continued on the flight to Johannesburg's OR Tambo Airport, and then had taken a short break to find the cargo area and check on Nsele, the honey badger, who was clearly impatient to get to the bush. He'd organised some food for the poor creature, and had then gone to the Emperors Palace Casino complex near the airport. Graham had continued drinking steadily, alone, until he could barely stand, and had then gone to his room in the adjoining Metcourt hotel and passed out.

The guilt woke him, still half-inebriated, at four in the morning, and he could not get back to sleep. In his drunken stupor earlier he had almost talked himself out of the mission he was planning, but his resolve returned. Costa had tried to kill Kerry, Eli, Bruce and him because of what he had done. He needed to end this blood feud, one way or another. With his hand still shaking, from the drink or fear or both he took out his phone and opened the Twitter app.

It was ironic that Sarah had set up a Twitter account for him, in the hope he might post pictures and updates to excite would-be paying volunteers, for his next tweet was aimed at her. *I hereby resign as assistant veterinarian for Animals Without Borders in protest over their criminally negligent plan to build a rhino breeding facility in Mozambique.*

Graham posted the message. Emboldened now, he continued, updating his status, or whatever it was young people did on social media. *Taking some solo time out at Boulders Camp in Kruger for a few days. Just me. After that I'm going to bring down this crazy rhino scheme.*

'That should do it,' he said to himself.

He lay in bed, unable to get back to sleep. He had wronged Kerry, a beautiful young woman, but he told himself that he had made the right decision, letting her know he had no desire for her to try and stay in touch with him or follow him. He had been an arsehole for so long that the act came easily enough.

Graham hoped Sarah would let Costa know what he was up to. Boulders was a remote camp, not far from the Mozambique border. Costa had taken the loss of his brother personally, which was understandable, and Graham was counting on the gangster having enough machismo to come for him in person. If he couldn't kill Costa then he hoped the man's hunger for revenge might be sated with his death, and that he might lift his fatwa against Kerry, her father and Eli.

With a bit of luck Kerry would be on her way back to Australia by now. He felt guilty about falling for her and sleeping with her. Even as he came to realise how much he wanted her, intuitively knowing she represented a possibility of salvation, he felt at the same time he was betraying Carla. What right did he have to happiness when his negligence had caused the death of the only other woman he had ever truly loved? And if he loved Kerry, what right did he have to make her fall for a broken-down drunk?

The sadness he self-medicated away with drink and *dagga* and his stupid wisecracking ways was flooding him from within like water filling a sinking ship. He did not deserve to live. Kerry did not deserve to die for his mistake nor throw away her life on him. He could see no other options than a showdown; even if he took Kerry away, to the relative safety of Australia, Costa would have won and he would continue his pillaging of Africa's wildlife, albeit in a suit of respectability tailored for him by Sarah. He knew Sarah; she wasn't naive, which meant she was acting out of some darker motive.

Graham got up, showered, and, steeled with grim resolve, caught the shuttle bus to the airport. He and the honey badger both took the morning SA Express flight to Phalaborwa. At the tiny regional airport he stopped to fortify himself with a chicken salad, though a good portion of the meat went to a fluffy feline, which looked part African wildcat, that clawed at his leg and threatened to eat him if he didn't share his meal with it.

A baggage handler helped him load the honey badger into the back of his Land Rover.

Des Hennessy was expecting him in Hoedspruit, but not until tomorrow. He had arranged by email for Thandi and her boyfriend to drive his Defender from Hoedspruit to Phalaborwa without giving them the details of exactly what he was up to. The boyfriend would then take Thandi home in his car.

Graham drove the short distance to the Phalaborwa Gate entrance to the Kruger Park – the airport, like the town and the enormous copper mine that employed most of the town's workers, were right on the edge of the national park. He checked in at the gate office, showing his Wild Card yearly entry to the park and giving the reservation number for his accommodation.

'You are staying at Boulders Bush Lodge?' the young woman behind the computer at reception said.

'Yes.'

She raised her eyebrows. 'You are just one, for three nights?'

'Yes.' It was an unusual booking. Boulders, in the central northern section of the park, was a private camp, which meant that only one group, or in this case an individual, took over all of the accommodation. It could sleep twelve people, and while it was good value for money if that many people were staying, the cost was extravagant for only one person. 'I like my privacy.'

The truth was that when Graham had seen online that the camp was vacant – most likely because of a last-minute cancellation – he thought it would suit his needs perfectly. With no other tourists in residence there would be no collateral damage.

'Hmm,' said the woman, clearly thinking he was some kind of insane animal lover. Graham didn't care.

'I have a firearm,' he said to the woman.

'OK.'

It wasn't illegal, nor overly unusual, for private citizens to carry pistols in South Africa, though gun licences were becoming harder to obtain or renew. There was an established procedure for bringing a weapon into the park. Graham filled in the firearms register and produced his nine-millimetre Glock pistol, which Thandi had left in the central cubby box of his Land Rover. That was illegal – leaving the Glock unattended overnight – but being caught with an undeclared gun in his vehicle in the park would have resulted in his immediate arrest.

Graham removed the magazine from the pistol, cleared it, and handed it to the woman he was dealing with. She inspected it then threaded a short length of wire cable through the slide and the trigger guard and then crimped the free ends together with a lead seal. She then placed the pistol into a bag and used another wire tie and seal to close the bag.

When she was done the woman gave Graham his national parks entry permit and wished him a pleasant stay.

Graham went back out to his Land Rover and had a quick check through the rear window. He had covered the badger with a plastic tarpaulin he had in the back of the truck and placed his jacket and backpack against the travel cage. He got in the vehicle, started it and drove from the car park to the entry boom gate.

The security officer on duty at the gate used a handheld scanner to capture the details from his vehicle licence disc on the windscreen and Graham's driver's licence. Graham should have organised the transport and release of the badger into the park with the South African National Parks head veterinarian at Skukuza. The vet knew Nsele was coming, but the animal should still have been subjected to a check and the full public relations spectacle by Sarah and the park's PR people. Graham didn't want Sarah getting another opportunity to tell the press about her harebrained scheme in Mozambique and if he had his way it would never get off the ground.

In any case, Nsele was carrying no injuries nor any diseases so the check would have been a formality.

'You have a firearm?' the guard asked.

'Yes.' Graham showed the guard the sealed bag, which satisfied him the correct procedure had been followed.

'Can I check in the back of the vehicle, please?' the guard said.

'Sure.' Graham got out and unlocked the back door of the Land Rover. He felt his pulse pick up as the man stuck his head into the luggage area, but the guard missed the animal and handed his permit back to him.

Normally when he entered the park Graham felt an instant lessening of any tension or worries that were burdening him. It was, to him, a place of refuge and tranquillity. However, because of what was on his mind, and the rendezvous he was heading for, he couldn't feel that sense of serenity. He found his senses were heightened in another way.

As he cruised along the tar road through this part of the park it was almost as if he was seeing the bush and its inhabitants for the first time in his life, instead of the last.

The sky was impossibly blue, still unblemished by the clouds that would bring the rain any day now; the mopane trees were a lustrous, rich red gold that would turn emerald after the first storms. The earth beneath the trees was the colour of blood. In this part of the park the vegetation grew thick so game viewing was not as easy as on the more open, grassier areas to the south.

All the same he slowed and then stopped to watch a herd of elephants munching away. A big cow snapped off a branch and held one end with her trunk. She rotated the limb in her mouth, like a human chewing on a corn cob, as she stripped off the nutrient-rich bark.

Graham looked at the eye that faced him and marvelled at the long lashes, and the enviable peace and calm that this giant displayed. Her baby wandered about her legs, its own trunk an as-yet-untrained appendage that flopped this way and that.

Moved by the simple sighting of the elephants Graham checked his phone and, finding that he had signal, he called his friend Juan, in Mozambique. Juan answered and they exchanged greetings.

'Tell me, Juan, did you ever see that baby elephant again, the one Retief and I were chasing when he . . .' Graham swallowed the emotions that rose up unexpectedly, 'when the chopper went down?'

'As a matter of fact, we did, Graham,' Juan said. 'You wouldn't have seen this from the air, but it had a distinctive feature; its right ear had a rip in it – maybe a hyena or lion had tried to get it. He was a lucky little guy, two times over.'

'How so?' Graham asked.

'One of my guides saw it a couple of days after all that drama you had in Massingir. It was back with the herd; it seems one of the other cows in the family had decided to adopt it after all. It was feeding and looking strong.'

Graham wiped his eyes. 'That's *lekker*, Juan. Thanks.'

'You OK, *boet*?' Juan asked.

'I am, brother,' Graham said, returning the term of endearment.

'You still need to be careful of Costa, my friend.'

'You won't need to worry about him for much longer,' Graham said.

'What do you mean?'

'Let me worry about him. Goodbye, my friend.'

'Graham, are you –'

'Sorry, losing signal,' Graham lied, then ended the call.

He turned on the engine again and continued his journey. Maybe he was reluctant, even a little scared, but he took the time to stop again to look at a male impala. These antelopes were the most common mammal in the Kruger and nearly all but first-time visitors passed them by for the most part. Today Graham saw the healthy shine on the fur on its flank, and the light twinkling in the ram's dark eye.

Even if he wanted to, he couldn't turn back.

Graham crossed the broad Letaba River, pausing briefly to take in a crocodile basking in the sun. A row of wicked teeth protruded from its lower jaw. The reptile looked fat and lazy, but Graham knew that it could snap into action in a heartbeat.

He had stayed at Boulders once before, and the camp held the last of his fond memories, probably with the exception of his time with Kerry. The last time he had been in love and truly happy in life had been ten years earlier, at Boulders, and at Victoria Falls.

First he had to drive to Mopani Camp. This was the closest main rest camp to Boulders. A trio of *dagga* boys, the local nickname for mud-plastered, dangerous old male buffalos, glared at him as he turned off to Mopani and drove up the hill. He went through the thatched entry gates and pulled into reception, on the left.

In the office he presented his permit and booking confirmation and the woman behind the desk processed the paperwork.

'You know there is no shop or restaurant at Boulders?' she asked.

'Yes.'

'You can buy whatever you need here at Mopani.'

'Thank you.'

Graham took the woman's advice and drove through the camp to the store. He bought a couple of nights' food, a sixpack of beer and a bottle of brandy. He didn't want to get blind drunk, and although he had booked out the whole camp for three nights he did not expect to need food or drink for more than two.

Near the store was the camp's restaurant and bar, set on a wooden deck overlooking a dam. Graham took his paper bag of supplies and walked across to the railing.

Out over the dam a fish eagle cried to its lifelong mate, and it took Graham only a few seconds to pick out its snowy white head at the top of a dead tree on the far side of the dam. The other eagle soared across the dark blue sky and landed next to its mate. They both threw back their heads and called.

That sound had always uplifted Graham, like a welcome home, but now the birds' lilting cries just sounded painful, and left him feeling sad. He left the scene, trying to imprint the beauty of the dam on his mind forever as he walked to his Land Rover, got in, and started the engine.

From Mopani Camp he headed southwest towards Boulders. Near the Shipandani Hide he saw another massive crocodile and was again reminded of the impending danger he was heading into.

The route to Boulders took him down one side of the Mopani airstrip, used by national parks aircraft to access this part of the park. As he cruised along he picked up movement on the strip in his peripheral vision and stopped. A pack of seven wild dogs broke from the line of trees and started running down the strip. Graham put the truck into gear and accelerated to catch them.

271

As he drove, trying to keep one eye on the road, he saw the dogs moving into a practised formation. Ahead of them, for the first time, he saw an impala ram, running at full pace and occasionally leaping into the air.

One of the painted dogs, as they were also known, left the pack and veered left, towards him, and Graham eased off, not wanting the animal to inadvertently run into him, or vice versa. Across the other side of the gravel airstrip he saw another dog pushing to the right, into the bushes that lined the runway on the far side.

These two, Graham knew, would be the flankers, and they poured on the speed, moving either side of the impala and corralling him, preventing him from breaking left or right off the cleared ground.

The main body of dogs had split into groups of two and three. The first pair were chasing the impala while the other three lagged slightly behind.

Graham accelerated again to keep up with the hunt and wondered if the dogs would run out of runway before they caught the impala, which might stand a better chance of losing them in the thick bush. Just as it looked like the antelope might outrun them, the game changed. The three stragglers, who had been conserving their energy, sprinted past the lead two pursuers, who moved aside, adding extra security to the flanks.

The outriders circled in, and as the three-dog killer group finally caught the impala, the remainders formed a circle around it. The expert example of teamwork and choice of ground had sealed the ram's fate almost from the start. When the dogs all closed in Graham stopped and watched through his binoculars.

The prey of wild dogs, Graham knew, died of shock and massive blood loss and the impala was literally torn apart in front of his eyes in a spray of blood and hair. To many humans it seemed cruel and horrible, but Graham contrasted it to the way leopards killed – slowly suffocating their prey – or lions, whose kills were often drawn-out affairs, where the feeding began before the victim was even dead.

Graham lowered his binoculars, but raised them again when he caught sight of movement at the far end of the airstrip. Through the lenses he saw the loping, hunchbacked figures of four spotted hyenas. It wasn't unusual for them to trail a pack of wild dogs, waiting for Africa's most successful predators to bring something down and then use their superior bulk to chase them off the kill. Graham thought of Gina, whom he had patched up and was recovering nicely. He would miss her and the rest of her clan.

The hyenas, however, were too late. The dogs had left little more than bones and some raggedy skin. Faces bloodied and rallying each other with squeaking calls, they turned and ran at the hyenas. The two families danced around each other, the hyenas whooping and cackling and the dogs almost playing with their adversaries.

Graham moved on again. He wondered how his own hunt would end.

Chapter 29

Kerry wanted to get to where Graham was apparently staying, at Boulders Camp in the Kruger Park according to the tweet Eli had seen on his phone, as quickly as possible, but it was a busy time of the year and the direct flights from Cape Town to Skukuza Airport inside the park were fully booked.

Instead, she and Eli flew to Johannesburg the next morning and caught a connecting flight to Kruger Mpumalanga International Airport – KMIA – near White River. The flight landed on time at four-fifteen in the afternoon, but there was no way they could make it to Boulders Camp before the park gates closed.

Kerry had called her father, and Bruce and his new friend Tamara Shepherd were waiting for them in the cool, thatch-roofed terminal. The pair had been travelling together, sightseeing.

Eli went to the men's room and Tamara excused herself, after greeting them, to go and pay for her car parking ticket.

'What's with you and the nurse?' Kerry asked her father now that they were alone.

'Tammy. She's bonza, isn't she?'

Kerry felt uncomfortable seeing her father acting like an excited teenager. She felt a pang of loss for her mother, but that had been two years ago and as far as she knew her father hadn't dated anyone else since. 'No one's said "bonza" since 1952.'

'But you do like her, don't you?' he said.

'I hardly know her, Dad.'

He blinked a couple of times. 'It's important to me.'

'What is? Having sex, ten minutes after having a heart attack?'

He gave her his lopsided grin, and despite his grey hair and wrinkles she saw the forever-young eyes looking back at her. 'How do you know what we're getting up to? What I meant was that it's important to me that you don't mind.'

'I'm old enough not to mind you seeing another woman. I know men have needs.'

'I need love, Kez, that's all.'

She swallowed hard. 'We all do.'

He reached out and gently clasped her shoulder. 'You OK?'

'Yeah. No. I don't know.'

'Are you really sure you want to go after that lunatic drunken vet?'

'Yes, Dad.'

'You could find another bloke in a heartbeat, Kez.'

She sighed. 'Even if you're right, Dad, after everything that's happened I can't just go back to my job in Australia and pretend that this was all a dream, or a nightmare. There's a war going on here and no one back home even knows.'

He took a deep breath, then noisily exhaled. 'When I came back from Vietnam – hell, when I came back from Somalia, East Timor, Afghanistan, all of them – I had this feeling that no one in good old safe and predictable Australia had the first fucking idea of what was going on out there in the rest of the world, where I'd been.'

275

Her father, although a soldier, had rarely sworn around the house, and when he did she took notice. He wasn't prone to anger or abuse, but her mother had told them, when they were growing up, that sometimes their father needed space, to be left alone, and that it wasn't because he didn't love them or didn't want to be with them. He was not one to tell war stories, but she wondered, now that she had faced death and gunfire for the first time in her life, how he had been able to hold himself together so well and for so long.

'I think I know what you mean,' she said.

Bruce nodded. 'It's not easy, coming home, but you've got to, sometime.'

She remembered seeing a video of the Vietnam Veterans Welcome Home Parade, from back in 1987. She had been a toddler at the time, but she had a memory of seeing her father on the television screen a few times when the video was replayed, the camera momentarily focusing on him. *Why is Daddy crying?* she had asked her mother. 'Because he is now home,' her mother had answered.

Eli came to them and, perhaps sensing they were deep in conversation, offered to take their luggage trolley out to the car. He left them again.

'I know I have to go home at some point, Dad,' Kerry said, 'but what if home isn't Australia any more? What if it's here?'

Bruce ran a hand through his hair. 'I'm worried sick about you and this Mozambican madman who's trying to kill you, but it's why I'm here, Kerry. I'll take you to find Graham. I know that if I told you that you were crazy and I flew home to Australia you'd just carry on with this mission of yours alone. At least this way I can keep a bloody eye on you.'

She kissed him on the cheek. 'Thanks, Dad.' They walked, arm in arm, towards the terminal exit. 'But I don't want to cramp your style with your new girlfriend.'

He laughed. 'Tammy's got to go back to work on Friday, but she's due three days' leave first. We were talking about going into the Kruger Park anyway.'

'This might not be a holiday,' Kerry said.

They went outside and Tamara was already at the collection point with her Nissan X-Trail and Eli on board. Kerry and Bruce got in and Tamara drove, following signs to the Kruger Park's Numbi Gate.

'We're booked into Pretoriuskop for the night,' Tamara said. 'It's the closest camp to the gate.'

'So we can make it to Boulders tomorrow?' Kerry asked.

'*Ja*,' Tamara said, 'it's a very long drive, but we can do it if we leave early.'

Bruce looked over his shoulder from the front passenger seat. 'Kez, Graham might have just booked out that big camp all by himself because he wants some peace and quiet, not because he wants a bunch of Australians and Americans crashing his hermit's party.'

'And a South African,' Tamara weighed in. 'Actually, I'd love to go see Boulders Camp. It's very hard to get a booking there and it's the only place in the Kruger I've never stayed.'

That swung it for her father. Bruce, in the first flush of romance, would say or do anything to impress his new girlfriend. 'Well, I suppose the old goat wouldn't mind a bit of company,' he said.

From the airport the countryside went from hills covered with farms and timber plantations to sprawling settlements. Schoolchildren walked on the roadside and minibus taxis weaved unpredictably in and out of the traffic. Kerry checked her phone. 'Bloody hell.'

Eli, sitting next to her, craned his head to look at her screen. 'More irate tweets from Graham?'

'Yes,' she said.

'His Twitter account's crazier than Donald Trump's,' Eli said, 'and that's saying something.'

'I'm worried about him,' Kerry said. 'He seems to be goading Costa into doing something, to having another go at killing him. He's trying to publicly shame him, and Sarah in the process.'

'Costa deserves shaming,' Eli said. 'I'm more worried about you than I am Graham. He gave you some good advice when he told you to take care of yourself and stick with me.'

'Hear, hear,' said Bruce from the front.

*

The following morning Fidel Costa sat in the small but tastefully decorated circular waiting area of Skukuza Airport in the Kruger Park, fanning himself with his Panama hat. The irony of the fact that he could see a life-size statue of a rhino just outside the terminal was not lost on him.

Even more amusing to him was the knowledge that a good stone's throw away from where he sat was the Mission Area Joint Operations Centre – the headquarters of South Africa's war against poaching in the Kruger Park. And here he was, right under their noses, a respectable businessman turned philanthropist and head of an NGO established to conserve the rhino. He allowed himself a self-satisfied smile.

The Airlink Embraer from Cape Town landed and Fidel joined a troop of khaki and green–clad safari guides waiting to pick up their tourist clients.

'Welcome,' he said to Sarah Hoyland when she appeared.

'Great to be back in the park again,' she said.

Fidel took her carry-on bag from her as she went to the national parks reception desk to organise her entry permit into the park.

Sarah travelled light, with no check-in luggage, so once the paperwork was done they walked straight out to the car park where a black Range Rover with Mozambican plates sat idling, air conditioning on to stave off the sweltering heat.

Sarah paused and looked at the writing and logo on the side. '*This* is our official Animals Without Borders Rhino Conservation Centre vehicle? A Rangie? This costs more than most people's houses here.'

Fidel nodded. 'Yes, much more. And it's not the only vehicle. Rest assured, however, the others are Land Cruisers so not nearly as expensive.'

His driver opened the back door for them and they climbed in.

'You don't think this vehicle is maybe a tad ostentatious?' she asked.

'Of course,' he said. For all her time spent in Africa she still had much to learn.

'So why buy it – with our donated funds?'

'Your aim is to make the people who live in Mozambique feel a sense of ownership of the rhinos you are bringing to my country, yes?'

'Yes.'

'Then they need to see that the animals are worth it, in monetary value – that there is prosperity in conservation.'

'Fidel, pardon my Australian slang, but that is kind of fucked up.'

He laughed. 'That's one of the things I like about you, Sarah, you are not afraid to speak your mind. Let me explain.'

'I'm all ears.'

'I am the chairman of your new rhino facility and conservation program in Massingir, yes?'

'Yes.'

'That makes me a chief, of sorts.'

'That's one way to put it.'

'A chief commands – and deserves – respect. The people around him need to be reminded that he is in charge, and that he is successful. A vehicle like this shows people that I deserve respect, that there is money behind this project, and that, there-fore, there is value in keeping rhinos alive.'

'Whatever.'

He felt she was being dismissive of him, but he didn't mind too much. She didn't understand the relationship he had with his constituency, with his people. Outsiders, non-Africans, often wondered why so many people in African countries who lived in abject poverty did not rise up in anger and revolution when they saw their elected leaders living in big houses, driving expensive cars and even flying in luxury jets. Politics and power meant wealth in Africa – Fidel Costa was living proof of it – and the average man on the street in Massingir aspired to a better life. It was how Fidel recruited, how he extended his patronage and shored up his web of support in the police, bureaucracy, and in the local business community – with money.

'I've seen you all over the internet,' he said, 'announcing our joint venture. There's been some opposition to it, quite a bit from Graham Baird.'

Sarah nodded. 'But mostly the coverage is good. Donors outside of Africa like the idea of uplifting local communities by giving people ownership of their wildlife.'

'Most of my constituents have never seen a rhino, let alone wanted to own one,' he said.

'True, but when they see the money rolling in to build the breeding sanctuary, and the dollars coming from tourism, they'll become instant experts. You have to spread the wealth around, Fidel.'

He held back the retort that instinctively formed on his lips. 'I hear you.'

'I'm worried about Graham.'

'I wouldn't have thought someone like him even knew what Twitter was. Also, I'm surprised he can even get phone reception at Boulders Camp.'

Sarah took her phone out, switched it on and waited while it connected to the local network on roaming. 'Bloody hell, Graham's tweeting again.'

'What is he saying now?'

Sarah frowned. 'He says, "*#dealwiththedevil – Animals Without Borders charity is sleeping with Moz's number 1 rhino poacher*".'

'He doesn't mention me by name?' Fidel asked.

'No, not yet. I'm just scrolling through his earlier tweets.'

'He's trying to provoke me,' Fidel said.

'Graham's posted some pics of where he is – a view of yesterday's sunset from the deck at Boulders Camp, another that show his feet and the waterhole below. He says in another tweet he's in heaven, with the camp all to himself.' Sarah tapped her phone's screen with two fingers.

'What are you writing?'

'I'm drowning him out,' she said. 'Every time he uses our twitter handle his tweets are seen by my supporters. Fuck him. I'm not going to have him cost us money or followers. And what the bloody hell has he done with my honey badger?'

Fidel settled in to the leather of the Range Rover's seat and took two small bottles of water from the chilled cubby box. He placed one by Sarah's thigh, then leaned a little closer and put his hand on her knee.

She glanced at him, then nodded to the driver in front.

'Roberto is my trusted man. He knows to keep his mouth shut,' Fidel looked up, to the driver's rear-view mirror, 'and his eyes on the road.'

Sarah's phone beeped.

'He's just instant-messaged me,' she said. 'He's seen me tweeting, I bet.'

'And?'

'He says: "*Welcome back to the lowveld. When you see Costa tell him he'll be seeing his little brother soon.*"'

'Bastard.'

'He's definitely goading you,' Sarah said.

'Yes. He killed my younger brother, the only other surviving member of my immediate family.'

'I seem to remember your brother was a poacher, and either he or one of his comrades shot down the helicopter Graham was in, killed the pilot, and tried to kill Baird as well.'

Costa knew the woman was right, but there was more to this. 'My brother, Inâcio, was the baby of our family. My mother had him during the last days of the war, before she . . .'

Sarah put a hand on his, which was still on her knee, and clasped it.

'Before she was killed by the RENAMO rebels. I was a fighter, I had survived the war, but my father had been shot years before and my sister was also dead. I raised Inâcio myself until I married. He was my brother, but in this strange way he was also like my son. I wanted the best for him, better than I had, but he always wanted to be like me, and that is my shame. That is how he came to die.'

'He chose his own path, Fidel.'

He moved his hand out from under hers and made a fist that he pounded into his own leg. 'Yes, he chose the path of the hunter, but he died like an animal. Do you know how Baird killed him?'

The woman shook her head.

'He shot him with a dart full of M99, you know, the opiate they use to drug big game.'

Sarah put a hand to her mouth. 'Oh no.'

'Yes. He had his bag of drugs in the helicopter. Inâcio was not even unconscious. That stuff, it just immobilises the animals. They can see, hear, smell all that is around them, they just cannot move.'

Fidel screwed his eyes shut. He had been through this, over and over, imagining the death of his brother. It must have been, he thought, like the stories the Jesuits had told him of people in the old times, in Europe, who had been mistaken for dead and buried alive, perhaps in a coma, only to wake up and find themselves entombed, waiting to die. He pictured Inâcio seeing the chaos of the crash and the gunfight around him, of feeling the painful prick of the dart. Perhaps his brother knew what had happened and was waiting, hoping, mentally begging the veterinarian to come and reverse the effects of the poison seeping through his body.

Sarah said nothing, her mind perhaps processing the same gruesome thoughts.

'Baird did nothing. He could have given him the same drug they give to heroin addicts, to reverse the effect of an overdose. The veterinarians all carry that. But he didn't. He chose to stand there and watch, and wait, as another *filthy poacher* died in front of his eyes.'

'It's brutal, I'll admit,' Sarah said.

Fidel slapped his hand on the leather of the seat between them. 'It is an insult.'

Sarah went back to her phone.

'What is it?'

She passed him her phone. Sarah had switched to her own Twitter page. He read the latest tweet from Baird aloud.

'"*I repeat I am hereby resigning from my position as assistant veterinarian for Animals Without Borders. They have signed a deal with a poaching kingpin and the charity is guilty of wasting supporters' funds.*"'

'He's overstating his own importance – he was only ever a back-up vet, but his number of followers has increased from virtually none to a couple of hundred already. Soon the bloody mainstream media will be on to this.' Sarah snatched the phone back from Fidel and spoke the words of the tweet she was composing as she tapped the screen. '"*Graham Baird complains of us wasting supporters' money while he drank the minibar dry during his recent visit to Cape Town in the hotel where we put him up!"'*

'This war of words is futile,' Fidel said. 'Baird is a liability. He needs to be struck off your balance sheet.'

'Just wait until the cyber media world finds out what a philandering old drunken bum he really is. I know where plenty of his skeletons are locked.'

'Yes, just as you know some of my skeletons, I imagine,' Fidel said.

She looked at him. 'I know your background, Fidel, and I'm taking you at your word that you're going to give up poaching, that you've been converted.'

He met her eyes. 'The loss of my brother still weighs heavily on my heart.'

'I want to believe you're sincere. But the fact is that you have the clout to get the rhino breeding facility off the ground in Mozambique, and a reputation fierce enough to make sure no other poachers try to get their hands on our rhinos once people know they are under your care.'

He brought his hands together as if in prayer. 'I am no saint.'

'Oh, I know that, but if you stick with me I'll use Facebook, Twitter and Instagram to make you one, Fidel.' She paused. 'What do we do about Graham Baird?'

Fidel tapped his fingers together. 'He is one stupid, washed-out old man. However, he is a threat to our venture. People, the media and politicians, listen to veterinarians. He has the potential to cause us harm, but equally important to me is that he deserves to die for what he did to my family. He has advertised to us and the world that he is alone in the middle of the Kruger Park. Of course, he could be setting a trap. You know him; what do you think?'

Sarah wasn't sure what to think, but what she knew was that

there was no way she was going to let Graham Baird scuttle this deal. The planned Mozambican rhino sanctuary was worth millions of dollars, over its life, to Animals Without Borders and that equated to hundreds of thousands for her.

But it wasn't just about money. She genuinely wanted to protect the rhinos. Also, Sarah secretly believed the rhinos could be a sustainable source of income for all them – the charity, her and Fidel – if and when the international trade in rhino horn was legalised. In the conservation-based NGO circles she moved in those in the pro-trade lobby, who wanted the sale and export of rhino horn to be legalised, were the enemy. Sarah couldn't wear her beliefs on her sleeve, but it was her view that giving rhino horn a legitimate market value was the only way to ensure the species' survival.

She was under no illusion that Fidel had experienced some kind of epiphany and was doing this for the right reasons. She knew she was doing a deal with the devil, but she also believed she could control Costa. He knew of her views on trade and she had obliquely hinted that until the market was legalised there would still be back-door routes for harvesting rhino horn and getting it out of Mozambique. That had played to Costa's lust for money and she was well aware of his other desires. It was plain he wanted to sleep with her. She would use any weapon at her disposal to hold him to this deal and keep him following her agenda.

What she hadn't factored on, in all her behind the scenes negotiations, was Graham becoming embroiled in all this by killing Costa's brother.

'I think Graham really is there by himself. He's a romantic at heart and I think he wants to take you on, man to man. It was a mistake for you to target Kerry, her father and Johnston.'

'Who said I did?'

She smiled, but let it rest. 'All I'm saying is that Graham is probably advertising where he is in the hope that you will do something to get rid of him, and perhaps consider the ledger wiped clean as far as the others go.'

Costa made no reply, but she knew he was mulling over the proposition. She did not want Graham dead, but nor could she afford his bleating.

'It is like he has a death wish,' Costa said.

'Graham's messed up because he's carrying too much grief in his life. His wife died ten years ago and he never got over it. I think he's sick of his guilt, tired of living.'

'Well,' Costa smoothed his moustache, 'maybe I can help him.'

Sarah closed her eyes and settled into the soft leather of the luxurious seat. She was pretending to be tired, but in reality her heart was thumping as the reality of what she was setting in motion pumped through her body like a dose of venom.

Chapter 30

L uiz, Fidel Costa's master tracker, stopped and tilted his head, listening to the sounds of the night.

A tiny Scops owl chirped to its mate, and somewhere far off a lion gave a low and wheezy call. One did not have to roar loudly to scare.

The team of seven men behind him were young, keen and inexperienced. More and more men from the villages around Massingir where Fidel had drawn his recruits were failing to return from the cross-border forays into South Africa. Sometimes the men were arrested and sent to prison, but more often than not their bodies were returned to Mozambique for burial. Fidel's recruits, like his late brother, were getting younger and less experienced by the day.

This was a big group, many more men than Fidel would have sent to hunt rhino. Perhaps it was because he knew these troops were so inexperienced that Fidel wanted to send a small army to take out one man.

Luiz had heard from Fidel how he would be changing his money-making strategy. Now he would rob in a different way, taking money donated by people from as far afield as America, Europe, Australia and even Asia, to put rhinos in a compound and breed them, like cattle.

He tutted, once more ridiculing the idea.

Luiz was a hunter, not a farmer, and it irked him that his boss had taken to acting like a woman or a peasant, feeding and watering animals instead of tracking them down and killing them.

Oh, there was money to be made, of that Luiz was sure. For if there was one thing Fidel loved more than stalking and shooting, or running a pack of dogs, it was making money. The ideals of the revolution counted for nothing. Fidel had been Luiz's commander during the war, when their quarry had been the capitalist dogs of RENAMO. The hated opposition were the puppets of the South Africans and, before them, the Rhodesians. The whites in turn were in thrall to the American imperialists.

Luiz hadn't really believed all the Cold War rhetoric. Communism, capitalism, socialism, they were all the same to him. They were ideas used to dress up or to camouflage the real business of life – hunting, killing, surviving. Luiz was a survivor. It was no accident that he was alive and so many young men from the villages were dead.

Luiz knew not only how to hunt, but how to hide. He could tie on his old shoes so that his feet were on top of the shoes, but facing back to front so that when he left the scene of a hunt it looked like he had been walking towards it. When hunting elephant he had hacked off the spongy footpads of one of the big beasts and, together with a shooter, they had tramped away from the scene of their crime, one in front of the other, moving their legs as an elephant would have. His feet had squished sickeningly in the blood and fat, but he had survived.

The men behind him made too much noise, with their incessant whispered bravado, and he smelled their tobacco, their *dagga* and their soap. They were chirping like guinea fowl, which the Shangaan called 'cackling women'.

'Be quiet,' he hissed to them. For a moment the youngsters were silent, but it would not be for long.

They had to be extra careful tonight, for their quarry was a man. Hunting humans, Luiz knew from his time in the civil war, was the most difficult of all tasks. An animal was predictable; Luiz knew where a rhino would go to drink or wallow, and what it would do if it detected its pursuers, most often by sound rather than sight.

A lion would flee, if it saw you first, but if you cornered it the cat would charge. Elephants rested in the shade of tall trees during the heat of the day, and would move more at night. A tracker could use these predictable traits to his advantage. But hunting men was different.

A man had a brain, and that made him unpredictable. Fidel had told them that the veterinarian, Baird, who had murdered Costa's brother, was holed up in the Kruger Park in the camp they called Boulders. He was alone in that big, rambling modernistic lodge that Luiz had seen once, while tracking a rhino that was heading for the camp's pumped waterhole.

That made no sense.

Baird had advertised his presence and Fidel had ordered Luiz and his team to go into the Kruger and kill the South African.

'*Comandante*, this is an ambush,' Luiz had said to Fidel.

'No,' his boss had replied, 'this is assisted suicide. Baird is taunting me, asking me to come and kill him, and I am complying. You know I have eyes and ears inside the national park?'

'*Sim.*' Luiz had nodded. It was true. There was a traffic policeman – the South African National Parks actually employed such people to set up speed traps and police the speed limits in the game reserve – who had been entertained in Maputo by Fidel on a number of occasions. The man had family and a mistress in Mozambique and, Luiz guessed, a growing bank account waiting for him when he chose to retire with his girlfriend.

'Baird travelled alone. There are no military or national parks patrols in the area around Boulders. No one is waiting for you. Go. Kill him. You will be rewarded, Luiz.'

And so Luiz had crossed the border, as he had done a hundred times before, but this time he was not in search of a rhino horn, but rather the head of a man.

Fidel had told Luiz the money would continue to flow, even after he set up his rhino breeding program with the woman from Australia and her benefactors' funding. But for that to happen Baird needed to go. The man threatened the whole project and, of course, there was the debt of blood to be paid.

'We are going to stop hunting wild rhino,' Fidel had said to him, 'for a little while, at least.'

Luiz had been surprised. 'You are going straight?'

Fidel had laughed. 'No, but I need to make it look like it. I cannot have any men, like yourself, who are so closely linked to me, caught poaching. In time, this rhino breeding centre will make us money, Luiz. We can drip-feed horns that we harvest to the Vietnamese. One day international trade in horns may be legal, but in the meantime we can corner the market.'

Luiz had shaken his head. 'I have bills to pay, women who rely on my money as much as my manhood. You are wealthy, *Comandante*, I am a soldier. I can't afford to wait for this scheme to start paying.'

'Are you disobeying an order, Luiz? You have been like an uncle to me.'

'I think this plan is a mistake,' Luiz had said.

They had left it at that. Fidel was clearly not happy that Luiz had not simply rolled over, like a dog, and accepted a change in their way of life. He would do this task for Fidel, kill the South

African, Baird, but he was not ready to hang up his rifle just yet, not even for Fidel.

Luiz came to a *koppie*, a giant child's pyramid of smooth red granite marbles balanced precariously on top of each other. Luiz told his young clucking chickens to wait while he climbed to the top. He felt the effort in his old heart and stiff limbs, but kept a watch in the moonlight for the adder or the mamba that might live in the rocks, still a little warm to the touch from the day's sun.

Once at the top, careful not to be silhouetted against the moonlit sky, he looked around. He saw the floodlight that illuminated the waterhole in front of Boulders Camp. A bull elephant was reflected in the silvery surface and Luiz heard it guzzling water. A fire flickered in the *braai* area.

Luiz felt his heart quicken at the prospect of the hunt, yet at the same time the blood that pumped forth chilled him to his core. He took out the satellite phone Fidel had given him, flipped up the antenna and waited for it to acquire a signal. When it did he sent an SMS to the only number Fidel had programmed into the phone.

Ready.

*

Graham fed the genet, even though it was against national park regulations.

The sleek, spotted cat-like creature had been his only companion for the past two evenings. Graham had politely, but firmly, told the attendant on duty at Boulders Bush Lodge – there were normally two but one was on leave – that he did not want to see him during his stay. He told the man he would do his own dishes, make his own bed and tidy up around the lodge. He reinforced his requirement for privacy with a two-hundred-rand tip in advance.

Graham could normally not abide people who fed wild animals. When monkeys, baboons, hyenas and even birds became dependent on humans for food they turned into problem animals. More often than not the creatures' scavenging habits led to them being shot.

The genet wolfed down the morsel of cooked *boerewors* that Graham had sliced off for it. He took half of the rest of the sausage from the *braai* grid and slid it onto his plate.

Graham wondered if Costa's men would come.

He doubted the gangster would come in person to finish him off. Costa had a reputation as a man of action during the Mozambican civil war – at least that was what his politician's backstory maintained – but he was no fool. It was one thing for him to come to Hoedspruit to oversee Graham's demise, but another for him to go wandering about the Kruger Park in the middle of the night.

It was quiet, save for the sizzle of the remnants of *wors* fat on the coals and a Scops owl calling nearby. The big bull elephant had finished his last slurp of water and had disappeared noiselessly into the mopane trees. It never ceased to amaze Graham how quiet these giant creatures could be when moving through the bush.

He ate from the plate on his lap, washing down the strong farmer's sausage with rationed mouthfuls of one of the two beers he had allowed himself for this evening.

It was eerie being in the camp alone. Boulders was a relatively new camp for the Kruger Park, having been built in the 1980s with funds from big business. As its name inferred it was built in among a series of granite *koppies*, elevated a few metres above ground level.

The camp had the air of a businessman's retreat; its finishes and design were more contemporary and luxurious than standard national parks accommodation in other rest camps, and the communal dining area was dominated by a long wooden-topped bar. Graham could picture nefarious negotiations and big deals being sealed during the apartheid era over brandies and Cokes at that bar.

In the well-appointed kitchen off the dining room were two fridges and an oven. The camp ran on solar power, which generated enough electricity to keep the lights going all night, including the floodlight out at the waterhole.

A timbered walkway linked the dining-cum-kitchen area with the four single-room accommodation units and one with two bedrooms, all strung out in a line amid the rocky outcrops, discreetly spaced apart. Four of the units looked out over the floodlit waterhole in the centre of a natural depression surrounded by mopane trees. One unit faced rearwards.

Where Graham sat, between the communal area and the first sleeping unit, there was an outdoor fireplace and *braai*, also lit by a solar-powered floodlight. Barred steel doors isolated the elevated walkway and units from the car park underneath the raised dining area. Graham had found a padlock and secured the door so that if anyone did try and storm the stairs from below they would be locked out. It wasn't much of a defence – the walkway and accommodation units could be reached by someone scaling the boulders – but it might give him some slim advantage.

Graham finished eating, swigged some more beer and looked up at the night sky. It was breathtaking, as had been the sunset off to his left, which he'd viewed from the dining area deck.

Darkness had brought a change in the wind direction and on the light, slightly chilly breeze came the scent of death from out near the big baobab tree that sat atop an island of red rocks.

A spotted hyena whooped long and low from the same direction. Graham had spied vultures in the baobab and other trees out that way, before sunset, so he assumed a kill had been made some time in the last few days.

Perhaps he had misjudged Costa, but he didn't think so.

To his right, in the east, were the Lebombo Hills that marked the border between South Africa and Mozambique. Most of the rhinos in the Kruger Park were located in the southern and central sections of the reserve, so Graham was betting on Costa's gang being able to make it across the border there without being detected.

He was sick of running.

Graham took the nine-millimetre pistol from the waistband of his shorts and set it on the table beside him. He had snipped off the security wire and seal that the woman had placed on his pistol at Phalaborwa Gate and unloaded, cleaned and reloaded the weapon several times, more for reassurance than anything else. If he left the park and the firearm was checked he would be in serious trouble and liable for prosecution. That, however, was all academic to him, as he had no reason to think he would be leaving the Kruger Park alive.

As well as the pistol he had taken a machete from the back of his Land Rover, and he had a hunting knife that had been left in the cubby box.

Graham finished his beer and left the dinner plate out for the genet to lick clean. He walked along the boardwalk to the first accommodation unit, opened the front door and the internal screen door and turned on the lights inside, then walked back to the communal area and turned off all the other outside lights.

Anyone watching would expect him to go to his unit, perhaps read for a while or have another drink before going to sleep. Graham walked back to the room, opened the front door and left it ajar, but slammed the screen door closed.

*

'I said be quiet,' Luiz whispered to the men behind them.

'Relax, old man,' said Julio, one of the gunmen, whose chunky gold necklace glittered in the moonlight. 'It is just one man we are hunting, right? And he is almost as ancient as you.'

Another snickered.

'If you are so certain of yourself, Julio, then you take the lead. There is no need for me to track any more, you can see the camp, see the floodlight. Are you man enough to take the point, and to go into battle first?'

The youth puffed his chest out and stared Luiz in the eye. 'Of course I am, especially if you, the great Luiz, have lost your nerve after all these years.'

Luiz said nothing. Julio moved past him, taking the lead and, for the first time since they had crossed the border from Mozambique, the youth brought his AK-47 up into his shoulder and looked alert. Luiz would see how long the young pup could maintain his concentration before he lapsed into his lazy ways. Such a boy would not have lasted a day in combat against RENAMO.

Luiz took up a position in the middle of the group of men, where he could better exercise command and control once the shooting began. He raised his nose and smelled the kill. The hyena called again.

'They frighten me,' said the boy behind him.

Luiz turned to him. 'Nothing to worry about, especially if the animal is calling. It is telling you, and any other creatures in the night, that it is here.'

'Is it true that witches ride on their backs?'

'Yes, that is true, Armando, but that AK in your hands is more than a match for any witch.' Luiz clapped Armando on the arm. He was a good boy, who should have been at university, but his parents were dead, both killed by the virus.

Luiz clicked his fingers. Julio turned back to him.

What now? the whelp mouthed.

'Slowly, slowly,' Luiz whispered back.

Julio scoffed at him and carried on, head high.

Luiz had seen the lone figure in the distance, turning off the exterior lights at the camp then retiring to his accommodation. The light was still on in the room.

'Approach from the rear, Julio, circle around the *koppies*,' he said.

Julio looked back again. 'Of course we will go in from behind. I am not so stupid as to advance over the open ground at the front where the waterhole is lit and the man will be watching for game. That would be too obvious.'

Luiz nodded. Yes, far too obvious.

*

Dave Corlett was reading a paperback by the light of a desk lamp in the Mission Area Joint Operations Command at Skukuza Airport, far to the south of Boulders Camp. The MAJOC was the headquarters for the combined South African National Parks, police and military effort against rhino poaching in the park.

Dave was performing one of his honorary ranger duties by spending a Saturday night manning the telephones in the nerve centre. Honorary rangers needed to do a certain number of duties per year to stay current. These could range from such necessarily mundane activities as picking up rubbish in the Kruger Park or checking visitors' permits and bookings to clearing snares in the bush or even taking paying guests on guided walks in big five country. Pulling a night shift in the MAJOC might have sounded glamorous to some, but in reality it was hours of boredom punctuated by the odd moment of excitement. He yawned and contemplated making a third cup of coffee.

The phone rang.

'Poaching hotline, hello.'

'Good evening. I will dispense with the pleasantries as I am calling about a crime that I believe is about to be committed.'

'Go on.' Dave slid the message pad across the desk and clicked his ballpoint pen.

'My name is Fidel Costa. I am a concerned citizen and elected representative of the people in the town of Massingir in Mozambique. I am in South Africa on important business relating to my charity work. I wish to report a possible armed incursion of poachers from my country into yours.'

Dave wrote down the name. It was familiar. He'd read it some-where, just recently, maybe on Facebook.

'Yes, Mr Costa, I'm listening.'

'One of my constituents, a woman, came to me just now and said she believes her son is part of a gang inside the Kruger Park who are planning to attack and rob one of the park's camps, as well as hunting rhinos.'

Dave licked his lips. 'Which camp?'

'The Boulder, or something like that; she was not sure of the name, and while I am an ardent conservationist and concerned for the plight of rhinos, I do not know all of the camps in the Kruger.'

'Boulders?'

'Yes, that was it,' the voice, Costa, said. 'The gang – they are all armed – left yesterday, according to the woman. They could be at your camp by now. She is most concerned about her son.'

'Thank you, Mr Costa. Now, if I can just get some more details please, I need –'

'Hello? Hello? The signal here is not good. I cannot hear you.'

'Hello?' Dave said. The call ended.

Dave was worried. With the war on rhino poaching having been fought for several years now, the unspoken fear of the security forces and national parks was that innocent civilians – tourists – might one day get caught up in the armed conflict between poachers and anti-poaching forces. Now it seemed even worse – a gang of armed poachers deliberately setting out to hit a national parks camp.

Dave sounded the alarm.

Within minutes the operations room had been stood up, with high-ranking rangers, police and military people roused from their beds. Outside, in the dark, came the whine of a jet turbine engine as a national parks helicopter's blades began to turn. A rapid reaction force of armed rangers was running for the aircraft.

Dave said a silent prayer that he hadn't set all this in motion for nothing, and that if the threat was real the reaction force would get to Boulders, in the far north of the park, before anyone was hurt.

Phones were ringing around him. He was given a job by his superior, to call Mopani Camp, the nearest rest camp to Boulders, and find out the number and names of all guests and staff staying at Boulders Camp. Already another parks ranger was on the radio, trying to raise the camp itself.

'Baird, you say? Bravo-Alpha-India-Romeo-Delta?' Dave asked the duty manager at Mopani Rest Camp.

'Yes,' the sleepy-sounding woman said, 'first name, Graham.'

'I know him. Thanks.'

Dave hung up and reported to the senior person on duty, an army colonel.

'There's only one guest staying at Boulders Camp, and it turns out I know him. He's a neighbour of sorts, a vet from Hoedspruit. I've got his number.'

'Then try him,' the colonel ordered. 'Phone signal in that part of the park is *kak*, but if you can get hold of him, tell him there's a load of shit heading his way.'

Dave took out his mobile phone and found Graham's number. As he tried to get through he said a silent prayer for his sometime golfing friend, and for the team that was flying into battle.

Chapter 31

The genet stayed close to Graham, hiding in the rocks, but occasionally raised its face above the parapet and sniffed the air, wondering if the human had another morsel of food he was willing to share.

After returning to his room and loudly closing the door, Graham had climbed down over the balcony railing onto the rocks below, and lowered himself to the ground. He had picked his way quietly, carefully, between the boulders and made his way up into the *koppies* behind the camp to a position where he could look down on the buildings and the walkway that linked them.

Graham heard a noise, rapid footfalls on wooden decking. He raised the nine-millimetre pistol and swung his aim to the path between the first and second accommodation units.

He drew a breath.

Then exhaled. 'Nsele.'

It was the honey badger he had released on the first day he had arrived at Boulders. It was back.

When he first opened the travel cage there had been an explosion of black and white fur and a maniacal growling and hissing as the honey badger, angry and frustrated at being cooped up so long, had erupted from its tiny prison. For a moment Graham had thought the wee but ferocious beastie was going to turn on him, and had jumped out of the way and up onto a nearby outcrop to escape the teeth and claws. But Nsele had shaken his head imperiously and scampered off, not to be seen again until now.

Graham watched the way he trotted along the walkway, head up, not caring about the noise he made. Honey badgers had the attitude of a black rhino in heat trapped in a body the size of a spaniel.

Nsele turned off the path and leapt up the steps to the fire pit and *braai* area. He jumped up onto the brickwork beside the barbeque and leaned over until he could lick the *braai* grid. Even though it still would have been too hot to touch, Nsele cleaned the remnants of sausage fat off the grid. Unsatisfied, he jumped back down and took to the walkway again in search of more food.

Beside him the genet took fright at the sight of one of nature's most aggressive little carnivores and bounded up higher and further into the fortified safety of the rocky hilltop.

'Go away,' Graham hissed at the badger.

Nsele raised his face to him, his downturned mouth looking confused. The poor thing had been around humans all its life – and spent a good part of that trying to escape from its enforced prison – and now here it was, still dependent on people. Graham felt sorry for it, and ashamed that he had fed the genet. He despaired of a world in which people killed each other and magnificent animals for something as stupid as rhino horn.

Nsele growled and hopped, all four paws off the ground as he turned within his own body length. The hairs on his back rose up, as did his tail. He was instantly alert over something. He trotted away from Graham, along the walkway.

Graham looked past Nsele and saw the first of the armed men heading, predictably, around the *koppies* on the ground below him, towards the one rear-facing suite.

He moved, as slowly and quietly as he could, until he could better see all seven of the men moving beneath, through a passage between two clusters of boulders. There was enough light from the moon for him to get a look at them.

The first man looked alert enough, youngish, wide-eyed, his AK-47 raised and ready. The second was older, with a tight cap of grey curls. His head never stopped moving, eyes scanning left and right, up and down. Graham melded his silhouette closer to the rocks in response. The third man was the opposite; he watched his feet, perhaps fearful of tripping over. The others trudged on, even less alert.

Graham switched his gaze back to the older man. He recognised him, his hair and his lean, muscled gait. It was the man who had fled from the scene of the chopper crash and who had later beaten him up in the prison cell in Massingir, just before Capitão Alfredo had intervened. Luiz was what the captain had called him. He would be the ringleader of this little circus, an experienced killer.

The role of the last of the seven was to cover their rear and he was doing a reasonable job of it. Every few steps he would stop and survey the trail in the direction they had just come, swinging his assault rifle in a one hundred and eighty degree arc. Graham watched and waited. The man bringing up the rear was excited, perhaps, by the promise of imminent action, because the delays between checking behind him were getting longer; he was too interested in what was ahead.

Graham clambered down from the rocks, timing his climb to arrive at ground level just as the small column of poachers passed him by. These men, he told himself, were here for one reason and one reason only: to kill him. He slid between two smooth granite monoliths and held his breath as the first and second men walked by.

The third man was picking his nose with his free hand; the rifle in his other was pointed down. He was close to the older man. Four, five and six were bunched together in a tight group, but seven, sweeping the rear, was a few lengths back from the others.

The young man had just completed a check behind him when he came abreast of Graham, who looked skywards, composed the briefest of prayers for forgiveness, and stepped out from between the rocks. He clamped his left hand around the man's mouth, hard and fast, drew him back into the crevice and slid the bone-handled hunting knife up under the man's ribcage and into his heart. He held the shuddering body, felt the hot wetness flood down over his hand and forearm, and kept the man silent until he died.

Shaking, Graham tried to calm the tremor that passed through his own body. Peeking around the edge of the boulder, he watched as the poachers moved on and the next man in line, who had been second from last in the group, failed to look back and check on the tail end man, as he should have.

Graham took the dead man's AK-47 and searched his body. He removed a satchel bag containing two spare magazines of ammunition for the rifle and a loaf of *pão*, Portuguese bread, from around the man's neck and looped it over his own. In the side pocket of the poacher's cargo pants was a hand grenade. Graham transferred that to his own pocket and climbed back up into his eyrie.

Below him the poachers kept moving. None of them had noticed that the man at the rear was missing, but they would, eventually.

Graham moved up and over the rocks, back towards the lodge, and could see the lead man approaching the rear-facing unit. He thought back to his military service. Like all conscripts he had gone through basic infantry training.

He now had an assault rifle, which could be fired on full automatic, like a machine gun. He needed to be able to employ it as an automatic weapon, to maximum effect, if he was going to stand any chance.

Graham paused, just as his quarries stopped, to assess the situation.

He had just told himself that he wanted to stand a chance.

Graham had come to Boulders, deliberately taunting Costa, because he fully expected to die. There had been times over the years since his wife, Carla, had died, that he'd felt like he wanted to disappear from this life, to end it all. He had felt that way on the flight back from Cape Town.

On the drive to the camp, however, he'd had mixed emotions. He had taken in the colours around him, the elephant's eyes, the simple beauty of the impala, because he thought it was the last time he would see them, but the truth was that these, too, were the things he lived for. Despite his cynicism and disgust at so much of what he saw around him on a day-to-day basis, he lived to care for the animals, birds and reptiles that could not save themselves. He existed for the love of nature.

The men who knelt in the darkness lived for the promise of money, and that cash came from destroying all that Graham held sacred.

He might – probably would – die tonight, but he would take as many of these bastards with him as he could. Graham removed the magazine from the rifle, checked it was full and that there was a round already chambered, and prepared for battle.

*

Nsele jumped down from the *braai* grid. It was his second attempt at finding food on the hot metal grill and it had failed. He was not happy.

303

He raised his face to the night sky and sniffed the air. He caught new scents on the soft breeze. Men.

Nsele tramped along the wooden walkway, squeezed through a couple of railings and jumped down onto a smooth boulder to investigate. He paused, looking, listening and sniffing.

There they were.

He saw them, crouched in the shadows cast by the moon. He sensed danger, remembered it from long ago. Just as he had all those years ago, when he had been little more than a cub, he recognised the weapons in their hands, remembered the boom of gunshots, the pain of the dart.

He needed to get away from these humans – and he still needed more food. Nsele looked around and saw that there was one room with a light on. The solid wooden door to the room was open, with just a screen door barring his way in. He could open that, easy.

Nsele growled.

*

'What was that?' Julio whispered. 'A lion?'

Luiz cocked his head. 'No, don't be stupid. Have you ever even heard a lion?'

Julio looked at him defiantly for a couple of seconds then, realising he could not hold the bluff, turned his face away. 'Once. In the zoo, in Maputo.'

Luiz shook his head. 'That was something small, maybe a honey badger.'

'Just a badger? Nothing to worry about then,' Julio said.

'Ha.' Luiz grinned to himself. He hoped the boy never had to confront one of those feisty little animals. 'You will learn. If you live that long.'

'Enough talking, old man, I say we go now, find the white man and kill him, dead. I'm going to bust a cap in his arse.'

Why, Luiz wondered, would this youth want to talk like American rappers and gangsters? 'We wait, and we listen.'

Julio flexed his fingers around the pistol grip of the AK-47. He was, Luiz saw, keyed up and ready for action.

Julio looked over Luiz's shoulder, back at the others. 'Are you ready, men?' he hissed. 'Or would you rather sit here sleeping like old men?'

One of the three looked to his two comrades. There were half-hearted nods. 'We are ready.'

'What about Batista and Alexo?' Julio asked.

Luiz looked beyond the three men he could still see. Batista was a lazy fool, half asleep or stoned on *dagga* most of the time, and Alexo was the youngest of the group. In Alexo's favour, the boy, just turned eighteen, was keen, alert and willing to learn, which was why Luiz had given him the important job of watching their rear, in case they were being followed by a clandestine patrol of rangers of the South African Army's elite Recce Commandos, who were also engaged in the war on poaching.

'Batista, wake up,' one of the trio said.

Luiz got up, slowly, so as not to dislodge any rocks, and picked his way towards the rear of their little column.

Batista yawned.

'Where is Alexo?' Luiz whispered.

Batista looked around him. 'I don't know.'

Luiz fumed. 'You were supposed to keep looking back to check on him.'

'I thought that was Alexo's job, to watch behind us, not mine.'

If he wasn't worried about the noise he would make or the yelp of pain it would elicit, Luiz would have punched Batista in the face on the spot. 'You idiot. Come with me, watch your step and stay silent.'

Luiz moved silently and as swiftly as he could, retracing their steps, eyes scanning the rocks and crevices around them.

He heard a movement up ahead, and another growl, but this was deeper, from a bigger animal than a badger.

Whoo-oop!

The hyena's cry was deafening this close, and echoed off the rocks. Luiz raised his rifle and glanced behind him. Batista was turning, his eyes wide with fear. 'Stay still.'

Luiz climbed the nearest rock, then hopped to the next boulder. Batista struggled up behind him. Luiz saw the slope-backed silhouette of one hyena, and another emerged from the gap between the rocks and looked up at him. The moonlight caught the white teeth, dripping silver strands of saliva. Their faces were wet. Luiz looked down. They were feeding.

On the boy, Alexo.

*

Julio crept along the wooden walkway, disdainful of old-man Luiz's dithering. He held the pistol grip of his AK-47 in his right hand and in his left he carried a Chinese-made hand grenade. Fidel had told them to not be afraid of using the grenades; the aim was to kill the veterinarian, not capture him.

'Let's do this,' he said to the man behind him.

Julio flattened his back against the wall of the illuminated accommodation unit. When he was next to the screen door he looked to his comrade, who nodded that he was ready.

Julio cradled his rifle in the crook of his arm and pulled the pin from the grenade. It was harder to extract than he thought, and he remembered Fidel telling them that pulling the pin with your teeth only worked in Hollywood war movies.

'One, two, three,' he mouthed silently, then kicked open the door and tossed in the grenade.

Julio was braced for the grenade to go off, but an explosion of black and white fur, snarling teeth and long claws erupted from inside. The man next to Julio yelped and tripped as the honey

306

badger ran between his legs, snarling and swiping as it went. The gunman fell over and, with his finger on the trigger, accidentally loosed a burst of rounds that slammed into the wall beside Julio's face and arced up into the overhanging thatch roof above him.

The grenade detonated, and the shock wave knocked Julio backwards into the railing. He ignored the other man's dangerous stupidity and charged into the room, now filled with smoke and shattered debris. He swung his torso right and raked the bathroom with gunfire, then carried on and emptied his magazine into the bedroom. There was no one in here, dead or alive.

'Julio,' said his number two from outside, 'the white man is running!'

Julio came out of the room, coughing. 'Where?'

'We just saw him, on the boardwalk. He had his hands up, not holding a gun of any sort.'

'Let's go,' Julio said. 'You first. Hurry!'

They gathered themselves and set off along the walkway.

*

Graham watched the men come. He had been up and down this path dozens of times in the last two days, scouting for vantage points and blind spots. He knew that when he rounded a bend he would not be visible from the accommodation unit he had left lit up, and which was now catching fire. The grenade blast had ignited the thatch roof.

Graham had left the young man's AK-47 under the table in the outdoor cooking area. After he ran from the men, empty-handed and in full view, he jumped over the walkway fence and made his way back, unseen, through the rocks to where the gun was stashed near the outdoor cooking area.

He grabbed the rifle, lay down on his belly and waited.

The men came into view, silhouetted by the blazing roof behind them. They had slowed, Graham noted, their bravery and keenness dissipating as they closed on him. There was no sign of the grey-haired commander.

Graham took aim, lining the sights up on the centre mass of the man in the lead.

The man's young eyes must have caught a glimpse of flame glinting off the barrel of Graham's rifle, or perhaps his pale skin or hair, for he brought his AK-47 up and pulled the trigger.

Graham fired at the same time, but his weapon was steadier, resting on a low brick wall. Bullets flew over Graham's head and ricocheted off granite behind him, but his rounds flew true and the first man slipped and fell, dropping his gun.

Graham kept his finger on the trigger, emptying the magazine into the tightly bunched group of men.

Another two went down. The third turned and fled and was lost from sight as he disappeared through a glowing shower of embers from the burning roof.

With no other poachers in sight Graham got up off the ground, changed magazines and cocked the weapon on the move. He relocated to a spot higher up in the rocks, overlooking the *braai* area, and with a better view of more of the walkway and deck.

He looked down at the men he had shot; the adrenaline pumping through his body dispelled any feelings of remorse or fear. He had survived. The first man he had shot and one of the other two were motionless and silent, presumably dead, but the third was screaming in pain. His cries began to cut through Graham's adrenaline haze. The man was talking in Portuguese, weeping and bellowing.

Graham raised his rifle to his shoulder and took aim at the man. The bloodlust subsided as quickly as it had risen. He was an animal doctor, but he could no more shoot a wounded man in cold blood than any other medico – or any decent human being – would have.

There had been seven men. He had killed the first with the knife, now these two, plus one more seriously injured. That left three.

Graham's phone, set to silent, buzzed in his pocket. The only spot he'd previously had signal in the whole of Boulders Bush Lodge was on the deck outside the dining area, but being high up on the hill behind the camp he must have come into range again. He took out his phone and answered it in a whisper.

'Graham, is that you, matey?' a voice with an English accent asked.

It took him a moment to place it. 'Dave? Dave Corlett?'

'Yes, how are you, Graham?'

'I'm under attack.'

'Bloody hell, then it's for real?'

'Whatever it is, yes, it's very real. Where are you?'

'I'm in the JOC, at Skukuza, on night watch; we had a tip-off from a Mozambican geezer that Boulders Camp was about to be hit by a gang of poachers.'

'Well, your tip-off was correct. I've killed three and wounded one, three more on the loose.'

'Bloody hell. Sit tight, Graham, a rapid reaction force of armed rangers is on their way to you by chopper and the police and army have been notified as well. Help is on its way. Are you injured?'

'I'm fine for now, but not for long, I expect. Have one for me at the golf club, Dave.'

'Will do, mate. Do you want me to stay on the line?'

'No, I've got my hands full with –'

A shot rang out and Graham heard it strike a rock nearby. Someone was probing, trying to get him to reveal his exact position by firing back. The wounded man continued to scream.

'Dave?'

'Graham, are you all right?'

'Yes. You said someone from Mozambique tipped you off. Who was it?'

'Bloke called Costa. Fidel, like Castro. Turns out he's some local politician, but a couple of the higher-ups here at head-quarters said he's also been implicated in rhino poaching.'

'Thanks, Dave. Got to go.' Graham ended the call and noticed that an SMS from Dave had also come through, giving him the same information.

Graham checked his ammunition and wondered what the hell Costa was playing at. Had he called the authorities with a tip-off to establish an alibi? And if so, did Costa assume his men would have killed Graham and melted away before any reaction force arrived?

Either way, he was still very much alive and a feeling that he wanted to stay that way was banishing his earlier feelings of despair and strengthening his resolve.

'Come on you bastards,' he whispered, 'come and get me.'

Chapter 32

Luiz grabbed Armando by the arm and dragged him down amid the rocks where he was hiding with Batista. Armando was shaking and had been running away when Luiz stopped him.

'Calm down.'

'Julio is dead,' Armando blurted, 'and Samora. Afonso is wounded. The white man is still alive.'

They could hear Afonso bellowing and calling for help, for his mother. The screaming was unnerving Armando, and even Batista was alert now, and worried. Luiz needed to rally them, and finish this job.

'He is one man. One old animal doctor. Who are you?' He looked into each of their eyes, but they were struck dumb. 'You are warriors!'

Batista blinked, then nodded. '*Sim.*'

Armando swallowed. 'Tell us what to do, Luiz.'

'Julio underestimated the man. He may be old, and just a man who cares for dogs, but he knows how to shoot. We must treat him like we would a cornered lion. He is dangerous, but if we work together, he will die. We must be quick, though.'

The two youngsters nodded.

Luiz roused them and pulled them back. He pointed left and right, explaining to the men how he would outflank Baird and trap him in the *koppie*.

*

Graham climbed down from his hilltop vantage point.

It was the screaming from the wounded man. He could not handle it any longer.

He dropped down onto the outdoor cooking area and, keeping watch with the dead man's rifle swinging left and right, he jogged over to the casualty. Graham knelt by the man, who he now saw was, like the first he had killed, little more than a boy.

The man had no strength to struggle as Graham slung his rifle and grabbed the youth under the shoulders. He dragged him along the walkway, across the deck where tourists would normally be enjoying a drink or an outdoor dinner, and into the internal dining area.

Graham went to where he had left his backpack, behind the bar. He picked up the bottle of Klipdrift that he had brought with him from the Mopani shop, undid the top and took a long slug.

Unzipping his backpack he took out rubber gloves, a couple of field dressings and scissors. He took the green canvas satchel bag from around the man's torso and cut away his shirt. He saw the wound to the stomach. It was bad, but if the man was lucky Graham's bullet might have missed enough of his vital organs for him to pull through.

Graham drew up a syringe of a sedative drug and injected it into the man's arm. That stilled him, and Graham applied a dressing and tied it tight. He took out a bag of saline and rigged up a drip that he hung from the bar top, then went to the glass sliding doors and cautiously stepped out onto the deck.

An explosion sounded in the rocks high above him, where he'd been hiding before. They were trying to flush him out with a hand grenade. He ducked back, half-in and half-out of the dining room, training his rifle on the *koppie* and watching for silhouettes.

Gunfire sounded and the plate glass next to him shattered. Graham fired up at the boulders then quickly moved inside to another window and dropped down out of sight.

More glass rained into the room and bullets ricocheted around the interior.

'You'll kill your own bloody man!'

He heard voices from the rocks, commands and acknowledgements. They were readying for a final assault. Graham crawled to the next window, popped his head up and saw a man making slow work of clambering over a large rock. He raised his AK-47 to his shoulder, took aim and fired twice. The man slumped, fell and slid, leaving a shiny wet trail on the stone surface.

That left two of them.

Graham saw another man moving amid the boulders. He shifted his aim and pulled the trigger, but the firing pin clicked on nothing. 'Shit.'

In the army they called it the dead man's click, that sound that told you that the magazine was empty of bullets. Graham removed it, tossed it aside and fished in the canvas bag next to him. There was one magazine, which he quickly fitted. He reached into his pants pocket and pulled out the grenade he had taken from the man he had stabbed. He placed it next to him, ready to use.

Bullets poured in through the window from which he had just been shooting.

Graham heard a gurgling noise in between the firing and looked across to the wounded man. He was having a seizure, but as soon as the shaking had started it stopped.

'Bloody hell.'

He crawled across to the man and saw that he had stopped breathing. He was so young. Graham set down his rifle and hand grenade on the cool tiled floor beside him, bent over the boy, cleared the airway and lowered his lips to the man's mouth. From outside he heard the thump of feet on the walkway, but he continued alternating between breaths and compressions.

The young man gasped and coughed and Graham put an ear to his mouth. He was breathing again. Graham looked up just as a figure appeared at the shattered remains of the sliding door, pointing a rifle at him.

Graham started to raise his hands but Luiz, the old poacher, had already pulled the trigger.

*

Dave Corlett keyed the radio handset. 'This is the JOC, over.'

'Roger, over,' said the leader of the reaction force of armed rangers, over the noise of the helicopter's engines.

'There is one man confirmed still at Boulders, Dr Graham Baird. Do you copy?'

'Affirmative, JOC, Dr Baird. We're approaching Boulders Camp now. There's a fire down there and I can see one . . . two bodies, over.'

Dave said a silent prayer. Graham was a curmudgeonly old bugger, but Dave wanted nothing more than to stand him a drink in the bar of the golf club again sometime. 'Any sign of Baird, over?'

'Negative.'

Dave held his breath.

'We're circling the camp,' the patrol leader radioed, 'coming in to land now. There's no sign of life here. Just bodies.'

Chapter 33

Kerry, Bruce, Tamara and Eli had risen early and driven north through the Kruger Park. Kerry was getting more worried with every hour that passed. She hadn't been able to get through to Graham on his mobile phone. Eli had said the signal at the camp was bad, but Graham's phone had been ringing, not just going straight to voicemail. He could, of course, simply be avoiding her – he had made it clear he had nothing more to say to her.

Kerry's mood turned even grimmer when they saw a pall of black smoke over where Boulders Camp would be, as they drove down the access road.

When they arrived, an armed national parks ranger stopped them at the top of the driveway. 'Sorry, no entry here,' the man said.

Kerry's heart started pounding. There were two police *bakkies* and a black Range Rover parked behind Graham's Land Rover, which was in one of the car spaces underneath the elevated dining area.

'Who's in charge here?' Eli asked.

'Captain Sannie van Rensburg, from Skukuza,' the ranger said.

'Can you please call her and tell her Eli Johnston is here?'

The man shrugged and unclipped his radio and made the call. A few minutes later Sannie van Rensburg walked up the dirt road. They all got out of the car.

'Eli, this is a crime scene,' Sannie said after the greetings were exchanged.

'Is Graham here?' Kerry asked.

Sannie frowned. 'We know he was here, Kerry, but there is no sign of him or . . . of his body. We have our crime scene people on the way and they'll be helping us investigate. Some of the parks rangers are following up some tracks and other signs.'

'We've been driving for hours through the park,' Tamara said. 'Please can we at least use a bathroom?'

'You could go in the bush,' Sannie said.

'*Ag*, not me. *Please?*'

Sannie exhaled. 'All right. I'll get one of the rangers to take you to one of the accommodation units we're not investigating. Come this way.'

The policewoman led them past the cars and Kerry noticed the Animals Without Borders logo on the side of the Range Rover. 'Is Sarah Hoyland here?'

Sannie looked back at her. 'The Australian woman, yes, she is. They're here with the national parks PR people. Dr Baird was supposed to be at a media event in Skukuza, but for some reason he ended up here and the parks people were not happy because he brought a honey badger into the park and released it without authority. There's an empty travel cage in the back of his truck.'

'You said, "they"?' Kerry said.

'Your Miss Hoyland came with Fidel Costa. They travelled here from Skukuza like VIPs on one of the park's helicopters with their PR people.' Sannie made no attempt to hide her disgust at the news. 'Costa's driver arrived a short time ago with his car to take them onwards.'

'My God,' Kerry said. 'Costa kidnapped me and tried to kill us!'

'I know,' Sannie said. 'I don't want you making a scene with him, Kerry. We need evidence if we are ever going to hope to charge him. You told me you didn't see him after you were taken prisoner in Mozambique?'

'Yes, that's right,' Kerry said. As a lawyer she had too much respect for the law to lie and try to place Fidel at the scene of her imprisonment. 'I was with him, at the police station at Massingir – Graham had gone to deliver the officer in charge's baby – and when I went outside Costa was nowhere to be seen and someone came up behind me, put a bag over my head and bundled me into a waiting four-by-four. I was held at his property, though. Eli confirmed it was his farm.'

'I checked on that,' Sannie said, 'after I spoke to Graham. Costa's clever. If he owns that farm where you were held – and we believe he does – it doesn't show on any record; it's in the name of his late wife's parents. My colleagues in Mozambique say Costa's places of residence are a villa in Massingir and another house in Maputo.'

'But he tried to kill Graham at Ukuphila,' Kerry said.

'Graham told me the man with the security guard at Ukuphila was wearing a ski mask,' Sannie said.

Kerry fumed. 'But Graham was sure it was him.'

Sannie's phone rang and she held up a hand to excuse herself and looked away.

Exasperated, but seeing her chance, Kerry strode past the policewoman and jogged up the stairs to the deck and dining area of Boulders lodge. It looked like a war zone. Out on the open area in front of the lodge were two national parks helicopters. Kerry saw a couple of armed rangers patrolling the area, looking for tracks.

'Hey!' she heard the detective call from behind her.

Kerry pressed on. There was a television cameraman and a well-dressed woman who Kerry took for a reporter interviewing Sarah Hoyland. Fidel Costa stood on one side of her and a man in national parks uniform stood on the other side.

Kerry strode over to them and stood between the cameraman and Sarah and Costa. 'You bastard. What have you done to Graham?'

The cameraman, sensing conflict the way a shark smells blood in the water, turned his lens on her.

'Kerry, not here,' said Sarah.

'I'm sorry, I don't know where Dr Baird is,' Costa said, his tone even. 'Miss Maxwell, isn't it?'

'You know bloody well who I am. You kidnapped me and later tried to have me killed.'

'Now, now, please don't go making any unfounded allegations, Miss Maxwell, or –'

'Kerry!' Sannie called. 'Come away.'

Kerry ignored her. 'Or what, you'll shoot me, Costa? Like you tried to kill Graham in Hoedspruit?'

'What's all this about?' the reporter asked.

Kerry looked around her. She focused on the young man in national parks khaki. 'Who are you?'

'I'm from South African National Parks public relations. Can I ask who you are?'

'Ask him,' she jabbed a finger at Fidel, 'who he is. He's the number one poaching kingpin in Mozambique. I can't believe you even let him *into* your national park.'

Sarah took her elbow, but Kerry shrugged it off. 'Kerry, listen to me. It was Fidel who alerted the national parks people that a hit squad was coming over the border to get Graham here.'

Kerry turned on Costa again. By now, Eli, Bruce and Tamara were arrayed in support behind her, the two groups facing each other down.

It was Bruce's turn to poke a finger at Costa. 'You're fucking dead, mate.'

'I won't dignify such profanity and threats with a reply,' Costa said to Bruce, 'but if you make them again I will ask the police to intervene.'

'Just try, mate.'

Sannie van Rensburg stepped between the warring parties. 'Everybody calm down. No more threats.'

'Thank you,' Costa said to her.

Sannie turned on him. 'Listen to me *Mister* Costa. I know who you are – half the South African Police Service knows who you are. You'd be well advised to keep quiet as well.'

'Can someone tell me what's going on here?' asked the public relations man. 'We brought this TV crew here to talk about the release of a honey badger, and the foiling of an attack on a national parks camp.'

Kerry was astounded. She looked around and saw an armed ranger kneeling by a man who lay wounded and bandaged beyond the shattered glass sliding door that led to a dining and bar area. 'What happened in there?'

'We found a medical bag inside with Graham Baird's name on it. It looks like Graham treated that man, who is outfitted like a poacher. We found more bloodstains and drag marks. We think Graham's been taken.'

Kerry put a hand on her forehead. She felt faint. She was sure Costa was behind all this, yet he was standing there, smiling, silently mocking them all. And Sarah was defending him.

'Look at me,' Kerry said to the cameraman. She pushed her way back into the shot. With a glance over her shoulder she saw Sannie standing on the outer rim of the action, not wanting to be filmed, hands on her hips. 'Start rolling.'

'No,' Sarah said.

'Yes!'

The journalist nodded to the cameraman.

'This man,' Kerry began, pointing behind her, 'Fidel Costa, who has gone into business with the Animals Without Borders charity, is a murderer and a poacher.'

'I will sue you,' Costa said behind her.

'Do your best,' Bruce said. 'She's a lawyer, and a bloody good one.'

Sarah looked to Fidel. 'I think we should go.'

He nodded and touched the brim of his Panama hat. 'Miss Maxwell, it appears Sarah and I must leave. I look forward to meeting you again.'

Eli's fist seemed to come from nowhere and Fidel's head snapped back, his hat tumbling over the railing of the elevated walkway as he fell.

'Nice one, Yank,' Bruce said.

Kerry spun around. She was as shocked as the rest of them. The cameraman zoomed in on Costa, then panned to Eli.

'Get up,' Eli said to Costa, fists raised and ready to strike again.

Costa gingerly fingered his jaw. 'Johnston, I know you.'

'I know you do. Just make a move. Please.'

Sarah extended her hand to Fidel but, with his ego as bruised as his jaw, he brushed her offer away and got to his feet. He squared up to Eli, but kept his hands by his side. 'I will see you, in Mozambique, some time.'

'You can bet on it, buddy,' Eli said. 'Make sure you're packing so it'll be a fair fight.'

'Bloody hell, enough with the machismo.' Kerry looked to Sannie van Rensburg again. 'Isn't there *anything* you can do?'

Sannie stepped in. 'Break it up.'

'A bit late, aren't you?' Sarah said to Sannie.

Fidel brushed himself down and he and Sarah walked away from the group.

Kerry started to follow them, but van Rensburg put a hand on her arm. 'Wait.'

'What is it?' Kerry said as Fidel and Sarah walked down the stairs from the deck to the car park below.

'We've been watching Costa, and so have some dependable police in Mozambique. We're building a case against him, Kerry. He's not fooling anyone with this born-again bunny-hugger act of his. And as for that woman, Sarah . . .'

'She's just after money. The more money she bleeds from overseas donors, the bigger her cut is.'

'We're already worried in South Africa about horns from de-horned rhinos being smuggled to Asia and if they start cutting off horns in this proposed sanctuary in Mozambique, as they say they will, then it's highly likely they'll be smuggled out to places such as Vietnam.'

'Yes,' said Kerry, 'and you need to see if there's a link between Costa and the man who tried to rape and kill me.'

Sannie nodded. 'But we must be careful, softly softly for now, hey?'

'Yes, I understand. But where is Graham?'

*

Sarah got into the back of the Range Rover next to Fidel. The driver already had the engine running and the air conditioning was kicking in.

The heat was oppressive outside and the cool air chilled the nervous sweat on her body.

'That was too close, with Kerry and the news crew, and now the television will have vision of Eli hitting you.'

'I will sue him for assault.'

Sarah sighed. 'I think you should just lay low.'

'That is not in my nature, Sarah.'

More machismo, she thought. 'What are we going to do about Kerry? She could go public in Australia, when she gets home, and cause some real shit for you, for us, internationally.'

321

Fidel faced her and looked into her eyes. 'She almost met with an unfortunate accident here in South Africa when she got a flat tyre. Africa can be a dangerous place. Something else might happen to her, just like it happened to that arrogant security man from Kwangela, Michael Collins.'

Sarah said nothing. She was so close to seeing the biggest deal of her career working with NGOs come to fruition. *The end justifies the means*, she told herself, clasping her hands to still the tremor she had just noticed.

'Our success in Mozambique, breeding and protecting rhinos, will speak for itself. She can be neutralised – one way or another, either drowned out by the positive PR you generate, or, as I say, something might happen to her.'

Sarah drew a deep breath. How had it come to this, she wondered, the two of them discussing hurting or killing people? Costa was becoming more and more open with her about his tactics. He was prepared to kill and to sell out his own men to see the deal went ahead. 'She might be too scared to speak out.'

Fidel nodded. 'I will see to it. It appears my senior man, Luiz, survived the counterattack by the national parks rangers. I could not see his body among the others.'

'You set him up,' Sarah said, 'calling in the national parks anti-poaching rangers last night, even before Graham was dead.'

Fidel nodded. 'It was not an easy decision for me to make, but Luiz is also opposed to me getting into bed with you, so to speak, for different reasons from the others. I will have to deal with him as well.'

'What about Eli Johnston?' Sarah asked.

'What about him?'

'I'm exposed,' Sarah said, 'particularly if he works out that I stole his phone in Cape Town and found his email chain to Michael Collins.'

Fidel stroked his moustache. 'Yes, I can see why you would be worried.'

'Eli lost a lot of support over the incident at Kwangela. It's going to take him a long time to rebuild his public image, and the cash flow to him and his rangers on the ground in Mozambique will be reduced to a trickle.'

'Which will make him very vulnerable to attack, perhaps even an ambush,' Fidel said.

Sarah nodded. The enormity of what she had set in motion, what might yet happen to Kerry and Eli hit her. She swallowed bile. Sarah knew Costa was crooked yet she had sought him and his money out nonetheless. She had chosen to believe his thin lies that it was not he who had tried to kill the others. Now, with their goal in sight, he had just about dropped all pretence. If she could get him on a digital voice recorder, explicitly admitting his part in the attempted murders and his future plans she could use it against him, or at the very least it would give her some insurance.

'Where to, boss?' the driver asked from the front seat.

'Let's take a drive through the park. I think we should make Nelspruit by evening. I'm sure we can find a nice hotel there. We'll cross into Mozambique tomorrow.'

'Sounds good. We need to get you out of South Africa for a while,' Sarah said.

'Agreed.'

'I wonder what happened to Graham's body?' Sarah felt nauseous. Her former lover, an irascible pain in the arse at the best of times, was most likely dead. *What have I done?*

Fidel shrugged. 'We will know once Luiz returns and gives me a debrief. Luiz has no way of knowing that it was me who alerted the parks staff. As I say, I will deal with him in time.'

'Whatever you say,' Sarah barely whispered. Her phone beeped. She took it out.

The message was from Graham Baird. Sarah's heart lurched as she opened the SMS. Fidel's driver began reversing up the long, narrow gravel driveway that led to Boulders Bush Lodge.

She read the words on the screen. *Get out.*

'What is it?' Fidel asked. 'You look like you have just seen a ghost.'

Sarah reached for the door handle. *Enough*, she told herself.

The Range Rover exploded.

Chapter 34

Nsele sat on top of the granite boulder, looking down at the people on the viewing deck below.

He was not scared of humans. He had been around them all of his life, imprisoned for their entertainment. But he had learned that by and large they meant him no harm and they were a good source of food.

It was the same with the man lying in the shade of the rock. There was food beside his body, left in a bag, but Nsele had eaten all that. He sat on the rock, in the sun, watching the humans below. If no one put a *braai* on soon he might just have to eat the man lying beside him.

*

'Check that *ratel*,' Sannie van Rensburg said, shielding her eyes from the sun and pointing upwards.

'That what?' Kerry walked across the deck to where Sannie was standing.

'Oh, the honey badger. We call it a *ratel* in Afrikaans.'

Kerry looked to where Sannie was pointing, in the rocks

above the lodge, near the peak of the mound of boulders. The badger sat, as if basking, head resting on its paws, looking down at them.

'I've never seen one as relaxed as that. Normally they're trotting about looking for something, or someone, to kill,' Sannie said. 'I wonder if this is the one Dr Baird released.'

'It must be Nsele, the one Sarah brought over from Australia. Funny that it's hanging around.'

'Tea?' Bruce said, walking out of the gutted remains of the dining room and kitchen. 'The gas stove survived the gunfire and explosions and I managed to get the kettle on.' He handed them each a mug.

They were all waiting at the lodge for a crime scene investigation team to arrive, along with the coroner's people. The rangers from the rapid reaction force had put out the fire that had engulfed the Range Rover and the people inside it. Kerry had been furious at Sarah and had wished Fidel Costa dead, but she was still shaking from the shock of witnessing three human beings incinerated before her eyes. Seeing the honey badger was a welcome relief.

Kerry took a sip of tea, then set her mug down, went to the railing and climbed over it.

'What are you doing, kiddo?' Bruce asked, his tone alarmed.

'I'm going to climb up, see how close I can get to it and get a picture of it in its natural environment.'

'Be careful,' Bruce said. 'Tammy told me those things can kill you by ripping your scrotum out.'

'Well, lucky for me I don't have one.'

Kerry started climbing. It was silly, she told herself, to be scrambling higher up over these often slippery boulders, heading towards an animal that did, in fact, have a reputation for ferocity.

But she didn't care.

She paused, halfway up the *koppie*, to turn and look around her. The view over Africa was spectacular. On the horizon to the east, over the Lebombo Hills, dark clouds were coalescing. The breeze, easier to feel this high up, was coming from the same direction, and she caught the scent of rain.

The badger growled at her as she came closer, then ducked out of sight, retreating down the opposite slope of the rock on which it had been perched.

'Where are you?' Kerry was breathing hard by the time she got to where the animal had been. Cautiously, she peered over the top of the boulder.

The badger scampered away into the deep shadows as she saw a body lying there, shirt covered in blood, bandages soaked through; his stylishly cut grey hair, a few days' stubble.

The face, though, looked at peace.

'Graham!' Kerry screamed.

*

Nurse Tamara Shepherd brought Graham back from the dead.

When Kerry discovered him he had stopped breathing, but his skin was still warm to the touch. Kerry had yelled for help and begun CPR. Tamara scrambled up the *koppie* and took over from her, and Graham started breathing again and came to.

'Whoever dressed Graham's gunshot wound knew what they were doing,' Tamara said as Bruce, Eli and two rangers carefully lifted Graham onto a stretcher that had been found in the reaction force's helicopter. Slowly and carefully they began the painstaking process of carrying Graham down the *koppie*, with Tamara walking next to them holding a plasma drip from the first aid pack that had been used to treat the wounded poacher.

Once they had made it down to the level of the lodge, Sannie van Rensburg stopped them. 'I need to ask him some questions.'

Tamara's expression was grim. 'He was nearly dead. We need to get him to hospital by helicopter. The wounded poacher is stable, but he should go with Graham.'

'All right,' Sannie said.

Graham lifted a hand. 'Wait.'

Sannie was on one side of him, Kerry on the other. Kerry was looking at the screen of Graham's phone. 'You tried to warn Sarah about the bomb?'

Graham nodded and the slight movement seemed to be an effort. 'Grenade. Luiz . . . Costa's man. He found me and took the grenade I had.'

'The man who was sent to kill you, along with the others?' Sannie asked.

'Yes. He . . . he shot me, but couldn't finish me off as I fell over the man I was treating, one of the poachers. How is he?'

'He's going to be OK,' Tamara interjected. 'You saved him.'

Graham coughed. 'Before Luiz could kill me I told him what Dave Corlett said . . .'

Kerry looked to Sannie, who said: 'Dave was the honorary ranger on duty at the JOC who took the message from Fidel Costa that there were men on the way to raid Boulders Camp.'

'Fidel was telling the truth? He set up his own men?' Kerry asked.

'Yes,' Graham whispered. He cleared his throat. 'Dave had tried me earlier – the signal is weak at the lodge – and I was able to show Luiz an SMS from him giving me the news about Fidel. Luiz knew then it wasn't a bluff. He patched me up and dragged me up into the *koppie*. I didn't see him again.'

Sannie looked over at the charred remains of the Range Rover and the blackened skeletons inside. 'Luiz must have set a booby trap.'

'Wedge or tie the grenade between the body and the chassis, next to the fuel tank,' Eli said, 'and tie some cord from the pin to

328

the spoked wheel rim. As soon as the car starts to move and the wheels turn the pin is extracted and, well, *ka-boom*.'

'I . . . came to . . . managed to get up and look over the rocks. I saw Sarah and Costa getting into the Rangie. I . . . I tried.'

'It's OK, Graham,' Kerry said. 'It's not your fault.'

The helicopter's engine was whining and the blades turning.

'We need to get him on board,' Tamara said.

Sannie nodded.

Kerry leaned over and, on impulse, kissed Graham on the lips.

Graham smiled and shifted his eyes to Tamara. 'Can I stay here instead?'

Tamara shook her head. 'No!'

The men carried Graham down the stairs and across to the waiting chopper.

Kerry held a hand to her eyes to ward off the cloud of dust and grit thrown out by the downwash, and watched as the helicopter lifted off, turned, lowered its nose and sped away.

Silence returned to the bush, though in the distance she heard the first rumble of thunder.

Kerry looked at the phone again, then turned her head at the touch of a hand on her shoulder.

'He's a tough old dog. He'll pull through,' Eli said.

The rangers had left them. Sannie van Rensburg had taken charge and was issuing new orders, for them to begin a new search, for the man who had booby-trapped the Range Rover.

Bruce and Tamara had sought shelter and shade inside the damaged lodge. Kerry and Eli were alone on the plain. An elephant, no doubt scared off by the earlier battles, was loitering in the tree line, waiting and watching for the right moment to come for a drink at the waterhole.

'I was wondering, Kerry, would you like to come over to Mozambique to see my anti-poaching rangers in action? Now Costa's dead you wouldn't be at risk.'

329

Kerry looked up at him. 'I don't know. But I do have a question for you, that I'd like you to answer honestly. Did the guy who was killed in the car crash, Collins, the head of security, know that you were intending on putting that rhino to sleep?'

He took his hand off her. 'I'm fighting a war, Kerry.'

She took a pace away from him. 'I know. I was almost collateral damage. What did you do? What were you trying to do, Eli?'

'The rhino would have recovered quickly, whether Graham reversed the drug or not. I wanted video showing how easy it was to kill an animal in captivity.'

'But your job, so you told me, was to test the security at the zoo by flying a drone over and dropping an apple – not sedating a rhino. Why did you do it?'

'This war's fought in people's minds, as well as on the battlefield. The media is crucial. I needed footage that showed a rhino passing out, as if it was dead.'

'But,' she said, 'you told me that this was done for internal reasons only. Are you telling me you were going to send your video to the news media or post it online and shame Kwangela when they were getting you on board to try and beef up their security?'

He looked away.

'Answer me, damn it,' Kerry said. Eli just looked at her. She remembered something else, a fact she hadn't been able to recall when they talked over lunch in Cape Town. 'The poison.'

'What poison?'

'Don't play dumb, Eli. When I heard on the radio you'd been arrested the cops said something about you being found with poison or pesticide on you. I know what it was about. You were going to make a video for the internet, or TV or whatever, weren't you, with props and all, showing the world how easy it would be to lace a bait with poison.'

He shrugged. 'Stuff gets leaked to the media all the time. Do you know how much it costs to relocate rhinos to different countries? Millions, Kerry. That's money that could be spent on guns, bullets, drones, thermal imaging cameras, night vision goggles. I could win the war on poaching in Mozambique with the sort of donor money Sarah and that criminal Costa were going to plough into their crooked, harebrained schemes.'

'So you lied to the head of security, supposedly your friend, and set out to shame Kwangela publicly, and shame the good people who want to ensure remnant breeding populations of rhinos might survive outside of Africa.'

He clenched his fists by his side. 'It's a *war*,' he said again. 'You win by killing people, not by trying to recreate Noah's ark.'

'You lied to them. They put you in a position of trust and you were going to abuse it.'

'It's a fucking *war*.'

Kerry stared at him. He was a zealot, prepared to break the rules, to do whatever it took to win. And that was the problem; he seemed as concerned, if not more concerned, about beating his competitors as about saving wildlife.

'I'm pretty sure Sarah stole my phone,' he said, filling the silence between them.

'What makes you say that?'

'She came to my dressing room after the gig in Cape Town, the fundraiser at the convention centre. I thought about it while I was in prison. I didn't have my phone from then on. She set me up, the bitch.'

Kerry turned and started to walk back to the lodge.

'Where are you going?'

'Away from you.'

Epilogue

Thandi collected Graham from the hospital and drove him home to Hoedspruit. It was oppressively hot. Dave Corlett's English wife, Veronica, he recalled, had said once in the bar of the golf club that the devil lived in Hoedspruit in October.

The blue sky was being subdued by a tower of ominously black cloud. There was precious little grass and the bare soil around his house was like an angry red graze.

Kerry had called him a couple of times during his stay in hospital, and emailed him, and while he'd been friendly to her he had been noncommittal about them meeting, assuming she was still in South Africa after he was released. He had asked her not to come and visit, inventing a story about a serious infection he had picked up – it was nothing to worry about, but he was in isolation, he said. She seemed to have bought it.

Thandi helped him out of the Land Rover and handed him his walking stick. The bullet had, Dr Bongi quipped, aerated his left love handle. It was still painful, but he had pills.

'I'll be right from here, thanks, Thandi. You can take the

Landy home with you tonight if you like. It will be a couple more days before I'm up for driving.'

'It is fine,' she said. 'I will get a taxi home.'

'Serious? There's no need. No one will be using the Land Rover here.'

'I'm fine, Graham, really.'

'Well, suit yourself.'

Graham found his key and opened the door.

Immediately he knew there was something wrong. He couldn't smell anything. There should surely be the stench of rotting leftovers, the overflowing ashtray, mouldy washing. He set his bag down on the *stoep*, unzipped it and took out his pistol.

With the stick raised in one hand and his pistol in his right he went in.

'Graham!'

'Kerry?' He lowered the gun.

'I called the hospital. I didn't expect you back until tomorrow.'

'Bongi changed his mind about my release date. More likely he got sick of my complaining about the food and my care. I've put neater sutures in a dog's ball bag.'

'I'm sure he did a good job.' Kerry had a spray bottle of household cleaner in one hand and a cloth in the other.

'I wondered what that foul smell was when I opened the door.'

'Let me help you.' She went to the door and picked up his bag.

'What are you doing here?'

'Waiting for you. I never gave you your key back.'

He looked around. The place was spotless. He suppressed a shiver. It was, however, good to see her. 'Where's your father?'

'In love.'

'Nice place to be. I went there once.'

'Would you like a drink, Graham? I found some beers and put them in the fridge.'

'Um, no, thanks. I've been dry these past five days in hospital and I'm enjoying not waking up with a hangover for a change. Water would be *lekker*, though, thanks.'

Kerry went to the kitchen and took a chilled bottle out of the refrigerator. Graham followed her in.

'I like what you've done with the place,' he said.

'It was a bio hazard.'

'Kerry . . .'

'Graham . . .'

'What are you doing here, really?' he asked.

She put her hands on her hips. 'If you think you can sleep with me and then walk out and have nothing to do with me, then you don't know women very well and you certainly don't know me.'

'Agreed, at least on the first count.'

'So, you reckon you know me?' She poured water for them both and handed him a glass.

'Yes. I know you're a good person, with a good heart, who is committed to conservation and the environment, who is principled and honest, and brave enough to travel across a border to try to free a man accused of murder – a man who you hadn't even met and who screwed up your booking when all you wanted was to come over here and help.'

Kerry swallowed.

Graham held up a hand. 'Let me continue. I think you might have learned, also, that if you want to do something that matters, it doesn't matter what cause you support or who you give your money to, it's what's in your heart. I also thought about my own life, and how I've wasted so much of it staring into the bottom of a bottle when all around us, here in the bush, is this incredible beauty that needs to preserved and protected. I've done my bit, over the years, but I realised my work's not over, and nor is my life, not while there is wildlife still injured or in danger.'

CAPTIVE

'You've given this some thought,' she said.

'Yes. Pretty deep, eh?' He forced a chuckle. 'I did all this thinking while sitting on a bed pan these past five days and, actually, since we, well, spent that time together at Kwangela.'

'Yes, about that – Kwangela that is, not the bed pan –' she said, 'why did you give me the cold shoulder afterwards?'

Outside there was a rumble of thunder and then the gunshot crack of a lightning strike. They both winced.

Graham gulped down some water like it was gin, his face serious again. 'You know my wife died of malaria?'

'Yes, you told me,' Kerry said.

'She wanted to move to Australia, for good, and as much as I am wedded to this screwed-up continent I loved my wife, Carla, more. We decided that before we left we would go on a final trip around southern Africa. We went to the Kruger – stayed at Boulders Bush Lodge; Victoria Falls in Zimbabwe; and we travelled up the Mozambican coast as far as Pemba.'

Graham took a deep breath and some more water. His mind and body were screaming for a cigarette, but he had decided to give up while in hospital.

'Does this have something to do with why you didn't want to go and see the falls when we were in Zimbabwe?'

He nodded and bit his lower lip. Tears welled up in his eyes, as they sometimes did, especially when he was tired. It felt as though there were enough to fill a dam inside him, and now that dam was threatening to burst. When he'd been thinking about Carla, and Kerry, and how close the Australian woman had come to dying because of him, he had started crying in hospital. Tamara Shepherd, now back at work, had sat with him and held his hand. He recognised that he had been fighting so hard, and for so long, to hold in his emotions that it had exhausted him, physically and mentally, to the point where he had welcomed the prospect of death at Boulders.

'When we were in Zimbabwe, at Victoria Falls, Carla asked me if I thought she – we – should take some anti-malarial pills. We live in a malaria area, in Hoedspruit, but none of the locals take prophylactics. It's not practical and probably not good for you to take them all the time, so we cover up, use mosquito repellent and sleep under nets, and when anyone develops cold or flu-like symptoms we go to a doctor, that's how we deal with it.'

'You checked on me several times, asked if I was taking pills and precautions against malaria.'

'Yes.' He gripped the glass in two hands to try and steady himself. 'But I said to Carla, "No, don't be silly, we'll be fine", and . . . and . . .' Graham felt his whole body start to convulse and the tears begin to flow.

Kerry came to him and he felt her arms around him as he buried his face in her freshly laundered bush shirt.

'I'm here, Graham. It's all right.'

'No,' he sniffed, 'it's not. Stupid, bumbling, drunken me told her, when I was half-pissed, not to worry about it. That was me, breezing through life thinking everything would be just fine and we had nothing to worry about.'

'Carla could have made her own decision.'

He cried some more. 'I know. I've told myself that, but she didn't. She listened to me. She contracted cerebral malaria, the worst kind, in Mozambique, and she fell ill and two days later she was dead.'

'Oh, Graham.' She moved him to the lounge room and they sat. She held him tighter and rocked him. 'Let it out.'

He had been bottling up the grief, keeping it at bay with booze and, sometimes, drugs, for a decade. Now he felt like he didn't have the strength to keep it in any more. He worried he might dissolve in the flood of tears now that he had started.

In time, he became still and could see again. Kerry held his hand.

'Sorry,' he said.

'Don't be.' She wiped her own eyes and it was only now he could see she had been crying as well.

Kerry stood.

'Van Rensburg came to see me in hospital, to interview me,' he said.

'What did she say?'

'They never found Luiz. But she did tell me that in the wreckage of the Range Rover, in Sarah's burned handbag they found a second phone – Eli's. The theory is that Sarah, directly or indirectly, set Eli up at Kwangela.'

'I see,' Kerry said. 'It doesn't change what Eli did, drugging the rhino, nor what he intended to do with the video vision he shot.'

'Yes, I got your email about that. I haven't heard from him.'

'Me neither,' she said. Kerry looked at her watch, then left him and went to the spare room, where she had stayed last time. She came out holding her bag and daypack.

'Where are you going?'

'My dad has gone animal crazy. He's been driving around these last two days – Blyde River Canyon and the Panorama Route up to Graskop and Sabie, but he's desperate to get back into the Kruger Park. He's coming to pick me up in an hour. I thought I might be gone before you arrived.'

'I'm pleased you were here,' he said. 'Even if I did end up blubbering like a child.'

'Don't discount your emotions, Graham.'

'That's what your father's girlfriend said to me in hospital.'

'She's nice,' Kerry said.

'She is.'

Graham didn't know what to say next. They stood there, in the lounge room. Thankfully, his phone rang.

'Graham Baird,' he said. He listened to the caller for a while. 'Shit. OK. I'll get my bag and be on my way soon.'

'What is it?' Kerry asked when he ended the call.

'There's a rhino that's been hit by a goods train. A railway line runs through the Olifants River Game Reserve, not far from here, and while the drivers slow down when they're passing through the reserve and are watchful for wildlife, accidents still happen. It's alive.'

'Are you fit to drive?'

'No.' He started to type Thandi's name into the contacts list on his phone. Hopefully she hadn't got far. 'Thandi will take me.'

'No.'

'What do you mean, no?'

'I saw her leave your Land Rover and walk away. She'll be in a taxi by now. Let me drive you.'

'What about your father?'

'He'll be happy to drive around Kruger by himself. Also, you still owe me a few days of my stint as a paying volunteer.'

'Are you serious?' he asked. His heart started to accelerate. 'Would you like to stay?'

She put down her bags. 'Can I?'

'Yes.'

'For how long?' Kerry asked.

'Forever, if you like.'

She grinned and came to him. Outside it started to rain.

ACKNOWLEDGEMENTS

There is a real-life veterinarian in the town of Hoedspruit and he has probably done more to save and protect African wildlife than anyone I know. His name is Dr Peter Rogers and he kindly provided assistance with some technical questions I had for *Captive*.

Peter is assisted sometimes by another veterinarian Dr Hamish Currie, who is also the director of the Back to Africa charity, which has done a fantastic job bringing animals from zoos around the world to their ancestral homelands. Hamish and his team have facilitated the return of northern white rhino to Kenya and roan antelope to Swaziland and South Africa and I am a big fan of their work. I'm very grateful to Hamish for reading and checking the manuscript prior to publication.

Unlike the abrasive fictitious Graham Baird, Peter and Hamish are very nice guys and they have my deepest respect.

There is a real Graham Baird and while it's probably an exaggeration to say he saved my life, I am sure he saved my left hand. Some years ago, while trying to extract ice from a frozen water bottle in the Kruger Park (to make a gin and tonic), I managed to stab myself in the hand with a very sharp serrated knife. I had just put up the roof tent on my Land Rover and, bleeding profusely, there was no way I was going to be able to drive myself to help. Graham and his wife, Sharon, who were camping nearby, drove me to a doctor's surgery where I was stitched up. Without Graham and Sharon's first aid it would now take me twice as long to write a book. I promised Graham that one day I would use his name in a book and I hope he likes his similarly heroic namesake.

Sarah Hoyland from the Sydney-based Classic Safari Company is a much nicer person than her fictitious alter ego and like a number of other good people, she contributed money to a worthy cause to have her name used in this story. Sarah's donation was to The Australian Rhino Project. I would also like to thank the following people and the charities they supported: Ruth Nicholas on behalf of Kerry Maxwell (Friends of Robins Camp, Hwange National Park); Kevin Johnston on behalf of Eli Johnston (The Askari Project, which supports elephant conservation in Kenya); Jenny Crameri on behalf of Tamara Shepherd (HEAL Africa, a charity supporting a hospital and community projects in the Democratic Republic of Congo and other African countries); and Chris Hennessy, on behalf of Desmond Hennessy (Guide Dogs for the Blind).

I'd like to thank my very good friends Charlotte Stapf and Annelien Oberholzer for reading early drafts of the book. Charlotte is a Sydney-based psychotherapist who helps me with matters of the mind and is an eagle-eyed editor, as is Annelien, who corrects my Afrikaans and cultural references every year.

John Roberts, an Australian Army officer who went to Mozambique on a UN mission to clear landmines fell in love with Africa and ended up becoming a Mozambican citizen. Thank you, John, once again for correcting my Portuguese and giving me some excellent insight into a part of the world that captured his heart.

Thanks, as well, to firearms expert Fritz Rabe, for his feedback on guns and ammunition; Wayne Hamilton from swagmantours.com.au who proofs each of my books and helps with my travels in Africa; Dr Neil 'Bongi' Taverner for his advice on heart attack treatment; and ambulance paramedic Ashley Lapham who showed me how to insert a cannula one day while we watched a herd of buffalo in Zimbabwe – as you do. Thanks also to Dave and Veronica Corlett and my other friends in Hoedspruit, who always make me feel incredibly welcome when I visit their lovely town.

As with all my books my hard-working team of unpaid editors – wife, Nicola; mother, Kathy; and mother-in-law, Sheila – helped make this story what it is when you read it. Thank you, all.

I'm also lucky to have fantastic professional editors, editor Danielle Walker, copy editor Brianne Collins and Alex Craig.

Thank you to the wonderful team at Pan Macmillan, in Australia, the UK and South Africa, and all the other publishers around the world who have stuck by me. I can't thank you enough for making my dream come true and giving me the job I wished for since I was child. Thanks, especially, to Pan Macmillan's publishing director, Cate Paterson, for giving me my big break and the life I always wanted, and for being a good friend.

Last, but definitely not least, if you've made it this far thank you – you're the most important person in the business of writing and publishing and I couldn't do this without you.

Tony Park
Africa 2018

THE CULL
TONY
PARK

The poacher becomes the hunted.

The war to save Africa's wildlife is fought on many fronts.

For former mercenary Sonja Kurtz, the opportunity to head up an elite squad tasked with taking down the continent's poaching kingpins is a chance to strike at the heart of the enemy. Financed by British billionaire Julianne Clyde-Smith, the pair hope to bring about real change.

But as their operation progresses, the new unit's activities soon draw them into the firing line of The Scorpions. A ruthless underworld syndicate willing to do anything to protect their bloodthirsty trade.

When Sonja's love interest, safari guide and private detective Hudson Brand, is employed to investigate the death of an alleged poacher at the hands of the team, their mission comes under intense scrutiny. As darker forces come into play and the body count rises, Sonja is forced to consider if Julianne's crusade has gone too far and what she could lose if she continues with the increasingly bloody campaign . . .

'No modern author writes with as much knowledge, conviction and love of the Southern Africa of today as Aussie veteran army officer Tony Park'
Crime Review